A Stitch in Time

Amanda James

Published 2013 by Choc Lit Limited
Penrose House, Crawley Drive, Camberley, Surrey GU15 2AB, UK
www.choclitpublishing.com

A CIP catalogue record for this book is available from the British Library

ISBN 978-1-78189-000-4

Printed and bound by CPI Group (UK) Ltd, Croydon, CR0 4YY

With much love and thanks to my husband, Brian
and my daughter, Tanya, for their love, encouragement,
patience and unwavering faith in me.
I couldn't have done this without them.
And to my darling grandson, Ronan. You bring light to
the darkest day and fill my heart with joy.

Acknowledgements

There are so many people I would like to thank but that would fill another book.

Firstly I want to thank Dr Joanna Cannon for being my beta reader. She read the first draft and loved it. She said she had forgotten that she wasn't already reading a published novel. I was over the moon as it was a first draft and a bit of a departure from my previous novels. And coming from such an accomplished writer, it meant such a lot. Her words gave me fantastic encouragement. Thanks so much, Jo.

I would like to thank all my family and friends who have been so thrilled with my writing successes, big and small. A special mention must go to my parents, brother and family for their love and encouragement.

I would also like to thank the many writer friends I have on Twitter and Facebook for their good humour and advice. We all know how difficult it is to become published nowadays and sharing our experiences really helped the writing process.

And finally, a huge thank you goes to the entire Choc Lit team for always being at hand and so wonderful to work with. My fellow Choc Lit authors are fantastic too. They welcomed me with open arms to the Choc Lit 'family' and are always so supportive, and encouraging. I of course am enormously grateful to the Choc Lit Tasting Panel, because without their acceptance, you wouldn't be just about to read this book!

Chapter One

The number 37 bus hurtled down the narrow street, its engine growling like an angry thunder god. Sarah froze rabbit-like and did a quick but futile calculation in her head. The distance to the safety of the café entrance, compared to the puddle (masquerading as Lake Windermere), which was about to disappear under huge rubber tyres = not a chance in hell.

'Oh no ... don't you dare! Can't you see me walking here, you—' The wind snatched her curse and tossed it up to the rain-soaked heavens.

In a desperate attempt at damage limitation, Sarah turned away from the road and flattened herself against the café window. Cupping both hands around her face, she closed her eyes, and set her back against the deluge. A second later, a muddy wave of what felt like the Arctic Ocean drenched almost every available inch of her from head to toe. Water trickled into her ears, under her collar, down her neck, into her boots, soaked through her coat, black velvet leggings, and worst of all, her new 'I cost an arm and a leg' red cashmere sweater dress.

A moan escaped from her lips as she realised that as well as the damage done to her clothes, a whole morning spent in the hairdressers had been undone in just a few seconds. Raising her hand to her head she could feel the lovely bounce of recently blow-dried hair at the front, and plastered rat's tails hanging at the back. She must look like someone had hit her on the back of the head with a water mallet.

Sarah blew heavily down her nose and tried to calm her rage. That bus driver had done this deliberately. He could have slowed down, moved out a little to avoid the puddle, but no. That bastard had been out to get her, and boy, did he get her. She swallowed the lump of humiliation forming in her throat. *Open your eyes, Sarah, before people inside the café notice.* On doing so, Sarah realised the 'before people notice' ship had well and truly sailed.

Through the clear spaces in the steamy window of the café, she could see customers reacting in a variety of ways to the bedraggled scarecrow of a woman peering in at them from the street. Some were nudging each other and laughing openly, others were more politely stifling giggles behind hands and one or two frowned and shook their heads in sympathy.

One customer, her best friend Karen, sat open-mouthed and then set down her coffee cup, pushed back her chair and hurried out into the rain.

'Oh my God, Sarah, come inside, let's try and get you dry somehow,' she said, grabbing Sarah's soggy arm and pulling her inside the door.

Sarah shook her arm free and looked around the pin-drop silent café. 'I'm not going in there now,' she hissed. 'I'm completely soaked and humiliated; I'll just go home instead.'

'Don't be daft, at least it's warm in here. By the time you get home you'll catch your death. I'm sure we could borrow a towel and there are hand dryers in the loo.'

Sarah glanced back outside at the torrential rain and then into the café where normal conversation had started up again. It *would* be daft to struggle home half-drenched in this downpour and the delicious waft of coffee and cinnamon rolls finally convinced her of Karen's argument.

At last, with the help of two towels and fifteen minutes with the hand dryer, Sarah could just about sit down at a table without squelching. The walk from the loo to the table had been less than silent however. Her boots had expelled damp air, making little farting noises each time her foot met the floor.

The café owner had been really lovely and insisted on giving Sarah coffee and freshly made carrot cake on the house. She'd also taken Sarah's coat and put it on the radiator through the back of the shop. The nasty 'laugh out loud' customers had left shortly after Sarah had walked in, and most people had smiled kindly or ignored her predicament.

Wrapping her hands around the big mug of coffee, Sarah relished the heat seeping into her chilled fingers. She sipped it as quickly as the scalding liquid would allow, feeling it melt a warm, comforting path to her tummy.

'Feeling better now, hon?' Karen asked, her head tilted to one side.

'Getting there, ta.' Sarah looked across the table at Karen. Immaculate as usual. Even though it was the middle of December and pissing down with rain, Karen always looked absolutely stunning. A cross between Angelina Jolie and Julia Roberts was how Sarah's neighbour had described her recently when she'd seen Karen giving Sarah a lift home. Sarah reckoned that she herself was average to fair on a good day, but right now people would describe her as a cross between Vicky Pollard and a loo brush.

They'd known each other since school and met once a month on a Saturday afternoon, regular as clockwork. Today, mindful of the fact she was the wrong side of thirty and feeling a bit dowdy, Sarah had bought new clothes and had her mousy blonde hair highlighted and restyled. Just this once, Sarah had wanted to feel attractive and make an impression when she met up with the glamorous Karen. Well, she'd certainly made an impression, hadn't she? Yep, an impression that she'd been hit with an ugly stick.

'I can't believe this awful weather lately,' Karen frowned. 'I think we'll need to build an ark soon.'

'We do live in Sheffield, Karen, and it *is* December; what do you expect?'

'OK, no need to get stroppy. It's not my fault you got drenched, is it?'

'No, sorry, I'll be alright when I've had a sugar fix.' Sarah sighed and dug her fork into the cake. She couldn't help noticing that all the male customers, while ostensibly chatting to their wives or girlfriends, kept sliding little surreptitious glances at Karen. Their eyes seemed to be attached by invisible threads to Karen's eyes, mouth, breasts and legs, though not necessarily in that order. Karen appeared oblivious to their worship, banging on about work and who said what to whom. But Sarah noticed Karen tossing her hair once or twice and licking cappuccino traces from her lips with a slow tongue.

Never mind, Sarah told herself; at least she had a husband who loved her. Poor Karen had a series of broken relationships as long as your arm. Even though she was such a lovely person, for some reason men didn't stay around. Perhaps they couldn't hack the constant predatory threat of other roaming males.

Sarah had once moaned to Neil that she always felt self-conscious when she met up with Karen. Neil had said all the right things: 'That's rubbish! Yes, I guess she's pretty, but she's not my type. I have the perfect woman right here.'

Sarah was not naive enough to believe she was the perfect woman, but it helped to know that he thought she was.

'This carrot cake is delicious, in fact I might get another piece, want some?' Karen asked, pushing her plate away.

Sarah shook her head and pulled a face. 'Another piece; you're throwing caution to the wind, aren't you?' She laughed. Karen watched her calorie intake very carefully as a rule, hence the svelte figure.

'You only live once.' Karen stood, inched her way between the table and chairs and walked to the counter.

Sarah nearly choked on her coffee; she couldn't believe it.

She'd been too preoccupied getting dry to notice anything before, but she could swear she'd seen a roll of fat when Karen's tummy had been at eye level. *And* she was getting more cake? There is a god!

Swivelling in her chair to get a better look at her friend's apparent weight gain, Sarah was afforded a profile view. Yes, definitely a paunch ... round, quite neat ... Sarah felt her own stomach lurch and her mouth fall open. *God, she's not getting fat you daft mare, she's ... no, that's crazy. Karen's always said that's the last thing ...*

'What are you gawping at?' Karen squeezed past again and settled back at the table, already sticking her fork into the generous slab of carrot cake.

'Err ... nothing, just not used to you eating cake like it's the new get-slim-quick fix.' *Go careful, Sarah. If she wants to tell you her secret then she will ...*

'What are you, the cake police? It's nice to have a little bit of what you fancy now and again. Aren't you always telling me that women are under pressure to conform to the stick-thin super model brigade and that we should fight against it?' Karen's brown eyes flashed and she rammed a huge forkful of cake into her mouth.

Sarah raised her eyebrows and held up her hands. 'Sorr-ee!' *Mood swings, weight gain ...*

Karen slammed her fork down and avoided Sarah's eyes. 'Look, I'm sorry, I'm a little emotional at the moment. I didn't mean to snap.' She looked back at Sarah, her eyes awash with sudden tears. 'You're the last person I wanted to get angry with ...'

'Hey, don't be silly, what's up?' Sarah reached for Karen's hand across the table. Karen snatched it away. 'No, don't be nice to me or I'll bawl my eyes out.'

'I think I can guess what's up. I hope I'm right or I'm probably going to get a slap ... it's not too many cakes that's caused your pancake washboard to bulge a bit, is it?' Sarah sat back in her seat, just in case.

Karen flushed and shook her head, no.

'Who's the daddy?'

'It's a mess; I don't want to talk about it.' Karen folded her arms and looked out of the window.

A mess? Sarah would give everything to be in Karen's platform boots. 'Was it a one-night stand, or ...'

'What don't you understand about the words "I don't want to talk about it"?' Karen cursed under her breath and shrugged into her coat. 'Look, I'm not in the mood for a heart to heart. I'm sorry, it's not you.' She picked up her bag and stepped into the aisle. 'I'll ring you, OK?' Karen briefly touched Sarah's shoulder and then rushed out into the rain.

The handbag was hurled with such ferocity that it scattered the carefully placed tower of exercise books across the back seat. Loose pages and colourful diagrams of the Dunkirk retreat plopped on to the floor and disappeared under the passenger seat. Yeah, that'd be right, not only did she have to mark them all, she now had to scrabble around with her arse in the air trying to retrieve the bits that had fallen out. *Serves you right, Sarah. You should try and calm your bloody temper.*

She slid behind the wheel and slammed the door on yet another miserable day. Three in a row – a hat trick. Saturday had seen the ruin of her new hairdo and clothes (the cashmere sweater dress would now just about fit the cat), and then the awful upset with Karen. Sunday, Neil had buggered off just as she was putting their seventh wedding anniversary meal on the table (which she'd planned for weeks and slaved over all day) – a mate of his was having a crisis, apparently. And Monday, today, the head teacher had announced Ofsted would arrive mid-week.

The imminent arrival of school inspectors was enough to

strike fear into the heart of even the most confident teachers at the best of times, but Sarah's mid-week timetable was definitely the worst of times. Both Wednesday and Thursday were full teaching days with the toughest classes in Years 9 and 10. There would be no hiding place.

Sarah tucked her shaking hands under her legs and leaned her head gently on the wheel. Bile rose in her throat and the school lunch she'd had, against her better judgement, hinted that it would like to get reacquainted. Dear God, if she felt like this on Monday, by Wednesday she'd probably vomit and pass out on the classroom floor. A coping strategy was needed pronto.

Two images were simultaneously offered for consideration courtesy of the panic section of her brain: 1) a few huge gin and tonics in the bath, or 2) a rigorous workout at the gym.

Sarah's heart lurched for the gin, while her head figured that she should steer clear of alcohol, at least until Inspector Gadget had finished with her.

She flicked open her phone and pressed speed dial. *Great, answerphone* ... 'Neil, it's me. Going to the gym. See you at home later ... Had a really, really awful day, tell you about it soon. And can you pop into Sainsbury's on your way home and get something quick for tea, a pizza or something? I can't be arsed to cook.' *Especially not after I spent so long preparing the meal yesterday, and then feeding it lovingly to the kitchen bin.* She chucked the phone over her shoulder and, instead of landing on her handbag, it of course decided to join the diagrams of Dunkirk.

To shower here or at home? Sarah glanced at her watch; time was getting on, even though she was as pink as a shrimp and covered in sweat, she'd best get home. The rowing machine, treadmill and weights had loosed a few feel-good endorphins, and the tension that had twisted her shoulders into a hunchback had begun to trickle away with her perspiration.

Picking up her fluffy towel she wiped her arms and face, shoved it into her gym bag and walked towards the exit. 'Sarah, hey how's tricks?'

Turning round she saw Natalie, a woman she often chatted to at the gym, hurrying towards her. Sarah groaned inwardly. Natalie was OK, but she was a huge gossip and Sarah avoided telling her anything too personal. Besides, she had to go home and have a shower, stuff some food down and then tackle those books. 'Hey, Natalie, I'm good. Can't stop though; I've got lots of school work to do.'

Natalie chose to ignore that and poked Sarah on the arm. 'Have you heard about the lovely Carlos?' Natalie's dark eyes shone with excitement. Carlos was one of the personal trainers at the gym.

Sarah sighed. 'No, what about him?'

'He's been sacked for shagging a client in the sauna.' Natalie leaned in conspiratorially. 'And the client was a bloke!' she hissed gleefully.

Sarah shrugged and turned for the door. 'Poor Carlos.'

Natalie put her hand on Sarah's arm preventing her from pushing the door open. 'Poor Carlos? Poor half the women here, including moi. Such a waste if you ask—'

'Yes, well I'm sure everyone will cope. Anyway, nice to see you but I must dash,' Sarah said, and once again made to leave. Natalie was beginning to piss her off big style.

But incredibly, once again Natalie put her hand on Sarah's arm. Bloody hell, couldn't this woman take a hint?

'Saw that lovely hubby of yours the other day. I didn't have time to stop and chat to him though as I was dashing to the library before they closed.'

Lucky Neil.

'He was just going in Mothercare with a drop-dead

gorgeous woman, long chestnut hair, tall, leggy,' Natalie nudged Sarah and winked, 'arm in arm they were, looked really cosy.' She gave a false laugh. 'Only teasing, pet. Your Neil wouldn't cheat, would he ... So who was she, his sister?'

Sarah put her hand on the door handle, more for support than intention to push it open. *No, please, no ...* Sarah's heart thundered against her rib cage and for the second time that day she thought she was going to lose her lunch. How many drop-dead gorgeous women with long chestnut hair did she know, and going into Mothercare ... no wonder Karen wouldn't tell her who the damned father was.

'Hey, are you alright, love? You've gone ever so pale ... I hope I haven't put my foot in it,' Natalie said. The nasty gleam in her eye and pretend concern on her spiteful face told Sarah that's *exactly* what she'd intended to do.

'What? No, course you haven't. Yes, yes, it's his sister,' she managed. 'I'm alright, just tired, Natalie. Bye.'

Sarah fled on jelly legs out through the changing rooms and into the car park. The damp cool of the night air rushed over her flushed face and neck, helping to steady her nerves a little. The clock on the dash said 6.05. Neil would probably still be in Sainsbury's and it was on the way home, anyway. Had the friend in crisis yesterday been Karen? The one he'd abandoned his anniversary dinner for? *Take deep breaths, you're overreacting, it will all be fine. Go and see Neil, he'll explain.*

As she drove, Sarah tried to focus. Neil and her oldest friend would never do that to her, surely. In fact, Neil had seemed surprised, almost shocked, when she'd told him that Karen was pregnant on Saturday.

'Really?' Neil's mouth had fallen open. 'Didn't think Karen was the mothering kind!' he'd said.

'Well, it obviously wasn't planned, and she's playing her "who's the pop" cards very close.'

'Blimey. So shall we have a takeaway?' Neil had walked into the living room and picked up the phone.

Thinking about it all again now though, Sarah remembered that he *had* turned very pink and hadn't looked at her directly. Perhaps Neil hadn't been shocked that Karen was pregnant at all. Perhaps he'd just been shocked because Karen had chosen to confide in her.

'And anyway, people may think *I'm* not the mothering kind!' she had yelled after him. 'Little do they know the reason we haven't heard the patter of tiny feet is because *you* have got cold ones where fatherhood's concerned!'

'Don't start on that again now; you're like a broken record with the baby thing. Do you want your usual?' Neil had dialled the curry house and there the matter had rested.

Sarah swung the car into a space and switched off the engine. She was getting ahead of herself. Neil probably went red on Saturday because he knew that Sarah would start on about babies again, would be jealous that her oldest (single) friend had become pregnant, while Sarah, a happily married woman of seven years, wanted to be, but her child-shy husband didn't think it was the right time yet, and hadn't done for the last three years. But would he ever?

She got out of the car and marched towards the brightly lit supermarket. There must be a rational explanation for why he'd been going into Mothercare (arm in arm) with Karen. She'd just walk up and ask him outright. No beating about the bush, no giving him time to think of some lame excuse. Sarah would know immediately if he was lying. If he scratched his left earlobe and swallowed repeatedly until his Adam's apple bobbed like a float on a lake ... then God knows what she'd do.

Neil was in the frozen food aisle when she pounced on him. 'Oh, hi!' He pinched her cheek. 'God, you look a bit messy, love.' He smiled.

'I didn't have time for a shower at the gym, but then I supposed you're used to your women drop-dead gorgeous nowadays, eh?'

Neil frowned, pulled his left earlobe and held up a pizza. 'No idea what you're on about. Your message said you'd had a really awful day, but don't take it out on me. Now, shall we have pepperoni, or four cheese?'

Sarah had to lean her weight against the freezer. He may just have an itch on his ear ... please don't let it be true ... please ... and not with Karen.

Neil was still holding up the pizza and frowning. 'Well, which one?'

'Are you the father of Karen's baby?' she whispered.

Neil flushed scarlet, put his hand to his ear, swallowed hard a few times and laughed a hard, brittle, and very false laugh. 'What? What did you just say?'

'You heard me!' Sarah screeched, making shoppers in their aisle, and the next three, stop dead in their tracks. An old couple deliberating over a packet of frozen Yorkshire puddings dropped it and stared open mouthed, a young couple pretended to read the instructions on a pizza, a middle-aged woman with a little boy slowed her trolley and shushed the child, and a young woman knelt to tie her trainers. Sarah could practically feel the curiosity emanating from all of them.

'You can't be serious ...' Neil stopped, but his Adam's apple jiggled for England. Sarah's vision seemed to have narrowed, tunnelled, until all she could see was that damned apple bobbing in his red blotchy neck. She shook her head, took a deep breath and blinked back tears.

'Oh, but I *am* serious, very serious.' She glared at the little audience they'd gathered and then back to Neil. 'So, are you the father?' Sarah flung her arms wide and thrust her neck forward. 'I need you to tell me the truth, and I'm sure all these nosy buggers listening in won't sleep until you do, either!'

Chapter Two

18 months later

The sound of the door clunking shut behind her, the cool touch of the hall tiles underfoot, and the lingering aroma of last night's curry, signalled she was home at last; another school day from hell was over.

Sarah wriggled her toes a little more on the smooth surface, and then dropped her sweaty shoes into the basket at the bottom of the stairs. Holding her aching back, she bent over, picked up the mail from the mat and flicked through the pile. *Crap, crap and more crap. Never mind about the decimation of the rainforests – the two-for-one garden gnome offer at Paradise Garden Centre is much more important.*

Bing-bong! She jumped as the doorbell chimed. Sarah rolled her eyes. *Who the hell is this, now?*

She sneaked into the living room and peeped through the blinds. It was damn near wine o'clock, and after the day she'd had, if it wasn't Johnny Depp out there, she wasn't interested.

Sarah could see that the caller was male, dark-haired, tall and suited. He had his back turned to her, and was tapping a clipboard on the side of his leg. *Nope, not Johnny Depp. Probably a time-waster, so he could bugger off.*

Just as she was closing the gap in the blind, the man turned and spotted her. He smiled, raised his clipboard and waved hello with his pen.

Bugger ... I'll have to open the damned door now!

'Hello,' she said, opening the front door slightly, 'I'm sorry, but I've just got in. I've lots to do, so I haven't got time to buy anything.'

‘Well, that’s alright then, because time is my business,’ he said.

Sarah noted that even though he wasn’t Johnny Depp, he wasn’t half-bad. He looked to be about thirty-five, had gorgeous sea-green eyes, a long aquiline nose and a full sensuous mouth. The mouth was curling at the edges in a slow smile.

She sighed. *Never mind his smile, Sarah, he’s a time-waster, get rid of him.* ‘As I said, I am really busy, and as you have just said, time is your business. Timeshares I expect, so I really must …’

‘I’m really not selling anything.’ He placed the pen between a set of perfect teeth, lowered his eyes and traced his finger down the pages on his clipboard.

‘Well, I don’t mean to be rude, but I must go,’ Sarah said, already starting to close the door. What she needed was a big glass of red and her feet up.

He looked up from his board and smiled again. ‘I think you *do* mean to be rude, actually. Don’t worry, I just need to go over a few instructions with you. You have a huge task to complete, and we need to make sure you know exactly what’s going to happen.’ He took a step towards her.

Sarah immediately slammed the door in his face. Who the bloody hell did he think he was, completely ignoring her? He was obviously a complete fruit loop – handsome, but a fruit loop nonetheless. A task to complete; now that was a new one.

Marching into the kitchen, she grabbed a wine glass from the cupboard and poured a big glug of red. Now, a comfy sofa and mind-numbing rubbish on the TV beckoned. Taking a mouthful of wine she walked into the living room, and nearly spat it out again. The fruit loop was sitting casually on her sofa, grinning from ear to ear.

‘Ooh, have you got a glass for me, Sarah? I could murder one.’

Managing to swallow the wine, she backed towards the door, gasping, 'How the hell did you get in here, and how do you know my name?' Frantically, she tried to remember where she'd put her mobile; was it still in her school bag?

Fruit loop held up his hands. 'Hey, sorry, don't be afraid. Asking for wine was crass of me. You must be freaked out. Look, I promise I'm not here to hurt you.'

Sarah inched out into the hall. Even if she could put her hand on the damned phone, she probably wouldn't have time to dial 999. No, the best solution was to make a run for it. She set down her wine glass on the hall table and turned for the front door ... only to see fruit loop standing in front of it.

She felt the floor come up to meet her, and leaned heavily against the wall. This was impossible; he was sitting on her sofa in the living room, wasn't he? 'How the ...?' He held up his hands again, silencing her. 'I told you, time is my business.' He shrugged. 'I can make it stop, go forward and back, but only for a short while, otherwise the dimensions get mucked up. I would certainly get into big trouble with the powers that be, too, but we'll talk about that another time; there's enough for you to take in at the moment, as it is.

'Anyway, suffice to say that I stopped time, walked round you, here in the hall, and then started it again. Same way I got in here, too. Now, we really must get down to business. I am not here to hurt you, I repeat *not here to hurt you*, Sarah. My name's John, by the way.'

John walked towards her, gesturing that she should return to the living room. Sarah led the way on shaky legs and then sank down into her armchair. She figured that the fallout from the Neil-and-Karen trauma and her stressful job had, at last, pushed her over the edge. Lots of her teacher friends had breakdowns ... this must be her turn. Actually, now that it had happened, she felt relieved, really ...

'So,' John's voice broke into her thoughts. 'Sarah Yates, thirty-four, divorced.' He looked at his clipboard. 'No children, history teacher at Grangeworthy High, stressed, disillusioned with the way teaching is going, though not with the subject of history, and not with most children, just the minority who eat you alive. The latest bane of your life is Danny Jakes of 9CM, who told you recently to "stick your detention up your fat arse!"'

John, now seated on her sofa, pulled a face of sympathy across the room, flicked over the page of notes and continued. 'Err ... husband ran off with best friend, they now have a child, you despise them both, especially him, because you gave him the best years of your life, and now think that your chance for kids has passed. You desperately wanted a child but your ex always put you off, always found some kind of excuse.' An even more sympathetic look found a home on John's face. 'Dear, oh dear.' He placed the clipboard down and looked across at her again. 'Now, I have got the right, Sarah Yates, haven't I?'

Sarah wished that he hadn't, but sadly he had described her life in a nutshell. Neil had indeed left with Karen about eighteen months ago now. It had been a drunken one-night stand apparently; the pregnancy had come as a terrible shock. They hadn't planned to keep the child, but then time went by and Karen found it impossible to have a termination. They started getting used to the idea, and Neil insisted on providing financial support, hence the trip to Mothercare.

Then, when Sarah had found out and everything was in the open, Neil and Karen had decided to make a go of it. So, it was Sarah's fault really – how nice for them to have it all magically and neatly resolved like that.

It was old news, but the pain was still as fresh as a daisy on a spring morning. Hearing the facts read out like a shopping list, even though John seemed sorry for her, did not help.

The pity of strangers ... wasn't that a poem, perhaps a film? She should audition for the lead role. Sarah sighed and rubbed her eyes.

'Yes ... yes that's me, unfortunately. Now, you need to disappear because I'm suddenly feeling very weary. I'll make an appointment with my Doctor in the morning, but for now, I just want to sleep.'

'Doctor, why?'

'To get some antidepressants or something for this breakdown I'm having.' She shrugged. 'I'm obviously talking to a hallucination.'

John threw back his head and laughed. 'No, Sarah, I'm as real as you. It's normal to feel shell-shocked, but you'll get over it quite quickly; people usually do.'

'So, I'm not having a breakdown?'

'Not as far as I know ... look, I am what's known as a Time-Needle. It's something you're born into and can't do anything about. My dad was a Time-Needle until his retirement a few years ago and so was his father. Our job is to sew together holes that have opened up in time using a Stitch. If they remain open, people will die. I find Stitches in time and you're a Stitch.'

Sarah looked at him open-mouthed for a few moments, and then, springing up, she wagged a finger at him. 'OK, that's it, and that's all! I need a drink!'

She shot out. John followed her to the kitchen. He watched, frowning, as she pulled a wine glass from the cupboard and picked up the bottle, all the while muttering under her breath.

'Err ... you have a glass out here in the hall already,' he said, going to the hall and returning with the glass.

'Oh, I'm terribly sorry, I forgot. How silly of me. I mean, I *am* behaving perfectly normally, aren't I? Talking to a Time Lord, Needle, or whatever the hell you are, listening to stories of sewing holes together in time, and what was the last thing?' she said, knocking back the wine in one gulp. 'Oh, yes, I'm a Stitch ... Yup, perfectly normal!' She poured more wine and glared at him.

'Oh dear, you really need to calm down a bit, Sarah. Do you mind if I have this one?' John asked, holding up the wine glass.

Sarah shrugged and stared out of the window. This was worse than she had initially feared. Not only was she having a full-blown breakdown, she couldn't make the damned hallucination stop. Her mind was totally out of control!

She closed her eyes and breathed in through her nose and out through her mouth, counted to three, and snapped her eyes open. No, he was still there, sipping her wine as if he was real! Her addled mind had conjured up a gorgeous guy and called him John. Johnny was apparently too obvious. God, how sad was she? Sipping her wine, she decided that the best thing to do was go with the flow. *If I play along, show myself ... my mind, that I'm not scared, perhaps the stress will go away ... and with it, the hallucination. And anyway, what choice do I have?*

'You look a bit calmer now,' John said, setting his glass on the table and drawing up a stool.

Sarah sighed and opened the fridge door. 'Yes, well I think it's sinking in a bit now. Would you like some crackers and cheese? Wine on an empty stomach isn't such a good idea. I was going to dial a pizza later, but I've gone off that idea; funny, that.'

'Yes, please if you're sure it's no trouble,' John said, peering round her at the contents of the fridge. 'Ooh, and a bit of that cold ham and pickles if there's some going begging.'

'Anything else, you know, while I'm here?' Sarah asked.

'Err ... is that Sainsbury's houmous?' John asked, licking his lips.

A few minutes later, Sarah, seated opposite at the kitchen table, watched as John made short work of his food. She decided he did look a bit like Johnny Depp, but his face was broader, his jaw squarer, and as far as she remembered Depp's eyes were brown, not green like the twinkly ones looking at her right now. Biting into a cracker, Sarah pointed a piece of cheese at him and asked, 'So, you're a time traveller; do you have a wife?'

'A wife?' John looked startled. 'No, but I think we need to keep our relationship platonic, Sarah. It's not that I don't find you attract—'

'No! It's a book and a film,' she said, horrified that he'd thought she was coming on to him. She sighed and shook her head. *Hang on? What the hell does it matter what he thinks, he's not bloody real!*

'Oh, I see,' John was saying. 'I don't keep up much with books and films.' He popped a pickled onion into his mouth. 'And, I'm not a time traveller; you are ... or will be, if you agree to it, of course.'

'Oh, right, yeah. I'm always zipping about the universe in my trusty TARDIS. More ham, John?'

'Now you are just being facetious, Sarah. Ham ... mm, just a couple of slices will be lovely, thanks.'

'Anyway,' Sarah said, with her head in the fridge, 'thought you said I was a Stitch in time, not a time traveller.' She forked ham on to John's plate, a thought suddenly occurring to her. 'Ha ha, "a stitch in time saves nine"! Mind you, that old saying means that if you don't attend to a problem immediately, the problem will get worse. God knows quite what *you* meant, John.'

John thanked her and took a sip of wine. He stared at her across the table while she crunched her crackers. 'Look, Sarah, I think you're ready to hear what this whole thing is about.'

Sarah drained her glass and folded her arms. 'Yup, I think I'm ready too, John; fire away, why don't you?'

'OK.' He leaned forward and pushed his plate to one side. 'The meaning of the old saying "a stitch in time saves nine" has become corrupted over the centuries. It actually means that if a hole in time isn't sewn up by a Stitch, nine people will die. Those nine people may, or may not, be pivotal actors on the stage of history, but if they die, or are never born, the effect on the future is always negative. The Stitch has to travel back through time to save them.'

Sarah swallowed a cracker and began to admire the capacity her brain had for such intriguing plots. She was even starting to enjoy it. Great-looking guy, wine, interesting conversation, even if it *was* all in her head; it was better than watching EastEnders on her own ... again.

'OK, John,' she said, rolling up a slice of ham and dipping it in the houmous. Sarah wasn't fussed about what a hallucination thought of her table manners. 'So, I'm this Stitch. Why are there holes, why me, and what do I have to do?' She shoved all the ham in her mouth at once.

John raised his eyebrows slightly as he watched her stuffing her face, but didn't comment. 'Why do holes appear? There are lots of theories too complicated to go into now. Why you? I have no idea, I just get the information. What you have to do, I *can* answer.' He took a dainty nibble of cheese and dabbed his mouth with a bit of kitchen roll. 'A stitch is a person but it is also the acronym for your task. You have to:

S-ave
T-hree
I-mportant
T-errestrials
C-lose
H-ole.'

Sarah frowned and dabbed her finger at the last few crumbs of cheese on her plate. 'Great acronym. It has just one dastardly flaw, Mr Depp.'

'Mr Depp?' John asked, draining his glass.

'Yes, you said earlier that I had to close the hole to save *nine*, like the old saying. Well, now, you just said *three* important terrestrials.' Sarah sat back, folded her arms and giggled. *Seems like my hallucination is having a breakdown, too!*

'No flaw, Sarah, you save three, and then the children that they go on to have, or sometimes, grandchildren, make up the nine,' John said smugly. 'Is it OK if I pour another?' He held up his glass.

'Yes, why not? And get one for me, would you?' Sarah held her glass above her head as he walked past. She'd already had one large glass, but hey, the wine was helping her relax, and she definitely needed that. With any luck she'd pass out and wake up tomorrow John-less. 'Oh, and I think we'd be comfier in the living room,' she called over her shoulder as she left the kitchen.

Sarah flopped on to the sofa, punched the cushions, and slotted them behind her back. She stretched and yawned loudly as John came in.

'Don't get too comfy and go to sleep. You need to understand what's going to happen,' he said, handing her the wine.

Sarah noticed it was a very small glass. 'So do you ever go back in time, John?' she asked, swirling the wine around her glass.

'No.' He looked at her aghast. 'If a Needle ever goes back in time without express permission there are always consequences for him. He would be seriously punished.' Sarah pulled a face but said nothing.

'OK,' he said, picking up his clipboard and sitting in the

chair opposite. 'Looks like the three that you are down to save are: a homesteader in the Old American West, someone caught up in the Sheffield Blitz, and,' he flicked paper, 'ah, yes, a suffragette in early twentieth-century London.'

'Well, *that* confirms it then. I am having a breakdown.' Sarah sighed, yawned again, and closed her eyes.

'What does?' John frowned.

'Well, it's a bit bloody predictable, isn't it? I teach all those things in my job, don't I? My brain has neatly woven them into my hallucination.'

'No, Sarah, you aren't having a breakdown. It's partly because of what you do, that *you* have been chosen as a Stitch. You have to know the period well, to be able to blend in.'

Opening one eye she said, 'I thought you didn't know why I had been chosen – that you "just got the information"?' Sarah waggled her index and middle fingers in mock quotation marks.

'Yes, that's true, I only know little bits.' John sighed and looked at his watch. 'But as far as I can tell, Stitches are chosen because they have hidden qualities, courage and stuff. They don't always recognise that in themselves and stitching brings it out ... in most of them. Look, I need to know, are you going to do this or not?'

Sarah closed her eye. 'Hmm, I don't think I'd be in the *most of them* category. I feel right out of courage at the moment, John, hidden or otherwise.'

'But will you do it?'

'Do I have a choice?'

'Yes ... though you will have deaths on your conscience if you don't.'

'Oh, that's nice then. Has anyone ever refused?'

'A few,' John said. 'One had devastating consequences. There was a guy a few hundred years ago, his name was

Norman. He refused, and someone who should have been born wasn't, and eventually someone who shouldn't have been born was.'

Sarah opened both eyes. 'Who?'

'Hitler.'

'Hitler! God, how awful!' Sarah said, reaching for her wine glass.

'Yeah, you know that saying, "time waits for no man"? It was originally time waits for Norman, but unfortunately, Norman didn't care.'

Sarah scratched her head. 'But I don't get it. If I go back to the Old American West and save somebody, their children or grandchildren will already have been born, had children of their own, grown old and may be dead by now. So how can all of that have happened if I haven't even gone back in time yet? And what I do back in time will totally mess up the future ... won't it?

'No, Sarah,' John said, shaking his head. 'You've just grown up watching films and reading books that *assume* that's how time works. Scientists have no real clue. They *say* they do and provide lots of equations and write books to prove it, but unfortunately, they have it all wrong.'

'Wrong? So, how ...?'

'Never mind all that now. We really don't have the time ... no pun intended,' John said, smirking.

Swinging her legs to the floor Sarah leaned forward and ran her hands through her hair. This was *beyond* crazy now. She decided the best option was to agree to everything and then hopefully John would go. He kept glancing at his watch, so must want to be off. *There you go again, Sarah; he's not real!*

'OK, I'll do it. What happens next, and who do I save first?'

'Now that's a little tricky,' John said, looking sheepish.

'We aren't told that bit. It will happen unexpectedly and you'll just have to cope the best you can … Also, there's no guarantee that you will pick the right person, and even if you do … no guarantee that you can save them. It's all part of a test to see if you're up to the job, I think.'

'Oh, this just gets better and sodding better.'

John ignored her. 'Anyway, other Stitches have told me that everything generally falls into place when they get there. So, Sarah,' he stood up and moved to the hallway, 'I'll bid you good evening. I need to check that everything is as it should be at the market garden. I have two staff, Roy and Helen, that lock up for me. They run the small shop that's attached to it too, but I always like to check everything.'

Sarah jumped up and followed him to the door. 'You're a manager of a market garden?'

'No, I own it. It doesn't really feel like a job; I love it,' he said, grinning. 'I don't really like this Time-Needling stuff, but as I said, I was born to it and can't do anything about it – awful really, so much responsibility.' John opened the door and stepped out.

Sarah shook her head. What kind of an imagination must she have?

John said goodbye and crunched a few steps along her drive. He hesitated and turned round. 'Oh, and don't mention anything about the future to anyone from the past. That would be problematic.'

'Yes, right, I can see how it would be. See you!' she called, quickly shutting the door.

Bewildered, Sarah walked round the house locking the doors and stacking plates and glasses in the dishwasher. Neil and Karen had a lot to answer for. She wondered if they would feel a tiny bit guilty when the men in white coats showed up at her front door with a nice strappy jacket. She poured a glass of water and opened her telephone/address book at the 'D' for doctor page, placing it by the phone. Snapping the hall light off, and the house into darkness, she trudged up the stairs to bed.

Ten minutes later, John stepped into the hallway. He flicked on a small torch and tiptoed to the bottom of the stairs. Reassured by thunderous snoring from upstairs, he carefully opened Sarah's schoolbag and slipped an envelope into it. He dropped Sarah's spare key, which he'd snatched earlier, back into his pocket, extinguished the torch and then quietly let himself out of the house.

Chapter Three

That cannot possibly be the right time! Sarah held the alarm clock an inch from her nose, trying to force her bleary eyes wide as the morning light seeped through her curtains. Yes, no doubt about it, the clock definitely said 6.30 a.m. Jeez Louise, it only felt like a few hours since she had flopped into bed!

The first coherent thought of the day flitted across her consciousness like a nervous sparrow. It eventually alighted and pecked painfully at her sense of wellbeing. *Tuesday ... ouch ... lesson one, 9CM ... Ouch, ouch ... 9CM means Danny Jakes ... OUCH, OUCH!*

Groaning, she pushed her face into the pillow and tried to dislodge the hammering beak with an image of a graceful swan, coming to land on the half-term holiday next week. Just as the swan touched down, stretching its beautiful neck of freedom, John's face and last night suddenly surfaced, throwing the swan into a flurry of flapping wings and mad panic.

Sarah leapt out of bed as if she'd been scalded. The awful prospect of teaching Danny Jakes suddenly seemed like a walk in the park compared to the experience she'd had the previous night.

Hurrying over to the window and peeping through the curtains, she half-expected to see John outside, clipboard in hand, looking back up at her. He wasn't there, thank goodness. No, everything was as it should be for a Sheffield suburban Tuesday morning in May.

The milk float hummed, the birds sang in the trees, and next door's cat prepared to take another poo in her flower bed. Sarah was so relieved to see life unchanged that she couldn't be bothered to rap on the glass to shoo it away.

After a shower, she was beginning to feel more like herself. Perhaps she wasn't having a breakdown, just a blip of psychosis due to stress. *I mean, if I was having a full-blown breakdown, I would be hallucinating again by now, wouldn't I?*

Sarah wiped steam from the bathroom mirror and pulled down her bottom lids. No, her eyes looked normal. She stuck out her tongue; yuck, normal. But then, what would she expect to find if she were mentally ill: spiralling eyes and little green men dancing on her tongue? *Come on; just get on with the day and stop worrying. You need all your energy for Danny Jakes.*

Breakfast over, Sarah collected her school bag from the hall. She remembered there were a few books she had meant to mark last night, but of course hadn't. Glancing at the clock in the kitchen, she realised she didn't have time to do it now. Oh well, can't be helped. Now, where were her shoes?

The shoe hunt proved futile in the kitchen and living room, but her eyes lingered on the doctor's number in her open telephone book. Sarah's fingers hovered above it but then made themselves busy plumping cushions instead. *Just see how it goes for now. And if you don't find your shoes in a minute, this whole morning will be a disaster!*

The shoes were eventually located in the shoe-basket of all places. Slipping them on, and grabbing her coat and car keys, she left for school.

'Hey, Sarah, have you got 9CM first period?' Gary Keynsham, Head of English, shouted across the staff room. Gary always shouted, even when there was no need. Sarah thought he just loved the sound of his own voice and was so far 'up himself' that he was insufferable.

She forced a smile. 'Yes, why?'

Gary closed the gap between them and stood inches from

her nose. 'Can you give a message to Danny Jakes?' The volume of his voice required a step backward.

She nodded.

'Tell him to come to my room at break; I have a reward for him. He's behaved brilliantly and is making fantastic progress!' Gary flashed a row of tombstone teeth.

'Really, well you must have something I don't; he's a complete shit in my lessons,' Sarah said.

'Yes, I have heard he can be a tinker, but he's *always* great for me. Must be the teaching!' He winked, punched her arm and let out a heehaw bray that rivalled any donkey's. 'Just joking, of course. Thanks for that, pet, see ya laters!' Gary shimmied off like a peacock in heat. He had his eye on the new student teacher, the lovely Jodie. Jodie, having seen his approach, ducked out into reprographics.

Sarah sighed and picked up her bag. Her watch told her it was 8:50. *Ten minutes to countdown, but I need a pee.*

After washing her hands, Sarah checked her appearance in the mirror. She wasn't too bad for thirty-four, was she? Her mousy blonde, shoulder-length hair could do with a trim and more highlights, but she'd managed to keep fairly slim and her light blue eyes still sparkled. Neil had once said that her eyes were 'wishy-washy' but then, he was a first-class toerag after all. She wondered what colour eyes his little boy had. Karen's were brown so ... *stop it, Sarah. For God's sake, why do you do this to yourself?*

She pulled lipstick out of her school bag and wondered if the assessment of her appearance was correct. Neil dumping her for the beautiful Karen hadn't done wonders for her confidence. But if she *did* look attractive, why she was 'on the shelf', as her mother called being single. Perhaps she'd ring her mum tonight, or her younger sister, Ella. A chat with Ella normally boosted her confidence and perhaps she could confirm her sanity or lack of it.

And 'on the shelf'? What a stupid expression. Women weren't tins of peas, or packets of biscuits, were they? Sarah applied the lipstick and blotted it with a tissue. Maybe her appearance wasn't the problem; maybe she was just boring.

'Morning, Sarah!' Janet Simms breezed in. She taught drama and was the personification of her subject. She was larger than life, both physically and metaphorically, and today was dressed in a flamboyant African-print maxi dress. Her flame-red hair clashed with the pink of her lipstick and her beady black eyes narrowed as they danced across Sarah's face.

'Now, what's up, tell your Auntie Janet.' She pinched Sarah's cheek 'My mission for this morning is to turn that frown, upside down!'

'Nothing, Janet, I'm OK.' Sarah managed a watery smile and put her lipstick away in her bag.

'Nonsense! If you're OK, then I'm a Dutchman!'

Immediately a picture of Janet wearing clogs, a Dutch hat and standing next to a windmill, popped into Sarah's mind. She shook it away and was about to close her bag when she noticed an envelope tucked down the side of her pencil case. Pulling it out, she saw that it had her name written in the top left-hand corner.

'Well, I'm popping for a little wee; when I come out I want the truth, kid!' Janet bellowed, stomping into a cubicle.

Frowning, Sarah opened the envelope, slid out a letter and tried not to listen to the thunder of Niagara Falls, which passed for Janet's 'little wee'. After reading the first sentence, the thump of her heart drowned out Janet's efforts and a troop of cartwheeling elephants showed up in her belly.

Hi Sarah, John here – hope you have recovered from the shock of meeting me last night.

Leaning on the sink with her left hand, she managed to control the shake in her right, just enough to read the rest.

There are one or two points I forgot to mention. When you have found the person you are supposed to save, you may get a sign. It could be itchy feet, tingling in your back, or perhaps hiccups. These are some of the things Stitches have reported.

Mind you, having said that, sometimes there is no physical sign. Sometimes there is just a feeling, you know?

Oh yes, and if you mention something we have in the present to someone in the past by mistake, you should get a warning. Ringing in the ears, belching uncontrollably or possibly a fit of the giggles have been known.

Sorry this all sounds a bit vague, but every Stitch is different. Anyway, just do your best, Sarah.

See you soon,

John ☺

'I feel better for that; nothing worse than needing a pee in the middle of a class, is there?'

Janet's attempt at hand washing was unceremoniously interrupted by Sarah, frantically waving a piece of paper in front of her face. 'Can you see this?' Sarah yelled.

Janet took a step back to avoid a paper cut to the nose. 'Well, of course, you're waving it inches from my face. What on earth ...'

'Yes, but what is it, what can you actually SEE?' Sarah held it up with both hands, wild eyes intently watching Janet's face.

Janet's normally confident, unruffled expression started to slip. She looked decidedly unsure, perhaps a little scared, and backed towards the hand dryer. 'It appears to be a letter, Sarah.'

'Appears to be, what do you mean, is it or isn't it?'

'Err ... it is,' Janet said in a small voice.

Sarah tossed her head back. 'Ha! I'm not crazy then. Here, take it, read it, tell me what it says!' She thrust the letter at Janet's ample bosom.

Janet, bewildered, eyed Sarah warily, took the letter and said soothingly, 'OK, calm down.' Janet read it and shrugged. 'Itchy feet, hiccups, it doesn't make much sense to me ... is it supposed to?'

'No, Janet, but incredibly ... it means this whole thing is real!' Sarah snatched the letter and squeezed Janet's shoulder.

Janet stepped back again and screamed, '*Eeee!* What the hell ...'

The hand dryer blew fiercely down Janet's back.

'It's OK,' muttered Sarah, grabbing her bag and rushing for the door. 'It's only a bloody hand dryer, God *knows* what state you'd be in if you had *my* life at the moment.'

Sarah ran across the playground as the bell for first lesson sounded. Why she couldn't work on one of those nice new compact sites instead of this sprawling 1950s' job, she didn't know. The history block was detached from the main school across two playgrounds and when the weather was bad she got soaked, along with her books.

Thankfully, it was quite a bright day today but very breezy, and the wind picked that moment to catch her light cotton skirt and reveal her knickers to the world. '*Aaaargh* ... bloody wind!' she yelled, dropping her bag and textbooks to the floor as she struggled to cover her modesty.

'HAHAHAHA! Oooh, Miss, red lace knickers. You hoping to get lucky tonight?'

With a face as red as her knickers, she looked for the owner of the voice. Little knots of kids making their way to lessons laughed discreetly behind hands, but to her left, Danny Jake's gang stood blatantly howling and pointing.

Danny swaggered over. He was tall, well built for his age and had his black hair spiked within an inch of its life with bomb-proof hair gel. 'Want some help picking up your books, Miss?' he said, an angelic look on his face.

'Was that you making disgusting remarks just then, Danny?' Sarah hissed, scrabbling to gather the spilled contents of her bag.

Danny stood up, his arms full of textbooks. 'Now, would I do a thing like that, Miss?' His eyes twinkled gleefully and he winked across at his gang.

The gang collapsed into more sycophantic laughter and Sarah decided to just leave it. She was really late for the lesson, completely thrown by the letter from John and, of course, now flustered and embarrassed by this hideous knicker incident. 'Just bring the books, Danny; we are late for lesson,' she snapped, marching to her classroom.

Behind the desk in her classroom, Sarah logged on to get the register up. She hid her hot face behind the computer screen, and tried to rescue some dignity and calm from the depths of despair she was drowning in. She should never have worn those knickers. Who was she kidding? Those knickers were reserved for sexy vibrant young women, not plain Jane, past their sell-by dates like her. *Deep breaths, only an hour to get through, then you have a free period.*

'OK, you lot! Try to keep the noise down to a dull roar whilst I get the register up. Sit down, books out, and be quiet!' she barked, trying to remember what the hell she was supposed to be teaching them. Her mind had gone blank. Her brain just showed acres of desert, where facts, fun teaching activities, and interesting anecdotes should have been.

'Miss, we're not doing about Jews and the Hollowcoast again are we? It's sad, and I've had enough of it, to be honest.'

Sarah peeped around the side of her screen to see who'd spoken. Oh, Kelly Anderson, the best-behaved kid in 9CM. If she was in a mood, then God help her, the rest would be unimaginable.

Sarah stood up and walked to the front of the class. 'No, Kelly, we aren't looking at the Holocaust today. And yes, of course that part of history is extremely sad, but we must learn the lessons—'

'So what *are* we doing then?' Danny Jakes interrupted, flicking the ear of the girl sitting in front of him.

'Danny, stop that!' Sarah said, taking a marker and turning to write the title of the lesson on the whiteboard. She hoped by the time the pen connected to the board she would remember what the hell she was supposed to do. *Look in your planner, you silly cow. Get a grip, Sarah, before you just completely fall apart!* But the planner seemed to have disappeared from the desk, and the noise of restless students was growing – along with her panic.

'What are we doing, Miss? My mum said that I need to write the title, lesson objectives and date, neatly every lesson. Mum says that it helps me concentrate on what's to come next. If you don't say what we are doing, I can't concentrate and everything will get messed up,' Kelly whined, tapping her pen on her glasses annoyingly.

'Err ... hang on, Kelly, I'm just looking for my planner.'

'It's on your chair, Miss.' Kelly sighed, rolled her eyes and folded her arms.

Grabbing the planner as if it were the last lifeboat on the *Titanic*, Sarah flicked to today's date. *Phew, yes that was it, the Blitz!*

'Right, Year 9, listen up—'

'Why do you always say listen up?' interrupted Danny, again. 'It's stupid. Why not listen down, or listen across, or lis—'

'Danny, just be quiet! Also get your book and pen out, everyone else is ready,' Sarah snapped, wishing the little shithead far away.

Danny made no move to comply; instead, he rocked on his chair and grinned nastily. 'I think you'll find, Miss, that there are at least three other people who haven't got their books or pens out.'

Sarah glanced around and noticed that these three were the members of Danny's crew.

'And, anyway, what's the point in getting our books out when we have no idea what the hell we're supposed to be doing, eh?'

Sarah folded her arms and fixed Danny with a hard stare. 'Right, Danny, you've just got your name on the board for being so rude. And today, everyone, we are going to be looking at the Blitz.'

She turned to write Danny's name and the title on the board, only to be stopped by a barrage of Jelly Tots pattering across her back. She whirled round, glaring at the now silent class.

'Was that you, Danny?' she asked quietly, feeling her heart rate start to climb steadily up the scale.

'Me?' His lips peeled back from his teeth in a vicious snarl. 'Why is it always me?

'Good, question, Danny!' Sarah threw back.

'You got no proof!'

'Well, I was in the middle of writing *your* name on the board, so we have a motive.'

'Well, you're wrong. For your information, it wasn't me it was her!' Danny stood up and pointed at Kelly.

'Kelly? I very much doubt ...'

'Yeah, it was smelly Kelly, with the big fat belly!'

A number of things happened next. Danny's gang howled with laughter and banged their fists on the desk, Kelly howled with misery and threw a book at Danny, and Sarah felt herself teetering on the brink of insanity.

'Stop that and sit down! Danny, you are in detention, I'm writing to your parents, and move to the front of the room where I can keep an eye on you. Kelly, put that bottle of water down. If you squirt it at him, you'll be in trouble, too.'

Sarah put her hands on her head and watched the ensuing mayhem. Nobody took a blind bit of notice and Kelly drenched Danny with the water. Danny changed his expression from evil snarl to terminator mode and began climbing over the desks towards a cowering Kelly.

To Sarah, the whole grisly floorshow seemed to be happening in slow motion. One last plan to stem the tide of anarchy in the classroom suddenly entered her head.

'Right! That's it! I'm going to get Mr Lockyear from down the corridor!'

The head teacher only taught one lesson a week, and lucky for her, this was the day he taught, just three classrooms down from hers. *Thank God for Mr Lockyear!* Sarah rushed for the door, opened it, but instead of stepping into the corridor, she stepped into a place that looked like a picture in the World War Two textbook she'd had open on her desk.

Sarah stopped in her tracks. Open-mouthed, she gaped at her surroundings. She was in a street in the middle of a city. Everywhere was silent. People in wartime clothes with gas masks slung across their shoulders shopped, cycled, jumped on and off trams and generally went about their business. They called to each other and chatted, but she was deaf to their voices. It was as if Sarah were watching from behind triple glazing.

Shock released her momentarily, and she whipped round to the door, but both the door and the classroom had disappeared.

CRACK! A noise exploded inside her head like a firework

in a dustbin. Sarah fell to her knees, holding her ears. As she did, her senses kicked into action. She could now see, hear, smell and feel her new surroundings. The immediate feeling seeping through the wet pavement to her stocking-clad knees was cold; freezing cold. *Stocking-clad knees? She hadn't been wearing stockings; and freezing? It was May, for God's sake!*

'Ee, Sarah, have you slipped on t'ice? Come on, love, give me your hand.'

Sarah looked up at an outstretched hand, and beyond that, to a moon-faced man of around fifty-five years of age. How the hell did he know her, because she'd certainly never seen him before. He sported a trilby hat and a neat moustache, and wore a brown suit. His eyes were blue, sharp and at the moment full of concern for her.

He waved his hand in front of her eyes. ''Ere, take my hand, love ... You alright, Sarah? You look right pasty.'

Having no better plan, Sarah allowed him to help her up. It was then that she became aware of what she was wearing. Flat brown lace-up shoes, a sage green, thick, knee-length dress with a round collar, a heavy, black winter coat, and a hat which appeared to be, she pulled down the brim, ah, yes, red. Sarah extended a finger and poked the frowning moon-face on the shoulder. He felt solid. *Not a hallucination then.* She pinched her wrist and winced. Moon-face peered at her more closely. 'What's up, love, eh?'

Sarah looked around again at the busy scene. *Shit, this is all real then*! She gawped, slack-jawed, at him. Not only was she really here, in the past, *she* had a life to save. This was 'way random and weird' as the kids would say. No wonder Norman had bottled it.

'So, do you feel able to walk, love? Take my arm; I think I'd better walk you 'ome.'

Sarah looked at him and said, 'Home ... Sheffield?'

'Of course. You don't have an 'ome anywhere else do you? Now, I think you've had some kind of a turn. Hold on to Albert's arm, yes that's right. Just take a few deep breaths and we'll trot on.'

Sarah trotted on with Albert, along what she imagined was the High Street. She could just about recognise it, but most of the buildings they walked past were long gone in Sarah's time. For a few moments she put her fears behind her and was entranced as she walked through the past. The history that she'd only read about and seen in photos lived and breathed all around her.

The smell of wartime Sheffield amazed her most. As the main 'steel city', the smoke from the many factories and foundries lay heavy in the air. People passing in the street looked relatively clean, but had a mixture of odours emanating from them that were hardly Chanel. Mothballs fought with hair oil, stale sweat and nicotine for precedence. The number of people, young and old, smoking like chimneys, really shocked her. Even though she knew that the dangers of smoking were not yet known, it was still hard to take in.

'So let's 'ope Violet has made that bread she was on about, eh? I could do wi' a cuppa and some nice bread and drippin',' Albert said, smacking his lips.

'Violet?' Sarah looked up at him.

'Aye, Violet, yer auntie. Crikey, lass, you must 'ave bumped yer head. I think you need a nice lie-down after we get back.'

Sarah realised that amnesia might be the best tack to take. That would account for her being totally bemused with the situation and would minimise suspicion. She glanced sidelong at Albert as he stopped and shook a cigarette from a packet. 'Want one, duck?'

'No, I don't smoke thanks, Alb—'

'Don't smoke, and I'm a Dutchman!' Albert chuckled, lighting up.

Sarah wondered if he was somehow linked through time to Janet. He stuck out his arm and they set off again.

As they walked, she figured the main thing she needed to do was to find out who she was, how Albert knew her and this auntie Violet woman, where *exactly* she was in time, and crucially, who she had to save. The sooner she did that, the sooner she could go back. Her heart did a little somersault; well at least she hoped she could get back.

'Albert, what day is it?' she asked, trying to keep the panic out of her voice. 'I think you're right, I have got a touch of amnesia. Must have happened when I fell.'

Albert stopped and stared, his cigarette stuck to his bottom lip. 'Bloody 'ell, you don't know what day it is? I reckon we'd best go to 'ospital, lass.'

'No, I'll be alright soon, no worries.'

'No worries? You're talking a bit odd, too,' Albert muttered, taking her by the elbow and setting off again.

'Yes, sorry, so what's the day and date?'

'Thursday, the 12th of December.'

'But what year is it, Albert?'

He stopped again and shook his head. 'Are you sure you're not just pullin' my leg?'

'No, I'm not, Albert … I wish I was.'

'It's 1940.' He sighed and took her elbow again. 'Now come on, let's get 'ome, it'll be dark by four o'clock and I'm bloody freezin' already. I'm due to go back out later and I need a warm first.'

Sarah hurried along next to him, numb from the cold, but mostly from the revelation that it was December the 12th. She knew that on that day, the Sheffield Blitz began in earnest around 7 p.m. and lasted until about 4 a.m. There would be another attack on the 15th and 16th, leaving over 660 people dead in total and over 80,000 buildings destroyed.

These grim facts circled around her head as they hurried through the darkening streets. After 10,000 incendiary bombs had done their work, 40,000 people would be homeless and large areas of Sheffield would resemble the fires of hell. Sarah shook her head and blinked back tears. Just before, in the classroom, she couldn't remember anything about what she was supposed to teach. Now, everything she wanted 9CM to learn screamed in her mind.

The weird and awful thing was it hadn't even happened yet. But it would, in just a few short hours, and she'd be right in the middle of it.

Chapter Four

The light was fading fast as they hurried along the freezing city streets. Sarah pulled the coat collar more closely about her neck, sniffed a few times and searched in her pockets for a hanky. The pockets were bare, so she dabbed at her nose with the back of her hand. Why did your nose always run in cold weather? Perhaps she should ask Albert; she was sure he'd love a conversation about snot after everything else she'd said to him so far.

A little while later, realisation dawned that they were making for Pitsmoor, the area where she had lived as a child. Sarah lived in Stannington now, and hadn't been back for years, but the railway viaduct of the Wicker Arches looked just the same, and she took some comfort from such familiarity in an alien world. Then she remembered Pitsmoor would be hit badly and the old arches would suffer damage by the morning.

Presently, Albert led her along a narrow street of back-to-back houses, very different from the 1930s' semi she lived in now, and turned into a narrow ginnel. At the other side was a large yard, containing six houses opposite the same number of outside toilets. These types of houses would be long gone in the present. Albert led her to the end house, knocked on the door and walked in.

'Violet! You 'ere? I found Sarah in town and she's gone a bit funny!'

Sarah sighed and shook her head. If only you knew the truth, Albert, you'd go a bit bloody funny!

A woman wearing a blue-and-white flower-patterned apron appeared from a door at the back of the house. She looked to be around her mid-forties, plumpish, with auburn hair rolled in the classic wartime fashion, and a kind open face in which two emerald-green eyes twinkled.

'Gone a bit funny? She was alus a bit funny weren't you, love?' Violet chuckled, drawing Sarah towards a cosy fire roaring in the grate.

Sarah was divested of her coat and made to sit in the chair by the fire. She took in her surroundings while Albert and Violet talked of rumours going around about the best place to get fresh meat and even a turkey for Christmas.

The living area was spotlessly clean, but tiny. Again, Sarah knew that houses like this were small and cramped, but to actually step inside one was a different matter. There was a ceramic sink and draining board under the window, a row of cups on hooks next to it on the wall, a kitchen table and chairs, upon which a teapot and sugar bowl sat, two wing-back chairs either side of the fire, and a few shelves, mostly empty save for a few items. These items were a jar marked flour, a smaller jar which looked to be jam, and various pickles. *Must have a cellar; that's where the cheese, milk, eggs and any cold meat would be.* Centrally on the floor was a large piece of flowered carpet that had definitely seen better days.

'So what's this about you being funny then, lass?' Violet was saying, sitting opposite.

'I think I have a bit of amnesia, think I bumped me 'ed when I fell on t'ice,' Sarah said, noting that her Yorkshire accent had suddenly become much broader than it was normally.

'Oh, dear. Well you know who I am, don't you?'

Sarah nodded. 'Auntie Violet.'

'Well, she knows that only 'cos I told her,' Albert butted in.

'And how long have you lived 'ere with me?' Violet ignored Albert.

Sarah shrugged.

'By 'eck, you don't know?'

'That's nowt, Violet; she didn't even know what year it was!' Albert said, taking his hat off and running his hands over his balding pate.

'Alright, Albert, can't you see that you're upsetting the poor lass? Look, love, you came to me nearly twenty year ago when your mum, my sister, passed on. She got tuberculosis. Your dad died of it five years before that.' Violet leaned across and took Sarah's hat off. 'We've been great company for each other ever since. You were on your own, and so was I, after my poor Billy was killed in t' Great War. Now, do you remember 'owt of that?'

'Err ... yes, a bit. I think I'm starting to remember now,' Sarah said. She figured that if she said no, they may cart her off to the hospital. That thought made her shudder.

'She's not that bad, Albert. Now you best be off, your Aggie will be wondering where you are.'

Albert remained where he was. 'I think she is, Violet. Ask 'er summat'; you've not asked 'er 'owt yet. And didn't you say you were baking bread? Thought I'd 'ave a slice before I went home.'

Violet laughed. 'Him and his bread, says I bake the best bread in t' yard. 'Ee'd better not let Aggie 'ear him say that.'

'Aggie's his wife and they live next door?' Sarah said, hoping she'd guessed right.

Violet's eyes twinkled and a huge smile lit up her face. 'That's right, love. Well, next door but one.'

Albert shook his head. 'Any fool could 'ave worked that out. I still think she needs looking at.'

'Be off with you, Albert. I 'aven't got round to making bread yet. I'll do it in a minute. Pop back in a few hours, should be ready then.'

Albert looked a bit crestfallen but did as he was bidden.

'Alright, I'm off then. I'll bring our lad round for a slice before we go out.'

After Albert had gone, Violet busied herself making a pot of tea. 'You'll feel much better after this, love. And I've a bit of tripe we can 'ave. I'll boil a few onions to it; you know it's one of your favourites.'

Sarah smiled politely but tried to stop the bile rising in her throat. Wasn't tripe cow's stomach? *God, if she puts a plate of that in front of me, I swear I'll puke.*

'I'm not that hungry thanks, Violet; just a cuppa will do.'

'Nay, you must 'ave summat, lass. What about a bit of cheese on toast? I've got a bit of cheese on t' cellar head.'

Sarah nodded. She had got a cellar, then. The cheese may not be as fresh as she'd been used to, but anything would be preferable to tripe and onions.

Sipping her tea by the fire, Sarah began to feel a little more like herself. But of course she wasn't herself. She was Sarah, Violet's niece, and living in 1940! How could that be? A thought munched its way into her mind like a grub through an apple. What if she wasn't herself at all?

Jumping up and nearly dropping the china cup and saucer in the process, she looked at her reflection in the mirror above the fire. No, she was herself. No make-up, apart from some garish red lipstick and pencilled eyebrows, but certainly herself. She placed the cup on the chair and patted her hair. It was rolled into a hairnet and looked quite glamorous. She was reminded of the old film star, Bette Davis. Karen, eat your cold little heart out!

'Here you are, love, take your toast. Now, I'm just going to put me feet up for two minutes, before I get to work on that bread.' Violet sat in the chair opposite Sarah and yawned loudly. 'I feel exhausted. It's all go at that factory.'

Sarah sniffed the cheese on toast and took a small bite. It was very cheesy but surprisingly good. Violet nodded off after a few seconds, snoring and whistling like a jet engine. Sarah polished off her snack and wished she had more. How could she have an appetite in this totally surreal situation?

She picked up her tea and drained what was left. She coughed and spat it out again into the cup. *What the …?* She swirled the cup. *Ah yes, tea leaves; these are the days of loose tea. Most folk didn't have teabags until the late 1960s.*

Sarah picked the remaining tea leaves from her tongue, stretched in the chair and yawned. The fire was making her feel sleepy and Violet snoring the house down didn't help. *Come on, Sarah, pull yourself together. You have a mission to complete and a plan to formulate.* She guessed that a plan to mirror Violet like two bookends, at each side of the fire, snoring for England, wouldn't be a good one. Nevertheless, two minutes later she was asleep.

Was she awake or asleep? She thought she'd heard someone's voice. Peeping from under her lashes, she sleepily realised where she was, and who was talking. Sarah groaned inwardly.

'Yes, they *are* in, they've just fallen asleep by t' fire … which is almost out,' Albert called to someone over his shoulder, flicked the light on and poked the dying embers. 'Good job we came by; they'd 'ave woken up bloody freezin'.' He threw a handful of coal on the now more lively looking fire.

Violet sat up and rubbed her eyes. 'Blimey, 'ave I slept all this time?'

'Aye, lass and young Sarah's still asleep. Does this mean there's no bread?'

'Albert, for goodness sake, yer obsessed wi' my bread! I'll get to it now.'

Sarah was not still asleep but really wished she was. Perhaps if she stood up and cleared her head, the whole scene would disappear. Hauling herself out of the chair, she rubbed her eyes; nope, no good. She blinked and gawped idiotically at Violet and Albert. 'I'm still here in 1940, then?' she asked.

'You weren't joking, then, Dad,' said a voice behind her, 'Sarah really 'as gone a bit funny.'

Turning, she met the eyes of a man in his thirties, dark haired and suited. The eyes were a sea-green ... and belonged to John, the Time-Needle.

Chapter Five

'John!' Sarah put a trembling hand to her mouth. 'I thought you didn't travel, just sewed.'

John raised his eyebrows and folded his arms. 'Travel, sewed? I drive trains and I've never picked up a needle in my life, what the 'eck are yer on about?'

'Well, at least she knows yer name, lad; there must be some improvement inside 'er noddle,' Albert said, chuckling.

'But, you *are* John ... I don't understand,' Sarah said, feeling the need to sit down again. He was identical to the John from the future, was even called John, but why? Was that a sign? Was he the one she had to save?

John's face softened. 'Never mind, duck, you'll get your noddle sorted soon. I'm on nights tomorrow, but on Saturday, we can perhaps go to t' pictures. That might cheer you up a bit.'

'You'll be lucky, son; she's never bothered with you before, why should now be different?' Albert said, sitting down heavily in the chair that Violet had vacated.

'Oh, shurrup, Dad. She seemed 'appy enough to see me just now,' John said, sitting at the kitchen table.

Sarah smiled inanely. Both men looked at her as if she were an exhibit in the curious creatures section of the museum. Violet pottered about mixing flour, yeast and water in a brown earthenware bowl. 'Stop gawpin' at her, you two. She'll not feel right till she's been through t' sheets if you ask me,' she said, adding water from a jug.

'Through t' sheets! It's a bit early for bed in't it?' John asked.

'Not now yer daft ha'porth, tonight. Look, make yersen busy and bring some more coal up from t' cellar,' Violet said, glancing at Sarah who had now taken off her shoes and was rubbing the underside of her feet vigorously.

'You alright, love?' Violet asked.

'Yes, it's just me feet; they're really itchy all of a su—' Sarah stopped, as a line from John's letter smacked her between the eyes. *When you have found the person you are supposed to save, you may get a sign. It could be itchy feet ...* It had to be John then! Her feet hadn't itched when she'd met Albert and Violet.

John clattered down the cellar steps with the coal scuttle and Sarah wondered what she would have to do to save him. Should she follow him down the cellar? This whole thing could be nothing to do with the Blitz; it could just be that he slips on a bit of coal and breaks his neck. If she went down with him, she could make sure he didn't.

Sarah half-rose from her chair and then sank back down again. That would be really unlikely. The 12th of December, hundreds die all around from bombs and fire, while John slips on a bit of coal. *Get real, Sarah.* She had a sneaking suspicion that she would be pants at this time-travelling rescue malarkey. She sighed, listening to the coal being shovelled below, and then her ears tuned in to the conversation in the room.

'So do they pay you for these birds, then?' Violet was asking Albert.

'Nay, lass. It's an 'onour to let me pigeons do vital war work. God knows I'd be fighting if I were allowed. Instead I 'ave to make do with t' 'ome Guard. It's not the same as being a soldier, Vi.'

Violet stopped kneading the bread and gave Albert a hard stare. 'Well, I wish my Billy were alive and in t' 'ome Guard. He were a soldier and a fat lot of good that did him!'

Albert shuffled in his seat and mumbled something unintelligible. Then his sharp eyes alighted back on Sarah's.

'You like me pigeons don't you, love?' he asked, returning to the subject at hand.

Sarah nodded; it seemed safest.

'Just think if one of 'em wins a medal for going behind enemy lines, getting vital information and saving folk.' He beamed at them both. 'That would be a grand day alright.'

Sarah realised he must be one of the many pigeon fanciers who had given their birds to the armed forces to carry messages during the war. She remembered that many pigeons did in fact carry vital information, and if they survived enemy fire, managed to save lives, or bring crucial information about the positioning of the enemy. They were dropped in containers by parachute and hopefully fell into the hands of the allies and the resistance. A message was attached and then the pigeon would be released back to Britain, or sometimes to mobile lofts on ships.

Sarah suddenly blurted without thinking, 'Oh yes, I think there were about 250,000 used in total. And they did get medals, but not until about 1943 ...'

Violet and Albert just gave her withering looks and carried on chatting. They obviously thought she was still suffering from her 'funny turn'.

Sarah breathed a sigh of relief that they hadn't made more of her odd outburst, but then immediately broke into a fit of the giggles. Little wiggles of laughter bubbled up from her tummy, escaping in high-pitched tones, reverberating manically around Violet's kitchen.

She felt very peculiar. There was absolutely nothing she found amusing. In fact, she felt mad panic as the giggles became sudden bursts of laughter exploding from her mouth like the ratta-tatta-tat of a machine gun.

Violet and Albert stopped and stared, frowning at her attempts to quieten her mirth. Sarah clasped first one hand, and then the other, tightly over her mouth and tried to hold her breath. Her face flushed and her eyes felt as if they'd pop out of her head under the pressure of restrained laughter. Her brain tried to process the total lack of control of her emotions. *Oh God, yes! This must be the warning giggles at letting knowledge of the future slip!*

'I told you she wasn't right in the 'ead, Vi. I reckon we need to send for t' doctor. Look at 'er, she's like a raving lunatic!' Albert pointed at Sarah, whilst backing towards the door.

Violet ran to Sarah's side and shook her shoulders roughly. 'What's a matter, Sarah, talk to me, girl!'

That did the trick and immediately Sarah felt the laughter disappear. She took her hands away from her mouth, let out a breath and inhaled another, while trying to regulate the panic coursing around her body like an electric current.

John, whistling 'We'll Meet Again', came up from the cellar and walked in to a stunned silence. The tune died on his lips as he looked at the three of them. 'What's up wi' you lot?'

Sarah shook her head and flushed crimson, Violet shrugged and sat down as if her legs had turned to string, and Albert stood by the door. 'Come on, John,' he said, 'we best leave the lasses alone. Vi's got bread to make and Sarah's ... well, I'm not sure what she's got to do. Anyroad, we'll be late for our Marples meetin'.'

'We 'aven't got to be there until half-seven, Dad, and it's only quarter past six.' John looked completely bemused.

They batted an argument back and forth about leaving too early, but Sarah had stopped listening at the mention of Marples.

The Marples Hotel on the 12th of December 1940 had taken a direct hit. Completely demolished, seventy people in the hotel had lost their lives; it would be the worst single tragedy of that terrible night. Crazily, it was to have been research homework for 9CM that morning.

A flash of clarity, and the first clear plan so far, did a little dance of triumph in Sarah's battered brain. That must be it. This is what she was here for! She had to stop John. Under no circumstances must he, or Albert for that matter, go anywhere near the place. In fact, she needed to make sure everyone stayed put. They all needed to get to the shelters in time for seven o'clock when the air-raid sirens would go.

She swallowed hard and walked over to John. She guessed that Albert wouldn't listen to anything she had to say after just witnessing her acting like a woman possessed. No, John had to be the one to convince, and she put her plan into action.

'Why don't we go to the pictures tonight, John?' she said, putting her hand on John's arm.

He took a step back and blinked at her owlishly. He opened his mouth but nothing came out.

'Eh, pictures? You pick yer times, alright,' Albert said, shaking his head. 'No, I told you, we've got a very important meeting with t' pigeon man from RAF Lindholme.'

John found his voice. 'Well, me and Sarah could go t' pictures and you could go to meet t' pigeon man, Dad.'

'Oh, charmin'! 'ow am I supposed to struggle all the way up to Fitzalan Square with two baskets of bloody pigeons?'

John straightened his tie and coughed. 'Well, couldn't we meet him tomorrow, Dad?'

Albert looked ready to blow up. 'No, we bloody well couldn't. We 'ave no telephone, remember. How would we tell t' bloke, eh? Send a soddin' homin' pigeon?'

'Albert's right, Sarah, he needs to take them pigeons and he can't do it alone. And to be frank, I don't think you should be going anywhere tonight. Yer still not right, not by a long chalk,' Violet chipped in, returning to her bread and turning it out on to a floured board.

An uncomfortable silence descended, broken only by the thump, thump, thump of Violet pummelling the bread around the board. Sarah glanced out of the window and saw that the full bombers' moon had risen above the outbuildings. And though the fire now burned brightly, a chill crept along her spine and tightened icy fingers around her heart.

John looked down at Sarah still holding his arm, shrugged and smiled sheepishly. 'Think we better leave it till Saturday, then.' She looked into his lovely eyes. *If I don't do something drastic, you'll never see Saturday ... never see the morning.*

Sarah looked at Violet. 'Can me and John talk private, like? I've summat to tell 'im and then 'im and Albert can go to t' meetin'.'

Violet stopped pummelling. 'Well, I'm not movin' from 'ere, not with this bread half-done. There's only t' parlour, cellar, or outside.' Violet pursed her lips and pointed a floured finger. 'There's upstairs, but I'm not 'avin you take a man in yer bedroom, even if you 'ave gone funny.'

Sarah tried to suppress a smirk and led John towards what she presumed was the door to the parlour. Violet's sense of morality took the biscuit; she was thirty-four for goodness sake, not fourteen.

'And don't take all night,' Albert said, pointing to the teapot and raising his eyebrows at Violet. She nodded. 'Me and Vi are 'avin' another cuppa, and then I want to be off.'

'Alright, Dad, don't fuss,' John said as he followed Sarah into the parlour.

John flicked on the light and moved Sarah to one side as he adjusted the blackout curtains. It was a small, cheerful room, but plain to see that it was only used occasionally. The items of furniture and ornaments were obviously Violet's treasured possessions.

A green leather sofa and two wing-back chairs, all sporting antimacassars, were carefully placed around a red-and-yellow Persian-type rug. A walnut radio, or wireless as it was known then, was highly polished and had pride of place on a shelf along the back wall. The mantelshelf held a selection of china figurines and an Art Deco Bakelite clock sat in the centre. Two china dogs guarded either side of the fireplace. The fire, Sarah noticed, was unlit, which accounted for the near-freezing temperature in the room.

She also noticed that John looked a bit uncomfortable, avoiding her eyes and hugging himself against the cold. 'I'll turn this lamp on, John. Turn t' big light off, and come and sit by me on t' settee; it'll be a bit cosier.'

John looked even more uncomfortable but turned the light off. Perhaps he thought she had turned into a loose woman! Sarah suppressed another smirk.

He sat as far away from her as was humanly possible on a two-seater sofa, leaned forward, blew into his hands and then rubbed them vigorously on his legs.

'Why don't you move up further to me, John? It'll be warmer and I won't bite you.' Sarah chuckled. Her boldness surprised her. She would never normally have talked like this to a man she hardly knew. This situation wasn't normal, though. It called for abnormal behaviour and she could safely say she had that in spades. *It's just like playing a part, Sarah, just like acting really. Do whatever's necessary.*

'Huh, you've changed yer tune. Last time I tried to hold yer hand I got a slap around t' chops!' John said, glaring at her.

'I slapped you for trying to hold my hand?'

'Aye, but I expect you've forgot that, like everythin' else.'

Sarah sighed and nodded. 'I 'ave, John, yes. I'm sorry I did that. I won't slap you now, though.' She reached over and took his hand.

He gawped at her and flushed red. Even in the low lamplight, his face looked hot enough to grill beef burgers. Sarah noted that, though embarrassed, he didn't take his hand from hers.

Taking encouragement from this, she inched closer.

'So why aren't you taken, you know, married? In fact, why are we both not married?'

John traced the side of her face tenderly. 'Ee, Sarah, love ... you really don't remember 'owt?'

Sarah took a few seconds to answer; she was too busy gazing into his eyes and enjoying the gentle touch of his fingers. 'What? Err ... no, I don't, why don't you tell me?'

John moved a bit closer and stroked her hand. 'Right, I'll tell you. I got jilted and you got jilted. Me and thee 'ad alus liked each other, but we were just mates, like. We'd been courtin' these other two chuffs for about five year. Ivy was yer best friend, and Bob was mine. I'd proposed to Ivy, and she'd said yes. Bob had proposed to you and you'd accepted. And then guess what 'appened about a three year ago?'

'They did the dirty on us and buggered off together?' Sarah said.

'Yes, you do remember, then?'

'No, it's just t' bloody story of my life.' Sarah couldn't believe it. Dumped in both past and future dimensions. *Doesn't do a whole lot for my ego. I should write a book: On the Shelf in 1940 and 2013 – the tragic tale of Sarah, the most dumped woman in history.*

'Story of yer life? When were you jilted before?' John broke in on her self-pity party.

'Eh, oh don't mind me, I'm muddled ... so anyway, how did I come to slap you?'

'It were about six months later. We'd gone t' pictures and I put my arm round you. You let me, then I went to 'old yer 'and, but I got walloped. Then you stormed out.'

The clock chimed 6.30. Sarah's heart rate went into overdrive; she was running out of time. She had to act fast now to make sure John would support her, no matter what Albert said.

'Well, I've changed my mind now, John,' she whispered,

moving closer still and resting her head on his shoulder. 'I was wondering if you'd like to kiss me. Promise I won't slap you.' She tilted her face up to his.

John, who looked as if he had been given a million pounds, was about to say something, but then just kissed her instead. It was a quick gentle peck on the cheek and then he sat back, clearing his throat nervously.

'Is that the best you can do?' Sarah murmured, putting his arm around her and her hand on his knee.

'By 'eck, that bump on yer 'ead must be making you forward, lass.'

Sarah laughed. 'Yes, it must be.' She leaned over and brushed her lips across his.

John needed no more encouragement and drew her tightly to him, kissing her hungrily. Sarah felt her libido go from nought to a hundred in less than ten seconds. His kisses were just as delicious as the rest of him, and she tingled all over as he ran his hand over her back and down her thigh. It had been over eighteen months since a man had so much as winked at her.

She could feel his heart thumping in his chest; as her own excitement grew, and before she knew what she was doing, she placed his hand on her breast. He stopped kissing her and looked into her eyes. 'God, Sarah, what are you doing?'

'Why, don't you like it?' she panted.

'Course I bloody like it, I just don't know if I can control myself … My dad and Violet are in t' other room …'

'Don't worry about it, just kiss me again.' Sarah unbuttoned the top buttons of her dress, pulled his mouth on to hers, and pressed her hips against him.

John moaned, slipped his hand inside her dress and then the light snapped on.

'What the 'ell's going on in 'ere, then!' Albert barked from the doorway.

Sarah and John sprang apart and jumped up. Sarah turned her back and buttoned up her dress.

'Well, do you 'ear me?'

John straightened his tie, said nothing and looked at the floor. Sarah thought he looked like a naughty schoolboy rather than a man in his thirties.

'In Violet's house an' all; bloody disgustin'. Come on you, we've a meeting to be at!' Albert turned to leave.

Sarah felt anger at Albert's words vying with panic at the thought of John leaving. Combining the two emotions to good effect she said, 'What's disgustin' about it? We're both single and we really like each other. And for your information, we're all going to the shelter, not to a meeting!'

John looked at her, puzzled, and Albert harrumphed and stomped out. Sarah followed hot on his heels, in time to see Albert push past Violet and grab his coat and hat from a chair. Violet, who was just putting a panshion pot of bread to rise by the fire, yelled, 'Oy, you nearly made me drop this! What's going on?'

'You'd better ask yer nutty niece! She's just been half-undressed in there with our John, now she's on about shelters and there's not even been a siren yet!' Albert snapped, slipping on his coat.

Sarah folded her arms and fixed him with a steely glare. 'Half-undressed is pushing it a bit, Albert, and there will be sirens ... very soon.'

'How the 'ell do you know that? You a witch, now?' Albert asked, ramming his hat on his head.

'No, it's just a feeling I've got. Besides, it's a bombers' moon.'

Albert gave her a withering look and made for the back door.

Sarah turned to John behind her and grabbed his hand. 'Please, John, you 'ave to trust me on this. Stop yer dad leavin' before it's too late!'

John pushed his hands through his hair. 'Dad, perhaps we ought to wait a bit if Sarah's 'ad a feelin'.'

'Ha! She's certainly 'ad a feelin' from what I saw in t' parlour.'

'Stop being coarse, Albert!' Violet said, planting her legs and putting her hands on her hips. 'Now, Sarah, what's this about shelters?'

'We have to get to t' shelters before t' sirens go. 'av we got an Anderson shelter nearby?'

'No. Have you even forgotten that? We use t' cellar.'

Sarah remembered that many families didn't have space for an Anderson shelter and felt safer in their cellars than going to a public shelter. That was good news regarding the time; it must be going up for 6.45. No need to leave the house. But were cellars safe? What if the house took a direct hit, they'd be trapped in the rubble.

'You comin' or what?' Albert asked, standing in the open doorway.

John looked at Sarah and she shook her head, no. He shrugged. 'Can't we just give it a bit longer, Dad?'

'No, we bloody well—'

'Violet, will we be safe in t' cellar?' Sarah said, cutting Albert off in mid-rant.

'I expect we'll be as safe as anywhere. Tom Butler reinforced it with steel sheetin' a few months ago and we 'ave a tunnel all t' way through this row of houses.'

'Oh, I see. Is the tunnel so that we could escape better if we did get flattened?' Sarah asked, stalling for time.

'No, it's to make sure that we 'ave a more direct route to the loony bin for you, yer daft mare,' Albert said from the corner of his mouth.

'Please, Dad, stop being so nasty. Sarah's really worried,' John said, putting his arm around Sarah.

'Albert, close t' door, yer lettin' all t' warm air out,' Violet said.

Sarah looked at Albert. He showed no signs of relenting and dug his hands into his pockets. If she could just get him to stay until seven o'clock, the sirens would sound and she'd have saved John, and Albert, too.

'Please, Albert; just come down t' cellar for ten minutes. You won't be late for yer meetin' then, and you will have helped me to 'ave peace of mind,' Sarah said, crossing her fingers behind her back.

'What do you think, Vi? What do you want to do?' Albert asked, stepping back in.

'I want you to close that bloody door for a start, and I suppose we'll do as Sarah wants. She's not 'erself ... not 'erself at all.'

Ten minutes later they were settled in the freezing cellar wrapped in an assortment of blankets. Albert sat on an upturned bucket, looking like he'd lost ten pounds and found sixpence. Sarah and John were huddled close on a bench, and Violet, in an old chair, was holding some green yarn up to the single light bulb, trying to cast stitches on a knitting needle.

'Why the 'ell you insisted that I stay 'ere instead of going down 'ome to Aggie I don't know,' Albert moaned.

'Because you'd probably sneak off to that meeting, Albert, and our Sarah reckons it's safer in 'ere.' Violet sighed.

John pulled Sarah closer and kissed the top of her head. He didn't bat an eyelid at the disapproving glower he got from Albert. A few seconds later Albert sprang up like a jack-in-the-box. 'This is daft. I'm o—'

He was cut off by the banshee wail of the siren signalling an air raid. He closed his mouth and sat down again. Sarah closed her eyes and tried not to cry. In her mind she could see the awful fate of so many poor people that night. She squeezed John's hand and took deep breaths. Violet put down her knitting and began to climb the cellar steps.

Sarah opened her eyes. 'Where are you going, Auntie Violet!'

Violet threw back over her shoulder, 'I'm off to change me vest. If I'm going to be killed, I want to make sure I'm clean.'

Chapter Six

Sarah snuggled closer to John's shoulder and squeezed his hand. She couldn't remember the last time she had felt so safe, warm and completely in love. In fact, she didn't think she'd ever been in love quite like this. 'I think the bombs have stopped falling now, John,' she murmured.

CRASH, CRUMP, SQUEEEE! 'Whoa, pull forward, Justin! You've only bloody reversed into three wheelie bins!'

Sarah's heart sank. The bombs must have started again ... but what was that about wheelie bins? They weren't around in the 1940s ... She felt herself rising from great depths. She opened her eyes to find that she wasn't in the cellar, that John's shoulder was a pillow, and that she was squeezing the paw of her old teddy, not John's hand. Realisation hit; she was in her bed at home and the row outside was a bin lorry.

Sarah felt terrible. Her head throbbed, her stomach bobbed on waves of nausea and the light shining through a gap in the bedroom curtains fired white-hot metal rods into her eyes. This was the mother of all hangovers. She placed a pillow over her eyes and tried to get a grip on what was happening.

How could she have a hangover? She'd not touched a drop since the night she'd first met John. Thoughts of John left a huge hole in her heart. What the hell was happening to her? How could she feel this strongly about someone who was alive in 1940? She hoped to God that she'd done enough to save him – save them all. And why on earth was she back in her own bed now? Shouldn't she be outside her classroom at school, instead? *Stop thinking, Sarah; clear your mind, have a shower and make a cup of tea, otherwise you'll 'go a bit funny' as Albert would say ...*

Sarah swallowed hard as she realised she'd never see the miserable old git, or Violet, ever again. Incredibly, she felt like she'd lost friends, good friends. But what about John? The Sarah of the past obviously loved him. That would explain her own feelings just before the row of the wheelie bins had rudely awakened her. She hoped that Sarah and John were safe and had been happy together.

But it was all so confusing. When she had looked in the mirror in 1940 she had seen her own face looking back ... so had the Sarah of the past looked exactly like her? John, here in the present, should be able to shed light on it all. That's if he ever pops up again, she told herself. Slowly, she put her feet to the floor and shuffled into the bathroom.

Slightly more shipshape after the shower, Sarah pulled on an old green sweater and jeans. Unable to face the noise of the hairdryer, she combed her hair through and left it to its own devices. The full-length mirror told her that it had seen her looking better, but that there had been one or two days after her husband left when she'd looked even worse.

Sarah sniffed a couple of times and frowned. *Bacon? Don't tell me my senses are mucked up now because of this time-travelling lark?* She opened the curtains and shielded her eyes from the glare. Betty Grenville, her neighbour, pulled her bin back up her path and waved cheerily. Sarah waved back. Betty was mouthing something and pointing at the window, gesturing that Sarah should open it.

'You don't look well, love; you off work?' she shouted up to Sarah.

Sarah's ears begged for mercy. The volume of Betty's voice could give a pneumatic drill a run for its money.

'Err ... I'm not great, Betty, I think I may have a day off, yes.'

'Well, look after yourself, duck. Anything I can do, just pop round!'

Sarah smiled, nodded, mouthed *thank you* and closed the window before her brain started to haemorrhage.

A worrying thought presented itself as she walked downstairs. Today was bin day. Bin day was Thursday; she'd popped over to 1940 on Tuesday, so what had happened to Wednesday? Also, she'd better phone school and think of a reason for skipping school today. Stopping at the bottom of the stairs, she sniffed again. Definitely bacon; bacon and coffee?

She walked into the kitchen and grabbed hold of a chair to steady herself.

''Bout time, sleepy head! Now sit down there; just got the eggs to finish, hope you like fried,' John said, pointing a spatula at her.

Sarah sat down and watched him for a few seconds. Her pulse raced and her heart mimicked a tumble dryer. Why was she so pleased to see him? Her brain seemed to have shut up shop and headed for the coast.

'Drink this, you'll feel better,' John said, setting a glass of orange juice down in front of her. Then, placing a cool hand on her forehead, he asked, 'Bit quiet this morning, aren't we?'

'Bit quiet?' Sarah removed his hand and folded her arms. 'Why on earth do you think that is, I wonder? I've just come back from the Blitz of 1940, feel like I've been run over by a truck, and appear to have lost a day of my life. And to cap it all, I get up to find you uninvited in MY house cooking bloody bacon! So, sorry if I disappoint; shall I do a few cartwheels and sing a rousing chorus from *Oliver*?'

John laughed out loud, picked up the frying pan and slipped eggs on to a plate. 'Well, it is one of my favourite musicals,' he said, and began whistling 'Oom-Pah-Pah'.

In spite of herself, Sarah wanted to smile, but took a sip of orange juice to stop herself. There was no way she wanted

John to think he was off the hook. And she needed to get any romantic notion about him *right* out of her head. The fluffy lovesick feeling that she'd had upon waking was just an aberration, an overhang from the Sarah in the past – a result of the emotional situation she'd left behind in 1940.

This John had much explaining to do, and she needed a clear head in order to find answers. Sarah just wished that he didn't look so damned attractive this morning. *I could try to superimpose the head of the insufferable Gary Keynsham on John's shoulders. At least then I could focus on the task at hand.*

As John poured coffee, Sarah noticed her own appearance and flushed as red as the crimson coffee mugs. Not only had she shoved on the oldest sweater known to man, but she'd neglected to put a bra on first! The sweater was threadbare in places and she could clearly see the outline of her breasts and, even more embarrassingly, her nipples. Coupled with her damp, roughly combed hair and her hung-over visage, bare of make-up, Sarah had never felt so unattractive and exposed.

She folded her arms tightly across her chest and sighed. Still, at least it would be easier to avoid any complications between the two of them. There was no way he'd fancy her looking like this. And that's exactly what she wanted.

'Now, *bon appétit*, my dear.' John smiled and, with a flourish, placed the bacon and eggs in front of her. It did look very appetising. Sarah remembered that she hadn't eaten anything apart from a small bowl of cereal and very old cheese on toast on Tuesday. Her tummy growled and bubbled in indignation and she realised she was ravenous. The trouble was, she'd have to unfold her arms in order to eat it. That would not be a good idea, given the nipple situation.

'Come on, dig in,' John said, through a mouthful of bacon. Even with bacon fat dribbling down his chin he would still win the hearts of her vegetarian friends. She tried the Gary Keynsham trick, but to no avail. Gary's head materialised in her imagination for a nano-second, but then, with a flash of his tombstone teeth, disappeared into the ether. Instead, looking back at her was a near-perfect face, at the moment wearing dark stubble on its strong chin, a sexy smile and a pair of sea-green eyes crinkling at the corners.

She looked at the table and shook her head. 'I'm not that hungry,' she said. 'Besides, I can't just start chucking bacon and eggs down my neck without some answers, John. My mind is in turmoil.'

John pointed his fork at her. 'You must be hungry after all you've been through. Just try and have a few mouthfuls, and drink your juice. I'll answer all your questions while we eat.'

For the next few seconds or so, John watched as Sarah tried to eat one-handed. With her left arm still clamped tightly across her chest, she attempted to cut the bacon with her fork and ended up catapulting one half of the crispy rasher into John's coffee.

'What the hell are you doing?' He frowned, picking the soggy morsel of bacon out and throwing it in the sink.

'It's your fault for making the bacon too crispy.'

'Oh, I see, nothing to do with you eating as if your left arm was in a sling, then?'

'I'm not,' Sarah said leaning forward on the table, her arms folded.

'No, not now, but you're obviously hiding something. Look, you still have your arms folded across your ... oh I see!' he said, grinning widely.

'What do you mean?' She looked away, her face aflame.

'If you're trying to cover your modesty, don't bother. I clocked that you were looking, shall we say, a bit perky, as soon as you came into the kitchen.' He laughed, and took a huge bite out of his toast.

Sarah opened her mouth and closed it again. She couldn't see the point of trying to make something up. She pushed her chair back and flounced out.

Reappearing a few minutes later, wearing a touch of make-up, a bra and a blue checked shirt, her hair in a ponytail, she sat down and proceeded to demolish her breakfast.

'Not hungry then?' John smirked.

'I lied, obviously. Now, put some more toast on, and tell me what the hell happened to Wednesday, why I feel like I've a hangover, why I didn't go back to my classroom but instead woke up in bed, and why the person I saved ... I suppose I did save him?' She looked at John anxiously.

He nodded.

'Good. What was I saying? Ah, yes ... and why he looked *exactly* like you.'

As John busied himself with the toast, he told her that she'd slept for an entire day as, because of the whole traumatic experience, and it being her first time as a Stitch, she'd been pulled out of the past and put into a deep sleep. She wouldn't have coped being sent straight back to deal with 9CM. The hangover was a result of the trauma and being brought back through time so rapidly.

'It's a bit like having the bends, you know like divers get when they come up from the sea bed too quickly. Nitrogen bubbles get in the blood or something,' John said, pouring more coffee.

'What, so I've got nitrogen bubbles in my blood?'

'No, but you have got this weird hangover due to the pressure of time on your body; you feel giddy, dizzy, sick and stuff. You're feeling better already though, am I right?'

'Yes, you are, but what worries me is what happened to school yesterday? They'll be wondering what's happened to me, not ringing in sick, *and* just disappearing in the middle of a lesson on Tuesday!'

'I fixed that, don't worry,' John said, waving the recently popped toast in the air to cool it down. 'I rang, said you were feeling under stress due to an awful migraine and "women's problems"; you had an embarrassing leakage and just ran home. I said you'll probably be in tomorrow, though. Your head of department is setting the work for the kids.'

Sarah stood up so fast she thought her head would explode. 'What! You told my school that I had ... I had ...' She couldn't bring herself to say it out loud.

'Yep, your period was majorly heavy, and you had to go home and change. What's so bad about that? I knew someone wh—'

'I don't care who you knew. How dare you! How dare you do that? I'll never be able to live that down, never!'

Sarah ran out into the living room and threw herself on the sofa, hiding her face with a cushion. Humiliation didn't begin to cover what she was feeling. *God, that's it then. My whole world has just crashed and burned.* She heard John come in and walk over.

'Sarah? Why are you getting so upset? I could hardly tell them the truth, could I?' He tried to pull the cushion from her vice-like grip.

'No, but you could have made something up less cringingly humiliating! Just go away!' The anger in her voice, though muffled, came through the cushion loud and clear.

John didn't reply and a few seconds later she heard the front door open and then close.

Damn him! Had he buggered off without answering the rest of her questions? Hurling the cushion across the room she leapt up and ran to the window. A quick glance left and right revealed nothing but an empty street. *Probably popped into another dimension; easier to get to his stupid market garden!*

Sarah marched into the hall and there was John, leaning with his back against the door, arms folded, head on one side, a cheeky smile playing over his lips and a mischievous twinkle in his eye.

'Suppose you think you're funny, eh?' she said, torn between wanting to slap him and kiss him. Kiss him? For God's sake, what was she thinking? *Must be bloody sex starved after all this time.*

'Yes, I do. I hoped I could make you laugh too, lift the atmosphere a bit,' he said.

'It will take more than a little prank to make me laugh today. I'm not sure how much more of this I can take to be honest.' Sarah felt tears pricking her eyes.

She turned quickly and walked back to the kitchen. There was no way he would see her cry. Picking up the frying pan, she squirted detergent and ran hot water into the sink.

'Leave that, Sarah. Why don't we take our coffee out into the garden?' John said, putting his hand on her shoulder. 'It's a lovely day ... and judging by the knots I can feel in your shoulder, I think you need to relax.'

She shrugged off his hand. 'I need to do this.'

'Why don't you put it in the dishwasher?' John asked, walking over to open the back door.

'Because I always wash pans by hand and because I WANT TO, ALRIGHT!'

John raised his eyebrows, shrugged and went into the garden.

Sarah stopped scrubbing and stared at the bubbles in the sink. She exhaled and, with that breath, most of her anger drained away, leaving her wrung out like the cloth in her hand. What exactly had made her so furious? Was it the humiliation John had caused by his stupid bloody phone call to school? Was it the whole extraordinary and emotional experience she'd just had in 1940? Was it the fact that when she'd gone upstairs to change, her hands had busily applied make-up even though her brain expressly forbade it?

She pulled two clean mugs from the cupboard, sloshed more coffee into them and gave a heavy sigh. *All of the above, Sarah ... all of the above.*

The sun dappled through the leaves of the old silver birch and on to John's shoulders, giving his white T-shirt a Dalmatian effect. Sarah's large and unruly garden was a burst of colour at this time of year. She mowed the lawn, but the riot of flowers and mature shrubs were the evidence of a previous owner's labours.

'What a lovely garden you have!' John said, watching her walk down the path, trying not to spill the coffee.

'Not my doing, I just tidy round. No idea about gardens really.' She nodded towards a bench under the rose-covered pergola. 'Do you want to sit down over there?'

Side by side they sipped coffee, while John prattled on about gardening and his love of nature. Sarah half-listened, but mostly enjoyed the soothing sound of his voice, the warm sun on her skin and the heady scent of roses permeating the air.

'So, do you want to see photo evidence of your neat stitching?'

'Mm? What?' she said, only vaguely aware that he'd asked her something.

'You're miles away, aren't you? Do you want to see a photo of John and Sarah?'

Puzzled, she watched as he stood up and pulled a wallet from his jeans' pocket. Flipping it open he extracted an old black-and-white snap and handed it to her. The photo depicted a laughing couple on their wedding day. The man was tall, sandy haired and moustachioed; the woman was short, raven haired and radiant. The usual gathering of friends and relatives surrounded the couple on the steps of the church; Albert and Violet were at the forefront.

Sarah looked up at John. 'You said it was a photo of John and Sarah? That's Albert and Violet, but I've never seen the couple before.'

He sat back down next to her. 'No, but it *is* them. They really were called John and Sarah. And, in order for you to achieve your aim of saving John and stitching up the hole in time,' he patted her knee, 'which I might add, you did brilliantly – you saw yourself as Sarah and John as me.'

She shook her head. 'But why? I don't understand.'

'Well, if you had looked in the mirror and seen a total stranger looking back, you may have quite possibly gone to pieces.'

Sarah studied the photo. 'Ah yes ... yes, I can see that, but why did I see John as you?'

He smiled awkwardly, scratched his nose and coughed.

'Well?'

John shot off the bench towards a clump of grass at the edge of the lawn. He knelt down and poked at it. She wandered over and peered at the grass, and then at John, noticing that his face was very red. He looked seriously embarrassed. 'What are you doing?'

He cleared his throat and looked intently at the clump of grass. 'I think this may be couch grass. You'll need to get rid of that. It can be very invasive.'

'Really? I think you are being very *evasive*, John. Why are you so embarrassed all of a sudden?'

John stood up and looked towards the house. 'Well, I'm worried about what your reaction will be if I tell you why I was John.'

Sarah stepped round to face him. 'Try me.'

'Well, John had to be someone you were, err ... familiar with, so you could feel comfortable,' John mumbled, his green eyes dancing away from hers.

'Familiar with? I hardly know you.'

'Yes, well I'm who you wanted to see, apparently. When Stitches are on a mission, the theory is that their brains often conjure up images of friends or loved ones; you know, to help minimise stress?'

Sarah frowned. 'But there are loads of people I know better than you, and ...'

'OK, Sarah, listen.' John took her hand and led her back to the bench. He sat down, pulling her beside him. 'Look, it was because you had to employ, let's say, delicate tactics to keep John from going out to that meeting. You needed to really feel something for the guy, in order to bring yourself to do ... what you did.'

Sarah was mortified. How could her brain be so stupid? Now John knew how she felt. Hang on, how did she feel? When she'd woken this morning, she'd felt in love with the John in the past, but that was just woven in with the experience. OK, admittedly she was attracted to *this* John, sitting gawping at her on the bench – who wouldn't be – but love? No way! And how arrogant was he to think that?

'Well, this time that theory is wrong, John!' She stood up. 'It's obvious that I cared for the other John because Sarah in the past did. You must just have been on my mind due to all the trauma of time travel and everything and my brain popped you out on to the other John. Now, I think I'm going back to bed for a bit, so it's time you left.' Sarah walked briskly down the path and into the house.

On his way out of the front door John turned to her. 'Look, I know you're angry for lots of good reasons, but please take my card,' he held out his hand, 'and call me if you need to ask questions or if ever you're worried about ...'

She pushed his hand away. 'I won't need it, thanks. Bye!' Sarah closed the door on him and with her back against it, shut her eyes and slid down to the floor.

After gathering her composure, a few minutes later she

dragged herself up and into the kitchen. On the table propped against her empty plate was a business card. Picking it up she read:

So, looks like he did his time-stopping trick again, then. Nipped round me in the hall and then out again. Sighing, she turned the card over.

Please don't be angry with me.
You have many adventures ahead
and you'll need a friend. John and
Sarah's grandson is apparently
going to be our PM soon.
All my best, John ☺

Prime Minister, blimey! She hoped he'd be a good one. Sarah stared at John's empty coffee cup and traced her fingers around the rim. She decided she'd had enough adventures for one lifetime. Nevertheless, she put the card in her pocket and took comfort from its presence as she cleared away the breakfast dishes.

Chapter Seven

'Dad, what are you doing here?' John asked, making his way through the tall rows of runner beans towards a kneeling figure weeding a patch of earth.

'Charming,' Harry Needler said, standing to a stretch. '"Pop over and see me anytime, Dad; I'll be glad of your help, Dad," he says. Now he wants to know what I'm doing here.'

John laughed, embraced his father, and then held him at arm's length. 'Let's have a look at you then,' he said, taking in his dad's twinkly eyes and scant grey hair. 'If anything, you seem to be growing younger lately; have you got a portrait in the attic that's grey and wrinkled?'

Harry pretended to spar with his son, thumbing his nose and dancing lightly on his feet over the damp earth. 'That's a backhanded compliment if ever I heard one. I'll have you know I'm only sixty-two, so why should I be grey and wrinkly, eh, eh? Come on, pud 'em up!'

'I'd rather have a cuppa. Come on, I have a flask and a spare cup in the greenhouse.' John chuckled, dodging his dad's half-hearted jabs.

'Gawd, you're no fun. Is there a portrait in your attic that is young and carefree?'

With feet on a bucket and a mouth full of biscuit, Harry looked appreciatively around his son's well-stocked greenhouse. 'So what's that plant there, then?' He pointed his mug at a spindly plant snaking along the high trellis.

'That's a rare chilli plant; I grow a few for specialist restaurants. That end of the business is doing quite well.' John smiled and drained his mug. 'So, why are you here really? You never just "pop" by to help with the weeding and ask about rare plants.'

Harry raised his eyebrows and assumed a look of cherubic innocence. 'It *has* been six months, John. I thought I'd take a break from my travels and see how you are.'

John said nothing but shook his head, folded his arms and waited.

'OK, I wanted to see how the business was going,' Harry said, taking another biscuit from the packet.

'It's going OK. People still need to eat even during a recession, but you could have picked up a phone to ask that, Dad.'

Harry sighed and dipped his biscuit. 'Not the market-gardening business; I meant *the* business.'

'Needling? Just as always ... Why, what's going on?'

Harry avoided his son's eyes, just held out his mug and nodded at the flask. While John busied himself pouring tea, Harry cleared his throat and said, 'I've been asked to have a word ... They dropped me an email yesterday. There's concern about this latest one ... this Sarah.'

'Bloody cheek! Why?' John asked. This time he was the one avoiding eye contact.

'I think you know why. She obviously likes you and it is thought that the feeling's mutual.'

John turned his back and picked up a pack of flower pots. He unpacked them one at a time, setting them carefully along a bench. 'Of course I like her; it would be impossible to work with someone I didn't in my line of work.'

'That's not what I meant and you know it. It was you who she chose to see to help her through the trip to the Blitz ... That should have given you a red light. But you going round cooking her breakfast and sitting under her rose arbour didn't exactly give her the "stay away" signal. It has to stop, John ... Think of the consequences.'

John whipped round to face his father. 'Give me a break! I just told you I like her, but that's all! I've only known her five minutes. God, isn't it enough that I do this crazy stuff without the puppet masters sending you to grill me?' he snapped, his face aflame and his eyes flashing.

A sad little smile replaced the sunny disposition on Harry's face and he stood up and set his cup down. 'Fancy a pint, lad? I saw a nice little boozer on my way up here, only about ten minutes away.' Harry slipped his jacket on and walked towards the door.

John frowned and dusted his hands clean. 'Right, so we can have a nice little chat and you can grill me some more about my feelings for Sarah, I suppose?'

'No. I *would* like a little chat with my only son, but as for finding out about your feelings ... you've already told me everything I need to know.'

Chapter Eight

Sarah felt as if she were wading through treacle the next morning as she walked heavy-legged through the school gates. Her heart rate went from a waltz to a quickstep and the voice responsible for maintaining her pride and dignity screamed 'Don't go in there!' But every atom of her rational being propelled her forward. *You have to go in there sometime, just get on with it.*

The first hurdle was to get past reception without being collared by Gillian, the 'I put my make-up on with a trowel' receptionist, who took calls about staff absence. Sarah knew she was a terrible gossip and would have already spread Sarah's 'condition' around the whole office of secretaries. What niggled her most was that the whole embarrassing debacle hadn't even happened; it was just a figment of John's warped imagination. Still, Sarah had purposely come in earlier than normal. Hopefully, she'd avoid having to speak to many people.

A quick glance on passing revealed not Gillian, but Jenny, sitting on reception. Phew, Gillian must be away herself or …

'Oh, you're in then. Alright now, Sarah?' Gillian popped out of the office door to Sarah's left. She wore a fake mask of concern, and an unquenchable desire for more juicy morsels of gossip flickered in her heavily mascaraed eyes.

'Yes, thanks, Gillian,' Sarah muttered, intending to stride through the doors to the staffroom corridor.

Gillian put her hand on Sarah's arm and looked around conspiratorially. 'Don't worry, love, your secret's safe with me. Your "friend" explained everything. It must be lovely to have someone like him to look after you.'

Sarah nodded and stepped forward, but Gillian leaned in again. 'I think it might be the menopause you know. My sister started about your age, fortyish, and it was the same for her.'

Menopause! Fortyish? The bitch! Gillian knew that Sarah was just 34, because a few of them had been out for a drink to celebrate her birthday. Sarah was about to let rip with a few choice words, but then decided to keep quiet. If she started, she was afraid she wouldn't be able to stop. Stepping forward, she pushed past Gillian and flung open the door.

'Well, really!' Gillian gasped.

In the sparsely populated staffroom, Sarah shuffled through the mountain of paperwork in her pigeonhole. Two days away and the pile rivalled the one she'd have to pick up from the mat at home later. Half were glossy ads for history DVDs and textbooks, the other half were from various members of staff reminding her about meetings, break duty, and detentions.

'Hey, Sarah!'

Sarah lifted her head. Oh joy, Gary Keynsham; did that man ever do anything else apart from hang round here like a bad smell?

He sidled up to her, flashing a smile at the lovely Jodie who'd just entered.

'Did you forget to pass that message on to Danny the other day? He didn't show up at break and—'

'No, sorry, I had one or two things on my mind, Gary.'

'Well, no matter, I caught him last night and—'

'So why bother me with it now?' she asked, walking to the door.

'My goodness, you're snappy this morning; must be the time of the month, eh?' He winked at Jodie and folded his arms.

Sarah whirled round, her eyes flashing. Had that nasty bitch Gillian been spreading it round the staff, too? Gary pulled a face and stepped backwards. He looked very wary and treated her to his biggest smile. 'Hey, it's just a joke, hon, no need to get angry.'

'Just a joke, eh? Making a joke about the personal workings of the female body is just a joke? How would you like it if I said, "bit snappy today, Gary, must be because you couldn't get an erection last night"?'

Gary flushed and his voice scaled up a few octaves. 'What do you mean? I have no problems there.'

'No? Well I have no problems with my "time of the month" either, hon. Just think before you open your big sexist trap in future!'

From the corner of her eye, Sarah saw Gary's big sexist trap gape open as he watched her exit the staffroom like a woman possessed. She took great pleasure from the look on his face as he caught Jodie smothering a giggle.

Sarah unlocked the door to her classroom. She shuddered when going over what she'd said. The personal workings of the female body, what was she thinking? That sounded practically Victorian. She'd called him sexist too, but it served him right; he was, and he was long overdue a slap down.

Setting her bag on the desk she drew out her planner. Flicking to lesson one, to her extreme delight she saw that it was in fact a free lesson and not Year 9. She must have got the weeks mixed up. Thank you, God! Some good news at last. And lesson two was … oh, good, Year 10. They were her favourite group and they were about to start a topic on why the homesteaders moved to the American West in the 1860s. Great stuff.

Sarah snapped the planner shut and then her legs turned to mush. She sat on the desk. Palpitations raced through her heart, her whole body trembled like an aspen leaf and her hands grew clammy. Homesteaders in the American West? Damn, didn't John say she'd have to save a homesteader? There was no way she was ready to jaunt off on another adventure yet. She needed a rest and time to get used to the idea.

The door opened and Robert, her head of department, popped his head round. The young, dynamic leader of history was normally chatty and full of some new idea he'd like to share with her, but today he seemed reluctant to even make eye contact.

'Good to see you back. Need anything?' he asked, already inching the door closed. Sarah realised he didn't know what to say to her. She felt her anger surfacing again – John had a lot to answer for.

'Hey there, Robert, yes I'm much better now, thanks. I would like a word with you about Danny Jakes, though. I think we need to think of a few strategies for managing his behaviour.'

'OK, can we do it Monday? Shouldn't bother yourself with it today, not with your err … problem. Have a nice rest at the weekend.' Rob smiled sympathetically, as if she had some incurable disease, and then ducked out.

Sarah put her head in her hands and gave a heavy sigh. God, how embarrassing! As if her life wasn't stressful and depressing enough, now it was going round that she was in the menopause and couldn't handle dealing with unruly kids. Well, to be honest the latter was the truth at the moment. *OK, Sarah, snap out of the self-pity mode. You'll need your wits about you if you're suddenly catapulted into nineteenth-century America!*

It'd just be her luck to find herself on the back of a runaway horse. That's how her life felt at the moment – as if she were galloping towards a ravine and she'd lost control of the reins. Sarah sighed, jumped off the desk and began to set up a PowerPoint presentation for lesson two.

'OK, then, Year 10, what do you think that is?' Sarah pointed at the projected slide depicting a tiny sod-built construction half-buried into a hillside. The endless plains of Nebraska rolled away as far as the eye could see on one side, and on the other, a bedraggled family posed for the camera. A man proudly held the rein of a bony horse and a woman and three children gazed woodenly into the distance. The smallest child clasped a pumpkin almost as big as himself.

'Is it a toilet, Miss?' Jamie Albright asked hopefully.

'A toilet!' Kirsty Grimshaw snorted. 'Duh! Of course not, you idiot, it's too big *and* it's got a chimney sticking out of it. It is a chimney, isn't it, Miss?'

'It is a chimney, Kirsty, yes, but please don't be rude to Jamie. Remember the rule: class-discussion is for everyone. Everyone should be made to feel as though they have important contributions to make.'

'So the whole family lived in that shack thingy, then?' Kirsty asked in disbelief.

'Indeed they did, Kirsty, and that shack thingy was called a sod dugout, and those people there are called homesteaders, or farmers.'

'Sod? Isn't that swearing, though?' Jenny Holdsworth giggled. One or two others joined her.

'It's mild swearing yes, but sod is also another name for earth. If you look closely you can see the grass sticking out of the sod bricks that they cut from the earth. They let them bake hard in the sun and then built this house.'

'Why didn't they use ordinary bricks or wood?' Billy Cardale asked.

'Does anyone know the answer to Billy's question? Look at the kind of environment they lived in. What seems to be missing?' Sarah looked round the class and could almost hear the cogs turning in their curious minds.

As she was about to tell them the answer, Harriet Summers, who was a bright, enthusiastic, but shy girl, suddenly blurted, 'Trees! They didn't have many of them so they didn't have wood. They didn't have bricks 'cos they moved west from the east and couldn't carry heavy stuff like that overland on their wagons. Sometimes, they had to dump their prized possessions on the journey, if the horses were too weak to pull the weight. People got lots of horrible diseases on the journey, too, and lots died. There was terrible lack of water, Miss, and droughts killed crops, people and animals off, left, right and centre.' Harriet stopped abruptly as if realising where she was. She put her hand to her mouth and went very red.

Jeremy Greer, one of the least attentive of the class, started to slow hand clap Harriet, until Sarah silenced him with her best contemptuous glare. She turned back to Harriet, and gave her a wide smile. 'My goodness, Harriet, you seem to know quite a bit about this subject already.'

'That's nowt, Miss. See what she's done for independent research,' Harriet's friend, Stacey Lombrook said, nudging Harriet encouragingly. 'Go on, show her.'

Harriet shuffled in her seat and shook her head, no.

Sarah had set them homework to find something out about the homesteaders. They would be a little bit prepared for the new subject and more confident as a result. 'What did you find, Harriet, a book on the homesteaders?' Sarah asked.

'No, she made a model, didn't you, Harry?' Stacey said.

Harriet sighed. 'I was going to show you it at break time, Miss. Everyone else will think it's lame.'

'Lame? They won't, and if they do, then they are lame themselves, Harriet,' Sarah said, shooting a warning glance at Jeremy.

Harriet pulled a carrier bag out from under the table and placed it carefully in front of her. Reaching in, she gingerly drew out a model made of lollipop sticks, matchsticks and rubber bands. Sarah walked over and carefully picked it up and held it for all to see. She had to swallow hard as she realised the hours that must have gone into the light construction in her hand.

This is why she'd gone into teaching in the first place, to inspire a love of history, learning and to make a difference to the hopes and aspirations of her students. She cleared her throat. 'Does anyone know what this brilliant model of Harriet's is?'

'Looks like a windmill to me.' Kirsty shrugged and studied her nails. She was obviously disgruntled at the praise Sarah was giving to Harriet.

'Nearly, but not quite, Kirsty. It's a wind pump. Harriet, would you like to tell the class what wind pumps were used for?'

'Not really, but I will. They have sails like a windmill, as you can see. The wind blew them round and they drove a pump which pumped water from deep underground. They could then use the water to feed the crops and animals.' She looked at Sarah. 'If you wind that matchstick up tight with that rubber band and let go, it should spin the sails, Miss.'

Sarah handed the wind pump back to Harriet. 'You do it, Harriet; I don't want to break it.' Harriet came to the front of the class and balanced the model on the front desk. She wound up the matchstick and released it. The sails whizzed round once and everyone clapped. It was genuine applause this time and everyone started asking Harriet questions about it. Sarah was amazed at the transformation of the shy girl who never normally spoke out in class. She even handled a facetious question from Jeremy.

'So these wind pumps, yeah, they must have been, like, thousands of 'em in one field?'

'No, there would only be one or two. They didn't need lots, and anyway they were expensive,' Harriet said, looking at Sarah for confirmation. Sarah nodded.

'So, one 30cm pump would bring enough water for, like, a whole field?' Jeremy asked, with a twinkle in his eye.

'Oh, ha ha, very funny, Jeremy. No, the pump I made is *not* to scale *obviously;* they were about 5.5 metres high.' Harriet smiled, shaking her head.

Sarah whistled a happy tune and picked two ready meals from the chilled cabinet in Sainsbury's. Hmm, chicken madras or beef stew and dumplings? Well, it's Friday night so it has to be curry – curry on Friday, it's the law.

On the way to the checkout she thanked her lucky stars again. The lesson on homesteaders had been one of *the* best she could ever remember and, most importantly, she'd not been transported back to the Old West. The rest of the day had been uneventful and much better than she could have hoped for.

Sarah had decided to cut down on her drinking, but on nearing the wine aisle, was pulled like a magnet to a shelf of half-price Californian zinfandel. *Oh well, can't ignore such a good offer.* She shrugged, placed two bottles in her basket and set off for the checkout again, but the checkout she had her eye on seemed to get further and further away. The more she walked, the further away it got.

Sarah halted, aware of a leaden feeling dragging her feet to the floor, as if she were wearing concrete boots. Looking down, she could see the supermarket floor disintegrating, breaking up and swirling around, as if made of gas. Misty tendrils drifted over her shoes until her feet were totally immersed in it. And then she began to sink.

Sarah tried to open her mouth to scream but an unseen pressure sealed it shut. She tried to open her hand and let go of her basket, raise her hand to the other customers in an attempt to attract their attention from their two-for-one offers and Friday night curry, but her hands remained immoveable – tightly clasped. The customers were slowly lost from view as she descended. She looked up. Sarah could see the bright lights and hear the noise and bustle of the supermarket, but after a few seconds the noises faded and the light grew smaller, until it was no bigger than a manhole cover.

Down, down she sank, trapped in an invisible, but tightly wrapped cocoon, into the thick gas. No, not gas ... she realised it was fog. Her skin was coated with moisture and her nostrils were invaded by the fog's smoky, leafy smell. And then at last her feet touched down on something solid. Rigor mortis released her body, and the fog drifted away.

Sarah blinked rapidly and rubbed her eyes. The something solid was a highly polished wooden floor. She was standing in the middle of a grand Victorian drawing room. Heavy oak chairs and settees upholstered in sumptuous crimson hulked around a marble fireplace. In high purple-painted arches either side of the fireplace stood alabaster full-sized sculptures of semi-nude maidens, arms raised above their heads with cherubs at their feet. An imposing grandfather clock marked time at one side of a floor-to-ceiling window, heavily draped in navy velvet curtains, and on the other side, a mahogany grand piano postured on lion-clawed feet.

Sarah, wide eyed and open mouthed, tried to register and process what she was seeing in her panic-stricken brain. She felt her stomach roll and her heart assume an irregular rhythm as her attention was directed towards what she held in her right hand. The basket containing a ready meal and wine had miraculously changed into a metal bucket full of coal and a box of matches.

Before she had time to think coherently, the door flew

open and a tall, beady-eyed, horse-faced woman of around her own age bustled in. She wore her dark hair parted down the middle and swept into a loose bun, a high-necked, long-sleeved, lemon, calf-length dress and on her feet highly polished laced boots.

'There you are,' she said, pointing her finger at Sarah imperiously. 'Get that fire made up, girl. We have the Pankhurst visit in a few hours. This room is old fashioned enough; she mustn't be cold into the bargain.'

Sarah gawped, her stomach rolled again and she feared she may vomit. Bollocks! Just when I thought I'd got away with not being dispatched to the American West, I end up in Edwardian England!

'Chop-chop; stop staring like an imbecile, you silly ninny, and do it!' The woman turned on her heel and flounced out.

Sarah ran to the fireplace, tipped out the bucket of coal and then knelt. With her hands on the rim of the sooty bucket, she vomited.

Chapter Nine

Trembling like a whippet in a strong wind, Sarah pushed the bucket away and sat with her back to the fireplace. Brushing a strand of hair from her eye, she took deep breaths and tried to quell her turbulent gut. Focus on one point and concentrate, her dad had always told her when she'd been carsick as a child. Replacing the nausea for an instant, a pang of sadness twisted her belly; God she missed her dad. Was it really seven years since he'd died? She could do with his strong, dependable, eyes-front support right now.

Sarah focused on her feet. They wore the same style boot as the woman in the lemon dress, though much rougher and heavier. As her eyes travelled along her body, she found she was wearing the black dress and long white apron of a traditional maid, and, patting her hand on the top of her head, felt a cloth hat of some sort. Sarah closed her eyes. *A mop cap. Oh God, I must look like an extra in* Upstairs Downstairs.

Her eyes snapped open at the sound of quick, light footsteps approaching outside. The door opened and a young blonde-haired maid, dressed in an identical uniform to Sarah's, came in. She carried a bucket and made a beeline for the window. Humming a merry tune, she set the bucket down and dipped a cloth into it. After wringing it out, she stood upright again, and that's when she saw Sarah.

'Bleedin' 'ell, Sarah, you gave me a start! What's happened?'

The maid hurried over and knelt at Sarah's side. 'Well, cat got your tongue?'

Sarah shook her head and shrugged. 'No, just came over a bit funny,' she whispered, wondering if Albert would suddenly pop up and nod, knowingly.

'Well you've got more soot on your face than all the sweeps here in London.' The maid dabbed at Sarah's forehead with the damp cloth. 'And I can smell sick ... have you chucked up in that coal bucket?'

Sarah flushed and nodded, though why she should feel embarrassed about it she didn't know. It's not every day you're in a supermarket going about your business one minute, and then getting sucked down a time tunnel or whatever the hell it was, and dumped in Edwardian London, the next.

' ... because if you have, Sarah, you'll be in right trouble and no mistake. She's sacked people for less.'

Sarah was aware the maid had said something but in her confused state, half of it hadn't registered. 'Who sacked people?'

'Who do you fink? Queen Victoria, of course, she came back from the grave and sacked the footman last week.' The maid tutted, and shook her head at Sarah, but she did have a twinkle in her pretty blue eyes.

'What did you say I had to do?' Sarah ventured and managed a little smile.

'Oh, lumme! I said get yourself up, empty that sick and get that fire lit before Mrs Pankhurst gets here. If you don't, Lady Attwood will have your guts for garters!'

'I expect you mean Mrs Pankhurst the suffragette?' Sarah asked, getting slowly to her knees.

'No, I mean Mrs Pankhurst the music-hall actress.' The maid shook her head in disbelief. 'Now, take my hand and let me pull you up.'

With grim determination Sarah struggled to her feet and immediately felt much better. She sighed and pushed her hair back under her cap.

'Stop touching your face with them hands; you keep smearing more soot all over you.' The maid took Sarah's hands and scrubbed at them with the cloth.

Sarah sighed again and wondered who the hell she was supposed to save this time. Perhaps Mrs Pankhurst would visit and slip on a blob of Sarah's sick. In her mind's eye she saw a slow-motion scenario of Mrs P falling, her head inches away from brutal contact with the edge of the marble fireplace. But then, in the nick of time, Sarah would launch a rugby tackle at her. Mrs Pankhurst would land heavily, but unharmed, upon Sarah's prone body.

Valiant history teacher provides a soft landing for the heroine of women's rights. Hurrah!

'What are you smiling at?' The maid was looking at Sarah as if she'd lost her marbles. *Not a bad assessment to be honest, my dear maid.* The girl picked up the sick bucket. 'Look, come on, I'll take you down to the kitchen, you'll have a glass of water and wash your hands, then you must get back to the fire, alright?'

The house was massive. As Sarah trotted after the slight figure down stairs and along corridors, she admired the beautiful but faded grandeur of the old building. Tapestries adorned oak-panelled halls, portraits, presumably of previous Attwoods, sneered down at her from high balustrades and landing walls and, in the main hall, suspended crystal chandeliers winked in the natural light cast down from a stained-glass domed ceiling.

The journey turned past a main hall, a dining room and down two flights of stairs. Sarah noted that the predominant smell of beeswax and old books gave way to boiled cabbage and cake. Scrubbed flag stones replaced polished floors and, entering under a stone arch, she found herself in a large kitchen.

A plump woman stood at a long wooden table. She wore a green candy-striped dress and white apron and sweat rolled from her brow, almost as fast as she rolled pastry on a floured board. A few other servants dashed here and there, carrying pots, jugs and plates, and a smartly dressed butler-type sat by a range reading a newspaper.

The plump woman glanced over at Sarah and the maid. 'Did you remember to bring the milk in, Rose?'

'Yes, Cook, I'm just going to sort Sarah out and then I'm back up to do the windows.'

'Sort Sarah out, why what's the matter with you?' The cook stopped, frowned over at Sarah and placed her meaty hands on her hips.

'I just felt a little dizzy, Cook. I'm alright now, thank you for your concern,' Sarah said, hoping she'd done the right thing leaving the vomiting episode out of her explanation.

The cook wiped the sweat from her brow with the back of her hand. '"Thank you for your concern" she says. A bit hoity-toity, aren't we? Next thing, she'll be joining the WSPU like madam upstairs!' She jerked a pudgy thumb skywards.

Sarah was unsure how to react to that. Thankfully, Rose grabbed her arm and bustled her through the kitchen to the scullery. 'Right, I'll empty this stinkin' bucket before Cook smells it. You get some water in the sink; wash your hands and face and then get back up to the sitting room. Cook's not in a good mood; she thinks the WSPU should be burned as witches. "Them's that play with matches deserve all they get," she says.' Rose giggled.

Left alone at last, Sarah turned the tap on over the big, white, ceramic sink. It protested, making a squeaky noise like a strangled mouse, but eventually gave out a stream of beige-coloured water. She made a face and scrubbed at her hands with a bar of rough soap and reminded herself to steer clear of any liquid that hadn't been boiled whilst she was here. Sarah replaced the soap and carefully dabbed her forehead with a sponge.

A cotton square was all she could find for a towel and she hoped that it wasn't Cook's best handkerchief. Sarah looked around the scullery and decided that although the house was grand, it seemed to be outdated for the Edwardian period and a bit shabby here and there. Miss Lemon Dress, presumably Lady Attwood, had said as much to her earlier.

That brought her to her next question. So, what year was she in, exactly? The cook had mentioned the Women's Social and Political Union. If memory served Sarah correctly, Emmeline Pankhurst, due here for tea later, had formed the WSPU in 1903. Their tactics to get votes for women hadn't got too militant until around 1911 when women, egged on by Christabel, Emmeline's daughter, were encouraged to smash shop windows with hammers, and throw stones at the windows of politicians. Sarah also seemed to remember that arson became a weapon of choice around 1913. Was that why Rose said the cook referred to matches? But then if it was 1913, George V was on the throne – Edward had died three years earlier.

Sarah sighed, straightened her cap and smoothed out the creases in her apron. She wondered if John would appear, or at least a John lookalike. She could use a friendly face and some guidance right about now. She took a deep breath. *Right, positive thinking, Ms Yates. No use moping in here; get your arse back upstairs.*

On her way past the range, the butler still in residence, she tried to glance at the newspaper's front page. His thumb obscured the top line, so she dropped to her knee and pretended to tie her bootlace, whilst cocking her head to the side in an endeavour to spy out any kind of clue about the date. The name Lloyd George was clearly visible over a crease in the broadsheet and a side panel advertised 'Bingley's Miraculous Tonics for every ailment known to man. Our tonics promise to revive and invigorate even the dullest appetite.'

Sarah racked her brains. Lloyd George ... he'd been

Chancellor before Prime Minister. If he was PM, that would make it at least 1916 and in the middle of the First World War … no, there had been no mention of war, and she felt that there would have been by now. Coupled with the WSPU information her gut gave her a ballpark figure of 1912–14.

'Seen enough, madam, or would you like me to hand the thing to you?'

Sarah raised her eyes from the newspaper to meet the bespectacled steely beads of the reader. He did not look amused, not even a little bit. 'Um … I was just tying my lace, Mr err …'

'Mr Err? I think you'll find it's Mr Grayson, and don't take me for a fool. And whilst it's admirable for a maid to want to know what's happening in the world, you will do it on your own time. Now go to work!'

Sarah nodded, jumped up and headed for the door. As she stepped through, she heard Cook say to Grayson, 'Why they have to educate females at all I do not know. I think a bit of learnin' leads to trouble if you ask me. I can't read nor write and all the happier for it.'

After a few wrong turns, and confirmation from the large hall mirror that she was once again 'herself', Sarah eventually ended up back at the drawing room. Rose was busy at her task; she wiped dry one half of the window, singing, 'Bird In A Gilded Cage'. The haunting quality of her voice brought a lump to Sarah's throat, though she didn't really know why. As far as Sarah knew, the song was about a beautiful young woman who had married an old man for money.

From the doorway, she watched the young maid for a few seconds, and concluded the reason for her emotion wasn't the quality of her voice, but poor Rose herself, doomed to servitude for the rest of her life. Another young woman, just like thousands of others of this period, lacking opportunity and escape from this grand, but crumbling, cage of employment.

Sarah sniffed and walked over to the fireplace. Rose turned, nodded and continued with her song and her task. Gleaming brass fire tongs, a brush and a poker hung in a rack by the side of the fire. Sarah selected the tongs but realised she had as much idea on how to get the fire alight as she did about the exact date. What should she do next? Rose couldn't be called upon to explain, because Sarah had the idea that fire lighting was a task given to more lowly members of staff. Even though Sarah was probably around ten years older, it was clear from the way that Rose had spoken to her earlier that she was above Sarah in the pecking order.

Sarah looked up to find Rose scrutinising her from across the room.

'Ain't you made a start yet?' She frowned.

Sarah thought quickly. 'I don't know what to do; every time I bend down I go all dizzy again, Rose.'

'Well, dizzy or not, it needs doing.'

Sarah looked beyond Rose to the view outside the window. From what she could see it looked to be a sunny day and the green leaves on the branches of a nearby tree waved in the breeze. 'Why do we need the fire lit on a summer's day, anyway?'

Rose tutted and shook her head. 'Because Lady Attwood ordered it, that's why. This old house is draughty on the hottest day, and more important, you know better than to question her wishes, Sarah.'

'Yes, Rose, sorry. I wonder if we might swap jobs, just this once? I feel much better standing up.'

Rose looked as though she would refuse but then shrugged and pointed her finger. 'Just this once, mind. And don't tell my auntie, or she'll be at you hammer and tongs.'

'Your auntie?'

'Gawd, yes, Cook, of course, you dozy article.'

Ah, Cook was her aunt, then. Sarah walked over to the

window and dipped the cloth into the water. That explained why Rose had a higher position. From the window, she found that the house looked over a park and the row of houses next to the park were of red brick and very grand in structure. They had at least five storeys and many had balconies and arched windows edged with white frames, from floor to ceiling. Some even had Doric columns supporting porch entrances. These entrances led up a number of steps to shiny front doors complete with brass knockers. Sarah presumed that Lady Attwood's house was similar from the outside.

It was fairly quiet on the street; only one or two people strolled past. Two women arm in arm twirling their parasols, and a chimney sweep pushing a barrow filled with tools.

Sarah knew that in the present these houses would be hotels or flats, but would, at the moment, house many of London's rich and famous.

The feelings she'd had when walking through wartime Sheffield began to surface again. Sarah thrilled at the prospect of experiencing the past at first hand. It would be nice, though, to have a timetable and set plan of what she was supposed to do on these jaunts. She stepped closer to the window and rubbed at a smudge on the glass.

When she got back she'd get some straight answers from John. Would it be too much to ask for a bit of warning, just to prepare herself? And she wanted to know about the 'powers that be' he'd referred to the first time she'd seen him and how exactly he got his information. If they'd set out to test her, as John mentioned, they were certainly doing a grand job. Sarah wasn't sure how much more her frazzled nerves could take, and she was getting more than a little tired of playing the dopey Dora.

A few minutes later, Sarah folded the drying cloth and turned to Rose. 'I think I've finished, Rose, how are you doing?'

'Nearly there.' She struck a match and held it to some rolled paper under the coal. The fire took hold but slowly. 'This bloody chimney could do with a fettle. Trouble is,' she lowered her voice, 'Lady Attwood is too busy saving her pennies.' Rose stood up, and dusted her apron. 'Leastways she is until she snags old Mr Darnley. She'd better do it soon or we'll all be out on our ear I reckon, even Cook and Mr Grayson, too.'

Sarah walked over and leaned her arm against the mantelshelf. It seemed that Rose wanted to share some gossip. Any information Sarah could glean without appearing to have lost her memory, or her marbles, was most appealing.

'So do you think that will be an end to her money worries?' Sarah whispered, looking to the door and back to Rose to show her that she was being careful.

'If she can get him, yes. I overheard her talking to Mrs Farmingdale the other day when she popped over for tea. Lady Attwood said that she was sick of these old Victorian decorations and once she had a new husband everythink would be different,' Rose said, sweeping the coal dust from the hearth with the brass-handled brush.

'Blimey, aren't you clever finding all that out, Rose. I wish I had your brains,' Sarah said, hoping that Rose would fall for flattery.

Rose obligingly swallowed the hook, winked and said, 'That's nuffink. I found out that old Lord Attwood left her with lots of debts on account of his gambling habit when he died. It's no wonder that she had to sack young Bill the footman and Daisy.' Rose put the brush back, folded her arms and sniffed. 'It was a real shame Daisy went. Even though she was her ladyship's personal maid, she never had no airs nor nuffink, did she?' She looked at Sarah expectantly.

'No, Daisy was a real good sort and no mistake, me old china.'

'Ere, don't let Mr Grayson hear you talk slang or you'll be first out.'

Sarah nodded and then leant in close to Rose. 'So, Rose, I bet you couldn't find no more out though, eh?'

Rose raised her eyebrows. 'I know stuff that would make your hair curl. Now I have to double up as her personal maid as well as everything else, I come across all sorts. For instance, I know that she's not bothered about no women's suffrage at all. She's only bothered about getting close to Mr Darnley, and he's big pals with all the top 'uns from WSPU. She only joined in with helping those "fallen women" last year 'cos he was doing it.'

'Oh, Rose, that's really shocking.'

'Yes, and talking of shocking, she'd be really shocked if she knew where I went on my days off and no mistake.' Rose inclined her head in a 'follow me' motion.

Sarah followed her out of the room and could barely contain her curiosity as they hurried along corridors, three flights of stairs and stepped into a laundry. Rose stood with her back to a mangle, looked at Sarah and put her finger to her lips.

'Look, can you keep a secret?' Rose's eyes danced with excitement and her face flushed.

Sarah nodded.

'Well, alright then. On my days off I go to WSPU meetings, but for God's sake don't tell Cook.' Rose giggled, picked up clean towels and ducked out of the room.

Sarah smiled and felt her spirits rise as she stood by the door watching Rose step lightly along the corridor. The bird trapped in the servitude cage had suddenly grown wings and was preparing to fly.

Chapter Ten

Were parents gifted with a special 'insight' button immediately after spawning their first child? It certainly seemed that way to John. He watched his boot lock on to the spade again and force another clod of earth from the ground. Sweat trickled from damp hair into his eye and he flicked his head in annoyance, but didn't slow the punishing pace he'd set himself. Spade in, boot locked, arms flexed, spade out, spade in ...

Harry could always see straight through him, him and his bullshit. His mum, on the other hand, had been a different story. In her eyes he could do no wrong, and if he told her something, she'd believe it hook, line and sinker. God, how he missed her. Of all the people in the world he wished to see right now, she was the one. She'd know what to say, to advise, she'd help him make sense of the tornado of confusion whipping through his heart. But she'd died of cancer two years ago, and no matter how hard he wished, he couldn't bring her back.

Flinging the spade aside, John sank exhausted to his knees. His breath came heavy and his shirt was soaked through. With the back of his forearm he pushed his hair back, grabbed a water bottle and tipped it to his mouth. Eyes closed against the noonday sun, he gulped half the bottle in one and thought about the day his dad had visited again.

Harry was no fool. But then he did have help from insightful sources – insightful sources that had controlled John from the age of eighteen. The powers that be had guided his every move as a Time-Needle. Of course, Harry had helped, too and by the age of twenty-three, John had become almost as good as his father and his father before him.

When he was about ten he'd asked his father when and why the Needler family had been chosen. Harry had told him that it had all started with his six times great-grandfather, William. He had been a farmer and one day while weeding around the cabbages, he'd picked up an old wooden needle. The needle was one of many artefacts that he discovered in his day-to-day work and thinking that his wife might like it because their name was Needler, and also because she sometimes collected things that he'd found, he took it home. She *had* liked it and placed it in the box with various coins, bits of pottery and even an ancient Roman ring.

Apparently when they'd gone to bed that night William had been visited with what he described as a 'shining vision from up above'. The vision told him that he and his children would be Time-Needles and described the duties expected of him. The Stitch he was supposed to find was a young woman who lived in his village. Which young woman it was, he wasn't told, however. Furthermore, the reason why he had been chosen was because he had picked up the needle. Needles belonging to the 'shining visions from above' had been dropped here and there over the centuries and only those who were worthy of the job could find them.

At first he thought he'd dreamt it all, until he was shown a glimpse of a Roman amphitheatre while eating his lunch in the top field the next day. There was a gladiator fighting a lion and the lion seemed to be winning. William felt that this was a deadly warning of some kind and, terrified, threw down his lunch and ran back down the lane to his farm. Upon passing a neighbour's cottage he noticed their daughter, Ann, sitting outside sewing a blanket. Without a shadow of a doubt he knew that she was the Stitch he'd been told of and he somehow managed to persuade her that his ramblings were true.

Ann was transported back in time the next day, somehow prevented the gladiator from being selected to fight that day and the gladiator went on to lead a slave revolt against the Romans. The rest, as they say, was history. John was at the end of a long line of Needlers, but there were others around the world who were his contemporaries apparently, and all with similar tales to tell.

Of course John had felt proud and very special when his dad had told him their history, but there were many times when he wished that he was just an ordinary guy. Life would be so much simpler.

Harry had known exactly how to play John when they'd gone to the pub the other day, John remembered. They had played pool, had a meal, and sunk a few pints without even a mention of Sarah or even *the* business. As ever, John had been lulled into a false sense of security and then, near the end of the evening, he'd been tricked into revealing much more than he'd intended.

'So Josephina is still in Italy?' Harry asked, wiping the froth from his pint off his top lip.

'Yes, and she can stay there as far as I'm concerned,' John said.

'Perhaps, but I think she did care, John ... You just never showed her the love she needed. Always a bit standoffish I thought.'

'Thanks, Dad, but I think that *you* think too much. It was Sarah earlier, and now Josephina. And is there any wonder I was a bit standoffish? It's not the easiest thing in the world to keep our other business hidden. I'm not sure I will ever settle down properly. I mean, how can you give yourself wholly to a person when they only know half of you?'

Harry nodded sympathetically, took another drink and then remarked casually, 'Sarah seems to be doing quite well in 1913, I'm told.'

'You got the same email I did, then? Nice that they feel the need to still keep you in the loop ... not!' John frowned at his dad. 'And yes, considering it's only her second trip she should be very pleased. She has a way to go before she comes back though, I think.'

'Are you unduly worried?'

'Err ... no, though of course I'll be glad to see her back.'

'And I think she will be glad to see you too,' Harry said, taking a sip of beer.

'Oh, here we go again ...' John sighed.

Harry put his hand over his son's and leaned across the table. 'You can't fool me. You care for her but won't admit it to yourself. If your mum was here ...'

'Well, she isn't, is she?' John snapped and stood up. 'Do you want a last pint or what?'

'So you do care then.' Harry said the words as a statement not a question.

'Shit, Dad, I don't know ... no ... yes, I guess.' John ran his hand through his hair. 'I know it's not a good idea, but ...' He tailed off and shrugged.

'But I am the last one to talk, eh?'

John nodded. 'Yup, you said it.'

'And though you've only known her five minutes as you say, there is such a thing as love at first sight ... it was like that with me and your mum. I remember it like it was yesterday. She'd just come back from her second trip and was in a hell of a state because she'd appeared in the middle of town on a busy Saturday afternoon instead of at work in the bakery where she'd left from. Arriving in town like that had completely thrown her and she had nearly run under a bus apparently.

'Anyway, I took her to a pub to try and calm her down and, as she sat there nursing her sherry, the light from the open fire dancing on her face, I was furious at the powers that be for putting her through that. I knew Stitches had to be tested, put under stress, but not my Stitch, not my Patricia. It was then that I knew I wanted to marry her, even though I knew the consequences and the heartache that might entail.'

John looked at his dad. 'So, all the worry, stress, danger and everything else you both went through while Mum was on missions was worth it, then?'

Harry took a hanky out of his pocket and blew his nose. 'Oh yes, lad. What we had was worth all that ... and much more.'

John finished the bottle of water and, with the help of his spade, dragged his aching body up from the damp earth. Love at first sight was something he'd always pooh-poohed. But what exactly did he feel for Sarah? He was buggered if he knew.

What he did know was that he shouldn't even entertain the idea of a relationship given the rules of Needles and Stitches; his dad might look back with rose-tinted specs now his mum was gone, but John could remember how worried, stressed and sad he'd been when his mum was on a mission. He didn't want that for himself, and certainly not for Sarah, especially as he knew she had been almost destroyed by her husband's affair with her best friend. She needed a 'normal' guy, someone to depend on, someone in an ordinary job, not someone like him, constantly worrying about other Stitches and their missions. After she'd finished these jobs, she should go back to her life and find happiness.

But try as he might, he couldn't get her out of his head. Sarah was the first thing he thought of in the morning and the last thing before he closed his eyes at night. He'd been on tenterhooks ever since she'd left the present and his stomach churned at the thought of her getting in trouble, or worse, getting stuck in the past. It had happened to a few Stitches before ... ones who had been over confident, or too careless, or they'd just had bad luck. He hadn't told her that, of course; she had enough to worry about.

A short while later, John set off for his cottage just a few minutes' walk away. All that digging had left him tired and very hungry. His mind connected to food also presented a picture of Sarah trying to cover her boobs while eating bacon. He grinned at the memory and he felt a twinge of excitement as he thought about what those boobs would look like without that old jumper. His pulse quickened when he thought about what the rest of her would look like naked, too.

John shook the image away. He cared for her, but perhaps his feelings were just based on lust in the end; she was an attractive single woman, he was a single man, and it had been a while since he'd slept with anyone after all. Yep ... that was it. He needed to get a grip and see things for what they were. Sarah was a lovely woman who deserved a second chance with someone who would treasure her. And John Needler was definitely not that man.

Chapter Eleven

Having no better plan, Sarah decided to return to the kitchen. Perhaps there'd be a chance of food. It may be mid-morning in 19 whatever it was, but it must be near seven o'clock in the evening back in the present. Though, of course, she had no real idea; she suspected that time didn't work like that. And any suppositions she'd had about time before had been pooh-poohed by John. An image of John cooking breakfast in her kitchen flashed across her mind. He certainly looked good enough to eat. She shook her head. No point thinking about him now; it wouldn't do any good.

She walked down the corridor and followed her nose. Her tummy rumbled and the Friday-night curry and wine danced tantalisingly in her head. Sarah yawned and wondered if she would get a kind of time-travelling jet lag. She also wondered when she'd get her stitching done and return to normality – well, as normal as her life could be at the moment. There was still no clue as to whom she had to save, no itchy feet or hiccups – nothing. It had certainly been a lot easier in 1940. *It had been a lot easier in 1940? Ha! That must be at the top of the list of my all-time surreal thoughts.*

'There you are, Miss Hoity-Toity. I expect you've been off thanking people mightily for their concern and reading newspapers, eh?' Cook snapped, as Sarah entered the kitchen.

Sarah stared at the floor. She figured that this was a rhetorical question and the cook would presently continue her barracking. Sure enough, Cook marched over and prodded Sarah on the shoulder.

'There's potatoes to peel and floors to scrub, and you better get to it, gel, or you'll feel the back o' my hand!'

The back of her hand? Jeez Louise, were folk still allowed

to physically reprimand like that? Sarah wanted to call Cook an 'overblown maggoty bully', but for one, this sounded more like an Elizabethan term of abuse, and for two, and most importantly, she'd get the sack.

'Look at you stood staring at me like I'm a curio. Get to them potatoes!' Cook pointed to a mound of potatoes masquerading as Mount Everest at the end of the table.

Sarah puffed out her cheeks and let out her tension in a slow stream of air, then walked over and picked up a small vegetable knife.

'Stop sighing, or so help me!' Cook pointed a ladle at her. 'And there will be no bread and cheese for you in half an hour when everyone else has some.'

Sarah rolled her eyes and ran the knife under the skin of a potato. Oh fantastic, bread and cheese ... again. What is it with these people in the past? Don't they ever eat anything else?

'Ruby, looks like you're slacking on that brass cleaning. Run into the scullery and fetch a pot of water for Lady Sarah's taters,' Cook said to a mouse of a girl polishing a candlestick by the fire. *Oh, please. A Sarah, Rose and now Ruby? She really was in* Upstairs Downstairs.

Ruby scuttled off and then Grayson appeared at the door. 'Cook, Her Ladyship wants a word with us both about the Pankhurst visit.'

Unexpectedly alone, Sarah was free to do a spot of snooping. She dashed to the fireplace and knelt by the chair that Grayson had been sitting in earlier. Under it was a stack of newspapers, and Sarah selected the first in the pile, hoping it was the most recent. *The Daily Telegraph* had lots of information about the recent war in the Balkans splashed all over the front page, but the top strip of the page had been torn off.

Damn! Where the hell had that gone? Sarah's eyes fell on the brassware that Ruby had been cleaning. A few scraps of newspaper sat under the tin of polish. She snatched the newspaper, knocking over the polish in her eagerness. Smoothing out the pieces on the flagstone, she read: Monday, the 2nd of June 1913. 'Ha!' she said aloud. 'I was right!'

'Oh, my giddy aunt! Look at my polish, it's staining the floor!' Ruby wailed. She set down the pot of water on the table and ran over to Sarah.

Sarah looked up at the poor girl's panic-stricken face and then back at the puddle of polish. Bloody hell, Cook would go apeshit!

'Quick, Ruby, get a scrubbing brush and some soap and water.'

Ruby ran back to the scullery and Sarah grabbed the main part of the newspaper and blotted it over the spreading purple stain. Her heart sank; she realised she was probably going to get in big trouble for this. *Come on, Ruby, the evil weevils will be back in a minute.*

Right on cue, in walked Grayson and Cook. 'What on earth has happened here?' Grayson barked and stomped over to Sarah.

'You bloody tripe hound!' Cook said, lifting the corner of the newspaper. 'Can't leave you for a minute these days, and where's Ruby?'

'Here, Cook, I was just getting soap and water to clean it,' Ruby panted, slopping the water on the floor as she hurried to join them.

'Who's fault was it, I would like to know?' Grayson asked, arms folded, tapping a shiny shoe inches from Sarah's hand.

'Mine, Mr Grayson. Ruby had nothing to do with it.'

'I might have known. Too busy trying to read your papers again I shouldn't wonder,' Cook said, bending to Sarah's level and shoving her sweaty face close. 'I'm right, aren't I?'

Sarah recoiled. Sodding hell, that woman's breath stank bad enough to fell a skunk! 'Yes, I expect you are, Cook,' she said, keeping her head turned away.

'Well get it scrubbed, madam. There's definitely no bread and cheese for you now, or supper for that matter if you don't get it spotless!' Cook marched back to her table, muttering.

'It's a good job it was yesterday's newspaper, Sarah, or I would have docked your wages,' Grayson sneered and left the kitchen.

Sarah scrubbed furiously at the stain, imagining it was Cook's face. God, how she'd love to give both her and Grayson a piece of her mind.

After about twenty minutes scrubbing the floor was back to normal, but Sarah wasn't. She wanted to go home, was tired, fed up and ravenously hungry. She was just getting back to the potato peeling when Rose breezed in.

'Her Ladyship is fuming up there,' she said to Cook, perching on a stool at the table to cut a slice of bread from the board.

'What do you expect? We're all fuming, now that that bloody witch Pankhurst has decided she's too busy to bother herself,' Cook replied, pushing a cheese plate and butter dish along to Rose. 'I baked my best fruit cake and all sorts; waste of time and money now.'

Sarah raised her eyebrows. Mrs Pankhurst wasn't coming? That was one person to cross off her 'to be saved' list.

Rose stuck her nose in the air. 'She has apparently gone to a political engagement that she cannot possibly put off,' she said, mimicking Lady Attwood's accent perfectly. She took a bite of her bread. 'That's what Her Ladyship said to Grayson, but when I was leaving the room, I heard her mutter, "They should stick her in jail and let her rot next time." Shows you what she really finks 'bout women's votes, eh?'

'Don't talk with your mouth full and don't mimic Lady Attwood like that neither, Rose. Remember your place, my gel.'

Cook went off muttering that she needed to sit 'quiet a

bit' in her room. Ruby and the other maids took their bread and cheese and then were out and about elsewhere. Grayson apparently was on his afternoon inspection of the house, and Rose and Sarah were left alone.

'Cut me a bit of bread and pass the cheese down will you, Rose. I'm starving.'

Rose did as she was asked. 'Why didn't you say you wanted some before, when I was having mine?'

Sarah told her of the spilt polish and that Cook had forbidden her to eat as punishment.

'She can be such a cow at times. If she weren't blood, I'd bop her on the nose, job or no job,' Rose said, pouring out a cup of tea for them both.

Sarah was glad to have a bit of time to gather her thoughts and assess the information she'd acquired. A few choice questions to Rose should help.

'So, is it the 3rd today, Rose? I lose track of the days.'

'Yes, because it's my day off tomorrow and that's definitely the 4th. I know that 'cos I have a very important WSPU meeting ... so to speak.'

'What do you mean, so to speak?'

'Can't say no more than this.' Rose looked around to make sure nobody was within earshot. 'I'm meeting an important member of the WSPU and we're going to do something a bit different.' She tapped her finger on the side of her nose, nodded, and then sipped her tea.

Sarah worried that poor Rose would end up in prison if she did anything involving criminal damage. 'I hope you aren't going to get involved in smashing windows or arson, Rose; that won't further your cause, in fact it helped set things back until after the war.'

'War? What war?'

Shit, I mentioned the future again! Hope I don't start giggling again like last time. 'Did I say war? No, I meant to say law. The law won't like it and criminal damage will get the law after you.' Sarah smiled. Quick thinking, Batman.

Rose looked a bit puzzled but said, 'No, to tell you the truth, I'm not happy about the arson, but we have to do somefink to bring us women to the government's attention.'

'Yes, but trust me, being banged up, going on hunger strike and having a force-feeding pipe shoved up your nose has its place, but I think peaceful campaigning *will* help in the long run. Real education for women is a must. You'll get your vote in the end ...' Sarah tailed off. She felt an enormous bout of wind rumbling up from her stomach like gas in a geyser.

Rose sat back on the stool, put down her cup and frowned at her. 'You seem to know lots about everythink all of a sudden, Sarah ... and you seem to be talking right clever an' all.'

'*Buurgh! Boulgh! Yarrup!*' Sarah belched three times in succession louder than she'd ever belched before. She put her hand to her mouth in shock. Not the giggles this time; but this was one of the warning signs for talking about the future.

'Well, how rude! You'd better not do that in front of Cook or Mr Gr—'

'*Berrumph*!' Sarah clamped a hand over her mouth and shook her head at Rose and pointed to the cheese.

'The cheese made you belch like that, you mean?'

'*Yerrowgh!*' Sarah nodded.

'Cheese? I told you not to eat anything, you disgusting little guttersnipe!' Cook bellowed from the doorway.

She came over to Sarah and shook her by the shoulders, her face only inches away as she yelled 'You're a nasty deceitful little—'

Sarah took her hands away from her mouth and let rip right into Cook's eyes. '*Breuwrgh!*'

Cook jumped away as if she'd been scalded, which was

quite an amusing sight. Her jowls shook like jelly and her eyes popped open in disbelief. Rose slid a stool under her aunt's behind and eased her on to it. 'Sit here and calm down, Cook. I'm sure Sarah didn't mean it. She's not been well all day, have you, Sarah?'

The wind left as quickly as it had come and Sarah found that she was able to speak unhindered. 'No, of course I didn't mean it, it just slipped out.' She winked at Rose over the top of Cook's head. 'Better out than in as my old granddad used to say.'

'You cheeky mare, what's come over you? Have you no respect?' Cook asked, struggling to her feet.

'Now, what's all this then?' Grayson barked, strolling in.

'It's that Sarah.' Cook waved her fist. 'She's gone funny in the head. Belches right in my face she did, and stands there smirking as large as life.'

'Is this true, Sarah?' Grayson asked, polishing his gold-rimmed spectacles on a handkerchief.

'*Yerugsh!*' Sarah said.

Grayson took a step back and shoved his glasses back on. He stood blinking at her like an owl plucked from its nest on a sunny day. Sarah blinked back. Where the hell did that one come from? Still, it felt good to see the evil weevils in a pickle.

'See, I told you!' screeched Cook. 'It's all that reading she does, giving her ideas right above her station. She'll be wearing trousers next!'

Sarah stood up and folded her arms. She wondered if some mischief-making spirit had hitched a ride across time with her, because before she could stop herself she said, 'Trousers are very popular where I come from; they free the legs from these cumbersome drapes we are forced to wear. Moreover, literacy ...' she inclined her head towards Cook, ' ... that means reading and writing, Cook. Now, where was I? Ah, yes, literacy is crucial to the betterment of the human condition, and absolutely necessary to fulfil one's individual potential.' She began to pace back and forth across the kitchen with her hands clasped behind her back. Then she stopped and peered haughtily at Cook.

'It is clear that your condition is poor and your individual potential is sadly lacking, both as a woman and a human. I suggest you learn to read, madam, and perhaps when you do, you may feel the need to have some trousers specially tailored for your alarmingly large derrière.'

Cook, Grayson and Rose gawped open mouthed.

Sarah couldn't help it; she threw back her head and laughed like some villain in a play. She felt as if she had been dropped on to a stage at an amateur dramatics evening.

The other three looked at each other in disbelief and then back to Sarah. Grayson recovered his composure first.

'Right, Rose, escort Miss Heggarty to her room and lock her in. I do not want to see her for the rest of the day and I will speak to Her Ladyship about her conduct and further action.' He pointed to the door and dabbed at his forehead with his handkerchief.

Rose led the way out and up a flight of stairs. She didn't speak to Sarah on the short trip and kept her eyes averted. Sarah was at a loss to why she had just behaved like that and said those things to Cook. If she were locked in a room, how the heck would she complete her task?

Rose opened a door to the shabbiest room that Sarah had seen so far. Two small beds were placed either side of a stand bearing a tin basin and water pitcher. On a metal rail along the back wall hung two dresses and two coats, and two pairs of shoes were placed neatly underneath. A small chest of drawers stood next to the door.

Rose made sure the door was closed and then said, 'My God, that was bleedin' marvellous!'

'It was?' Sarah was pleasantly surprised; she'd assumed Rose's silence was down to disapproval.

'Yes. I didn't understand all of what you said, but it certainly put old Cook and Grayson in a spin. I wish I could use all them big words like you. Some of the leaders of the WSPU don't even sound as grand as that.'

'How much education have you had?'

Rose shrugged. 'Same as everybody. I learned my letters and numbers until I was twelve and then I came into service.'

Sarah sat on the edge of one of the hard mattresses. 'Well, that's a start, Rose. If you keep at it and get help, you'll be able to use the kind of words I did.'

Rose came and sat on the opposite bed. 'Yes, that's what I don't understand. How the bloody hell did you do it? You never talked like that before and I've known you for nearly a year. You seem all brainy and confident like.'

'I'll tell you about it one day, but not today. Let's just say I kept it under my mop cap.'

Rose laughed out loud. 'You're a caution and that's the truth.' She stood and moved to the door. 'Look, I'll sneak you some grub up later when I come to bed. I better not risk it before, not with things as they are. Borrow my pillow till then; may as well be comfy while you're cooped up in here.'

Sarah was relieved that it was Rose who shared the room. Just as she was slipping out Sarah whispered. 'So, who are you secretly meeting tomorrow, Rose?'

Rose popped her head round the door and rolled her eyes. 'If I tell you it won't be a secret, will it? But I do trust you ... It's Miss Davison. Keep it all under your mop cap, mind!'

Rose closed the door and locked it behind her. Sarah groaned and flopped back on the bed. That must be it then ... she'd found the person she had to save.

Emily Davison, well-known member of the WSPU, had thrown herself under the King's horse on the 4th of June 1913 and died four days later.

Chapter Twelve

The sound of snoring woke her. Sarah looked across at Rose's bed and found it empty. She ran her tongue over her dry lips and realised that she had been the one snoring. Sarah couldn't remember falling asleep, but she figured that she must have needed it after the shock of arriving here in 1913 and then finding out who she had to save.

Plumping the postage-stamp sized pillows, she propped herself up a little, closed her eyes and sighed. This was crazy ... more crazy than normal. Last time she saved someone who was obscure, just another person. OK, yes he was the grandfather of the next PM, but somehow it didn't seem as crucial to the march of history. Everyone had heard of Emily Davison, purely because she had thrown herself under the king's horse. It was one of those things people always said when they talked about the suffragettes. So, if Sarah saved her tomorrow, where would that leave history? She was buggered if she knew.

Caw! Caw!

Sarah's eyes snapped open. On the grimy skylight above her head sat a crow. Its beady eyes found hers, and it turned its head first on one side and then the other. Sarah had a crazy notion that perhaps it was John. Perhaps he doubled as a shape-shifter and had flown through time to help her. The crow deposited a squirt of white liquid and flew off. *Yeah, that'd be right. That's John all over. He dumps me in an impossible situation and then he dumps on me from a great height, too. Damn him ... Why had all this been placed at her door? And why did he make her feel so ... so ...* She shut her mind to him and sighed.

The blue sky, well what she could see of it through the

grime and crow droppings, was handing over to dusk. A half-hearted sunset muted through the dirty clouds and a single star winked in the darker blue. Sarah wondered what her fate would be when Lady Lemon Features had been told of her impudence. She shuddered. If they decided to sack her tonight, God help her. Out in London with nowhere to go didn't bear thinking about.

The key rattled in the lock and the door opened. Rose came in with a glass of milk in her hand, and a piece of fruit cake and an apple bundled in her apron.

'Ere, eat up quick. I heard Grayson tell Cook that Her Ladyship will be calling for you presently.'

Sarah rolled her eyes. 'Thanks for the grub, Rose; I hope she doesn't sack me on the spot.'

'Yes, well you will just have to be polite and say that you are dreadfully sorry. I'm not sure if you should use any of them big words. She might fink that you're too clever by half.'

Sarah took a bite of cake. 'Don't think the upper classes are too fond of us hoi polloi being educated, eh?'

'No. There's some who say Mrs Pankhurst and them are too snobby as well. They say that they're only interested in votes for middle-class ladies first and then us working-class women can come later. There's Annie Kenney, though. She's one of the top 'uns and she used to work in the cotton mills. When she was only ten a bobbin tore her finger off.'

Rose went over to the chest of drawers and pulled out a cotton nightdress. She held it up to Sarah and wiggled her finger through a hole under the arm. 'Better get this mended before I put it on later.'

The thought of stitching brought Sarah back to her task. 'So, tomorrow when you meet this Miss Davison, what will you be doing?'

'As much as I like you and that, I can't tell you all of it. Just to say we are going to the races.'

Sarah took a gulp of milk and said, 'The races? I'm not sure that would be a good idea. Why don't you persuade Miss Davison to throw a few stones at a politician's window instead?'

Rose frowned. 'Eh? You said earlier that breaking the law wasn't the answer. And anyway, what's wrong with going to the races?'

'Um ... well, you might lose your bet and then the bit of money you work so hard for will be lost.'

'No, Miss Davison said we're not going to bet. She said we're going to make a statement,' Rose said, opening a sewing box.

'Are you sure that you know what she's going to do there?'

'Not really, but whatever it is, it will be "Deeds not words". That's our motto, you know.'

As she watched Rose thread the needle, Sarah wondered what her plan for tomorrow should be. Perhaps she should follow Rose and somehow try to persuade Emily Davison to stay put. But how would she do that if ...

'Sarah? Get to the drawing room immediately, Lady Attwood wishes to speak to you,' Grayson barked outside the door.

'She's coming, Mr Grayson, sir!' Rose said, because Sarah just sat with her head in her hands.

'Come on, Sarah, better get it over with. You'll be alright if you do what I said ... hopefully.'

Sighing, Sarah stood up and brushed crumbs from her apron. 'Can't you come with me?'

'Crikey, no, that wouldn't be allowed. And anyway, I have to get this hole stitched. You know what they say, "a stitch—'

'—in time, saves nine", yes, I'm very familiar with that one, Rose.'

Lady Attwood had changed into a crimson velvet evening

gown, and was warming her hands at the fire Rose had lit earlier. Sarah entered and coughed. Lady Attwood turned and picked up her long black evening gloves from a chair. She didn't even acknowledge Sarah standing just inside the door.

Finger by finger she pulled the glove over her right hand and rolled it up her forearm. The heavy diamante necklace and matching comb in her upswept hair shimmered in the gaslight. To Sarah's nose, the heady scent of the lily of the valley perfume she was wearing was almost cloying. She must have poured a bucket of the stuff on. Still, it was better than the unsavoury body odour that clung to most people around the place. Personal hygiene amongst the servants in 1913 was much worse than the folk she'd encountered in 1940.

Lady Attwood eventually deigned to look in Sarah's direction. 'Apparently you have been extremely rude to Cook.'

Sarah sighed and bowed her head.

'Look at me, you stupid girl.'

Sarah raised her head and met the other woman's eyes. She tried not to look defiant, but it was so hard. Who did this snotty bitch think she was? She couldn't have been much older than Sarah and to talk down to her in that rude manner made her furious.

'Well?'

'Well what, my lady?'

'Well, answer my question!'

'I wasn't aware that you had asked a question, my lady.'

Lady Attwood stopped putting her left glove on and glared at Sarah. 'Not aware I had ... pah, the impudence! I said apparently you have been extremely rude to Cook.'

'Begging you pardon, my lady, that is a statement, not a question,' Sarah said.

Lady Attwood's mouth fell open and her ample bosom

began to rise and fall as her breathing quickened. She picked up a fan from a side table and fluttered it theatrically across her face and neck. 'In all my life I swear I have never been so rudely addressed by a ... by a scullery maid! How dare you?'

'I didn't mean to be rude, my lady. I was just stating fact.' Sarah tried to keep a smirk at bay that insisted on twitching the corners of her mouth.

'Well, really!' Lady Attwood thrust the fan on a chair and dragged her glove along her arm. 'I have no idea what has happened to you, Sarah, but you are certainly not yourself. Where did you learn to speak in such an educated manner?'

'Err ...' Sarah made a face. 'I loved reading when I was a child. It just progressed from there.' It wasn't a lie, just not the whole truth.

'But you never used to speak this way before.'

'No, I normally keep it hidden. I have found that certain classes of people find it quite off-putting, my lady. I was upset this afternoon when Cook was being horrid to me and it just came out.'

Lady Attwood picked up her fan again and wafted it gently; her forehead furrowed in a frown deeper than a field's in autumn. She seemed at a loss and paced up and down in front of the window. Sarah thought this may be a good time to try to make her exit.

'Begging your pardon, my lady, is that all?'

Lady Attwood stopped and slapped the fan shut on her wrist. 'Yes, that will be all ... and it will be all from you, too, I'm afraid. I want you to collect your belongings and leave this minute. I cannot have educated servants in my house. It just won't do.'

Bloody hell! That's all I need. Sarah needed to come up with a plan and fast! A plan wafted over to her courtesy of Lady Attwood's fan and over-applied perfume.

'Turning a woman out on to the streets of London at

night won't go down very well with Mr Darnley, my lady. And may I say, you have made yourself very attractive for him this evening.' Sarah smiled sweetly.

Lady Attwood's fan flicked open again and went into overdrive. 'What do you mean?' Her face flushed and her bosom rose and fell quicker than the fan. Sarah was dying to tell her to get a grip and that she was about a hundred years too late to behave like a virgin in a Jane Austen novel. Though that would please Sarah enormously, it would perhaps be taking things a little too far. She opted to keep it buttoned.

'How do you know I was meeting Mr Darnley this evening, you impudent, rude ne'er-do-well?'

Now if that wasn't taking things too far she didn't know what was. 'Ne'er-do-well? What a lovely old fashioned phrase. I'd quite forgotten about it.' Sarah said, folding her arms and perching on the arm of the chesterfield sofa.

Lady Attwood pointed the fan at Sarah. Her hand shook. 'You are sitting in *my* presence without leave!'

Sarah put her hand to her mouth in mock horror. 'Gasp, so I am! Now where was I, ah yes, Mr Darnley. I know quite a few things about him; for instance, a good friend of his helped me with my reading. I can't divulge his name, of course; he helped me leave, shall we say, my "questionable" career to find an honest job, too.'

'Questionable career? You mean you were a common street walker, a fallen woman?'

'You said that, not me,' Sarah said, thoroughly enjoying herself now. This whole fabrication was just tripping off her tongue. Such a great idea to bring Darnley into it. She admired her own ingenuity.

Lady Attwood flopped down in a chair like a puppet cut from its strings. The fan fell from her hand and she shook her head, as if denying Sarah's existence.

'And what I don't understand, Lady Attwood, is why it

"just won't do" to have an educated servant working for you. Mr Darnley would be more than pleased to find that you have a staff member who wanted to improve her life and keep on the straight and narrow. He is very much for the education of women and a champion of votes for women, too.' Sarah leaned forward and stared at Lady Attwood intently. 'So, why aren't you? I'm sure he'd be very upset, not to say ashamed, of the way you have behaved towards me. If you sack me I shall be loath to tell my tale to him, but tell him I will ... You can kiss goodbye to your happy-ever-after fantasy then, Florence.'

Lady Attwood's head bobbed like a pigeon's, her eyes blinked rapidly and her face grew as red as a tomato. She looked like she might spontaneously combust due to the shock and anger of having a scullery maid metaphorically tear her limb from limb.

'How dare you speak to me this way!'

'It's easy. You have precious little respect for any member of staff and are only chasing a good and caring man like Mr Darnley for his money. You are a disgrace to womankind and quite frankly, my dear, you have about as much likeability as a full chamber pot on a July day.'

Sarah stood, swaggered to the door and called over her shoulder. 'So, I take it that you have changed your mind about throwing me out on to the mercy of the streets?'

Silence.

Sarah turned round and glared at Lady Attwood. 'Well?'

'Yes, damn you!'

'Good, well let's forget this whole nasty episode then. I bid you good evening, my lady.'

Sarah ran back along the corridors, her mop cap slipping crazily to one side. Little giggles of mirth tickled up from her tummy and eventually, as she burst into her room, she let forth a guffaw loud enough to rival a thunderclap.

Rose looked up from her sewing, startled. 'Blimey, did she let you off, then?'

'She did indeed, my dear Rose.' Sarah belly flopped on the bed and then wished she hadn't as she'd forgotten it was as hard as iron. 'Ouch, how the hell do we sleep on these?'

'Never mind that, how did you get her to let you off?'

'I just said there had been a misunderstanding and I was very sorry for what I said to Cook. I did use a few big words and she seemed to like that.' Sarah hated fibbing to Rose, but it couldn't be helped.

Rose tied a knot, bit the cotton free with her teeth and placed the petticoat she'd mended on top of her patched nightdress. She smiled across at Sarah and said, 'I'm really glad that you're staying. We're just getting to be real pals, aren't we? You never said much at all to me before today.'

'Yes, I wanted to keep my education hidden, I suppose.'

Sarah wondered what would happen to the Sarah of 1913 after she herself had gone back to the present. She'd most probably return to the way she was before. That would be a shame for Rose and for Sarah, too. Also would that Sarah remember everything that had happened just now with Lady Attwood?

Sarah sat up on the bed. The whole thing was way weird. Back in 1940 and now she was herself, but someone else at the same time. She hadn't 'possessed' them like some crazy invasion of the body snatchers type of thing, because all her bits were definitely her own. Where exactly was the 1913 Sarah? Parked in the universe hanging about like some empty vessel? Another puzzle that John must have the answer to. Hopefully, after tomorrow, she would be able to ask him.

Rose went to the door. 'I'm just off to tell Cook what happened and then I'll be back for the night. I need my beauty sleep for my trip to the Epsom!' She giggled and left the room.

Sarah lay back and looked at the stars. She wondered if Emily Davison was making plans for a much longer trip right now. The jury was out on whether she'd intended to commit suicide, or whether she just wanted to make a statement. Davison had a return train ticket to Victoria station in her bag, and some say she only wanted to attach a WSPU banner to the king's horse. Apparently she'd ducked under the rail at the edge of the racecourse and ran in front of the horse. She'd tried to grab its rein, but the impact had sent her flying. She fractured her skull and never regained consciousness.

Sarah closed her eyes. On the other hand, there was evidence against it all being unintentional. Davison had hurled herself from a balcony at Holloway prison the year before. And it did seem unlikely that an educated woman would not have calculated the risks of running out into the path of a racehorse thundering towards her at full gallop.

Poor Emily, right at this moment she was somewhere not too far away, breathing the same smoggy air, planning for the next day, and very much alive. Sarah hoped to God that she still would be at the end of Derby Day tomorrow.

Chapter Thirteen

An earthquake of at least seven on the Richter scale shook the heavy iron bed with Sarah in it, as if both weighed no more than a feather. Sarah closed her eyes tight, curled her fingers around the metal bed head and hung on for all she was worth. What was happening? They didn't have earthquakes of this strength in Britain ... perhaps she'd been taken to the American West somehow before her mission was completed ...

'Sarah, what are you doing? Can't you hear me? Let go of the bed, and get up; you've overslept!'

Forcing her eyes open, Sarah realised that the earthquake was in fact Rose shaking her shoulder and the bed head roughly. 'Mm ... What do you mean, overslept?'

'Oh, at last! I've been shaking you for ages and you just lay there as if you were a dead fing. It's 6.30 and you have to get the floor washed outside the kitchen. Ruby dropped a coal scuttle and soot's gone everywhere.'

Sarah sat up and rubbed her eyes. 'Hang on, if Ruby dropped it, why have I got to clean it up?'

Rose gave a sad smile. 'I'm afraid Cook has got it in for you now, love. She'll make your life hell, and Mr Grayson will, too. I heard them saying that they'd make life so uncomfortable that you'd be glad to leave.'

'Oh, great,' Sarah said, dragging herself out of bed and pulling the uniform on over her head. 'What time are you meeting Miss Davison, where are you meeting, and is it just you two?' She tried to make her voice casual as she splashed water into the basin from the ewer.

'I'm meeting her at 9.30, we're getting the ten o'clock train ... there may be another friend, I'm not sure.' Rose knelt by the bed and pulled out a box containing a green hat with a small black plume. 'Do you fink this hat needs a spruce up?'

Sarah patted her face dry with a parchment-thin towel. 'Err, I think so, yes. Perhaps you could find another feather. The ladies will all be wearing their finery after all.' She swept her hair up into a clip and fixed her cap on top. 'Whereabouts in Victoria station did you say?'

Rose looked up and made a face. 'I never did say Victoria as it happens.'

'Didn't you?' Sarah's heart fluttered. She hoped she wouldn't start belching, giggling, or pulling brightly coloured scarves out of her mouth, because she nearly let slip that Davison had a return ticket to Victoria. 'Oh, well I assumed that's where you would go from. It's not too far away, is it?' She held her breath, hoping she'd guessed right.

Rose looked back at the hat and dusted the brim. 'It's a good half an hour's walk, but I'm not wasting my pennies on an omnibus.'

'And are you meeting on the train?' Sarah pushed, lacing her boots up.

'Lord love a duck, you're a nosy parker, ain't ya? ' Rose shook her head. 'No, we're meeting at the entrance, is that alright for you?'

'Just taking an interest that's all,' Sarah said, patting Rose on the shoulder as she hurried past and out of the door.

Two hours later, Sarah had cleaned the floor, peeled potatoes, scrubbed the range, and had been allowed five minutes to drink a cup of tea and eat a dry crust of bread. Cook hadn't said very much, just barked orders and clapped her hands, as if Sarah was a performing seal. Sarah didn't really give a damn about that. She was worried about catching Rose before she left, though.

Whilst she had scrubbed and peeled, Sarah decided that

the best option wasn't to follow Rose as she'd first intended and persuade Davison not to go, but to stop Rose from going to meet her in the first place. Sarah would then go to meet Davison alone and say that Rose was in trouble because of her affiliation to the WSPU. Cook had locked her in a cupboard and Grayson was preparing to give her the belt. A scenario like that didn't seem too farfetched for the time. Hopefully, that would lead Davison to abandon the Derby and come to Rose's rescue. It didn't seem like a bad plan, and besides, she couldn't think of anything else. Trouble was, how was she going to stop Rose?

'Right, I'm just going to polish my shoes, and then I'm off for the day, Cook,' Rose said, popping her head round the kitchen door a few minutes later.

'Right you are. Where are you going today?'

'Probably just around the park and then see what they're giving away at the market.'

'Hmm, mind you don't talk to no young men, and don't have plums again. You know how your stomach don't agree with 'em.'

'Yes, Cook,' Rose said, and nodded briefly at Sarah before disappearing.

Sarah jumped up. 'I better use the privy before I carry on with my jobs, Cook.'

'Well don't you be too long, madam, be back here in five minutes.'

Sarah hurried out of the kitchen. Bloody hell, five minutes to get to the loo, do your business, and back again? Cook ought to be a prison guard. Luckily she didn't need the loo; she needed to find Rose. Rose was out in the yard by an old table, a tin of polish and her good shoes sat upon it.

'Hello, Rose, I was hoping we could spend a few hours together today, you know at the park and at the market?'

Rose frowned, spat on her shoes and dipped a cloth in the

polish. 'You gone cuckoo? You know as well as I do I'm off to the Derby.'

'Yes, but seeing as how you said we were getting to be pals and that, I thought it might be nice to do something together instead.'

Rose pressed the cloth on to her shoe and rubbed in quick circular motions. 'Well, even if I wasn't going to the Derby, which I am, we couldn't both be off work at the same time, you ninny.'

'No, but I may have a sick stomach again like I did yesterday. I could pretend to go to my room and then come and meet you.'

'No, Sarah. It's too risky.' Rose spat on the other shoe. 'If we were found out we'd both lose our jobs, even if Cook is my auntie ... Besides, I want to go to the Derby. I may not get a chance like it again.'

Sarah sighed and folded her arms. She could tell by Rose's tone that she wouldn't change her mind. *There must be another way to stop her ...*

'There you are, skiving out here! Get back inside. Ruby has spilt milk on the floor in the passageway. Get it cleaned up!' Grayson clapped his hands and shooed Sarah past.

As Sarah mopped, she decided that she'd have no choice but to tell Cook what Rose was really up to. Her gut told her that this was not a good idea, but her brain was going from a slow simmer to a rolling boil under the pressure of getting it right.

Rose tiptoed through the milk. 'Gawd, just polished these shoes, that's all I need. Anyway see you later ...'

Before Sarah knew what she was doing, she dashed the mop under Rose's feet and down Rose went on her knees, with her left leg twisted awkwardly underneath her bottom.

'*Arrgh*, what the bleedin' 'ell did you do that for, you mad cow!' Rose stretched her legs out and gingerly prodded her ankle.

'Sorry, Rose it was an accident!'

'An accident? You jabbed that fing at me feet on purpose!'

Grayson, Cook and Ruby came running out into the passageway. 'What on earth happened here?' Grayson demanded, struggling to help Rose to her feet.

'She tripped me with that bleedin' mop!'

All eyes focused on Sarah. 'It was an accident,' she said in a small voice and wondered how she was going to get out and away to Victoria. The clock in the kitchen said nine o'clock.

Cook strode forward and grabbed her shoulder. 'Get in the kitchen, my gel, and we'll get to the bottom of what you've done to my poor Rose.'

Luckily, Rose wasn't too badly hurt. Grayson thought the ankle was slightly sprained and that a cold poultice should do the trick. She would have to take to her bed now, and miss her day off. Rose looked at Sarah with undisguised contempt and kept shaking her head when Sarah pleaded that it was an accident.

That wasn't surprising; because of course it had been deliberate. They'd questioned Sarah for about five minutes and, obviously, had taken Rose's word over hers. The whole circular argument struck up again, but the tedious repetition and recriminations were seriously eating into the time left. Sarah held up her hand to silence them.

'I'm sorry to inform you that I have an urgent message to take for Her Ladyship. She asked me expressly, on account of my excellent vocabulary and confident manner. I have to meet with an important personage at 9.30 and I fear I shall be late if I listen to any more of your inane prattle.'

'An important personage ... at 9.30?' Rose said, her eyes flashing. Those flashes said, 'You dare go to meet Miss Davison and I'll murder you.'

Grayson drew himself up. 'I think you are a liar and a danger to all in this house, madam.' He pointed a finger and backed to the door. 'You will stay there while I confirm this with Her Ladyship! Make sure she stays put, Cook.' He dashed out.

'Sit down there and don't move, you witch!' Cook snapped, her bosom heaving and her eyes lit with vengeance.

'I'm sorry, no can do,' Sarah said, turning to leave.

Cook ran to the door and blocked her way. She was surprisingly light on her feet for one so large. Her face flushed and sweaty and her feet splayed, she spread her arms each side of the door.

'Out of my way, you big tub of lard, before I tweak your nose off!' Sarah said, trying not to giggle, given the situation.

Cook's hands flew to her nose as protection against the threatened tweaking, so Sarah stamped on her foot. '*Ow!*' she shrieked, hopping on one foot as Sarah pushed past and ran for the main entrance.

Once outside, Sarah removed her hat and apron, wedged them down beside the steps and ran. Minutes later, she leaned on a lamppost, breathless, and tried to get some sense of where she was. She had only been to London a few times, but the last time was with a school trip about six months ago. They had actually visited Victoria Station to look at the architecture and Sarah remembered it was on Victoria Street, but where was she now?

The area looked very upmarket. A few horse-drawn carriages rattled past and one or two cars, but the only people she could see were a group of five or six businessmen. As they rushed along the street towards her, dressed in dark suits and top hats, she plucked up courage and said, 'Excuse me, could you tell me the right direction to Victoria Station, please?' The men looked at her disdainfully, carried on walking and didn't reply.

A younger one at the rear said, 'Well, you are at the end of Pont Street now. I think you need to—'

The one at the head of the group said, 'Come, Rupert, we have no time to dally with the likes of her. She looks like a deranged scarecrow, *and* she's hatless in public; one can't be too sure these days.'

Rupert looked sheepish but ran after the others.

Deranged and hatless? Good grief, they would have a shock if they could see how women dressed in the present. The scarecrow bit she could identify with. Her hair had come free of its clip and must look a fright to the eyes of 1913 folk. Sarah was just glad the weather was pleasant. Even though she expected the 'done thing' was to wear a coat, the black dress would just have to do.

Putting her hand to her head she turned in a circle and then followed the men. They looked like they were on their way to somewhere important, so she guessed that they might lead her to a more densely populated area. Turning a corner, she saw an old-fashioned bobby on the beat, strolling across the road. She ran up to him. 'Excuse me, Constable, could you tell me the right direction for Victoria Station, please?'

He stopped and folded his arms. 'Now are you sure you wouldn't like to sit down on that wall over there and get your breath, miss? You look most giddy.'

'No, thank you, I'll be alright; I'm just in a hurry.'

He frowned and waggled his Kitchener walrus moustache at her. 'You must be, to come out without a hat and coat, and your hair …' He flapped his hand. 'Right, if you're sure, miss, now let me see.' He pinched his chin between forefinger and thumb. 'I think this might be the quickest … no, on the other hand …'

'Oh, please, just give me a clue and I'll be on my way.' Sarah hopped on one foot and then the other. At this rate she'd get there by midnight.

'No need to be impatient.' He pointed to his right. 'Right, you need to go along this road here and left on to the King's Road, then right into Grosvenor Gardens and then you'll see the station, I shouldn't wonder.'

'Thank you very much, and can you tell me what time it is?'

He raised his eyebrows. 'Of course I can. We policemen always have the time, you know.' He patted his pocket and pulled out a watch on a chain. 'It is nearly five and twenty past nine. Now can I help you with anything else ...?'

Sarah never replied as she was already haring off like a speeding bullet towards the King's Road. Dodging a few carriages, people and omnibuses, Sarah, hot and sticky, eventually arrived at the station. The large clock above the main archway entrance said 9.50.

No, the train leaves at ten! Sarah scanned the length of the entrance and though there were lots of people milling around, she could see no one who was obviously Miss Davison. There were women waiting, but with men and children, with older women, with dogs, but not alone, or even in pairs. *Damn it!*

Sarah flew through the entrance and towards a gate manned by a station porter.

'Help, I need to get on the platform for the ten o'clock train to Epsom. I need to give someone a message, urgently!'

The porter looked at her over his half-rimmed spectacles. He looked less than impressed and wrinkled his nose as if he had a bad smell under it. 'Have you got a platform ticket, madam?'

'No, I haven't, but you need to let me through; it's a matter of life and death!' Sarah tried to squeeze past him.

The porter took her firmly by the arm and dragged her back. 'Excuse me, but I think you'll find that I don't! How long do you think I would keep my job if I let every tomfool through who said it was a matter of life and death?'

'Well, I'm sure it doesn't happen every day, for God's sake! What does it matter if you let me through ... What do you imagine I'm going to do, steal a train?'

The porter shook his head and pointed over her shoulder. 'If you wish to behave like a polite human being instead of a fishwife, buy a platform ticket from over there and I will consider letting you through.' He inclined his head and looked down his nose. 'I will, of course, expect an apology.'

Sarah patted the shallow pocket in her dress. She had no idea why she did, as she knew it was empty. 'I have no money. Please, I'm sorry for being rude, I must get through!' She tried to barge past again.

'And I ... must ... stop ... you!' Each word was punctuated by a push or a pull on her arm.

'Let go of me, you ridiculous man, before I slap you.' Sarah stepped forward and stuck out her chin. The porter raised his hand to signal a policeman who had just happened to wander through the entrance.

'OK, shove your platform ticket up your arse, it's probably too late now anyway, you moron!' she hissed, and turned for the entrance.

The policeman blocked her way. 'What seems to be the matter, madam?'

'Is it ten o'clock yet?' Sarah whispered, aware that tears were brimming in her eyes.

The policeman checked his pocket watch. 'Yes, it is that time exactly; now tell me what the matter is.'

Sarah shook her head and stumbled over to a bench, sitting down heavily, her head in her hands. Seconds later, a shiver travelled the length of her spine as she heard a whistle blow, saw smoke billow and heard the *chug, chug, chug* of a train pulling out of the station.

That's it then, Sarah, you've failed. Tears ran unchecked down her face as she stared after the departing train.

The policeman walked over, blocking her view. 'You look most upset; would you *please* like to tell me what's going on?'

Sarah would like to tell him, but how could she? He wouldn't believe a word she said about Miss Davison, and because she would have to mention the future, she would probably belch in his face or something. That would probably get her locked up, knowing her luck lately. Perhaps she could try a half-truth?

She wiped her eyes and looked up at him. 'I can't tell you everything, Constable, but could you contact Epsom races? As you may know, it's Derby Day and I feel something bad is going to happen ... Tell them to watch out for a woman.'

'Watch out for a woman?' He frowned, folded his arms, and rocked on the balls of his feet. 'I think I'll need a bit more than that to go to the trouble of sending a telegram.'

Sarah realised it was futile. He was already looking at her as if he thought she belonged in an asylum. *Jeez, I'd better get away before he arrests me.* 'Yes, of course you do. What must I be thinking? Don't worry, Constable; I think I'll just return home now.' She stood and tried to tidy her hair.

'And where would home be, madam? I think it's best if I escort you back, seeing as you're in a bit of a state.'

'No, that's alright, I'm sure you are busy enough.' Sarah started to panic. The constable's eyes had narrowed and his concerned smile had evaporated like the train smoke. What would he do when she couldn't tell him the address? 'I'm actually feeling much better now,' she said smiling and starting for the entrance.

The constable grabbed her arm. 'I insist; I wouldn't rest if I let you go off all confused like.'

Shit! What am I going to do? Sarah thought quickly. She put her hand to her head. 'Do you think I could have a drink of water first? I do feel a bit confused, as you say.' She let her legs buckle slightly and leant her head on his arm.

'Oh dear, oh dear,' the constable said, leading her back to the bench. 'Now sit here while I go and get that water, alright?'

Sarah nodded and put her hands over her face but peeped though her fingers at him as he ran to a nearby tearoom. As soon as he'd gone inside, she sprang up and hared out of the station.

Half an hour later, Sarah stopped at the same lamppost she'd leaned on earlier. She had run nearly all the way back in case old plod had tried to follow her. Her breath came in short huffs as she checked behind, yet again. Closing her eyes against images of Emily Davison under the hooves of the king's horse, she tried to calm herself. *Please, just let me go home now.* One thing was for sure, when she got back, she would tell John that there would be no more missions. She was through with stitching, done, finito, over and out.

At Lady Attwood's door she grabbed her apron and cap, and then let them fall from her hand again. She couldn't face going back in. Besides, she doubted that she'd be let back in after what she'd done to Rose and Cook. Thoughts of leaving Rose under such awful circumstances tugged at her heart, and her conscience. And all the people she'd met, seen in the streets. What would happen to them when war was declared next year? Their lives would be turned upside down. And many young men, like the one who'd said she was a deranged scarecrow, might not even survive. These thoughts and ones of a similar vein, whirled around her head like leaves on a windy day, until she felt totally hopeless.

Walking slowly down the steps to the street she felt tears prick her eyes again. Her legs buckled for real this time and she sat on the pavement and sobbed. Aware of footsteps approaching, Sarah placed her hand over her mouth and dashed away tears. She felt a hand on her shoulder.

'My dear lady, may I be of assistance?'

The blurred figure of a well-dressed, sandy-haired man in his late fifties stood before her. He removed his hat, leant on his cane and lowered himself down beside her.

Wiping her eyes again, she looked into his kind blue eyes. 'I don't think you can help me, I don't think anyone can, but thank you for asking.'

'You may be surprised; Edward Darnley has a reputation for being able to help people in sticky situations.' He smiled.

'Mr Darnley! Oh, I am pleased to meet you; I have heard marvellous things about your work,' Sarah said, clasping his hand.

'Really? Well that pleases me greatly. Where did you learn of my marvellous deeds?' His mouth twitched mischievously.

Sarah told him all about Rose and her involvement in the WSPU and how she had to keep it a secret from Lady Attwood and Cook. Sarah also mentioned that Lady Attwood frowned upon educated servants and had even considered dismissing Sarah yesterday.

'Ah, now that does distress me,' Darnley said, shaking his head. 'And tell me, Sarah, where did you receive your education?'

'I'd rather not say, sir. But Rose is so eager to learn. I would be eternally grateful if she could somehow receive the education she desires.'

'And would that put a smile on your pretty little face and dry those tears?'

Sarah smiled and nodded. She thought a lecture on patronising sexism could wait, under the circumstances.

'Then consider it done, my dear. Now then ...' Mr Darnley said, getting to his feet, '... let us enter this house together and I shall see to it that no harm befalls you.'

'If you don't mind, sir, I think I'll wait in the park across the road. I need to gather some composure before I meet the lady of the house again.' Sarah was beginning to feel peculiar. Her fingers tingled and her nerves felt as tightly strung as a violin bow. Instinct told her she'd be home very soon.

'I quite understand. I'll come and find you when the coast is clear.' Darnley placed his hat back on, touched the brim at her and set off up the steps.

Breathing slowly in and out, in an attempt to still her racing pulse, she crossed the road and entered the park. The scent of flowers and mown grass was intoxicating; Sarah stopped, closed her eyes and lifted her face to the sun. Her fingers still tingled, but the sun shone gently down, melting away the ice in her blood and loosening jangled nerves.

Sarah wrinkled her nose. An altogether more unpleasant aroma jostled aside those of grass and flowers. It smelled like manure ... She opened her eyes and looked down. It *was* manure and she was standing up to her knees in it. *What the ...?*

Blinking, she looked up. The park had been replaced by a market garden, and squelching through the mud towards her strode a man, wearing wellies, jeans, a red waterproof and a huge grin.

He waved enthusiastically. 'Hey there, Sarah, welcome back!'

Chapter Fourteen

A gamut of emotions starting at relief, and ending at anger, poured through Sarah's heart like water from a burst main. She folded her arms across her chest, pursed her lips and glared at John as he came to a stop a few feet away from the manure heap.

He gestured at the stinking pile. 'At least you had a soft landing ...' He looked at her face. 'Err, sorry, I guess you don't find this funny.'

Sarah couldn't speak. A gentle breeze wafted his dark curls around his forehead, his face was tanned from his work in the open air and his eyes looked as green as a field in spring. The smile he had been trying to hold back because of her predicament suddenly broke free of its fetters and reached from ear to ear.

Relief to be back in the present, and seeing him again, had another bit of a tussle with anger at the fact she was standing up to her knees in manure, and in her good school clothes, too. Anger twisted relief's arm up its back, securing quick submission.

'No, John, I don't find this funny ... Why would anyone find *this* fucking funny?'

John's smile made a swift exit. 'Hey, I'm sorry, I know you must be uncomfortable. No need to get so angry though.' He stepped closer and held out his arms. 'Come on, let me lift you out.'

Sarah bit back a reply as John slid his hand along her back, under her bottom and told her to put her arms around his neck. Because her legs were subsumed in manure it took one or two pulls before he could free her, but eventually he lifted her out, accompanied by a *shluck shluck* as her feet popped free of the gloop. Carrying her a little way from the muckheap, he stopped and looked into her eyes. He showed no sign of putting her down. Sarah struggled to remain angry, feeling the strength of his arms around her and the warm comfort of his body.

He nodded at her feet. 'Think you may need a new pair of shoes.'

'Oh, don't tell me, you just happen to have a pair in your pocket, do you?' she snapped, trying to keep a little bit angry, though his mouth so close to hers was giving her another feeling entirely.

'No, but I do have a hot bath, a pair of overalls, nice ones with sleeves and a zip and everything, no expense spared.' He twinkled. 'Oh, and a lovely pair of wellies that might fit you, too. You will find all these exciting garments at my house over there.' He nodded along the rows of vegetables and flowers to a cottage – a brown smudge against the green fields and blue sky.

'I see. Well hadn't you better put me down? You can't carry me that far,' Sarah said, but hoping he would.

'I'll carry you a little way, I think. You could slip over, the state your shoes are in and going barefoot would hurt on this open land. Besides, I think you could do with a bit of TLC after your latest ordeal.'

His look of concern, his kind words and the aftermath of her latest experience brought a lump to her throat. She laid her head on his shoulder. 'Thanks, John. Just a little way then.'

The cottage was the kind of place Sarah would have imagined if someone said 'picture a traditional English stone-built cottage in the middle of the countryside.' Barefoot, and leaning heavily on John's arm, she tiptoed along the cobbled path that led to the door. He had carried her for a good five minutes before putting her down. The rest of the way was slow going due to her ruined shoes and eventually she had taken them off.

The conversation had been confined to the market garden and how long he'd lived at the cottage. Neither had felt ready to launch into a huge question-and-answer session about 1913. Sarah had been relieved by that. She was happy to pretend that they were just friends out on a spring day. Her heart yearned for normality, and for the last while it had been delivered.

'OK, stay there and I'll get a bowl of water for your feet and a bin bag for the shoes. Once your feet are clean you can come in and I'll run you a bath.' John unlocked the door and disappeared inside.

Sarah stood with her back to the door and looked over the rolling hills to the moors beyond. Rarely venturing beyond her suburban street and the area around school, she had forgotten how beautiful the countryside just outside Sheffield could be. It felt like afternoon. The sun was high in the sky and, judging from the wet grass and the fresh earthy smell, it had just rained. Charcoal-grey clouds rumbled away over the hills and new white fluffy ones blew in to take their place.

Calm descended across the landscape and seeped into Sarah. She didn't want to move, breathe, or avert her eyes in case the whole lovely scene was suddenly whisked away and replaced by another time, place, and hideously surreal situation.

'OK, just step into this and I'll get to that bath,' John said, setting a bowl of soapy water and a towel by her feet.

Standing in the bowl and looking over the landscape immediately brought surreal back, leaping and yelling over the hills, chortling like some deranged garish cartoon character. Sarah giggled and shook her head. *Picture this, a beautiful English cottage with ivy growing along ancient walls, rolling green countryside fading to the purple of the moor, a blue sky recently washed of grey cloud, and a woman covered in horse shit standing in a bowl outside the front door.*

Having dried her feet and tipped the water away, Sarah ventured inside. There was a tiny entrance hall leading to a large kitchen. Even though the cottage was ancient, the kitchen was kitted out with every modern appliance, but tastefully done, and in keeping with the surroundings. Sarah loved the light, airy feel of the place. The lemon and white of the walls complemented the original stone flags and the light wood cupboards. A tall sash window looked over the fields and the afternoon sunlight angled in, painting everything in muted gold.

'Bath's ready, up the stairs and to the left. Hope everything is OK; I left overalls on the landing. I have a few here for the casual workers that help pick the veg at certain times; if that one doesn't fit give me a shout. I couldn't do anything about clean underwear ...' John shrugged and then added, 'Not that I'm suggesting you *need* clean underwear, it's just that I thought that once you have had a bath ...'

Sarah laughed and held up her hand. 'I know what you meant. Thanks, I can't wait for this bath.'

The bathroom was small but again fitted with appliances in keeping. An original, white, claw-foot tub filled with bubbles stood next to a small shower cubicle. Alongside that, a deep-set window-shelf displayed an array of old-fashioned soap, shampoos and lotions. Peeling off her filthy school dress and underwear, a grimy, tousled-haired, exhausted woman caught her eye in the mirror above the wide, square washbasin.

Sarah stepped closer. Beyond the exhaustion in her eyes lurked something else ... something that brought a lump the size of an apple to her throat. Failure. Emily Davison was dead and it was all her fault. *Too late now, Sarah. Get in the bath. And look on the bright side ... you could always fall asleep and drown.*

The unmistakable smell of curry wafted into her nostrils as she walked down the narrow, twisty staircase half an hour later. The green overalls were a little baggy, but serviceable, and she had dried her hair in John's room, which was equally as lovely as the rest of the house. It had a four-poster bed, simple pine furniture and was painted in pastel blues and white. The stripped floorboards were made warmer underfoot by a large, handwoven, yellow rug, and a beautiful painting of children running through a cornfield hung on the wall. Sarah hadn't noticed photos of anyone around so far.

The absence of a significant other gave her hope on the one hand, and a swift kick in the pants on the other. The kick was accompanied by a stiff talking to regarding the futility of having a romantic relationship. And certainly not with a Time-Needle; life would never feel normal again. Also, hadn't she decided against any more sewing trips? After today, she wouldn't be seeing him again. Besides, she'd only known him for five minutes, and love at first sight was just a crock.

Perhaps one day she may venture back out into the world of coupledom, but not yet. Neil and Karen's treachery had done great damage. That damage would take more than a handsome face and kind word to put right. Nevertheless, because she had no make-up to hand, she took extra care styling her hair, and pinched her cheeks a few times to try and look at least half in the land of the living.

'You're cooking curry? This is getting to be a habit, John,' Sarah said, pulling up a chair at the scrubbed wooden table.

'Curry? I cooked bacon and eggs last time, how soon you forget ...' He put the back of his hand to his forehead and sighed.

'Ha ha! You know what I meant – you, cooking for me.'

'Yes, well, you missed out on your evening meal last night; it was the least I could do. So the overalls fit then?' He pointed a wooden spoon at her.

'Yes, they're fine.' She smiled and then gave a heavy sigh.

'What's up?'

'Much as I'd like to, I can't put it off any longer. I need to do the twenty questions bit.'

'OK, ready when you are. Excuse me if I carry on cooking at the same time; these onions and spices will burn if I don't.'

'Right, so first and foremost, Emily Davison threw herself under the king's horse and died, so I failed, yes?'

'Yes, she did, and no, you didn't. Would you like a glass of wine?' John said, pulling a bottle from the rack. 'We have red, and I think there may be some white in the fridge. Perhaps lager would go better with curry ...'

'Will you stop wittering about drinks and explain what you mean. How can I not have failed if Emily Davison died?'

'Because the person you were meant to save wasn't Emily,' John said, his head in the fridge. 'Yep, we have lager.'

'Not Emily? Then who the hell was it?' He was beginning to irritate her again now.

John cracked open a lager and set it on the table along with a tall glass. 'Rose,' he said grinning widely, 'and save her, you did!'

Rose? Bloody hell! Sarah downed half the lager in one and wiped the back of her hand across her mouth. God, that felt good. Her pulse was racing ten to the dozen and relief jumped up from its arm lock and ran around her consciousness in perfumed slippers. Thank heaven she hadn't screwed up.

'So, are you going to explain what happened or do I have to kill you?' she asked, pouring the other half of the can.

John brought poppadoms and a chopping board over to the table and began slicing spinach. 'This spinach was growing in the ground this morning, can you smell how fresh it is ...?' He laughed out loud at the murderous expression on her face. 'OK, OK, I'll tell you.'

Sarah sipped her drink and broke off a piece of poppadom. 'So, get on with it!'

'If you hadn't have tripped Rose up in the milk, she would have rushed out of the house, down the road and under an omnibus – death would have been instant. She wouldn't have gone on to be educated by Mr Darnley, wouldn't have married his nephew and wouldn't have given birth to a daughter who grew up to be one of the early female surgeons of the 1930s. That surgeon wouldn't have gone on to win prizes for pioneering all sorts of new and marvellous medical stuff and save loads of lives.'

'Oh, how wonderful! I'm so pleased Rose had a happy life ... She did, didn't she?'

'Yes, as far as I know. She also set up a night school for working women to improve their literacy.'

'Really? I'm so pleased. I never had the chance to say goodbye and we parted on such bad terms, though I only saved her by accident, didn't I? '

'Not really; when you tripped her with the mop it was on a whim, instinct, but deliberate nevertheless, wasn't it?'

She thought about it. 'Um, yes, I guess it was.'

'There you go, then.'

Sarah drained her glass and then something she'd thought to ask John when she'd been in 1913 came back to her. 'How does it work when I was the Sarah in 1940 and 1913? I didn't occupy their bodies, I was definitely me ... and how will Sarah in 1913 cope, did she get the sack, and how did

Rose react to her, and how did Sarah explain her loss of extended vocabulary and—'

John held up his hand. 'Hey, no more "and hows", please. Slow down and I'll try to answer.'

John got them both a refill, tipped the spinach into the curry pot, and returned to the table with mango chutney. 'OK, as far as I understand it, a Stitch kind of works in tandem with the person from the past. They don't possess the body, but have a kind of spiritual and cerebral link.'

'You say "kind of" a lot. Don't you know *how* it works?' Sarah asked, trying to burp quietly behind her hand. The lager was very gassy. It reminded her of burping at Cook and she smiled wryly.

'Oh, you may smirk, Sarah, but it's very complicated. We Needles only get to learn what is absolutely necessary. The powers that be are very secretive.' John folded his arms and looked disgruntled. She'd obviously hit a raw nerve.

'I wasn't smirking; I was smiling at something else. Right, I get that there's a cerebral and spiritual link, but what happens to the body of the Sarahs from the past? Do they just float around in space or what? And do they remember what I did when I was being them?'

John scratched his head and sighed. 'As far as I understand it, the spiritual link makes them feel like they are dreaming, and so in that way they remember, like you might remember a vivid dream. That's why some of Sarah's extended vocabulary was retained; her brain had somehow stored it from yours. But the actual memory of the dream fades quite quickly, more or less, depending on the person.'

'But what about their bodies?' Sarah pressed.

'OK, I'm getting to that; blimey, you're so impatient. Because your connection is one of brain and spirit not physical, there is a melding of minds but not a physical meeting of bodies. When you are in the past you feel and see your own body, but Sarah in her dream state still has hers. She isn't in some space car park or whatever you said.'

Sarah sighed. 'That sounds surreal and a bit difficult to grasp.'

'That's because it is.' John nodded. 'I think you hit the nail on the head before when you said "when I was *being* them". Because you aren't them, physically, but you're like a spiritual presence outside *but* alongside them. In tandem, like I said earlier,' John finished with a shrug.

Sarah nodded and was quiet for a few moments while she digested that. It seemed to be going in a bit more now. She finished her drink and remembered he'd still not answered everything. 'So, how exactly *do* you get information, then, and who are these powers that be?'

'I learnt some from Dad, and I get emails of instructions and reports of a Stitch's progress.'

Sarah looked at him in disbelief. 'You're pulling my chain, right?'

'Nope.'

'But you haven't said who the powers are. Where are the emails from, some extraterrestrial, Time-Needle agency?'

'I really have no idea. I know that they are infinitely powerful and keep time running smoothly. My dad told me never question, or seek more answers about them, as bad things would happen. And to be honest, Sarah, you have asked quite enough questions for one day. You know when people say "pressed for time", meaning you are too busy or running late?' Sarah nodded. 'It originated from a Time-Needle who was far too curious for his own good. One word is wrong, it isn't pressed *for* time, it is pressed *in* time. This guy was actually "pressed *in* time"; he was flattened like a butterfly in a lepidopterist collection.'

'That's terrible!' Sarah said, wondering if John was fibbing to shut her up. But then, given the crazy things that had happened to her lately, she thought it was probably the truth. 'And how were Time-Needles contacted before email?'

'My dad used to get telegrams when I was young; why, what does that matter?'

'I'm a historian, curiosity comes naturally.'

For the next half an hour, while John busied himself stirring, tasting and putting the rice on to boil, Sarah got the answers to the rest of her questions.

Sarah hadn't got the sack. Mr Darnley had spoken up for her and Sarah and Rose mended their friendship when Darnley explained how Sarah had put a good word in for Rose. A few months later both Rose and Sarah had gone to work for him. They were employed as filing clerks and that's where Rose had met Darnley's nephew. Sarah had kept some of her extended vocabulary and was an eager student; as a result, she ended up teaching in the night school Rose set up.

Needless to say, Mr Darnley didn't marry Lady Attwood; in fact he dropped her like a hot coal very soon after Sarah came back to the present. She had to sell her house and let her servants go. She moved to the countryside and lived in a modest (by her standards) country house. She retained Cook and Grayson however, and all things considered, Sarah thought they had all got off a little too lightly.

Sarah ate the last bit of poppadom and said, 'Another few things I'm confused about ...' John rolled his eyes and put naan bread in the oven. 'No point rolling your eyes, John; after the things I've been through the least you can do is answer my questions.'

'OK, but I *have* been answering them for most of the time you've been here. Do you want to end up pressed in time?' He laughed. 'Besides, I thought you'd want to relax a bit and try to enjoy yourself.'

Relax and enjoy myself, with you? Was he just being nice

or was he attracted to her after all? Her eyes met his. 'Well, I do ... These are the last two questions for now. First question – why did I go through some kind of fog tunnel to 1913 but in 1940 just stepped through my classroom door, and then my senses were as if trapped behind glass for a bit, whereas in 1913, I felt travel sick and dizzy? And second question, I was in 1913 much longer than in 1940. Why?' Another question had been buzzing in and out of her thoughts like a wasp at a picnic too lately. 'And isn't it a coincidence that you managed to find a Stitch with the same name as the Sarah's in the past?'

John brought two plates and cutlery over to the table and sat down. 'I think you sneaked more than two questions in there, but never mind. Firstly, when you travel in time you have to adapt to the hole that's appeared. Sometimes it's a substantial tear; sometimes it's just a few threads that have snagged or something. The 1940 hole was substantial, so you had to be shoved through at some force; the time it took to travel was too quick for you to notice. The 1913 hole was shallower, so you could have a more leisurely entrance.

'The sickness and the loss of senses, I don't know. Everyone is affected differently and sometimes, as in your case, in any number of ways. Secondly, you were longer in 1913 because you're getting used to the experience of being a Stitch; it's not such a strain on your mental state. The next time, you may be there even longer. The powers test Stitches, as I said before. They try to make situations stressful and unpredictable to see if you can cope and are, therefore, the right choice. For example, you landed in a muckheap today and back in your bed the first time. And one of the reasons you were picked is because of your name. It wasn't a coincidence. It's much easier for all concerned if we can find a match and an awful lot of women through the ages have been called Sarah. It dates back to the Bible I think, or before.'

'Oh, I see … I think. But you never told me about that when I asked why I was chosen.'

'No. It would have been far too much information at the time. Now, let me get this show on the road.'

'It still seems a bit hard to believe that you just happen to find me, with the right name *and* the knowledge needed.'

'You think *that's* hard to believe when you have just travelled through time twice and saved the bacon of future generations? Hmm. What is wrong with *that* picture?'

Sarah sat back in her chair and watched John potter around collecting naan bread and making ready to serve their meal. Not such a strain on her mental state, he'd said. Well, he ought to spend a few hours in her head while she was on one of her missions. And she may be longer next time. How could she bring herself to tell him that there wouldn't be a next time?

Apart from the fact that her nerves couldn't handle a next time, she didn't think seeing more of John would be a good idea. The day under the pergola, when he'd told her that she'd imagined the 1940s' John as him because she cared about him, she'd got angry and dismissed it as just part of the emotional rollercoaster she'd stepped off. And in the light of the fact that she had been riding an emotional tandem with Sarah of the Blitz, it made sense that she would form an attachment. John had been the last fanciable man that she'd seen before going back to 1940, so it stood to reason that her brain had portrayed the John of 1940 as the present-day John. The 1913 experience had been too stressful for her to really analyse how she felt.

But if she were honest, when she'd seen him walking towards her today, even though she'd been standing in the manure, she'd been overjoyed to see him. Her heart had thumped in her chest and giddy excitement had whizzed adrenaline around her blood stream. The talking-to she'd given herself earlier in John's bedroom, about romantic relationships being futile, *was* logical and definitely *the* best course to take – a safeguard against potential future heartbreak must be achieved at all costs. Trouble was, now, though he was just going about mundane everyday tasks in his kitchen, she couldn't take her eyes off him.

He moved so beautifully, sensuously, light on his feet, almost catlike. He had an aura of confidence that was almost palpable, and when he stretched to one of the top cupboards for something, his toned upper body was clearly defined under his thin, white T-shirt. Sarah lowered her eyes and felt a slow blush creep along her neck. *This is no good, Sarah. It can't happen and remember, he said before that the relationship was strictly platonic, so just eat your curry and bugger off home.*

'My goodness, this is absolutely delicious, John. I didn't realise how hungry I was, either,' Sarah said, fanning her face and helping herself to more rice.

'Thanks. I thought you would be. This is Saturday afternoon – you left here last night about five o'clock and you didn't really eat anything substantial in 1913.'

'But it was Wednesday when I left there,' Sarah said through a mouthful of curry. 'Oh, never mind, I'm just going to give up trying to rationalise everything as the whole bloody thing is totally irrational.'

'That's the attitude. You don't want to end up like old Jeremiah,' he said, mopping up his second helping of curry with a bit of naan.

'Jeremiah?'

'The guy pressed in time.' John grinned, bringing the bread to his mouth, but a blob of curry slid off on to his T-shirt. He didn't notice and tucked in again. Sarah pointed her fork at the yellow stain seeping along his chest.

'Oh, bloody typical, I should have known better than to

wear this.' He stood up, stripped the shirt off and hurried to the sink. 'Not sure it will come out even if I soak it; what do you think?' he said over his shoulder, running water on to the shirt.

I think I would like to kiss every inch of your back and chest for dessert. 'Err ... not sure, it may do, you caught it early,' Sarah managed, taking a gulp of lager. Please let him put another shirt on.

John returned to the table. His chest was muscular, mostly smooth, but had a track of dark hair leading from below the waistband of his jeans to his navel and then it feathered out higher up across his pecs. 'You don't mind if I finish my grub semi-naked, do you? I'll get a shirt when I've finished; don't want to ruin another.'

Sarah shook her head and fixed her eyes on her dinner plate. She needed to leave as soon as was polite. The lager had gone to her head and she was worried that she would say or do something ridiculous if she stayed much longer.

Sarah helped him clear the table and insisted on washing-up. He wiped the table down, put things away whilst chatting about his market garden and how business was doing. She smiled and nodded but didn't initiate conversation.

'Well, thanks for a lovely meal, the bath, and everything. I had a great time, but I must be off,' Sarah said, folding the washing-up cloth.

'Off already?' He frowned. 'I have some great coffee and some chocolate cake we could have later.'

'No thanks, I have taken up enough of your day. Don't you have to get back to the garden shop?'

'No, I took the afternoon off to be here for you and I usually work in the garden, anyway. I have a few casual workers at busy times, but Roy and Helen take care of the business side of things. I'm sure I told you that.'

'So you did, sorry, I was miles away.' She gave him a watery smile. 'Now, can you call me a taxi, or is there a bus stop handy?' She folded her arms and looked out of the window.

'OK, you're a taxi.' He grinned at the old joke. Sarah didn't. He walked over, gently took her chin and tilted her face to his. 'What's the matter?'

'Nothing's the matter,' she said, her voice sounding like she'd borrowed it from Minnie Mouse. She could feel the heat from his body and his breath on her hair – he was so close.

'Hmm ... I think that's a big fat lie,' he said, brushing a stray hair from her cheek. 'You desperately wanted to be sent home, but not to your house, here. In fact you wanted to be as close to me as we are now, except the muckheap got in the way.'

Sarah's heart banged in her chest and her whole body had begun to tingle; either she was about to be carted off to another dimension or she was about to have an altogether more pleasurable experience. When John gently kissed the corner of her mouth, she banked on the latter.

'The muckheap got in the way; what do you mean?' she mumbled as he kissed the other side of her mouth.

'Your heart's desire was to see me above all else when you were in the 1913 park. It was unfortunate that you landed where you did, kind of ruined the moment.' John started to unzip her overalls.

Sarah put her hand over his. 'Did I? I don't remember wishing to see you ... and what are you doing? I thought you said this relationship had to remain strictly platonic.'

'That was then; this is now. I know we shouldn't, but I for one can't hold back anymore ... Of course, if you don't want to ...' He pulled her to him and kissed her tenderly.

Sarah held back a little. She couldn't face being hurt

again. But then his kiss became more passionate, demanding and his tongue parted her lips, flicked over hers. Her body dictated proceedings. *What the hell, Sarah ... go for it.* Running her hands over his back and tight bum she kissed him back, matching his passion. He pulled her zip lower and showered her neck and breasts with hot kisses. When his mouth found her nipples, she could barely keep standing.

Pulling the zip to its furthest extent and letting her overalls fall to the kitchen floor, he whispered, 'So, you decided to leave all the underwear off, then?'

Sarah looked him square in the eye. He had the look of a hungry wolf. 'Yes. Are you complaining?' She smiled, and started to unzip his jeans. John moved her hand lower and pressed it to him. 'Does it feel like I'm complaining?' he murmured, picking her up and carrying her upstairs to his bedroom.

Chapter Fifteen

Waking from sleep, Sarah thrilled at the feeling of a warm body entwined around hers. After John had fallen asleep earlier, she had lain with her head on his chest, listening to the steady beat of his heart. Closing her eyes, she'd prayed that she would still be holding him when she awoke, instead of just a pillow, or her old teddy bear, like last time.

Through the window she watched the sun slowly sinking over the hills, leaving a burnished copper glow in the sky; the silver vapour trails of distant planes crisscrossed through, like ribbon on a gift. A blackbird's song started up in the meadow, a cow lowed, and a breeze rustled the ivy along the ledge outside. Just wonderful.

Feeling John stir behind her, she wondered if she'd be asked to stay the night. This was all so perfect. Sarah wanted to stay in his arms, his bed, and his life forever; the intensity of her feelings both exhilarated and scared the pants off her. A cheeky smile crept on to her face. *Well, she wasn't actually wearing any pants at the moment.*

A cup of coffee and the cake he mentioned might be a nice surprise to wake up to. She lifted his arm carefully and slid out of bed. She noticed a black dressing gown hanging on the back of the door and shrugged into it. It smelled of sandalwood aftershave and was deliciously soft next to her bare skin; it fitted her well.

Nipping to the loo, she saw that the face in the mirror looked much happier than it had a few hours ago. Her eyes sparkled and her skin seemed to have a healthy glow. Sarah winked at herself. *Not surprised given what you've been up to all afternoon, you hussy.*

Waiting for the coffee in the cafetière, she found chocolate cake in the fridge, cut two slices, and then wandered into the living room. It was much bigger than any of the rooms she'd seen so far and French doors at the far end opened on to a generous patio, overlooking a stunning view of the valley beyond. How she'd love to live here. *Stop that right now, Sarah! You need to take things easy, slowly, not get carried away on some pink fluffy romantic cloud.* In her experience, pink fluffy romantic clouds tended to turn grey and rain on her parade, leaving her dreams floundering in a mucky puddle.

The decoration was just as tasteful in the living room as the rest of the house. The original Victorian fireplace and stone hearth would be a lovely focal point on cold winter evenings. A comfy-looking, red leather three-piece suite was the only bold colour, against oatmeal walls and a stripped pine floor and, on a large sideboard near the door, a number of ceramic plates and photographs were carefully displayed.

Sarah went over and bent to examine the photos. One was obviously of John and his parents when he was about ten. They were walking along at the seaside and a girl of about eight, presumably his sister, was dragging a stick behind her in the sand. They looked happy and windswept and ... who the hell was that?

Behind more photographs of his family and one of John graduating from university, a small photo of John with a woman caught her eye. She picked it up. It was fairly recent as he looked much the same. They were sitting at a table with a bottle of champagne in the foreground and two glasses raised to the camera. She was stunning. Raven haired, dark-eyed and a celebrity-white smile that lit the whole restaurant. A diamond ring winked from the third finger of her left hand. Sarah thrust it back where she'd found it; it suddenly felt alien, dirty. She wiped her hand on the dressing gown and hurried back to the kitchen.

The coffee was done. Sarah sincerely hoped that she hadn't been. God, that woman was so beautiful. A little voice of reason hopped on to her shoulder and whispered in her ear. *Stop getting ahead of yourself; he's not the type to two-time, is he? She's just his ex and is well and truly off the scene.* She sighed and took two mugs from the draining board. Yes, that would be it. Hope started to return tentatively from the despair that the photo had flung it into.

A little voice of doubt kicked reason into touch as she poured coffee. *But what if she's not off the scene, what if she's very much on the scene and he's a complete arsehole? Remember what Neil and Karen did? Do you want that again? And that dressing gown you're wearing, Sarah, is only a good fit because it's not his. You did wonder as soon as you put it on, but your pink fluffy cloud brain dismissed it.* Her hand shook as she poured the second mug. But what about the aftershave? *It's not aftershave, it's perfume, you silly cow.*

Doubt settled heavily in her chest as she carried the tray of coffee and cake upstairs. Pushing the door open with her foot she saw that John was still sleeping, one arm flung across her pillow and the other hanging loosely to the floor. The quilt had slid down to just below his navel and his face looked as innocent as a child's. He was beautiful.

Beautiful or not, Sarah wanted answers before she even thought about getting back into bed. She set the tray down, flung the dressing gown on a chair and slipped the overalls back on. She couldn't bear the thing next to her skin a moment longer.

'Hey, gorgeous, is that coffee and chocolate cake I can smell?' John said to her back as she looked out over the valley.

'Yes, hope the coffee's not too strong.'

John yawned, stretched and said, 'Why are you dressed? Thought we may have an encore for the earlier performance.'

'Who's the woman with the long dark hair in the photo downstairs?' Sarah turned, folded her arms and scanned his face intently.

John nearly spilled his hot coffee. 'Come straight to the point, why don't you?' He frowned, putting the mug back on the tray.

'The reason I'm dressed is because I slipped your dressing gown on to make the coffee ... I took it off again when I realised ... it isn't yours, is it?'

John's eyes met hers. 'Hop back into bed and we'll talk about it.'

'No, I'll stay where I am, thanks.'

He folded his arms, and the frown deepened. 'Suit yourself. The dressing gown isn't mine, no; it's Josephina's. We were together about three years and the photo you're so steamed about was taken the night we got engaged. She left me about six months ago, and went back to Italy.'

Sarah blinked a few times and swallowed hard. Italy, eh? She'd rather it was Australia, but Italy would have to do. John picked up his coffee and sipped it, keeping his eyes on the mug. She couldn't read him completely, but from his tense posture, she could tell he wasn't best pleased. In her brain, the words 'you overreacted you daft mare!' flashed neon on, off, on, off, on. Did she think he'd lived the life of a monk before her? And to even think that he would be the kind of man to cheat. Why the hell did Josephina leave him, anyway?

She perched at the end of the bed and picked up her mug. 'Why did she leave you, anyway?' She glanced sidelong at him and gave a little laugh. 'She must have been crazy.'

'Really? The way you behaved just now, you'd think I was a lying, cheating sleep-around!' He picked up a slice of cake, took a big bite and chucked the remainder down on the plate.

God, he was really angry, but then what did she expect? 'John, I'm sorry, I overreacted. I was just so happy being here in bed with you, pottering around in your home and then I saw the photo. I was jealous, worried and most of all stupid ... It's no excuse but after my husband—'

John held up his hand. 'That's enough apologising. I overreacted, too. It was a kick in the guts when she left. But she said she needed the smell of olives in her nostrils instead of cabbages. I guess I was angry because I kept the dressing gown and then you put it on. I hate it that you're upset.' He took her hand and kissed it.

'I'm not upset with you now. I'm just upset because she hurt you. If she wanted bloody olives she should have popped down to the deli.' She giggled. 'So how did you meet?' Why that mattered, Sarah didn't know, she just wanted to assess the situation a little more, she guessed.

'She was over visiting relatives here and a friend of her cousin is my friend, too. We went for a drink one night and she came along. We just got on, I thought I loved her, but in the end she was just a bit high maintenance for me. She "helps out" in her parents' vineyard, but is mostly cosseted and spoiled. They are stinking rich and pay for all of her whims – clothes, cars, trips to England. I think she expected me to become a well-trained little lapdog; she had to think again.'

'Well I'm glad she went back to Italy, that's all I can say,' Sarah said and kissed his shoulder. 'Seeing her photo gave me quite a turn.'

'You won't have to see it again, don't worry.' Smiling, John fed her a piece of cake with one hand and tugged at her zip with the other. 'And why don't you hop back into bed with me. I'm sure I could make you feel much better.'

Sunday morning saw Sarah up with the larks and striding over the fields. 'The best thing for a troubled mind is a good walk,' her gran always said. Considering that the woman was always moaning about her troubles, and rarely left her chair and the TV, it was a bit rich, but there was truth in every word, nevertheless.

Worries had wound around Sarah's mind like a jungle creeper when she had started from John's door an hour ago. After their misunderstanding last night, they had made love again and then stayed up watching an old Bette Davis movie. The question of her going home hadn't occurred to either of them. It was just so natural and easy being together. This morning, however, she knew she had to bite the bullet and tell him that she didn't want to stitch anymore, but she didn't want that to be the end of their relationship. Half-truths had been an option, but after the early morning sun and fresh breeze had worked their magic, her head was free of creeper, and indecision.

'There you are, I was worried that you'd left me – walked home in just old overalls and wellies,' John said. He was fresh from the shower, a green fluffy towel wrapped round his waist. 'Tea?' He ran water into the kettle and flashed her a smile bright enough to challenge the sunbeams dancing over the sill.

'Yes please, and I'm in no rush to leave.' She smiled back.

John poured the tea and indicated that she should follow him. He led the way through the living room – now Josephina-less, Sarah noticed on glancing at the sideboard – and out through the French doors to the patio. Sarah felt a little twinge of shame that he'd removed the photo because of the fuss she'd made yesterday, but it was a nice gesture and showed that he wanted to please her. Outside, a jug of orange juice, toast and vase of yellow roses sat on a wooden picnic table set for two.

'So if you thought I'd left, who's this for, eh?' Sarah poked him in the back.

'Tarnation, I guess you've plumb found me out, li'l lady,' he said, pulling a chair out for her. 'Do you fancy having a look around the garden after breakfast? Don't worry if not, I know not everyone gets excited about carrots and taters, Master Frodo.'

She laughed. 'Of course I'd love to, but I do want to have a serious talk first, if I may.'

'Uh-oh, sounds ominous.'

John ate his toast and sipped his tea while Sarah launched into a big spiel about not feeling able to cope with any more adventures. She felt that it was more luck than judgement that she'd saved Rose, and that it would only be a matter of time before that luck would run out. Three things bothered her most. One was the complete lack of control she had of exactly *when* she would be whisked back to the past; two was the fear that if she stopped stitching, John would despise her and end things; and the third thing was that she didn't really understand why the damn holes opened in the first place. Sarah looked at John with 'I hope you don't hate me' written across her forehead.

John wiped his mouth, nodded and said, 'Yes, I do despise you and want you out now ... and if you believe that, you're a nut job.' He leaned over and kissed her. 'Everything you said is all perfectly understandable and I think there may be things we can do about it. Firstly, you are a great Stitch. You may feel like you're out of control but the reports I have received about you are outstanding. Loads of Stitches just give up halfway through if they can't do the job immediately.'

'Give up halfway through, how do they do that?' Sarah was pleased that he still wanted her but tried to act cool. *'Don't let men think they have you dancing attendance.'* Another one of her gran's. Stupid, really.

'Oh in a variety of ways; they may just take to their bed and refuse to do anything, or they'll run away from where they end up – fugitives in another dimension. They're brought back and that's the end of it. In truth, they don't really care enough to save anyone. You should be proud of your achievements. And the ones that are found to be great at the job, despite the obstacles deliberately placed in front of them, often do get warnings about *when* they have to go back to the past. Some even get a hint as to where they have to go, too. It's a reward, I guess. As I said, your progress reports are excellent.'

'Really?' She liked the idea of getting good reports; must be the teacher in her. 'But you talk about Stitches as if there are loads of us knocking about the place. I've never met one ... or are they sworn to secrecy like spies, or are they just afraid to talk about it in case they get accused of being mentally ill?'

'There are thousands of Stitches, but let's go back to the question about holes.' John took a sip of tea and fiddled with the petals on a rose. Sarah had the feeling he was sidestepping the Stitch issue, but she let him continue uninterrupted.

'Like I said when we first met, there are a few theories but I favour this one. All the dimensions of time are linked by a living, breathing thread. From the beginning of time until the present, the deeds, emotions, memories and spirits of the players on this vast stage of history, all become part of this thread.' John paused and steepled his fingers. 'I guess it's like a strong, tightly woven cord of human essence, keeping time interlinked, balanced and enabling progress to the future.'

'What? How the hell does *that* work exactly?' Sarah asked.

'That isn't known, or at least I don't know it.'

Sarah said nothing but raised her eyebrows, sat back and folded her arms.

'Life isn't a romantic novel where all ends are sown up neatly, all questions answered and problems magically resolved, Sarah. Time is messy and the holes that appear take a lot of sewing up, as you've discovered. Sometimes there *is* no happy ever after.'

Sarah held her hands up. 'Hey, I didn't say a word.'

'No, but the look you're giving me speaks volumes. So do you want to hear the rest?'

'Yes, OK, Mr Grumpy.' She took his hand across the table. The whole thing seemed incredible, but then why should that surprise her? She *had* recently returned from 1913.

He squeezed her hand. 'OK, the holes appear because the link between past and present in certain areas becomes weak. As a history teacher, you know how important it is to know where we all come from and to learn from our mistakes. Also, we all know on Remembrance Day that we should be grateful to those who have made sacrifices for the wellbeing of others and stuff. Well, too often people forget. They just pay lip service to the past. Then holes open up in time's thread and can only be strengthened by the bravery, determination and love of people like you, Sarah. Stitches must go in and demonstrate that they are prepared to undergo traumatic situations in order to save the lives of others. The past isn't dead and gone; it's crucial for our passage to the future and even our very existence.'

Sarah felt strangely emotional all of a sudden. She loved the idea of past, present and future being held together by love and determination and other emotions. What had John called it ... human essence? But why weren't important events affected by a person from the future like her, just dropping into the past and changing things? And why hadn't he answered her question about other Stitches?

'That sounds incredible, John. So you say Stitches save lives to make the future as it should be, and when people muck up, bad things happen?'

'Yes, like when Norman refused and we got Hitler.

Apparently he'd agreed at first and then pulled out at the last minute; no one else was available at such short notice.'

'But like I said the first time we met, how can I be alive now and change things in the past that have already happened in the present. It makes my mind boggle, to be honest.'

'Again, it is a bit complicated, but like I said yesterday, you aren't really yourself in the past, are you? You don't appear to others as you, you appear as the Sarah they know. You kind of work in tandem, your spirit is with them, rather than you physically intervening as a separate entity. So even though you go back in time, *you* are not wholly you. Most importantly, time isn't set in stone, it's in flux, and changes can be subtle or dramatic depending on how good or bad a Stitch is at their job.'

Sarah sipped her tea for a few minutes. It all made a weird kind of sense, but there was just the question of why, if there were thousands of Stitches, didn't anyone know about them? Even if they were all sworn to secrecy, one of them would have let something slip over the years. She put down her cup and said as much to John.

He had a shifty look about him and fiddled with a spoon this time. 'Err ... there's no easy way of saying this. Once the mission is completed they—' he swallowed and looked over the fields '—they have their memories wiped of all connection to the mission.'

Though the morning was warm, a cold wind seemed to blow right through her. Sarah shook her head. 'Will that happen to me? And all connection ... that must include you, us?'

John looked back at her; his green eyes seemed darker, drawn, and full of uncertainty. 'Not if you listen and agree to what I'm about to tell you. There have been quite a few trusted Stitches over the centuries who were allowed to keep their memory intact. The powers that be were a hundred percent sure that they would never divulge their experiences to a living soul. The thing is, Sarah, if you give up now...' He set his mouth and shook his head.

'So if I give up, I get my memory dry cleaned and you'll disappear along with 1940 and 1913?'

He nodded.

She stood up and kicked the chair. 'Oh, great! So I have no choice then, again ... just for a change. One minute I'll be, oh I don't know, let's say on the toilet at home, the next I'll be in the Old West in a stage coach with my knickers round my ankles, huh?'

John shook his head and pursed his lips. Sarah could tell he was trying not to smirk at her scenario. 'No, that won't happen next time,' he said, standing and drawing her close. 'For those trusted and exemplary Stitches like yourself, there can be leeway in when you go. You have been tested and passed with flying colours. So next time – if you choose to have a next time – I'm guessing that you'll be able to be a bit prepared at least.

'You should take your time to think about it. Until I saw you standing there yesterday up to your knees in muck I *had* thought about it and decided it just wouldn't work, wasn't worth the heartache, but then when I looked into your eyes, my heart soared and I knew you were the one. If you choose to stitch – choose me – our life won't be ordinary, and it certainly won't be easy ... This game can take its toll. I know from experience ... You see, the same thing happened to my parents.'

'What? Your mum is a Stitch, too?'

He blinked and swallowed hard. 'She was, Sarah, and a bloody good one. She cared so much about her job. She died a few years ago and I miss her so much.'

'Oh, I'm so sorry ... Did she die because of a trip back ...?'

'No, nothing like that. It was cancer ... but perhaps the

stress of such a, let's say, "unusual" life style for Mum and Dad didn't help.'

'Ah, I know what that's like. My dad died of it, too. There's not a day goes by that I don't think about him. My mum was a mess at the time, but she copes the best she can now. She has a job in a charity shop, and that keeps her mind occupied, but she's not the same mum anymore. She just goes through the motions sometimes, alive but not living, you know?'

'I do know; my dad is much the same,' John whispered into her hair. 'So taking all that into consideration I wouldn't blame you if you wanted to call it a day, nobody would.'

Sarah was at a loss for words. She rested her head on his chest and listened to his rapid heartbeat. He was obviously anxious about her response. He smelled of lemon shower gel and the fresh sunny morning and she was shocked to realise that even though she was apprehensive about all the problems their relationship was sure to face, she had never felt as happy, safe or calm as she did right at that moment.

Despite everything he had told her, the logical, sensible, safeguard-against-hurt argument had at last been defeated. There was no way she would run the risk of losing him, and if that meant a trip to Mars without oxygen and a fire hose, she'd do it. And why would she do such a crazy thing? Because even though she'd known him for a just a nano-second in the marches of time, she felt right then that she would love him for eternity.

She lifted her head and looked into his eyes. 'I don't need time to think about this, John. I'm back on the job,' she said, and pressed her lips to his.

Chapter Sixteen

John had negotiated the next two weeks as 'time travel free' for Sarah. The first week was half-term and the two of them spent every minute together. Sarah spent more time at his house than hers; she had to keep pinching herself to check that she wasn't dreaming. And floating all along her blue horizon were pink fluffy clouds as far as the eye could see.

Although Sarah had tried to get more information about how he negotiated, and who with, she was none the wiser. He just said he did it by email and he didn't know who the powers that be were. It was something that they would never know and had to live with. In the end, she believed him. As he said, life wasn't a romance novel. But lately, when she was in his arms, Sarah felt that's *exactly* what life was.

The question about why she had been selected as a Stitch had been answered, though. As John had said the first time she had met him, in general Stitches were chosen because of their strength of spirit, courage and potential to do the right thing. It was because of this, her job, and equally importantly, John surmised, because the powers that be had decided that it was time for him to settle down. He had been sadly mistaken with Josephina, but perhaps they thought that Sarah was a good match.

There was maybe some connection between them that only the powers could see; he didn't know, but that was his best guess. Because of the obvious problems associated with living such a life, most Needler wives hadn't been Stitches and were oblivious to their husband's Time-Needling. Keeping something like this hidden was very tricky, but necessary. John had asked his dad once if all Needles were men as his personal history seemed to bear that out, and were all Stitches women. His dad hadn't known for sure but he thought that these jobs were interchangeable. Once again, secrecy prevented knowledge of all the facts. He'd also guessed that women were better at stitching given their natural intuition and innate sense of caring. John wasn't too sure about this assumption. He'd met a few women who would give Genghis Khan a run for his money.

Most Needlers abided by the sensible rules of never getting romantically involved with a Stitch, too. If they had flouted the rules like his father had, and now, John himself, was doing, it was a good indication that the match was a good one because there were so many problems associated with such a relationship; both parties would risk heartache and sadness. His dad suspected (because he had never been told explicitly) that his mum had been chosen for him in this way, but had had to prove that she was determined to stick at stitching *and* by her husband when the going got tough.

The powers had made it as difficult as possible for the relationship to flourish between his parents, but they had stuck at it and in the end the powers were satisfied. Sarah was determined that they would be satisfied with her and John too, even though she had a sneaking suspicion that it wouldn't be easy.

Wandering around the market garden with John had been informative and interesting. She had learned more about vegetables and flowers in a few hours than she'd learned in her whole life. John was in his element there. His face lit up when he showed her this type of onion, or that particularly juicy vine tomato. Roy and Helen, the husband-and-wife team who ran the shop selling his produce and taking orders for larger concerns, were lovely. They welcomed her with open arms and she felt like she'd known them forever. Helen had taken her to one side as they walked along the cabbages. 'I've never seen John so happy; he obviously adores you.'

Sarah's heart did a happy dance. That must mean he was happier with her than he had been with 'not tonight Josephina'.

The following Sunday evening crept up on them, as, unfortunately, they are wont to do. John had brought her home and Sarah was torn between asking him to stay and doing a bit of work for the next school day. She hadn't so much as marked a textbook and felt woefully under prepared.

'I'll get off home and you do the work, hon; I would hate to think of you more anxious than you need be in the morning. Don't forget that by next weekend you will probably be asked to stitch again, so best get school work sorted.'

She kissed him goodbye, watched him walk down the path, get into his car and drive away. They had arranged to meet mid-week, but she felt as if her soul had just left with him. They hadn't said the L word to each other yet, but she guessed it would be soon. In fact, she would say it to him on Wednesday; bugger what had happened in the past with Neil and Karen and bugger her gran's daft sayings.

The school week hurtled past at breakneck speed. Sarah always felt as if she'd stepped into a whirlwind from the minute she entered school to the minute she left. The fact that she had loads of work to do and things to catch up on because of her lazy week with John, made it pass even quicker. But she didn't regret even a second of their time together.

The only slow spot had been the meal on Wednesday. It was like a clear cool oasis in the middle of a desert. They'd opted for Chinese and during a lull in conversation, Sarah had plucked up her courage. She took his hand and looked into his eyes, opened her mouth and then *he* said, 'I love you, Sarah.'

She laughed. 'That's just what I was going to say!'

He frowned and then a smile curled his lips. 'My name's not Sarah ... or did you mean you were about to tell me how much you love yourself?'

'Just shut up and kiss me.'

John had obliged and as he pulled her on to the bed later that evening she said, 'I never did say it properly earlier. I love you, John ... I love you more than I ever loved anyone in my whole life.'

Their eyes met and both were suddenly filled with tears of happiness. 'I feel exactly the same,' he said, kissing the salty moisture from her cheeks.

Friday morning found Sarah in the middle of the staffroom, laughing her head off. A few members of staff looked at her sidelong and nudged each other, but most were too busy to notice. In spite of worrying about what was to come over the weekend, Sarah enjoyed the light relief Gary Keynsham was providing.

'I don't see what's so funny, I only asked if you had been anywhere interesting over the holiday,' Gary said, flushing at the attention Sarah was drawing.

Sarah fought to get her giggles under control. 'I have as a matter of fact, Gary, though why you are pretending to care, I don't know.'

'I'm not pretending.' He frowned. 'I realise we parted on less than good terms on the Friday before the holiday. I just thought I would try and be more polite, I guess.'

'Well, I'll let you into a secret,' Sarah said leaning in close. 'On that very Friday night, I shot back through time to the year 1913. Had such fun, I can't tell you. I think I'll shoot off again somewhere over the weekend, too.'

He shook his head. 'That's the last time I'll make an effort with you, madam, that's for sure!' Gary stomped off, his 'peacock in heat' shimmy well and truly absent.

In the corridor on her way home, Sarah saw Janet Simms emerging from her classroom with an armful of folders. She hadn't yet seen Sarah and was juggling folders and keys whilst trying to lock the door.

'Let me help you, Janet,' she said reaching her hand for Janet's keys.

Janet leapt in the air a good few inches, which was no mean feat for a lady of her stature. 'God, Sarah you scared the bejesus out of me!'

'Sorry, I guess I'm light on my feet,' Sarah said, noticing how wary Janet had become of her. The other woman's eyes darted up and down the corridor as if looking for help.

Janet jiggled the key in the lock. 'Oh, don't bother, I can do it. You must be exhausted at the end of a long week, eh? Perhaps you should just go home and rest.'

Go home and rest? What was she on about? Sarah suddenly realised that perhaps it was because of the last time they had met in the toilets. A little giggle capered up from her tummy and demanded release. 'Ha ha, you think I have gone a bit potty don't you, Janet?'

Janet backed away slowly. 'No, of course not, perhaps you are under stress.' The backing away strides got longer and quicker. 'I blame this teaching lark; there's never enough time to do anything properly, is there?'

Sarah giggled again, 'To be honest, there's loads of time, but it sometimes gets big fat holes in it; that's the real stress maker.'

'Holes in it? Hmm, yes, I've noticed that before.' Janet

flashed another hopeful glance at the empty corridor. 'Anyway, must be off, have a nice weekend.' Sarah watched her haring away, her red hair pumping up and down like a huge candyfloss confection. As Janet disappeared round a corner, Sarah expelled a huge guffaw that echoed around the empty corridor like the call of a giant Kookaburra.

The light relief, courtesy of Janet and Gary, buoyed Sarah's spirits a little and she could almost forget about the next quest. Almost. Back home, the scent from the honeysuckle in her garden wafted enticingly, beckoning her outdoors.

Cup of tea in hand, and barefoot, Sarah enjoyed the feel of the grass underfoot and the warm, late afternoon sun on her face. The tinkle of her mobile phone broke the calm. A message … Sarah read:

Hey, Sarah, sorry to ruin your weekend but you knew it was coming. Your next trip will be tomorrow morning around 6 a.m. You will be in Kansas 1874, and the sister of a Martha Klearny. More than that, I can't say. I have been forbidden to see you before you go. It is believed I may unwittingly reveal too much and cloud your judgement. I love you, and we'll be together again soon. Be brave, you can do it, John xxx

Though the afternoon was still warm, the scent of honeysuckle still lingered and birds sang in the trees, Sarah felt a deep chill, as if she stood in a winter garden, or a freezer. All she wanted to do was have a quiet weekend with John, a normal couple, in love and enjoying each other's company. They weren't a normal couple though, were they? He was a Needle and she was a Stitch. 'Needle and Stitch'; that sounded like some crazy detective agency or children's animated movie. She pressed the keys on her phone and sent back just four words:

I love you, too. xxx

Sarah walked inside and ran upstairs. Her hands grabbed a tower of books from the shelves in the study and then, returning downstairs, she spread them all out on the floor in the living room. For the next three hours she pored over every little bit of information to do with the Old American West she had, just to make sure she was as prepared as she could be. Sarah realised that she knew it all anyway, and that it probably wouldn't make much difference when deciding who she had to save, but at least it made her feel like she was doing something to feel more in control.

At bedtime, the alarm clock felt heavy in her hand as she set the time to 5 a.m. Didn't they say time weighed heavy on your soul? It was certainly true this evening. Still, the early bird catches the last stage to Kansas, as they say. Closing her eyes, Sarah was determined to look on the bright side. This time she knew when, where, and the date of where she was going. Hopefully she shouldn't have to act like a dopey Dora too much. Most importantly, she was doing it to save lives, to strengthen the ties of humanity across time, and of course, to make sure she and John could be together. *Positive thinking, Sarah. This will be the last time and then everything can get back to normal.*

In the end, the alarm clock wasn't necessary, as by half past four, Sarah was up, dressed, breakfasted and wondering if she should try to smuggle some painkillers and travel sickness pills in her bra – just in case she felt nauseous or had a headache. John hadn't mentioned anything about not taking physical objects through time, just that it wasn't a good idea to mention anything from the present in the past.

The packet of paracetamol looked light, innocuous and very necessary as she tossed them from one hand to the other. She sighed and put them back in the medical box. Better not tempt fate. Running back upstairs she pulled a scrunchie and a few grips from her bedside table and tucked those down her bra instead. If she was going to be out on the windswept plains, she wanted to be able to keep her hair tidy. Sarah shook her head. That wasn't the reason at all. She just wanted something familiar to help her through whatever crazy plan the powers that be had up their sleeves.

Sarah spent a few moments wondering what kind of sleeves powers that be would wear. Did they have arms, or were they just ancient entities, shapeless, formless, controlling time and mortals and whirling about being powerful? If they did have sleeves, they would probably be long and sparkly, perhaps a bit medievally? She went back downstairs. Next time she saw Janet she'd share these thoughts. Sarah giggled at the imagined expression on Janet's face if she did.

The kitchen clock said 5.45 a.m. Time for a last cup of tea? She checked herself; she wasn't going to the gallows, just to 1874. A blue tit perched on the cherry blossom tree outside the window as she filled the kettle. The garden looked so mysterious and otherworldly in the grey morning light. She flicked the kettle on. Perhaps she would take her tea outside; there may be a nip in the air, but a bit of fresh air would ...

Before her eyes, the garden began to waver and flicker, as if seen through the intense heat of a summer day or an open fire. Though the kitchen window was closed, her hair was lifted from her forehead by a warm wind, and the smell of detergent in her washing-up bowl was replaced by wild sage and dust. The waving and flickering quickened and then, creeping up from the grass, like watercolours seeping across a canvas, an entirely new scene pushed her little garden out of existence.

Grabbing the sink for support, Sarah was surprised to

find warm, rough wood beneath her hands instead of cold steel. Glancing down, she saw that the sink had turned into a wooden railing. Sarah took deep breaths and tried to calm her heart rate. Her heart was having none of this and insisted on doing a perpetual drum roll against her ribcage. *Come on, you expected this, go with it, don't fight it. This trip through time is a damned sight easier than the last.*

The scene settled like the dust at her feet. A vast flat plain rolled to an endless blue sky as far as the eye could see, but immediately in front of her was one of the weirdest sights she had ever witnessed. What looked to be a large cornfield, or *had* been a cornfield, had silvery brown mounds of soil moving and writhing at its roots.

At first, Sarah imagined it to be the last little bit of transition from present to past, but everything else remained still. She rubbed her eyes and looked again. Inhaling sharply, she realised what was happening. The writhing mounds were not earth, but thousands of heaving grasshoppers clambering over each other trying to reach the last vestiges of corn foliage.

Stepping forward tentatively, she watched as some of the creatures devoured others and her stomach rolled with fear and revulsion as two or three took flight and landed on her head and arm. The vile thing on her arm was trying to bite through the cloth of a long-sleeved grey dress that had replaced her sweatshirt. Shrieking, she batted it off and flapped her hands at her head to remove the ones tangled in her hair. They felt dry and papery but their legs were strong and hooked into her scalp.

Panicking now, she swallowed her revulsion, grasped hold of one particularly stubborn insect, yanked hard, hurled it to the ground and stamped on it. It wriggled its legs feebly then lay still. She turned to run, still flapping her hands at her head. *Oh, thank God, another human!* Sarah could see a running figure draped in a blanket, hurtling towards her from a small homestead about fifty feet away.

'Hell, Sarah, what are you doing outside without a blanket? Get over here and away from those devils!' a man's voice shouted. From under his arm he tossed her a rolled-up blanket. She quickly wrapped herself in it and hurried with him back to the homestead.

Once inside, the man slammed the door shut and removed the blanket. He wore rough blue overalls, was in his late thirties, tall, tawny haired and amber eyed. Sarah was reminded of the cowardly lion in *The Wizard of Oz*. Well, they *were* in Kansas after all, Toto. The cowardly lion rushed over to help a heavily pregnant woman tip a pot of boiling water into the fireplace, which was full of wriggling grasshopper bodies. Sarah shuddered. They must have flown in down the chimney.

The woman wore a long navy dress buttoned at the neck, similar to the grey one Sarah was wearing, with a stained apron over the top. She looked to be in her late twenties, with curly, light brown hair and chocolate brown eyes. Sarah was reminded of Dorothy in the film, but this woman was obviously older. Perhaps the lion and the girl had got married and she was about to give birth to a scarecrow?

On the other hand, perhaps one of the grasshoppers had bitten away a piece of Sarah's brain that was normally responsible for rational and calm.

While the man and woman were busy scooping the insect bodies into buckets, Sarah looked around. The dwelling had a dirt floor and two walls were built of sod. The third and fourth were constructed of various types of wood and had obviously been begged, borrowed, or stolen from the look of the irregular strips and planks roughly nailed together. Two small windows allowed in some natural light, but overall the room was a little dark.

In the centre stood a rough table and chairs, in one corner was a rocking chair and a footstool on which knitting was placed, a battered armchair kept it company nearby, and in the other corner, looking strangely out of place in such rustic surroundings, a Welsh dresser displayed a few prized ceramic plates. My goodness, Sarah thought, Harriet Summers would be in her element here, though she imagined that a wind pump would be beyond this couple's financial reach.

Noticing an internal door, Sarah walked over and opened it. A short passage showed two small bedrooms at either side. Drawing aside a curtain in an offshoot, a smaller bed was revealed, and a few books and a writing slate propped on top of a chair were squashed in next to that. Sarah deduced that a child must be lurking somewhere.

Through the tiny window Sarah watched the relentless devouring of the grasshopper army as thousands covered the ground like a wriggling, writhing carpet. She knew what was happening as soon as she'd seen them outside. This was the great grasshopper plague that had hit the Midwest and Great Plains in the summer of 1873, and had returned in even greater numbers in July 1874. Though they were called 'hoppers', they were actually Rocky Mountain locusts and literally millions of the creatures had descended on the prairies, eating everything in their path.

Tales had been told of swarms so big they blocked out the sun, and the beating of their wings sounded like the buzzing of gigantic bees and heavy rainfall. They had eaten anything growing – even the wool off sheep's backs and the clothes off humans. They even bit through skin, as Sarah had witnessed firsthand; she was lucky that her arms hadn't been bare, as the reports of grasshopper bites described them as more painful than a bee sting.

Last night Sarah had read the heartbreaking reports of the poor farmers as all hope for a new life disappeared into the bellies of those insects. Most of the homesteaders had left the overpopulated East Coast, or had even come from outside the United States to escape poverty or persecution. All had come with a hope to find a patch of land they could call their own and build a future for their families. The Homestead Act of 1862 had done much in fostering the American Dream. Under the Act, up to 160 acres of free land was allotted to a person. If the homesteader built a house and worked it for five years, it became theirs. This was something most poor people had only dreamed about and most had risked everything to realise it.

'Sarah? Will you come out and help Joe burn the damned things? Hoppers or no hoppers, I have to prepare our meal,' 'Dorothy' called. Sarah wondered if 'Dorothy' was Martha Klearny. Just in case Martha hadn't yet stepped on to the set of *Little House on The Prairie*, Sarah decided to answer from the offshoot. If she was wrong, then at least she wouldn't be standing face to face with the woman when she said, 'What in the world has come over you, child? I ain't Martha, I'm Dorathee!'

'I'm comin', Martha!' Sarah called and was shocked to hear an American drawl come out of her mouth. Why she was shocked, she didn't know. She would hardly fit in if she spoke with a modern English accent, now would she?

Peering round the door at the woman, Sarah was relieved to find that she was arranging flour tins and various other tins on the table. Must be Martha then ... but was Joe her husband, brother, or what? Joe looked like he was preparing to go back outside. He shook out one of the blankets with his big farmer's hands, doubled it and placed it back over his head.

He lifted the blanket and peered at her like a lion from a cave. 'Quit gapin' and get the kerosene from the barn while I start rakin' 'em, woman,' he said, striding outside.

Sarah turned to Martha. 'I thought you meant burn the ones you just dowsed?'

'Why'd we do that? We need to burn them live uns in what's left of our field. This mornin', Greg Olson told Joe that's what they done yesterday. Damn critters stayed away after that, on account that they smelled the smoke of their brothers' burnin' bodies.'

Sarah nodded and folded her blanket. She knew that burning hadn't done much good. Whatever the farmers had done or not done, after a day or two, depending on the area, the grasshoppers had taken to the air swarming in formations resembling big black snakes as they moved south leaving bare earth where crops had once stood.

Outside, from under her blanket, Sarah could see what must pass for the barn. A long lean-to shack was situated just behind the house, and as far as she could see was thankfully free of hoppers. Her rough work boots kicked up red dust as she made her way over. She wondered where the child was. It would be unlikely that it would be in school in the middle of a plague like this. Besides, many children were taught at home, if they were taught at all.

Opening the heavy wooden door, she stepped inside. When her eyes got used to the dark interior of the barn, she could see a variety of tools, sacks of grain and a couple of horses tethered to a hitching post. A milking cow stamped at flies and six or seven hens scratched in the dirt. A ladder led to an upper level, presumably a hayloft, and a large jar marked kerosene stood just inside the door. *That grain needs protecting, it's a wonder the hoppers haven't been at it already.*

'Be sure and plug the gap under the door, Ma! I burned a few that came in up here, but I don't think it'll be long before more come.'

Ma? Sarah looked up. A pair of forget-me-not blue eyes

peered down anxiously at her from the top of the ladder. The eyes belonged to a boy of around ten years old; he had a shock of white blond hair and held aloft a flaming torch. Sarah thought he was the personification of Ralph in *Lord of the Flies*.

'Ma, are you listening? Plug the door with those kerosene rags!' He ducked back into the gloom, gave a whoop and she heard his feet stamping on presumably a few more hoppers.

Sarah looked down at a line of rags by her feet that she had disturbed when entering. Kicking them back under the door, she cursed John. How could he let her go on a mission knowing that this Sarah had a child? Didn't he know that for the past few years she had yearned for one? Didn't he know that her husband had started a family with her best friend, leaving Sarah wondering if she'd ever get the chance to have one of her own?

She knew the answer to these questions was yes. The first day she'd met him, he'd read out her life story from his clipboard. One thing was for sure; he would get a piece of her mind ... if she had any of it left when she returned. Another thing was for sure; whoever she had to save had better be bloody well worth it.

Chapter Seventeen

No sooner had Sarah plugged the gap under the barn door than it was flung open again and in stomped an angry Joe. 'What's keeping ya, woman? I raked a pile o' hoppers as big as Artie up there, but the damned kerosene didn't show!'

'Sorry, Joe, I'm comin' now,' Sarah said, hoisting the heavy jar into her arms.

'Artie! Git down here too, bring another rake,' Joe yelled, and then ran back outside.

When Artie and Sarah arrived at the field a few minutes later, Joe had managed to rake another pile of grasshoppers. Sarah felt her stomach roll at the sight of the tangle of legs and bodies writhing in a heap. Artie set to raking more of the creatures from the cornfield and Joe wrenched the kerosene from her grasp.

'I swear to God, Sarah, you are acting like a sleepwalker today!' He dipped a piece of rag in the jar and threw it on the pile. 'Matches?' he snapped, glaring at her.

Sarah felt in the pocket of her apron. Nothing. 'Um … I don't have any …'

Her shortcomings were interrupted by a *THRUM, THRUM, THRUM* … The ground under foot seemed to shudder and the air around their heads suddenly vibrated with the beating of thousands of tiny wings. Sarah looked up in awe as the hoppers took off as one into the sky. Even though she had read reports of the scale and shape of the swarms, now she was an eyewitness to it, she could hardly believe what she saw.

A huge undulating black 'S' stretched from the field and high into the blue like some hideous Biblical pestilence. A few minutes later, they had disappeared over the plain, ready to wreak havoc on the next homestead. Apart from the tangled pile at her feet and a few injured hoppers in the ruined field, the whole lot had vanished in a matter of minutes.

Sarah looked at Joe and Artie. If anyone wanted a definition of utter despair, they could forget the dictionary and just look at Joe's face instead. Sarah had the strange feeling that he had turned from a living, breathing man into a sepia photograph. His shoulders slumped, the passion in his unusual amber eyes was snuffed out like a candle, and the corners of his mouth endeavoured to reach the red dust beneath his feet. His huge capable hands hung limp, as if paralysed.

Artie looked from Joe to Sarah. An ocean of tears swelled in his blue eyes. Utter despair had somehow travelled across the few feet of dirt from Joe and seeped into his every pore. The ocean crashed on to his cheeks and his wave of sadness washed Sarah's own eyes.

Brushing her tears away, she looked at the ruined fields. Just a few pathetic stalks of corn sprouted from the ground, like a few unshaved hairs on a man's face. Sarah knew that this might well be the end for all of them unless there was enough food in the barn to get themselves and the animals through the winter.

'Joe! Thank God, they've gone ...' Martha hurried towards them holding her bump, her face smudged with flour. Then she saw the destroyed fields and gave utter despair a voice. An animalistic wail left her mouth, piercing the hot, dry air; a cry so gut wrenching that it chilled Sarah's blood. Putting her hands on her head, Martha let out another anguished cry. Her legs buckled, refusing to support her any longer, and she knelt in the dust crying over and over, 'Why, why, dear Lord, why!'

Sarah realised Joe was oblivious to anything except his

own private misery and Artie gave a strangled sob and sped back to the house. She knelt next to Martha. 'Come now, Martha, we'll survive … we'll get through somehow …'

Martha stopped wailing, threw back her head and laughed humourlessly. 'That's what we always say. We moved from Missouri when we couldn't make ends meet just two year ago, came here to this land of milk and honey … remember, Joe? Remember that's what *you* said, Joe, a land of milk and honey? Well, the milk's curdled and the bees forgot to come to this Godforsaken land.'

'Hush your mouth, woman!' Joe strode forward and towered above them both. His whole body trembled and his hands, having shaken off the paralysis, clenched and unclenched. Joe's eyes had re-found passion but a red mist had kindled it.

Before things took an uglier turn, Sarah stood and dragged Martha to her feet. 'Let's git you inside. It's not good for the baby gittin' all distressed like this.'

Once inside, Martha went to the rocking chair, sat down and stared vacantly at the wool on the footstool. Utter despair must have squeezed in under the door as it shrouded her from head to toe. Sarah could hear Artie sobbing in his room and right at that moment, if she had a choice, she'd have demanded a return ticket to the present.

Sarah put a kettle on the stove and looked for coffee. She didn't have a choice though, did she? No. And why didn't she have a choice? Because she would lose John, and with him would go her heart, neatly broken into a million pieces and shortly after that, her sanity would follow. She looked at Martha, drained of all spirit. *There's another reason, too, isn't there, Sarah? You could never live with yourself if you abandoned these poor folk now.*

The door crashed back against the wall and shuddered on its hinges. Sarah, nearly dropping the tin coffee mugs, whirled round to see Joe framed in the doorway, his hair blowing in the wind like a great lion mane, hope and anger vying for dominance in his eyes. 'I'm packin' a bag and goin' to Wichita,' he growled, rushing past her and into one of the bedrooms.

Martha heaved herself up and put her hand to the small of her back. 'I'd better go see what he's talkin' about.'

Sarah put the tin mugs down and followed her out into the bedroom, scared of what Joe may do in his feverish state.

'But what if there is no work in the stockyards, Joe?' Martha was saying.

'I'll find work somewhere else. I have to, Martha; we have food to last a few weeks but that's it.'

'But you'll be so far away, must be twenty mile or more and ... we ain't never been parted afore, not since our wedding day,' Martha whispered, her eyes filling with tears.

Sarah folded her arms and leaned her head on the wall. That answered the 'are they married?' question then.

'No we ain't, Martha.' Joe finished stuffing clothes into a canvas holdall and turned to face her. 'But we ain't ever been as near to destitution as this before, neither.'

Joe pushed past them both and hurried outside to the barn. A few minutes later, he drove a big black horse hitched to a small cart up to the house. Martha and Sarah stood in the doorway, but Artie pushed past and ran out to meet him. 'Take me, Uncle Joe. I can work with you.' He put his hand on the horse's reins. 'Just gimmee a minute to pack my bag and ...'

Joe flicked the rein and backed the horse up. 'No, boy, you gotta stay here and look after the women; no telling what would happen if they were left alone.'

Artie looked as if he might argue, but then seeing the set expression on his uncle's face, he looked to the ground. 'Yes, sir, I'll protect 'em.'

Yeah right, a ten-year-old boy? How sexist is that? Sarah shook her head. Perhaps not the best time to foist modern opinions on the situation, though.

Joe held his hand out to Martha. She walked out, stroked the horse's neck with one hand and gave her other to Joe. 'I'll be as quick as I can, hopefully no more than a few weeks. I'll return with this here cart full of provisions.' He looked lovingly into his wife's eyes. 'We'll survive … we always do.' He smiled and kissed Martha's hand.

Sarah swallowed a lump in her throat. 'We'll be fine, Joe. Me, Martha and Artie will keep this place safe until your return.'

Joe nodded at her and Artie, flicked the reins, and kissed his teeth at the horse. The horse tossed its head and set off at a fast trot out on to the plains, churning up a red cloud as it went. The three of them watched until Joe became a little dot on the horizon, and then they went back inside.

Sarah wished that utter despair had hitched a ride with Joe and jumped out on route, instead of choosing to keep them company. Artie shoved his hands in his pockets and mooched, whilst Martha just shook her head at Sarah and sighed heavily enough to plunge the house into the centre of the earth.

'Do you want me to finish making bread?' Sarah asked, hoping that the answer would be no, as she hadn't a clue how to do it.

Martha shook her head again and poured water into a bowl from a ewer similar to the one Sarah had used in 1913. Scrubbing her hands with a bar of rough soap she said, 'I'm not making bread, I'm making pancakes, and I need to keep busy anyways.'

Sarah drew a chair up to the table and paid careful attention to what Martha did with the pancakes in case she may be required to make them. As she watched Martha's spoon measure and beat, she wondered where her husband was – Artie's father. It didn't seem likely that he was around, or surely Joe wouldn't have asked Artie to take care of them. This thought comforted her, as performing wifely duties in the bedroom would be above and beyond the call of duty ... unless by some miracle Artie's father turned out to be John.

Sarah placed her elbows on the table and cupped her hands under her chin. How she missed him. She'd only been away from him for a few days and her body yearned for his touch. If only she could hear his voice on a telephone line across time, she'd feel less lonely. But that wasn't going to happen and so she'd better stop mooning over him. Besides, he was going to get an earful over Artie before he got sweet nothings.

A few minutes later, Artie quit mooching and joined them at the table. 'Ma, can I go over and see Abe Reimer? He said they were getting a new cow.'

Sarah felt a warm glow in her belly. She was someone's mother and it felt good. 'Well, don't you think you'd better eat your pancakes first?' She smiled, ruffling his unruly mop of hair.

Martha stopped beating the mixture and pointed the dripping batter spoon at Sarah. 'Just because my Joe has gone don't mean that you can go over his head. You know Artie ain't allowed by that Mennonite place.'

Mennonites? Now why did that ring a bell? Sarah remembered. Yes, they had been an immigrant group that had settled in the area and elsewhere around this time. They had come from Russia and had, she thought, German origins, too? Why wouldn't Joe want Artie to visit them? Artie looked at her, obviously expecting an answer. Sarah shifted uncomfortably in her seat. How could she ask why, without asking why?

'I know Joe said that, but they're not that bad, are they?'

Sarah asked. She thought that if a thoughtful and caring little boy like Artie wanted to visit this Abe, he must be OK.

Martha frowned and continued to beat the batter. 'Well, your Arthur gave his life fighting in the war for what was right. Them folk don't raise a finger to no one. Joe's says as how they hide behind this fancy "pacifist" word, but really, just plain cowardly is what they is.'

Sarah sighed. So, that's what had happened to her husband. The American Civil War had ended in 1865; poor Artie must have only been a baby when his father was killed, or perhaps Sarah had been pregnant at the time. Whatever the scenario, it was incredibly sad. Not only had these people struggled with the harsh winters, the droughts, and now a locust plague, they had recently been through the bloodiest war in American history. New weapons for the time, such as hand grenades and machine guns, were used, alongside swords and rifles. Over 600,000 had been killed in total.

'So what do you say, Ma?' Artie looked up at her hopefully.

As much as Sarah wanted to let him go, because if these people were pacifists, they had her vote, she thought that may cause more tension in an already tense atmosphere. 'Perhaps another time, Artie. Why don't you go and make sure that all those hoppers are dead out in the field and in the barn?'

Artie looked at her as if to say 'that's a cop out', but he nodded. 'Yes, Ma,' and slipped out.

Sarah left the table and from the door watched him run to the barn. If the situation hadn't have been so hopeless, the scene before her (apart from the ruined field) was breathtaking. Sarah had never seen a landscape as vast. From her front door back home, she could see a row of houses, and though the scene from John's door was beautiful, she felt as if the next hill was within easy reach, the next tree a walk away, but here – the great flat expanse of land joined hands with the sky and rolled away to infinity.

The scent of wild sage drifted on the wind, so relaxing. Sarah closed her eyes and leaned her head against the rough wood. If only she were here on a time-travelling holiday instead of a mission to save a life. Now, that could catch on back home; she should open a business. A smile flickered across her lips as she pictured a customer going to the counter in the time-travelling agents. *Morning, madam, please take a seat. Now we have Rome, Paris, or an 1830 holiday? Yes, madam, I do mean the real 1830!*

She opened her eyes and yawned. So, who the hell did she have to save this time? Joe had gone, so that left Artie or Martha. No itchy feet, tingling in the back, or hiccups so far, but then she had had none of those in 1913, either. And what harm were they likely to come to in the middle of nowhere? Certainly in the 1860s Indians may have attacked them, but not now.

The aggressive expansion of the great American dream had forced the Native Americans off their homelands and ever westwards, into smaller and smaller reservations. One of the last big battles was set to take place when Custer would get his comeuppance, but that would be two years into the future and in Montana. No, though it wasn't impossible, it was unlikely that they were in danger from Indians. Much more likely to be bitten by rattlesnakes, struck by lightning, or get a disease due to the dirty conditions they had to live in. Mm ... lovely.

'Hey, Sarah, can you wash these dishes while I cook us some pancakes?' Martha called, halting her contemplation.

'Yes, I surely can.' She laughed at the 'surely'. It was as if someone in her brain was rifling through the 'stereotypical Old Western speech' section and emailing appropriate words to her tongue.

Sarah looked past Martha at two big buckets of water. There was no sink. One bucket looked decidedly scummy, and on its surface a few flies were doing a few lazy circuits on their way to a watery grave. The other one didn't look much better, but at least it looked a little cleaner. Picking a dish from the table, Sarah went to dunk it in the clean bucket.

'Whoa there! What do ya think you're doin'? Martha shrieked.

'You asked me to wash the dishes ...'

'Not in the drinkin' water. I boiled that this mornin' and you gonna dump the dirty plates in it?'

'Then where?'

Martha shook her head in disbelief and pointed at the scum bucket.

'But ... it's dirty, Martha.'

'It ain't too bad. You know as well as I do that we have to be careful. We have a few barrels of water in the barn and the well is half-full but there's no tellin' how long Joe'll be. Until he comes back with the wagon we can't haul no extra water from the creek. And our once-a-week bathing will have to go to two weeks for now, I guess.'

Sarah nodded but couldn't bring herself to answer. The details about lack of water and consequent lack of hygiene of the homesteaders were not news to her ears, but it was one thing knowing about it and quite another having to physically live like it. Could she really bring herself to eat the pancakes Martha was now flipping on the stove? On the other hand, if she was here any length of time, she wouldn't survive if she didn't eat. Perhaps the Sarah she was 'kind of working in tandem' with, to quote John, had built up immunity to most of the dirt over the years.

The bathing once every two weeks was equally alien to a woman who showered daily. Strange that she couldn't smell much body odour. She had been able to in the last two trips. Perhaps she had been spared that, as it must be pretty fearsome.

'Pancakes are ready; you'd better call your boy in,' Martha said, setting three dubiously smeared plates at the table.

Sarah went to the door. 'Artie, pancake's ready!'

'He won't be able to hear that, go out and git him.'

Sarah set off to the barn. It was clear that Martha was the woman of the house, even though she was the younger sister. She and Joe had obviously taken pity on Sarah and Artie after her husband had been killed. A quick reccy of the barn revealed a missing Artie. The remaining horse and saddle had gone and hoof prints led away across the dirt path and then were lost in the yellowing grass of the plains. The direction pointed towards a black smudge on the far horizon. Shielding her eyes from the sun, Sarah thought that the smudge was possibly another homestead, though she couldn't be sure. Another smaller smudge appeared to be moving away from her and towards it. She sighed. That must be Artie.

Damn him, he's obviously gone to see Abe whatsit, after all. There was no way she could go after him; it looked to be a good five miles she guessed.

Sarah walked back to the house. Martha wouldn't be pleased, heavily pregnant in this heat, the crops eaten by hoppers, her husband gone until God knows when, and now her nephew goes AWOL and ignored pancakes wasting on the fly-ridden table. *Hm, things could be worse I guess.*

'*Aaarghhh*, Sarah!' Martha's fearful yell carried towards her on the hot prairie wind.

Shit, sounds like things just got worse ...

Sarah raced the last few feet, hoping to God that she wouldn't find a rattlesnake side winding away under the table, or a Native American with Martha's hair in one hand, his scalping knife in the other.

Sarah smashed the door open, adrenaline coursing through her veins like a freight train, and expected the worst. Of all the fearful scenarios that had hurtled through her mind over the last few seconds, this wasn't one of them. There was Martha on all fours in the dirt, sweat pouring down her face, her eyes bright with pain.

'Do somethin', the baby's comin' early!'

Sarah's heart plummeted and her legs shook ... damn it, why the hell couldn't it have been a rattlesnake?

Chapter Eighteen

The send key was jabbed with such ferocity that it stuck in the keypad, and then the mobile phone flew across the room and smacked into the cushions on the sofa. Who the hell did these creatures think they were? John poured himself a whisky and paced the length of his living room. The report had just come through saying that Sarah was getting bogged down in feelings surplus to requirement. Surplus to requirement? Feelings were feelings weren't they?

The boy Artie had apparently stirred deep emotions in Sarah about the loss of opportunity to become a mother. Time taken up with this could lead to a clouding of judgement, and for the moment, John's request for permission to be with Sarah was therefore on hold, pending the outcome of this mission.

John marched to the phone. The only person who would understand what he was going through was his dad. 'Dad, you'll never guess what the arrogant bastards have said now! I told them in no uncertain terms where to shove it!'

'Calm down, John ... Right what's happened?' Harry soothed. John told him. 'Well, they do have a point. I told you it wouldn't be easy when I came over the other week, and—'

'Oh, that'll be right, take their side. I thought you'd understand because of you and Mum,' John said bitterly.

'It's because of me and your mother that I'm saying all this. Don't you remember that Christmas Eve when she got stuck in that Cuba job in the middle of the sodding missile crisis? You were only ten and cried yourself to sleep. Neither of us knew if she would be back at all!'

John sighed. How could he forget? When she had returned

on Christmas Day morning it had been the best present they could have wished for. 'Yes, Dad, but that was a one-off; she never got stuck after that and it wasn't her fault either ...'

'Trying to brush it all under the carpet won't help. If you and Sarah stay together, then the road ahead will be far from smooth and plain sailing and you know it.'

'But they said that she is getting emotional ... Isn't that what it's all about, getting emotional? Actually caring about putting things right, mending the holes of despair opening up in time everywhere?'

'Of course, and that's why your mum was one of the best. But there is a point when your heart needs to take a back seat to your head in order to complete a mission successfully.' Harry sighed. 'Anyway, you know all this ... Just be sure that she's the one for you and—'

'She is, Dad. I'm sure of that,' John interrupted. 'I know I said I wasn't sure the other week, but I am now.'

'I know that, but if you'd let me finish. I was going to say that the powers that be will only agree to it if she loves you back one hundred per cent, too. If she's not strong enough then, well ...'

Harry left the rest unsaid.

John chatted to his dad about more mundane things for a while and then ended the call. He walked through the house and out on to the patio. There was a nip in the air that hadn't been there earlier. Perhaps it was a chill in his heart and nothing to do with the temperature at all. The rolling Yorkshire hills before his eyes gave way to the flat plains of Kansas in his imagination. He so wished he could be there with Sarah to help her through, to tell her it wasn't his idea to send her to be Artie's mum, that it was just unfortunate and that it couldn't be helped.

He also wanted to take her in his arms and kiss her. She'd only been gone a short while, but his body ached for hers.

The breeze blew up the valley, stirring the meadow grass and scudding clouds danced over it, casting shadows on a green sea. John shuddered and hugged himself. He had thought himself in love with Josephina, and when she had left him he had been devastated. But what he had felt for her could be placed on the head of a pin compared to the all-consuming, world-rocking love he felt for Sarah.

He smiled at the memory of her kisses and the way she pulled a face, her head on one side and her nose scrunched up, when she didn't understand something. His name on her lips sounded new and fresh, and the way she slipped her arm through his and looked into his eyes when they were walking made him feel like he was the most important man in the world.

John's smile slowly faded and a frown furrowed his brow. Something that his dad had said niggled him. What if Sarah didn't love him enough? What if she couldn't handle the job and everything that would come with a relationship such as theirs? And anyway, wasn't it selfish of him to expect her to? Right now she was in another dimension and he could do bugger all to help her. Was that fair; did he have the right to ask her to give up normality and everything she had been used to?

John gave a heavy sigh, and with one last look across the hills to the imagined landscape of nineteenth-century Kansas and Sarah struggling alone in emotional turmoil, he turned and walked back into the house.

Chapter Nineteen

Hot towels and water ... or was it hot water and towels? Sarah's brain had turned to guacamole. She gaped at Martha panting on the floor, and was totally incapable of rational thought or movement.

'Sarah, help me!'

The panic in Martha's voice helped Sarah find her own. 'When you say early ... how early?'

'What? You know it's due August ... so about a month I think ... git some sheets off the bed.'

Sheets off the bed, yes that's right, she can't possibly give birth on to the dirt floor.

Come on, Sarah, get your act together. Sarah raced into the bedroom and stripped the bed of sheets and pillows. She noticed a few stained towels on a chair and grabbed those, too; boil some water next, that was it, yes, hot water and towels. She thought of the water in the other room, and shook her head. God knew if any baby would survive this standard of hygiene ... let alone a premature one.

'Sarah?'

'Yes, I'm, *hic*, here,' Sarah said, easing a sheet under Martha. She noticed the floor was damp. That must mean her waters had broken. She also noticed she had hiccups. That must mean that this was the life she had to save. Great, thanks for that, John.

Martha hitched her dress up. 'I feel like I need to push ... God, it hurts so much ... how did you ever get through this? *Aaargh!*'

Given that Sarah hadn't actually had a child, she had no clue, but said, 'It'll all be, *hic*, over soon, honey. Bite on that, *hic*, pillow and just keep, *hic*, goin'.'

She ran over to the stove and put a pan of water on to boil. Now what else? In her mind she saw the baby slip out, her washing it with warm water and ... ah yes, cutting the cord. Sarah's hands hovered over a knife and a pair of scissors. She picked up the scissors and dropped them into the pan on the stove. Then she ladled 'clean' water into a cup and dropped a rag into that.

Rushing back to Martha, she kicked dust into her eye. 'Damn it, doncha think I'm in enough pain?'

'Yes, *hic*, sorry, *hic*!' She dipped the rag into the cool water, bathed Martha's forehead and wished she could do more. There would be no pain relief available here. Chloroform and ether had become fairly common for some sections of society at this time, but there was still opposition to it and there could be side effects.

Martha screwed her face up and turned a deep red as she pushed. '*Gahh!* Can you see anything back there?'

Sarah took a deep breath. She much preferred being at the 'mopping end' with a rag. Still, she had to look sometime. She shuffled along and took a peak. God, she could see the head! Her squeamish feelings disappeared as she saw a new life ready to enter the world. All of a sudden the hiccups went, new confidence arrived, and Sarah was ready.

Perhaps it was an autopilot instinct that comes to all women at these times, or perhaps it was the episodes of *One Born Every Minute* that she'd watched; whatever it was, she felt more in control and relatively calm.

'Won't be long now, Martha. Just a few more pushes and then the head should be ready to be born. When that happens, I want you to pant, like this, *huh*, *huh*, *huh*, not too quickly, OK?'

'What? Why?'

Sarah didn't really remember one hundred per cent, but said, 'Because that will stop you having a tear ... hopefully.'

That's all she needed, being a Stitch in time *and* having to stitch up a woman after childbirth, too.

A few minutes later the head was on its way out. 'OK, do the panting thing, like I told you. The head should come out by itself now,' Sarah said, mopping Martha's head again.

'It's stinging, *huh*, *huh*, *huh*.'

'That's it, it's comin', you're doing grand, Martha,' Sarah said, watching the baby turn and then slip free of its mother into her hands. 'It's a girl!' she yelled, grabbing the cleanest towel she could find to wrap gently around it. Another instinct/memory told her the next move. 'Right, Martha, can you git round and lie with your head on these pillows, the baby needs to be on your chest, next to your skin.'

Martha took a second to get her breath, undid the buttons on her dress, and crawled round and on to her back. Sarah placed Martha's tiny daughter on her chest and blinked back tears of joy when she saw the tender look of love in Martha's eyes as she lifted the baby's tiny hand. Martha stopped smiling. 'She ain't breathin'.' She looked up at Sarah with terror in her eyes. 'She ain't breathin'!'

Sarah fell to her knees and lifted the little body. No, she wasn't. OK what now? Smack its bottom, didn't they do that in the movies? Rub it with a towel was something else that whispered in the recesses of her TV-watching experience. Placing the child back on her mother, Sarah rubbed her back vigorously with a towel *and* gave her bottom a few taps.

The baby snuffled and then *Awaaaaaa!* bawled from her lungs. 'Thank God!' Martha cried. Tears poured down her cheeks and she kissed the infant's head.

Sarah wiped her own head with the damp rag and exhaled in relief. '*Phew*, I was worried there for a while.'

After a few minutes, Martha looked puzzled and then screwed up her face again. 'I got pain.'

Sarah ran to get a bowl. 'Yep, it's the afterbirth, Martha;

give a few pushes, it shouldn't take long.' Placing the bowl between Martha's legs, Sarah gently pressed her stomach; she had seen that done on *Casualty* once when a woman had given birth in a derailed train. Luckily, ten minutes later, the afterbirth was out too, and all that remained to be done was the cutting of the cord.

Sarah closed her eyes and tried to see the train scene in her head. The paramedics were directing the whole thing on a mobile phone as the woman and her partner couldn't be reached until the train was made safe. Had he tied a shoe lace round the cord and then cut it, or had there been two shoelaces?

'What's wrong, ain't you gonna cut the cord like you said?' Martha asked.

'Yes, I'm just trying to think of the best way. I ain't done this afore you know.'

'You'll do it fine. You have been a saviour so far and that's the truth. What I'd have done without you, I don't know … and when the little 'un weren't breathin' and all …' Martha shook her head and sniffed.

Thank the BBC, honey …

Sarah stood and went back over to the stove. She lifted the pan of boiling water on to the table and looked around for string or any likely substitute. The only string she found looked like it had been dragged across the entire length of the plains. It was thick in grease and sticky.

She looked down at her bootlaces; they, of course, were in a similar state to the string.

'Martha, have we got any clean bootlaces, or anything like string? It is gonna be used for tying round the baby's cord, so I want it clean.'

Martha thought for a few minutes. 'We got wool, that's clean, I guess.'

Ah yes, there it was on the footstool. It wouldn't be spotless, but it was the best they had.

Sarah wound a strand of wool around both index fingers and broke two pieces off. Then with a spoon, she hooked the scissors out of the hot water and set them on a clean area of the sheet to become cool enough to handle.

'After you cut the cord can you bathe her and dress her in her special baby clothes I sewed for her? They're in my chest.'

'Of course I will.'

'And then I'll try and suckle her. She looks like she's trying to suck now, don't she?'

The baby was staring intelligently at her mother and opening and closing her mouth slightly. Her tiny hand gripped Martha's finger, and she seemed perfectly alright, even though she had arrived unannounced and unprepared for. Sarah felt a huge sense of achievement looking down at that tiny bundle. She also felt the old yearning tugging at her heartstrings.

When will it be you lying there, Sarah? When will you have a precious child cradled in your arms?

The shoelace question was solved. As Sarah tied the first bit of wool around the cord about three inches away from the baby, she remembered that the actor had tied a second bit about a half an inch beyond that and had cut between them. The scissors felt ridiculously heavy and shook a little in her hand. Then, taking a breath, she opened the blades, positioned them between the bits of wool and closed them again before doubt set in.

Thankfully, everything seemed fine. Yells of pain and fountains of blood didn't pour from the baby; she just continued to look at her mother unperturbed. 'Looks like that's done it, Martha.' Sarah smiled, dipping a clean rag into warm water. 'I'll get her washed down and, if you can manage it, I suggest you try to clean yourself a little, too. We'd better get you and your daughter off this floor and settled in bed before Artie comes back.'

'I want to name her first. Me and Joe settled on Elspeth after our poor ma and Charlotte after his. Do you like it?' Martha asked.

'Little Elspeth, that's just beautiful. She would have been so proud.' Sarah wondered what had happened to their 'poor ma'.

Martha's face lit up. 'She would, wouldn't she? I don't know how she survived all them births; mind you, that's what done for her in the end, weren't it?'

'Yes, poor ma. How many did she have, I forgit?'

'How could you forgit? She died pushing our Billy out and he were the only boy, number twelve.'

Sarah gulped. Twelve babies in these conditions, with no pain relief; our 'poor ma' was a bloody hero.

An hour later, Martha and Elspeth were in bed. The little girl was feeding contentedly and Sarah had cleaned the birthing area as much as she could. The afterbirth was a problem. They didn't want Artie seeing it and if they left it indoors it would attract flies, even if they covered it well. Martha told Sarah that she'd heard that it was practice out on the plains to take it a good way from the house and leave it for crows, vultures or coyotes. Other women had buried it deep in the earth, or burned it.

'OK, Martha, I'm going to take this here bowl out on to the plains. Looks like it'll be sundown in a few hours, so it's contents will be gone quicker than you can say baby.' Sarah smirked, thinking that she could get used to speaking like this. She may even keep it up for a while back in work, particularly when Janet was around.

'It's only four o'clock honey; it won't be sundown till eight, but I guess you better do it now before that naughty boy of yours comes back. Are you gonna whup him?'

Sarah frowned; did Martha expect her to give him a good hiding? 'Whup him?'

Martha changed the baby on to the other breast and tutted. 'Yeah, whup him. He never gonna learn if you let him disobey you like that. There's one of Joe's belts in the trunk.'

Sarah tried to conceal the revulsion she felt at such a suggestion and shook her head. 'Not this time. We'll see what he has to say for himself when he comes home.'

Just as she was leaving with the fly-ridden placenta bowl under her arm, Martha called, 'And can you collect some more buffalo chips while you're out there? I don't think we got enough cow chips for the next while since Joe cut down to one feed a day.'

Sarah groaned. This day was getting better and better. Not only had she just had to deliver a baby, and was off out of the door with a bucket of blood and membrane to the plains where dangerous animals lurked, now she was expected to collect buffalo shit for fuel. This was an idea the homesteaders had borrowed from the Indians, as coal was expensive and wood scarce.

'OK, is the wheelbarrow in the barn?' she yelled over her shoulder.

'Yeah, and when you git back, will you milk Nellie? We missed eatin' them pancakes so you'll have to make porridge.'

Sarah presumed Nellie was the cow in the barn. Something else she'd never done ... but then, how hard could it be? She thought of a lame joke and grinned, more from the need to release tension than through humour: *Pull the udder one, Sarah, quit milking the situation and take the bull by the horns.*

In the barn, Sarah nodded to Nellie. 'See ya later, Nellie; I'll make sure my hands are warm.' And then she placed the bowl carefully into the heavy wooden wheelbarrow. Hopefully, when her next three chores were completed she'd be allowed back to the future.

She made a face as she manoeuvred the bulky contraption through the barn door and on to the prairie; the palms of her hands were already beginning to rub on the rough wooden handles, and the wind whipped her hair from under the stupid bonnet she'd been required to wear and into her eyes, up her nose and in her mouth. *But don't you have a scrunchie?* Undoing the buttons on the dress, she stuck her fingers down her bra and pulled out the band and grips. They *had* survived time travel then. Sarah giggled, scraped her hair up and secured it tightly. How could such small everyday objects fill her with delight? She guessed it was because they represented the future and allowed her to feel a little more in control. Also, in a small way, she had triumphed over the powers that be.

Ten minutes or so later, Sarah's dress was soaked in sweat and blisters were beginning to form on her palms. She stopped by a rocky outcrop; huge brown meatballs on a yellowing grassland of shredded wheat. Nice, but she couldn't eat three, as the advert had it. These were the first rocks she'd come across and perhaps the only ones for miles around by the look of it.

Under the shade, Sarah lowered her bottom on to a smaller boulder. Phew, it felt good to escape the baking yellow ball up there. If it was as hot as this at after four in the afternoon, what must it be like at noon? Looking back the way she'd trudged, she could make out the homestead shimmering like a mirage in the heat. This was about as good a place as any to leave the placenta. It was far enough away to ensure animals didn't come snooping round the house looking for more juicy morsels, and besides, Sarah couldn't go any further; she was well and truly pooped.

Come on, Sarah, the sooner you get this done, the sooner you can collect the buffalo chips, push the barrow back in the baking heat, milk the cow, make the porridge, and then go home to John. Not such a bad to-do list ... if you say it quick.

Standing up, Sarah stretched her hands high above her head, yawned and cracked her knuckles one at a time. One knuckle sounded very odd, it was more like a rattle than a crack. She rubbed her middle knuckle again and looked closely. Nope, nothing out of the ordinary. OK, get this damned placenta tipped out ...

Sarah bent to pick up the bowl and froze. The rattle she'd heard earlier sounded again, but this time it lasted much longer. Slowly she straightened up again and raised her eyes. This noise had nothing to do with cracking her knuckles, but everything to do with the vibrating tail-end of a huge rattlesnake.

Blinking rapidly, she took in its diamond-shaped head and slowly undulating, dark, oval-blotched body, as it looked down at her from a sun-drenched boulder. *Shit, it must have been having a sunbathe, and then you interrupted it by clicking your stupid knuckles right under its bloody nose.*

Was the damned thing going to strike? Sarah thought they rattled to warn, so if she slowly backed away, she would show it that she meant it no harm. Didn't those wildlife programmes say that dangerous animals were normally more scared of us than we were of them? Looking into its beady eyes and watching its forked tongue slither in and out inches in front of her face, Sarah doubted that the makers of those programmes had been in the position she was in right now.

As smoothly as she could manage it, in a long dress and heavy boots, Sarah put first her left foot slowly and carefully behind her and then brought the right to meet it. She repeated this twice and the snake ceased rattling. It still continued to smell her with its tongue and remained coiled, however. But the immediate danger had passed. There was no way she was in striking distance now, and she felt relief rippling through her heart like a fresh mountain stream.

She grabbed the handles of the wheelbarrow and backed it away over the short prairie grass. Unless the snake suddenly became turbo powered, it couldn't get her, but there was no way she was turning her back on it for a while yet. The placenta still sat in the bowl, covered in a towel at the bottom of the snake's boulder. Martha would have to buy another bowl.

On the way back, no buffalo were in evidence, but Sarah could definitely see evidence of them having been there. The dung was in no short supply, and by the time she'd walked a few hundred yards, she nearly had a barrow load. The chips, as the dung was called, were dry, smelled mostly of grass, and after a while, picking up the light, disc-shaped pats didn't bother her too much. But she was bothered by the blisters on the palms of her hands and fingers. How was she going to milk Nellie properly with those?

At last back in the barn, she ladled water into a bucket from a barrel labelled *Drinkin' warder*. The large messy chalked letters indicated Artie's hand and perhaps the spelling too, but Sarah couldn't be sure as many of the homesteaders were illiterate. Though her mouth felt as dry as the dirt at her feet, she was loath to take a sip and instead, sat on the floor and eased her sore and tender hands into the bucket. The stinging sensation quickly gave way to cool relief and she sighed and leaned her head on her arm.

Soft hoof falls and a horse blowing down its nostrils behind her made Sarah turn her head. Artie, the naughty wanderer, had returned. He slipped from the horse's back and started to remove the saddle. He hadn't spied her sitting on the ground in the corner and whistled as if he hadn't a care in the world.

'Now you stay and rest up, boy. I'll git you some cool

water to slake your thirst.' Sarah noticed the animal was white with sweat; Artie must have ridden him like the wind to get back so quickly.

He wiped the sweat from the horse with a twist of straw and then picked up a bucket. Stepping round the horse's stall to get to the barrel of water, he saw Sarah, and nearly jumped three feet off the ground. 'Snakes alive, Ma, you scared the sh ... life outta me!'

Despite her painful hands and the fact that she was supposed to be angry with her son, she threw back her head and laughed. She couldn't believe that people really did say snakes alive! And she certainly thought the phrase was apt, considering her recent encounter with old 'hissy fit' out on the rocks.

'Aren't you angry with me, Ma?' Artie asked, smiling with relief.

'A little. You were told not to go out to Abe's but you went anyways. But, life's too short and too precious to waste it whuppin' ya. Just milk Nellie for me and we'll say no more.'

He nodded, a grin splitting his handsome face from ear to ear. 'That's what Abe's daddy says. He don't never whup Abe.' He gently lifted one of Sarah's hands out of the bucket. 'What's happened to your hands?'

Sarah nodded at the wheelbarrow full of buffalo chips.

'But you fetch those chips all the time and your hands are OK.' Artie ran his hands through his shock of blond hair.

'Well, never mind that. Milk the cow, water the horse and then I have a surprise waiting indoors for ya.'

'You do? What is it?'

Sarah put a wet finger to her lips and shook her head.

'Well, I have one for you, too. Mrs Reiner sent us some bread and fresh churned butter. They got plenty up there.' Artie ran back to the horse, grabbed the saddlebag and showed her what was inside. 'Oh, and some jam, too. They said now Joe's gone, we need all the help we can git. Ain't that kind?'

'It sure is, boy, it sure is,' Sarah said, wishing that Joe would be friendlier to the Mennonites. Artie was certainly being influenced by their ways and that would bring a clash between uncle and nephew when Artie became a young man.

Later that evening, Sarah sat at the foot of Martha's bed and smiled as she watched Artie holding his new cousin as if she were made of china. In the lamplight, the house looked more cosy and welcoming. Sarah had made the porridge with Nellie's milk and though it was lumpy, it hadn't tasted half-bad. Martha hadn't raised the issue of Artie running off and seemed as pleased as punch as she looked fondly at her nephew cooing over her sleeping daughter.

Sarah sighed and felt that her mission was over. Every muscle in her body ached and her brain cried out for sleep. Perhaps tomorrow she'd wake up in her own bed … or even better, John's.

Chapter Twenty

Four days later, Sarah still hadn't woken up in her own bed at home, or John's. She was still stuck in 1874 and was beginning to panic. She had saved little Elspeth, hadn't she? She'd had hiccups so she must have been *meant* to save her. What if she was stuck here permanently? Perhaps the powers that be had decided she had to be punished because she'd said before that she was going to stop stitching, or because she'd had the audacity to smuggle a scrunchie.

Sarah could see them in her mind's eye, pointing spindly fingers at her from their medievally sparkly sleeves. In Munchkin voices they'd say, 'Sarah Yates, you will be doomed to collect buffalo shit, live in filth, suffer tornados, torrential rain, drought, grasshopper plagues, rattlesnake strikes, and lumpy porridge for the rest of your unnatural life!'

John had said that some reluctant Stitches had legged it and were brought back in disgrace. Others had just taken to their beds and refused to do the job once they were in the past. But Sarah hadn't done any of these things; she'd accomplished her task and willingly, so why was she still here, for God's sake? And there wasn't a damn thing she could do about it, was there? And what had happened about work? She could only hope that time had passed much slower in the present, like it had when she was in 1913.

So … day four. Artie had gone off to the Reiner's again, this time with Sarah's permission. They had done an hour of learning his letters and numbers together, he'd done a few chores, and then he'd been allowed out. It was as Sarah had expected. The nearest school was fifteen miles away, so Artie's schooling was down to them.

Martha had insisted on getting on with things as normal

and was making bread, and Sarah had cleaned the house as best she could and was now minding little Elspeth. She was a delight. She only cried when she was hungry or needed changing and she seemed to take a genuine interest in her surroundings.

'Can you see if she needs changin'?' Martha asked. Her lips were drawn into a tight pucker, the middle of her forehead folded to a frown. Sarah had noticed that she'd been in a foul temper all morning; she'd assumed it was down to discomfort from giving birth, but Martha had just shaken her head and tutted when Sarah had suggested this.

'I just changed her about half an hour ago, Martha. What's the matter with you anyways? You said you weren't in no discomfort but something's eatin' you, just spit it out,' Sarah snapped. She wasn't in the best of moods either, trapped in another time, not knowing when, or if, she'd ever get home.

Martha dusted her hands of flour and put them on her hips. 'I'll tell ya what's wrong. I don't like the fact that Artie's gettin' all cosied up to them Mennonites. Joe'll be crazy mad when he gits back.'

'Oh, for Pete's sake, they're good folk. Didn't they send us some vittles the other day?'

'They just did that so they can git on our good side. We don't want Artie gittin' all yeller.'

Sarah shook her head. 'If you think not killing other folk is cowardly, or "yeller" as you say, then I want my boy to be just like 'em. Don't you think over half a million dead Americans are enough?'

A flicker in Martha's chocolate brown eyes told Sarah that she had made sense, but she sniffed and said, 'Well, all I'm sayin' is, Joe won't see it that way.'

'Move your arse over a bit, Nellie,' Sarah puffed, leaning into the cow's flank. She grabbed the milking stool in one hand and the bucket in the other and prepared to do battle. Nellie had stood as meek as a kitten when Artie had milked her, but every time Sarah went near the beast, she kicked up her back leg, or twisted round on her rope, anything to make Sarah's milking career a troubled one.

A dribble and a splash was all Sarah had collected five minutes later and she was getting hot and bothered. 'Damn you then, you silly cow!' She got up from the stool and walked over to the barn door for some air. That, like the milk, seemed in short supply. A hot breeze, hardly strong enough to blow an ant over, puffed intermittently, and the heat haze over the plains moved everything under it in a crazy dance. To Sarah's eyes, every blade of grass, insect, and buffalo in the distance flickered and shimmered under the relentless July sun.

She took an iron bar leaning next to the *Drinkin' warder* barrel and prised the wooden lid off the top. Quickly, before any dust or flies could enter, she dipped a short ladle in and drank deeply. Phew, that hit the spot. She wiped her chin with the back of her hand and wondered how long it would be before she had the luxury of just turning on a tap ... or pulling a flush. The outside toilet here was unbelievably disgusting and Sarah had opted to use the bushes instead.

Fixing the lid back on the barrel, she turned to resume the fight with Nellie. As she did, her eye picked out a couple of dots drawing closer across the prairie. After a few minutes it became clear that there were three dots – horses and riders, and one of the figures took off his hat, waved it to and fro, and yelled. Sarah thought she caught the word 'Ma!' Walking out to meet them and shielding her eyes she could make out Artie, but the other two were strangers, of course.

The horses put on a bit of a spurt and soon they all trotted up to the barn. 'Hey, Ma, this is Abe and a friend of the family, George. They come to visit and they brought seed for plantin' and more vittles.'

They all dismounted and George strode towards her, removing his brown felt hat and clutching it to his chest. He was tall, muscular and, though he wasn't John, did resemble him, especially around the eyes. 'I am pleased very to meet you much,' he said, and then turned bright pink.

Sarah nodded, shook his hand and tried not to laugh at his muddled sentence, though not in a derogatory way. She thought it was most endearing, and the way his eyes crinkled at the edges made her heart miss a beat. What the hell? Crinkly eyes, most endearing? Hang on, Sarah; don't start getting gooey over another one.

'Pleased to meet you too, Artie's mother,' Abe, a tall, gangly, red-haired youth stuck out his hand.

'I am very pleased to meet you both, and thanks for our vittles the other day, and today,' Sarah said, nodding towards the bulging saddlebags.

'We got some sacks of seed too, Ma. Abe's Pa said it's tougher than the seed we git from back east. Where they come from in Russia the land is like arn, hot in summer and cold in winter,' Artie said, dragging a sack in to show Sarah. 'It's wheat, not corn, and we gotta plant it in the fall but it won't die through winter – ain't that summin'?'

'It sure is summin' but it ain't stayin' here,' Martha's cold voice came from the other door across the barn.

Everyone gawped as Martha strode towards them with a hunting rifle over her arm. Her mouth was set into a thin line and she stomped the sack of seed hard with the heel of her hobnailed boot. The sacking ripped a little, releasing a trickle of reddish tinted seed.

Sarah put her hand to her head. *Red seed ... Doh! Of course!* That's why Sarah had heard of the Mennonites before. Yes, they were a religious group, pacifists, strict

Christians, but the most important thing was that they had brought Turkey Red wheat seed with them from Russia. As Artie had explained, the wheat could survive extremes of weather and so did just fine on the plains. Reports said that the wheat saved many homesteaders' lives and had helped turn Kansas into a top wheat-producing state, right up to the present time.

'Git that sack back on the horse and then y'all git off my property,' Martha spat, cocking the rifle.

'Whoa, Martha, you don't want to be doin' that ... Just let's all calm down and talk this out,' Sarah said, stepping towards the sack of precious seed.

'Nothin' to talk about as fer as I can see. These folk ain't welcome and neither is their seed.'

George stepped towards the sack and twisted his hand around the neck. 'Looks like there's no pleasin' some, ma'am. Don't worry, we'll be outta your hair now.'

'Wait a minute, George, I'm sure Martha will see sense,' Sarah said, turning to Martha. She realised two things. One, she had to make Martha accept the seed, because that was obviously the key to their survival, *and* the reason that Sarah was still trapped there, and two, if Martha relented, Sarah could be home in a matter of hours or even less.

'Why don't you just accept it, Martha? What's it gonna hurt?'

Martha looked at George. 'You carry on, Mr Mennonite; I ain't listening to my sister.'

George hoisted the sack over his shoulder and narrowed his eyes at Martha. 'For your information, ma'am, I ain't Mennonite, but they have been real kind to me since my wife passed on and our crop failed. They gave me work and food in my belly, and they just wanna help you too, if you'll let 'em.'

Martha snorted. 'My husband ain't passed on, unless you

think Wichita is heaven.' She took a step towards George. 'Now this here rifle is loaded and cocked and if you don't git, I swear I'll part your hair with it, Mennonite or no.'

Just then, from the house, baby Elspeth sent up a plaintive wail. This gave Sarah a crazy idea. Crazy or not, that's all she had. She marched past Martha towards the door of the barn. 'You need to come with me back to the house now, Martha; I have something to tell you that's strange but true.' She stopped and turned to the others. 'My sister and me got some talkin' to do, just wait a minute till we come back, OK?' She looked at George and he nodded.

Martha shook her head. 'I ain't goin' nowhere till they're gone.'

'Oh, yes you are. I got a message from our poor Ma that's for your ears only,' Sarah whispered, stepped out of the barn and hurried back to the house.

That did the trick. Martha went after Sarah and walked into the bedroom just as Sarah was lifting Elspeth out of her cradle. 'There, there, my sweetheart, did you wonder where we'd all got to, huh?' Elspeth stopped crying, opened her mouth and pushed her head into Sarah's chest. 'She wants feedin'; now I suggest you tend to your baby instead of trying to kill the neighbours.'

'I'll git to feedin' her as soon as you tell me what you meant about our poor ma,' Martha said, walking out of the bedroom and sliding on to a chair next to the table. Pink spots of colour flushed her cheeks and her breath came in short huffs. Sarah realised she must still be exhausted from childbirth and the heat was making things worse.

Sarah walked over to Martha and handed Elspeth over. She pulled up a chair, leaned her elbows on the table and looked into her sister's eyes. 'OK, you are gonna find this real hard to swaller, but last night I had a dream.' Sarah wondered if Martin Luther King would pop up and tell her off for what she was about to say. 'In this dream, three men came a-ridin' across the plains with gifts for little Elspeth here ... It was kinda like in the Bible, with the wise men an' all.'

'What's this lollygagging'? I don't see what this has gotta do with our poor ma, or those Mennonites,' Martha said, swatting a fly from her nose and putting the baby to her breast.

'I'm comin' to that. So these three men bring grain and vittles ... and wait for it, Martha.' Sarah jumped up and raised her hands above her head. 'Our poor ma appears right by their side, points to the men, raises her hands to heaven and ses, "These are the friends of the child that bears my name; we accept your gifts with thanks, and forever shall you be welcome in my heart and in my home."'

Martha's mouth fell open and she blinked. 'You saw our poor ma in a dream, and she said that?'

'She did, indeed.'

'But, we ain't seen no three men, there's only a man and a boy in the barn.'

'Yes but they came a-ridin' over the plains just like in my dream,' Sarah said, with a faraway look in her eye. 'Artie, George and Abe, I saw them as I was takin' a drink and I felt all peculiar like.'

Martha shifted in her seat and Sarah could see she was swallowing this hook, line and sinker. 'All peculiar like, what do ya mean?'

'Like our poor ma had her hand on my shoulder. I could almost feel her fingers, a cool, light touch. And a perfume hung in the air ... couldn't quite put my finger on it ...'

Martha leant forward, her eyes shiny with tears. 'Was it that Florida water she had once, smelled of oranges?'

'That's it, exactly like oranges.' Sarah nodded. She felt a fraud, but if it meant that the seed would get planted and Martha's family would survive, then so be it.

Martha stood, handed Elspeth over to Sarah and buttoned her dress. Tears streamed down her face, leaving little traces in the film of dust that had settled over her cheeks while she'd been outside. She nodded to herself as if answering an internal question and then walked out of the door.

'Where ya going?' Sarah called.

Martha's voice carried back to Sarah on a sudden gust of wind. 'To invite our neighbours for a bite to eat.'

A good few hours later, they all gathered once more in the barn. George, Abe and Artie hadn't been told of the reason behind Martha's change of heart, just that it had to do with her poor ma. They had enjoyed a nice early supper of the bread that Martha had made, and some fresh boiled eggs from the barn chickens. The vittles of butter, cheese and pickles that George and Abe had brought added to the banquet. Artie remarked that they hadn't eaten as well for some time.

After George and Abe had saddled their horses and made ready to leave, Martha took Abe to one side and showed him Joe's tools. 'Because you have been so neighbourly, anytime you need to borrow anything just ask. Joe won't mind,' she said. Artie joined them, saying how his uncle was one of the strongest men he knew and that he could work out in the fields all day without stopping to rest once.

George nodded over at them and said quietly to Sarah, 'I guess your boy misses havin' a pa. He told me he died a few months before he were born.'

Sarah nodded, looked into George's eyes and was relieved to realise that she was only attracted to him because the 1874 Sarah was. George was sweet but he wasn't John. She sighed. 'Yes, I guess he does miss having a pa, and I miss having a husband.' She looked down and fluttered her eyelashes. The least she could do was give the right signals.

OK, perhaps not the most subtle signal, but Sarah figured that guys in the Old West needed a clear map to follow.

Perhaps soon Artie would get a pa, the 1874 Sarah would get a husband and they all would live happily ever after. Well, as happily as anyone could on the plains in those days.

George leaned in close and whispered, 'Would it be alright if I stopped by again, Sarah? Perhaps next week, we could—' he cleared his throat and ran his hands through his hair '—we could go for a ride together.'

She gave him her widest smile. 'That would be a nice thing to look forward to, George, thank you.'

Martha, Elspeth, Sarah and Artie watched George and Abe ride away, literally into the sunset.

Not long after, Sarah slid into bed, pulled the sheet over her and looked out of the tiny window at the black velvety sky sprinkled with diamond chips. A coyote howled at the full moon hanging in the firmament like a giant Christmas bauble, and Sarah closed her eyes. Such beauty should be shared lying next to the one you loved. So, all happy ever afters here, but would she ever get hers? A tear ran from the corner of her eye, but before it had soaked into the pillow, Sarah was sound asleep.

Chapter Twenty-One

Washing-up liquid, in the bedroom? Sarah sniffed again. And anyway, where the heck had Martha got that from? Not even the industrious Mennonites could have manufactured modern-day mild, green and kind-to-your-hands detergent. Opening her eyes Sarah found herself not in bed, but back in her kitchen standing at the sink in exactly the same position as when she'd left. Lowering her eyes she found that the long dress, apron and boots had been replaced with her jeans and sweatshirt.

Through the window, the garden had lost its mysterious and otherworldly look, as the grey morning was now bathed in warmth and light. The birds sang, the green grass rippled in a slight breeze, and next door's cat prepared another hole under the Silver Birch.

Sarah glanced at the clock – 11 a.m. My God, she'd left at 5.45, that was only five and a quarter hours, and she'd been away four days. 'Time flies when you're having fun' didn't begin to cover it. She sighed and rubbed her eyes. Well, all things considered, this had to be a bonus. Even though the whole thing felt very strange, she at least had the rest of Saturday and Sunday to recover before returning to school. Apparently she'd been asleep, but felt in shock at the mismatch in time, bone weary and decidedly grimy. A nice shower and a cup of tea seemed like a plan and the height of luxury compared to the way she had recently been living.

Turning from the window, she immediately noticed a piece of paper folded in half on the kitchen table. She picked it up and flicked it open, her heart turning somersaults when she saw who it was from:

Hey, the hero returns! The report this time was phenomenal. Not only did you save little Elspeth, you saved the rest of 'em too. Martha persuaded Joe to let them plant the seed and they prospered so much in the next few years that they could afford one of those wind pumps you told me about.

Now I expect you're wondering what happened to Sarah and Artie. Well, George and Sarah got together, they planted the Turkey Red too, Sarah had another child, a girl who she called Martha, and Artie grew up to be a senator! He was responsible for paving the way for all manner of early civil rights bills, and little Elspeth ... wait for this ... are you sitting down? No? Well sit down now then.

Sarah laughed aloud and sat at the table.

OK, she was the great great great grandmother, of, let's just say one of the most important leaders of the free world. And no, I can't be more specific ... but he's fairly recent.

'Oh my God!' Sarah said out loud and punched the air. 'Woohoo!' All of a sudden everything she'd been through over the last four days seemed very much worth it.

So, I understand that you will be back in the present at around 6 p.m. this evening. I have taken the liberty of shopping for a special meal and have splashed out on champagne. You deserve it, given everything you have been through, and ... I do realise it must have been difficult finding out that you were a parent.

We'll talk more about it all this evening. I am desperate to see you and long to kiss your beautiful lips and a few other places as well!

Come as soon as you are ready,

Love you indescribably, everlastingly and forever and more gooey stuff like that too,

John XXXXXXXXXXX

Just reading the letter made Sarah go weak at the knees, her heart skip a beat, the colour rise in her cheeks and every other cliché used to describe how a woman feels when she's in love. Bringing the letter to her face, she inhaled every trace of faintly lingering cologne, kissed his name and each kiss he'd placed at the end. Then she put it back on the table and dragged her weary arse upstairs to the bathroom.

Slipping her clothes off, she wondered why John assumed she wouldn't be back until this evening. Perhaps the powers that be weren't as accurate as they thought they were, or perhaps they were rewarding her. She *had* saved the life of the great, great, great granny of one of the most important men in the world right now, after all.

The hot water pounding on her head felt heavenly and she set to work scrubbing the dust out of her hair with a liberal application of her favourite shampoo. '*I'm gonna wash the plains right outta my hair and send them on their w-ay …*' she sang, wiggling her bottom and flicking water from her feet in time to the tune.

She spent a good half-hour getting scrupulously clean. Her awareness of body odour had returned with a vengeance and she realised she stank horribly, probably worse than the skunk she'd briefly encountered near the barn the other day, if that were possible. This prompted another song, to the tune of 'Two for Tea' but the lyrics were entirely made up. 'Slam dunk the skunk, 'cos I'm meeting me hunk, and he ain't no monk, da da da dada …'

Hair dried, nails filed and painted, various hirsute regions shaved and waxed, and every inch of skin clean and moisturised. So, was she ready for action? No. She obviously couldn't have slept long when she'd gone to bed under the full Kansas moon. Time traveller's jet lag leadened her limbs and her eyelids felt as if they'd been replaced by two copies of *War and Peace*.

Now the big fat question was, did she have a few hours' snooze and go over early to surprise John, or did she sleep a little longer, do a bit of school work and go over for around seven? The sensible part of her brain opted for the latter, though Sarah didn't feel particularly sensible today. Setting the alarm for 3 p.m., she conked out as soon as her head touched the pillow.

By 4.30 p.m. Sarah was up, wonderfully refreshed and dressed in a red, silky, low-cut dress and strappy sandals. Her hair and make-up were perfect – well, as perfect as Sarah could get them without going to the salon and beautician – and a cloud of expensive perfume accompanying her every movement wafted sensuously into her nostrils. John wouldn't know what had hit him.

The expensive perfume was courtesy of a tester spray in Boots. She'd popped into town to buy John a surprise gift, and had only passed the perfume counter on her way through. An assistant had pounced on her and asked if she'd like to try a squirt. But she was now proving difficult to shake off.

The young woman held up the perfume again, one hand on the stopper, the other underneath the bottle, as if presenting it as a prize for being the most gullible person in the shop. 'Oh, but it *is* a very good offer, madam, and we of course will gift wrap it for you today,' she said in a particularly annoying sing-song voice. Sarah thought she could give the evil school receptionist, Gillian, a run for her money regarding the thickness of her make-up, and her eyelashes looked as if a tarantula had taken up residence, dangling thick black hairy legs from each lid.

'Gift wrap it today?' Sarah asked mischievously. 'So if I came in tomorrow would you refuse?'

The assistant looked confused and blinked the tarantula legs a few times. 'Oh no, madam, we always gift wrap for our valued customers.'

'So, what about your unvalued ones, do you just chuck it in a scabby carrier bag and that's it?' Sarah couldn't help it; the assistant had only pounced because she was dressed up. If she'd been dressed as normal in jeans, she wouldn't have warranted a second glance. Sarah had also told her three times she didn't want to buy the stuff. Maybe one day when she had won the lottery, but her purse wouldn't run to it just now, especially since she had set aside quite a wedge for John's gift.

'*Hee-hee-hee*, I think you have a great sense of humour, madam. No, all our customers are valued,' tarantula eyes said, shifting from one leg to the other, already looking around for more 'normal' potential buyers.

'I'll tell you what,' Sarah said, leaning in close. 'If my boyfriend asks me to marry him tonight after wild passionate sex because of this stuff I've got on, I'll pop back and buy some. I'll even let you gift wrap it for me, how's that?'

The assistant turned bright red, difficult to do under so much slap, and said, 'Err, yes, ha ha, hope you have a nice evening.'

Still grinning five minutes later, Sarah stopped outside a jeweller's. The joke about marriage had been just that, but was she perhaps, on some subconscious level, expecting that tonight? The diamond rings in the window certainly looked very attractive. *Here you go again, running before you can toddle*. Sarah wasn't here for those; she was here to buy John a very appropriate gift – a time piece.

Pulling up outside John's cottage half an hour later, she flipped open the black case and examined the watch again. Was it too much? They hadn't known each other for long and here she was buying a watch that had cost a week's wages. It had a chunky silver strap and so many gadgets that it could probably travel through time, as well as being able to tell it. Its face was unpretentious yet beautiful. A bit like it's soon-to-be new owner's. Taking the lid firmly in her fingers she pressed it shut for the final time. *Stop faffing and get in there, you daft bat. He loves you and is dying to see you.*

Walking on her tiptoes, so her heels didn't click-clack on the hall tiles, Sarah sneaked into the kitchen to surprise him. A few large potatoes sat on the table. A potato peeler was propped up against one of them, and what looked to be two steaks marinated in a bowl. Bottles of olive oil and wine vinegar were open and a lemon had been cut almost in two, but the knife hilt still stuck out halfway down. That was odd. Perhaps he'd left everything and gone to answer the phone or something.

A little giggle of excitement and a tickle of mischief ran around her tummy. She'd carry on tiptoeing and then when she saw him, she'd yell, *OK, FBI, you're under arrest for Time-Needling without a warrant!* That should be a laugh.

Sarah put her head slowly round the living room door. All clear … perhaps he was upstairs then. Ah, no, the gauze curtain at the end of the room caught her eye as it puffed and fell. The patio doors must be open; John was probably setting the table outdoors. It had been a pleasant day and it should be warm enough to eat out, she imagined. Holding her breath, she tiptoed in and towards the patio doors. She could see that they were indeed ajar and heard music, she thought Coldplay, wafting in from outside. How perfect was this guy? Champagne, cooking a lovely meal, setting the scene outside with music and ...

The tinkle of a woman's laughter cut across the music like a knife wound to her ears. Sarah halted abruptly, mid-tiptoe, in the middle of the room. The little gift bag containing the watch swung to and fro from her wrist and her heart thumped to ground floor. What the hell should she do now? There could be a simple explanation and she could be a friend ... or his sister, yes, Sarah remembered that there had been a little girl in the family photo she'd seen. She exhaled and continued her approach in half-tiptoe mode. If his sister was out there, Sarah was hardly going to leap out yelling FBI, was she, but at the same time she wanted to keep her arrival fairly quiet just in case. *Just in case of what, Sarah?* The little voice of doubt had showed up again. *Just in case the laughter belonged to the other female on the other photo, Sarah, is that what you mean?* it said, gleefully.

Sarah reached the curtain and through it, could see two figures sitting at the table outside. Her heart was beating faster and her mouth was dry. They appeared to be drinking wine, but she couldn't see properly as the gauze obscured a clear view. Her hands shook as she nipped the edge of the curtain between forefinger and thumb and drew it to one side slightly. Her throat thickened and tears sprang into her eyes. The figures were drinking wine. One was John and the other wasn't his sister, or just a friend, it was Josephina.

In that instant, the dream of a lovely reunion, a night of passion, a diamond ring and a happy ever after, bounced off her radar, out of orbit and into the stratosphere. In her haste to get out of there, she span round and, unused to wearing high heels, tottered to one side, knocking over a side table complete with china vase. Cr-a-sh! *Bollocks! They couldn't have failed to hear that!*

Setting off at a run, her heels did for her again when her left one got stuck down a join in the stripped pine floor and down she went, pain shooting through her ankle as she joined the side table and vase on the deck.

John burst in, closely followed by Josephina. 'Sarah? What are you doing here and what the hell happened?' John asked, kneeling by her side.

Sarah bit the inside of her cheek to stop herself from losing control and bawling her eyes out. She rubbed her ankle; it was sore but she could wiggle it and it wasn't as bad as she first feared. 'I don't know, I just turned and tripped ... I came back early.' She looked up from her ankle at his worried face and lowered her eyes again. She couldn't cope with his pity.

'Oh dear, si, that ankle looks fat and puffy, Seera,' Josephina breathed, her eyebrows knitting together and blinking her stunning dark eyes in an attempt to show concern. Sarah knew that her ankle looked perfectly normal; the woman was just being a bitch.

'It's fine actually,' she snapped. 'If you'll help me up, John, I'll get going.' There was no way she would try to hoist herself up in *that* dress, with a sore ankle, in front of someone who looked like she'd just stepped out of *Vogue*. Sarah imagined that she'd either fall over again, or rip the dress from top to bottom. That would be the final insult to injury.

Josephina had on a similar style of dress to Sarah's, but it was a deeper red and infinitely more expensive than her high-street number. It clung to her immaculate body and rode up her tanned, toned thighs as she crouched by John. She managed to balance on heels twice as high as Sarah's without any trouble whatsoever.

'What do you mean, you'll get going? I'm cooking us a meal, remember?' John said, putting his arms under her arms and yanking her up.

Sarah put her foot gingerly to the floor; it would hold

her. She had to get out of there before she burst. 'Yes, but I just got a phone call from my sister, she came round to mine unexpectedly, she wants to talk, must be her husband upsetting her again.' Sarah hobbled towards the door.

'But ...' John began.

'Is this yours, Seera?' Josephina interrupted, waving the little gift bag she'd picked up from underneath the broken vase.

'Err ... yes, well it *was* for ...' Sarah shook her head and grabbed the bag.

'Can't you stay a little longer, Sarah?' John walked over and took her hand. 'Josephina just dropped by on the off chance ... She'll be going soon.' He looked at Josephina pointedly.

'Si, I guess I should call a taxi soon, though it would be nice to raise a glass to my Johnny's new friend.' She flashed a row of perfect teeth at Sarah, but the warmth of the smile stopped short of her eyes.

Her Johnny indeed, and new friend? God, Sarah would love to pull out Josephina's shiny long tresses by the roots. 'No, I must go, Ella needs me,' Sarah muttered and limped out to her car.

Where are the fucking car keys! Behind the wheel now, she rifled through her handbag for the third time. The tears in her eyes didn't help and then John banged on the window.

'Sarah, come on, please stay a little longer ...' he shouted, motioning that she should lower the window.

She flicked her tears away and opened it a crack. 'I can't and to be honest, John, this was never going to work, was it? I mean, the whole time-travelling thing is mad. I want a normal relationship, with a normal down-to-earth man.'

He put his palm on the window and shook his head. 'You don't mean that. I know how you feel, you said you loved me and ...'

'Yes, well, it wasn't real, not properly. I was just caught

up in the emotion of it all I guess.' Sarah found the key and thrust it into the ignition. Why was she saying all this to him? It was certainly a heap of crap; it felt as if her mouth had a mind of its own. 'So I suggest you go back to the lovely Josephina. She's incredibly beautiful and obviously thinks she made a mistake dumping you, or why would she be here?' Sarah started the engine.

Right on cue Josephina walked out of the cottage and raised a glass in Sarah's direction.

'So why did you come here today dressed like that and with a gift for me?' John asked, his brow furrowed, his mouth a hard line.

'Oh, it was a goodbye gift, I guess. An appropriate one to mark our relationship such as it was, and I thought I'd dress up for our last dinner, that's all.' She shrugged, opened the window more and shoved the watch at him.

John didn't open it. His eyes met hers and she noticed tears forming. 'Josephina means nothing to me now, Sarah. You know that you're probably just being tested, too? Look me in the eye and tell me I don't mean anything to you.' His voice cracked.

She looked at him and then at Josephina and then back at John. She saw Karen and Neil all over again. There was absolutely no way that her heart could go through all that again. She would love to believe him, but how could she be sure that it was just the powers testing her? He might have just said that to cover up his philandering. Sarah looked at the pain in his eyes and wanted to say I love you, I adore you, I worship the ground you walk on. She heard herself say, 'I'm sorry but you don't. Bye, John.'

Sarah reversed the car and drove away. Through her tears, in the rear-view mirror, she saw John open the gift box and put his hand to his head, and just as she turned the corner, Sarah saw Josephina walk over and take him in her arms.

Chapter Twenty-Two

Someone had got their hand clamped over her mouth. Sarah lay still and forced her eyes open. It was light, she was belly down on the settee in the living room, the television in the corner displayed static dots and she felt something hard against her groin. Hell, was someone trying to rape her? Quickly reaching for the hand, she pulled it from her mouth and twisted off the settee on to the floor in one fluid movement. Ouch! The heel of one of her shoes stuck into her bottom, and pins and needles raced through her hand like a nettle sting.

She was alone. No rapist lurked behind the settee. She realised what had happened and gave a wry smile. She had slept on her hand which had caused it to feel like someone else's, and the hard thing pressed against her groin was ... an empty wine bottle that had somehow become wedged underneath her after her binge-drinking session.

God, she felt rough. On her hands and knees she crawled to the bottom of the stairs. She was still in the red dress from last night, though it appeared to have acquired a few dubious stains since then. The stairs towered above her like the summit of K2 but she needed the loo and so there was nothing else for it. By the time she had crawled to the landing, beads of sweat were standing all along her top lip and a wave of nausea started a tsunami roll deep within her gut. *Oh shit, there's only one way this wave is going and that's up!*

The cool of the ceramic toilet bowl felt soothing on her forehead. It wasn't the most hygienic of resting places but she had no choice. The first tidal wave was safely in the toilet, but another was on its way. How had she got so shitfaced? Yes, there was one empty bottle on the settee, but she'd had a bottle before, not often, but when she had, she'd felt queasy but not completely ruined like this.

The answer came after vomiting a second time. She splashed water on her face and then went in search of a clean towel. Opening the airing cupboard another empty wine bottle presented itself. What the hell …? Ah, yes, a flashback … Sarah sitting on the loo singing 'I'm Not in Love' at the top of her lungs, whilst drinking the last few drops of red wine straight from the bottle. Then, finding she was out of toilet roll … opening the airing cupboard and taking a roll out with one hand and shoving the empty bottle in with the other. Yep, it had all seemed perfectly logical … last night.

Squeezing toothpaste on to her brush, she gently cleaned her vomitty mouth. So, what exactly *had* she done after she got back? Sarah remembered all the pain and humiliation of what had happened at John's and then returning home, but that was about it. The reflection in the mirror of a woman at least a hundred years old said *don't even ask*.

An hour later, showered and wearing clean clothes, she felt little improved, so decided to return to bed. There was serious wound licking to be done. Lying there with her eyes closed she felt the room spin. Opening one eye she half-expected to have arrived in ancient Rome and been tasked with trying to warn Caesar about keeping his knife drawer locked, or speeding up to JFK's cavalcade and throwing herself down before it in the road, shouting, 'Turn back, Mr President, or you may lose your head!'

She wasn't in either of those places though, sadly. She was in her bedroom, imitating a wet lettuce, a slug sliming under her soft green folds and munching its way through her brain. The room was only spinning because she'd poured two bottles of wine down her gullet, and judging by the carton on the kitchen floor, a family sized pizza from the freezer. Luckily she had been conscious enough to cook it.

Turning carefully, she pushed her face into the comfort of her pillow. Was it just because every fibre of her being yearned for him, or could she actually smell John on it? He *had* stayed here last week; it felt like a lifetime ago. Inhaling again, she decided she was just being fanciful.

Why had she told him a pack of lies yesterday? His lovely green eyes had been full of love and pain in equal measure when he'd asked her if she still loved him. How could she have been so cold, so cruel? Sarah drew her knees up and hugged them to her chest but found no comfort. A foetus in a cold womb, devoid of compassion and humanity, that's what you are, Sarah.

Beep, beep, bee, bee beep!

A message on her mobile. It sounded as if it was in the hallway. Did she have enough energy to get all the way down there?

Wrapped in a duvet, she perched on the bottom step. The pounding, rushing sensation in her head started to abate enough for her to lean forward slightly and retrieve the mobile from the scattered contents of her upturned handbag. Three missed calls with voicemails and four text messages, all from John. The first one was at 5 p.m. yesterday and the last one was just now. She checked them in order.

Voicemail 1 – Saturday – 5 p.m. – Sarah, please come back, I know you didn't mean those things, I can see why you were upset. You must have thought the worst seeing Josephina here like that. I swear she just turned up out of the blue. She'll be gone in a minute; I'm ordering her a taxi. It is you I love.

Voicemail 2 – Saturday – 6 p.m. – Josephina has gone;

she hung around insisting that I needed a friend as I was so upset. She even suggested that she stay for the meal I was preparing for you! I told her I was in love with you and her ship had sailed. Please ring me. And did your sister really come round, or was that an excuse?

Voicemail 3 – Saturday – 7.30 p.m. – Please, Sarah, ring me or text, anything to let me know you are alright … that we are alright. I can't drive over as I've had a drink, but I could get a taxi. I need to know if your sister is there, as I'd feel a proper Charlie turning up if she's pouring her heart out to you … She's not there is she, Sarah … I can feel it. You're breaking my heart here.

His voice broke on the last word and Sarah felt her eyes fill up and brim over. Another flashback … her flipping open the phone, seeing the texts from John and each time flipping it closed without reading … Her again, swigging wine and stuffing pizza, ignoring the insistent ringing from her handbag, turning some music up on her CD player and tossing her hair defiantly. Sarah shook her head now. What a stupid bitch.

Text message 1 – Saturday – 9.15 p.m. – *I really hope you will be back to normal tomorrow. You had a very tough time in Kansas and that may have clouded your judgement. It can't have been easy being Artie's mother, too – knowing how you feel about wanting children. I need to see you. I won't come round until you ask, but don't leave me like this for too long. I can't bear it. And the watch is so beautiful, thank you, I always wanted one like this. xxxx*

Text message 2 – Saturday – 10.15 p.m. – *OK, I'm*

getting the hint. I won't try to reach you again. I know you're upset about Josephina, but we were having a drink, not in bed together, for fuck's sake. I've poured my heart out to you tonight, begged you to come over and you just left me drangling ... dangling, as you can tell, I've had a drink can't spell for toffee... and now I'm going to bed ... do what you like. xxxxx

Text message 3 – Saturday – 10.30 p.m. – *Goodlight, Sarah, please contact me tomorrow, I do love U and I'm sorry I wasangry in th last message, it was just grustration. xxxxxxxxxx*

Text message 4 – Sunday – 11.15 a.m. – *Sarah, I'm worried about you. Text me back just to let me know that you are alright, or I'm coming over. Don't you realise that this is just another of the obstacles put in your way? My parents had ones just like this but they overcame them. You should have had time to think by now, and if you meant what you said yesterday, I'll have to accept it. I can understand that our life together would be hard, and as I said the other week, nobody would blame you for opting out. I can't make you love me, but just know that I will always love you, John. xxx*

Sarah stood up and went to the kitchen to get tissues. What should she do? Her heart, predictably, said, 'ring him and tell him you're sorry and get over here pronto.' Her head said, 'there is no way you could stand to be hurt again like last time.' A flashback of herself a year and a half ago on hearing her best friend Karen had given birth to her ex-husband's baby ... drunk, in the bath ... one hand tipping a bottle of painkillers into the other ... the hand coming up to her mouth.

She had come close, too close for comfort. And now she'd found John, loved him so much that it hurt ... and then this catwalk model waltzes back into his life. Yes, he'd said it was over between them, that the powers were testing them, and that she was the one, but Josephina *was* back. Sarah had seen in the other woman's eyes that she wasn't about to give John up without a fight.

Sarah blew her nose and poured a glass of water. Was she ready for a fight? She thought about her behaviour last night. That'll be a no then. And besides, wasn't the bit she'd told John about wanting a normal relationship and settling down true? He would always be a Time-Needle and that was about as far away from normal as you could get.

And it sounded as if his parents had a rough time over the years, too. No, it wouldn't work. Also, she'd always be wondering if he'd go back to Josephina and that would do her head in ... *Face it, Sarah, you're a mess and a hopeless case. He'd be better off with Josephina anyway ...*

In her pyjamas, Sarah wandered into the garden and sat under the pergola. The roses growing over it nodded their heads on a warm breeze, their perfume sweet and fragrant. Was it only a few weeks ago that she'd sat here with John? She smiled as she remembered how he'd revealed that the 1940s' John looked like him, because Sarah had wanted him to look like someone she cared about. *Ha! That was the understatement of the year.*

The mobile sat on her leg like a tiny weapon of mass destruction. What she was about to do would destroy her happiness, but hopefully would preserve her mental state (such as it was), and protect her heart from being ripped out and shredded. There were only so many times a heart could stand that kind of treatment.

She took a deep breath, opened her phone to messages, and typed:

John – don't come over. Sorry I didn't answer your texts and messages. My sister Ella didn't come round, you were right there. I was angry and upset because of Josephina, but to be honest it really doesn't change much. The rules against Stitches and Needles being together are sensible. We need to end it. I can't see how we could be happy, so I guess I have been tested and found wanting. Josephina can make you happy if you let her, I'm sure of it. Our time together was great fun, if off the scale in terms of surreal! I expect I will have no memory of you or my adventures soon – better that way. All the very best for the future – Sarah x

A message came back in a few minutes. Through her tears she read:

Then there is nothing more to say. I was kicked into touch by Josephina, and I mistakenly thought that you would never be so cruel. Seems I was wrong. It will be a very long time before I let anyone else go for the hat trick. And yes, apparently you have until the end of the week to keep our memories. There is one last job 'they' would like you to do because someone has dropped out, and because of your roaring success with the others. I told them that this was very unlikely, as you didn't even want to do the last one.

I was going to be churlish and just put 'John' at the end of this. But I can't be like that. Love you, John xxx

Sarah rocked to and fro, sobbing, for the next twenty minutes. Next door's cat startled her, by patting her leg with its paw, as if to say, 'Hey, what's wrong, is there something I can do?'

She was about to shoo it away, but something about its

beautiful green eyes made her feel closer to John and she scooped it up like a baby, squeezing it to her chest. The cat's sympathy didn't extend to scooping and squeezing, and it wriggled free, but it settled on the bench next to her, purring.

The cat's smoky-grey fur was warm from the sun, and as she stroked it, Sarah's sobs subsided. Didn't they say that stroking animals was therapeutic? Perhaps she'd get one; hell, she might even get six. When she had first moved to this house after her marriage had broken down, she'd considered getting a cat, but a kitten would have been too demanding – Sarah could barely look after herself at the time.

Now might be the time to rethink. She smiled. 'The Cat Woman' would be her new moniker. For miles around, people would talk in hushed tones about the nutty woman who lived on Meersbrook Street, with 125 cats, who never went out, apart from nights when the moon was fat and full, who always dressed in black and paced the alleyways yowling most horribly.

'Barnaby, where are you? Din dins!' On hearing his owner's voice, the cat flew from the bench, sped across the lawn and over the garden wall faster than a cruise missile. Sarah sighed, alone again … naturally. At times like these, a girl needed her best friend. Since hers had buggered off with her husband, Sarah didn't really have one. She had a few friends from uni she still kept in touch with, a couple of acquaintances from work, Ella, and her mum, but how would she go about explaining John to them anyway? Yes, the time-travelling experience could be omitted, but then the whole picture wouldn't be clear and … She shook her head.

Besides, they had enough of their own troubles, too; she couldn't burden them with it. Ella had problems with her husband being out of work and they argued loads, and her mum was still getting over her dad seven years on. The way Sarah was feeling she'd probably blurt out that John was a

Time-Needle and then they'd really have something to worry about. No, it wouldn't be fair to share … would it? *Oh, for God's sake, Sarah, what difference does it make anyway? You've made your decision, so live with* it.

Her tummy told her she should probably try to eat something, so she stood to a stretch and dawdled up the garden path, pausing to admire the herb pot John had brought over for her recently. 'Nothing like a few fresh herbs straight from the garden to perk up a meal,' he'd said, presenting her with a handful of basil for their bolognaise sauce.

Sarah bent over and rubbed a basil leaf between her finger and thumb and touched her fingers to her nose. The pungent aroma sent her straight back to that evening. John had thrown a strand of spaghetti at her kitchen wall. She wondered what on earth he was doing, until he explained that if it stuck, it was ready to eat, if it fell off, it needed a bit longer. She sniffed. Perhaps she was just a bit of undercooked spaghetti – too spineless to stick to anything.

Where the hell was the tin of soup she'd seen only the other day? Sarah shoved packets and tins around her cupboard as if they had personally affronted her in some way. One particularly hard shove sent a tin of beans rolling from the shelf on to her toe. *Thunk!*

Ouch! Serves you right, Sarah, bullying the contents of your kitchen cupboards; it's hardly their fault that you have wilfully dumped the love of your life, is it?

The tin of tomato soup had been found, heated up and now sat in front of Sarah on the table. She had added a few basil leaves for old time's sake and swirled them under the surface with her spoon. A few thoughts tumbled around her fuzzy head. What if the powers that be as part of the test had deliberately told John that Sarah would be returning from

Kansas later than he thought? What if they wanted him to spend time with Josephina, knowing that Sarah would walk in on them? What if they wanted them to split up because they thought that if Sarah needed to settle to a normal life, had the baby she so desperately wanted, she might persuade John to abandon Time-Needling? What if she'd just walked into their trap, and right at this moment, as she was sitting here eating the soup, they were rubbing their spindly little hands together and flapping their medievally sleeves at each other in triumph?

She took a sip of soup. Hang on, that couldn't be true, could it? John said that they wanted her to do another job. If she'd abandoned John and the whole time-travelling malarkey, then why would she do another job for them? She gulped another spoon of soup and a basil leaf. Unless ... it was a big fat double bluff ... and they thought that she'd take the mission because she was so miserable in the present, she would take the job because she was so desperate to escape. Yes ... they must be very clever these folk, entities, spirits, whatever they were, or they wouldn't be called 'the powers that be', would they? Ha! Well she was smarter!

But, as Sarah got ready for bed that evening and another school week stretched ahead of her like a death sentence, the idea of another jaunt started to seem more appealing. What did she have to lose, anyway? It couldn't fail to take her mind off John, and as long as she could communicate by text so she didn't have to speak to him, it would be fine.

Setting the alarm and turning off the light, Sarah admitted to herself that the only reason she was considering another time job, was that she wanted to keep contact with John. But no good would come of it ... What would be the point of delaying the inevitable? A picked scab never healed, her gran always said. John was probably being consoled with his head clasped tightly to Josephina's heaving bosom at this very moment. *Sleep on it, Sarah. See how the land lies in the morning.* The John substitute, Thomas the teddy, was bear-hugged to within an inch of its life and five minutes later, Sarah had slipped off to oblivion.

A little while later, the bedroom door opened quietly and John tiptoed over. He looked at her face illuminated by the moonlight spilling across the sill and before he could dash it away, a tear rolled down his face and splashed on to the teddy. He placed a gentle kiss on her forehead. 'Sleep well, my darling, I love you,' he whispered and then tiptoed out again.

Chapter Twenty-Three

Was he a wuss or was he a hero? John absently sprinkled three spoonfuls of brown sugar into his coffee and stared out of the café window at the passers-by. Half of his brain said the former, the other the latter. Perhaps, therefore, he was somewhere between the two. After all, he had heroically poured his heart out to her, baring his soul, declaring undying love by text and voicemail, but then he'd wussed out when she'd said that it was over; just rolled over – accepted it.

He spooned three more heaps into his coffee and stirred and decided the biggest wuss factor was not insisting that Sarah stayed put the other night when she'd come round and found Josephina at his. Yes, obviously Sarah had been in a rage, lashing out at him and saying things that he hoped she hadn't really meant. But that was to be expected given what she'd just been through. She was definitely not herself after spending the longest time in nineteenth-century Kansas, being Artie's mum, delivering babies, living in filth, and he could have tried a bit harder to make her see reason, couldn't he? Why hadn't he just told Josephina to piss off right there and then? That would have helped smooth the waters straight away. And on top of that, she was obviously terrified about him repeating what her ex had done to her.

John lifted the cup and took a sip of coffee and took all his resolve not to immediately spit it back out again. He screwed up his face and forced himself to swallow. The waitress noticed and she frowned in return. 'Something wrong with the coffee, luv?'

'Err ... no ... I mean, yes,' he mumbled, feeling like a chump. 'But it's my fault. I think I put too much sugar in.'

'Oh, right ... I could get you another?'

'No, it's OK, thanks. I have to be off anyway.' John scraped back his chair and stepped out into the street. The waitress had looked at him as if he was a bit simple. Perhaps she wasn't far wrong there.

Even though it was a lovely June day, John didn't notice. He thrust his hands into his jacket pockets and just let his feet carry him. The hero versus wuss debate continued unabated in his head. With the same absence of mind he'd had guiding the sugar spoon, he was surprised to soon find himself in a park a few streets away from the café.

The scent of the freshly mown grass and the sounds of the ducks quacking contentedly on the nearby pond muscled into his jumbled thoughts. A heartfelt sigh escaped his lips and at last he stopped and looked around at the lovely day. Children squealed and laughed in the nearby play area, dogs ran alongside their jogging owners, people cycled, others picnicked, made daisy chains, couples walked hand in hand and John's heart ached for Sarah.

A bench on a hill looked a good place to sort his head out, and once seated he looked across the landscape. From this distance the park looked like a Lowry painting but with added colour. So ... was he a wuss? John allowed himself to be brutally honest and examined his feelings objectively. He realised after a few moments that perhaps he was more of a hero, with only a smattering of wuss, but it brought him little comfort.

Josephina, he concluded, had been allowed to stay because he loved Sarah too much. Perhaps subconsciously he couldn't ask her to sacrifice her life to this crazy job after all, and Josephina's presence made it more likely that Sarah would leave him. Afterwards when Sarah said by text that she didn't want him, he'd continued to be a hero by rolling over – letting her go. Yes, he'd told her how he felt and begged her to reconsider, but had he gone round there, hammered on her door, camped out on her front drive until she'd changed her mind? No. Well, he *had* gone round when she was sleeping and then left again, but that didn't count and was firm evidence of wussdom.

John's fingers plucked a blade of grass growing through a gap in the bench. He chewed on the juicy stem thoughtfully. And now it looked as if she could be off on another mission anyway. Hopefully it would be her last, and in a short while Sarah's memory of stitching and him would be wiped, and then she could go back to normality.

What would his life go back to, though? Without Sarah he didn't have one, just an empty gnawing feeling in his chest where his heart used to be. Deciding that being a hero was pretty shitty, John stood and set off down the hill. If by some miracle Sarah came to him and told him she'd made a mistake, then he was sure that they could make it work somehow, but it would have to come from her. A grim smile played over his lips; only a wuss would ruin it all by giving in to his feelings now.

Chapter Twenty-Four

Three days later, Sarah splashed water on her face in the school loos. It was break time and she mentally crossed the first two lessons off her teaching day. Danny Jakes had taken the starring role as usual, but he'd not been anywhere near as bad as before. Perhaps she was getting the better of him, or perhaps she had just learned to ignore his annoying ways in return for a quiet life. She suspected the latter.

The next lesson was a free period, then lunch, then double Year 10. Not so bad. It would be weird talking to them about the homesteaders, having so recently been there, though. In an odd kind of way she was looking forward to it; at least her mind would be occupied and she would be afforded some respite from the pressing decision about whether to accept the job or not. All week that precise question had been buzzing incessantly round her brain like a demented bee. She was erring towards taking it. It was Thursday tomorrow, so she'd better make her mind up soon.

Janet Simms breezed in just then and stopped, caught like a rabbit in the headlights. 'Oh, hi, Sarah.' She sidled past, avoiding Sarah's eyes.

The poor woman was really freaked out by her. It wasn't surprising, given the way Sarah had acted the last time. Just at that moment, winding Janet up seemed a very silly idea. How juvenile she'd been.

'Look, Janet, I just wanted to say that I'm not mad … I'm just sad,' she blurted. 'Lots of odd things have happened in my life lately, the most recent being the break up with the love of—' Sarah's face crumpled like a screwed-up tissue, and her voice harrumphed out into a sob '—my ... my li-fe.' She covered her face with both hands and blubbed for England.

Sarah realised what the neighbour's cat must have felt like yesterday when she'd scooped it up and squeezed it. Janet stepped forward and was doing the same to her, and although she meant well, Sarah felt herself suffocating in Janet's candyfloss hair. Squeezing her thanks to Janet briefly, she stepped back, pulled a paper towel from the dispenser and blew her nose loud and long.

'I'm sorry, Janet. I didn't mean to lay all this on you. It just came out.'

Janet raised her eyebrows and put her head on one side. 'Now listen here, young lady, there's no need to apologise to me; I've been there, done that and bought a return ticket for more. Just tell me everything, get it off your chest, sweetie.' Janet had returned to her normal earth-mother self, and shot Sarah a wide smile of relief. She was obviously glad to find Sarah less unpredictable.

'No, I'm fine thanks, just got a bit too much that's all.' Sarah shrugged, dampening another paper towel and wiping the running mascara from under her eyes.

'Nonsense, let's grab a coffee and go to my room. I have some lovely choccie biscuits with your name on them, too. My ears are yours for the next twenty minutes.'

Even though she realised that her heart couldn't be mended with a few choccie biscuits, Sarah could do worse than use Janet as a sounding board. There was no one else to turn to, well apart from Ella or her mum, and she'd decided that wouldn't be fair. But she certainly needed to talk. 'Well, if you're sure ...'

'I wouldn't ask if I weren't. Now just tidy your face up a bit more while I have a little wee.' Janet entered a cubicle and locked the door.

Sarah rolled her eyes and stuffed bits of paper towel into each ear to avoid a Niagara rerun.

'So, that's about the size of it, Janet.' Sarah sighed, perched on the edge of Janet's desk and stuffed the remains of a third biscuit into her mouth. She washed it down with a gulp of coffee and wished that she could be like other people who couldn't touch a morsel of food when they were upset. It always worked the other way for her. Whenever she was seriously down, she ate anything and everything, as if she were a bear preparing to hibernate over a Canadian winter. When Neil had dumped her, she had gained a stone within four weeks. It had taken her three times that to lose it.

Janet picked up the box of biscuits and held them out to Sarah. 'Another?'

Sarah shook her head and folded her arms to prevent her hand disobeying her brain.

'Well, it seems to me that you overreacted. The poor bloke can't do much more than he has already to make you see sense.' Janet bit into a biscuit and wagged the other half at Sarah. 'And to be honest, I expected more from you. Josephina is determined to fight you for him, so what do you do? Wimp off home with your tail between your legs.'

Sarah's hackles went up at that. 'I told you why. My heart couldn't survive another pasting like last time.'

'Right, yes, so just roll over and die, huh? That's the best option. Go through life only half a woman, existing rather than living and, hopefully, in a few years' time, you'll get knocked over by a bus and all the pain will be gone.' Janet slammed her coffee mug down, jumping liquid out over her desk.

Sarah frowned. Janet's eyes flashed with frustration, anger, or both and her bottom lip was trembling, as if she were about to cry.

'Sorry to make you angry, Janet, but I nearly didn't make it the last time.'

'I *am* angry, but not with you per se, just I can see you making the same mistakes that I did. As I said before, I've been there done that … I had two marriages go sour on me when I was very young, so for years I kept my heart in bubble wrap for exactly the same reasons as you.' Janet paused and looked out of the window at the kids howling in the yard. 'One guy, Michael, was the nicest you could ever wish to meet. He kept asking me to settle down, but I strung him along over five years before I eventually said yes. We had two wonderful years together, but then he got cancer and died.' Janet looked back at Sarah and blinked away tears. 'That was five years ago and there isn't a day goes by that I don't regret being a stubborn, stupid cow for keeping him dangling.'

Sarah felt her throat thicken and lowered her eyes. The pain in Janet's was too much to bear.

Janet stepped forward and put a finger under Sarah's chin, forcing her head up. 'Don't be a stubborn, stupid cow like I was, Sarah. Go to him tonight … Tell him you were wrong.'

Sarah swung into a parking space in front of John's garden shop at 4 p.m. that afternoon. She'd flown out of the classroom bang on the 3.15 bell and driven like a bat out of hell straight there. Janet's story had put everything into perspective and Sarah had been so glad she'd chatted to her.

Wednesday was Roy and Helen's day off and so John ran the shop on that day. He had young Tanya from the nearby village to help out in the afternoon, but Sarah remembered that John had told her he'd be all on his own this Wednesday, as Tanya was on work experience at the vets. Sarah thought that after she'd eaten a huge slice of humble pie, she'd help him lock up and then she'd treat him to dinner out.

The old-fashioned doorbell jingled as she pushed the handle and walked in. Closing the door behind her, she took a deep breath. The smell of earth-fresh produce mingling with the perfume of a few gift items – scented candles and joss sticks – whooshed up her nose like the scent of heady perfumed blooms in a bouquet. Such a great shop, it had that old-fashioned appeal and did very well from the surrounding areas.

John didn't seem to be around. Perhaps he was in the back making a cuppa. She was just about to step through there, when she heard a voice from behind the counter.

'I weel be with you shortly, just opening a box, feel free to browse.'

Sarah felt as if she'd been run through with a corkscrew. Her gut twisted, contracted and she felt physically sick. Josephina appeared a second later with a million-dollar smile on her face, but it froze into a sneer when she saw that the new customer was Sarah.

Apart from mascara, her face was bare of make-up. She was dressed in jeans and a blue T-shirt and her lustrous hair was scraped back into a ponytail. Sarah thought she still looked better than she ever could, even after hours in a salon and a beautician.

'Oh, what do you want?' Josephina said, all pretence at politeness and nicety dropped like a ton weight.

'I came to see John. I know he works here on Wednesdays.' Sarah's voice sounded calm and normal. She ought to go on the stage.

'He has flu, so I am come to his rescue.'

Sarah felt a little relieved; perhaps Josephina was a last resort because he had no one else at such short notice. 'Oh, I'll pop up to the house and see him then ...'

'I'd rather you didn't, Seera.' Josephina narrowed her eyes and shook her head – a strange jerky movement as if she'd just got a nasty electric shock. 'John was very upset the weekend. I moved back in on Monday, he was feeling a little poorly and I have been looking after his every need.'

The 'every need' was said in a way that left Sarah in no doubt about what she meant by it. The bitch could just be lying, of course. Sarah would put nothing past her. 'I'll just go along and see for myself,' she said, turning for the door.

'If you want to be humiliated ... go along. You had your chance, but you didn't fight for him. "Finders keepers, losers criers", Seera.'

Sarah turned back to face her, a flush racing up her neck and cheeks. 'It's "losers weepers" actually, and what the hell do you mean, humiliated?'

Josephina shrugged and leaned against the counter as if she belonged there. 'He told me he loved you once, but he would *never* take you back now. He also said you were far too possessive and clingy.' A triumphant smile curled her lips. 'He couldn't believe that you were so jealous of our engagement photograph that he had to remove it. How insecure of you, Seera. John hates that. We were together a long time, I know him inside and out.'

Dumbstruck, Sarah stood there feeling like a complete idiot. He had told her about the photo? How could he have been so cruel? All the rousing words from Janet, all the taking life by the scruff of the neck speeches she'd given herself for the remainder of the afternoon, and all the girding of loins bravado act she'd practised, had turned out to be for nothing.

He didn't want her after all ...

The other night, John had told her in a text that the Josephina ship had sailed. Well, she looked like she was very much back in safe harbour, with her anchor dropped deep into his seabed. Tears tickled the back of her nose and she turned and fled before Josephina could gloat anymore.

The drive home gave her time to think and make a decision. She felt strangely calm, and, borrowing a title from an old rock song, 'comfortably numb'. The bee that had buzzed incessantly all week had been released back to the hive.

Three hours later, she'd marked a pile of exercise books and prepared lessons for the rest of the week and next Monday, too. Planning ahead was key; she'd be busy this weekend. Whatever happened she would take the mission, but there was a phone call she needed to make. Sarah took the phone in her hand and took a deep breath. 'John—'

'Sarah ... thank God!'

'I just rang to ask if it is really over with you and Josephina.'

'Yes, of course! She's nothing compared to you, you know that.'

Sarah closed her eyes and prayed he'd tell her the truth. 'So you haven't seen her since the time that I came back early and she was there?'

There was a pause on the end of the line and she heard him exhale. 'No, she left and that was it. I told her I wanted nothing more to do with her.'

Sarah felt her heart plummet. So why the bloody hell was the bitch in your shop? 'You're sure?'

'Of course.'

That response was about as honest as a conman. Sarah's hand gripped the phone so tightly her knuckles were white and her voice trembled. 'I've made a decision. Tell them I'm up for the job. Tell them I'll be ready early Saturday morning. Bye, John.'

'But why? Sarah, we need to talk about us.'

'There is no us, John,' she snapped and ended the call.

Sarah threw the phone across the room, punched a cushion and bit the edge of her thumbnail. The bitch had been telling the truth then. On the way back home in the car she'd told herself that even though John had clearly allowed her back into his life, as there she was, large as life in his shop, somehow Josephina must have had a stab in the dark about the removal of the engagement photo and come up with the right answer. After all, the woman would grasp at any straw to get John back.

Sarah had also told herself that she was stupid and weak if she just accepted what such a conniving cow might say, so the phone call was supposed to have given John a chance to come clean. She'd deliberately kept quiet about having been to his shop earlier to see how he'd reply to her questions. Now she had her answer.

The phone started to ring and of course the caller's ID was John. She didn't pick up. She didn't pick up the next twenty times, either. If this was part of some big test, she had SO had enough of it. If she allowed this to carry on she'd be back in the bath, drunk with tablets in her hand and there was no way she'd let that happen. Life was too precious; her dad would have certainly agreed with that.

Sarah dashed tears from her eyes, turned off her phone mid-ring and went to bed.

Chapter Twenty-Five

Sarah woke early on Saturday morning with the smell of lemon in her nostrils. The alarm clock, inches from her nose on the side table, said 5.45. Déjà vu. Had it only been a week previously that she'd stood at her sink and then stepped into a ruined cornfield? At least her life hadn't been in ruins then. Sarah had been in love, and confident that she'd be with John for the rest of her life. Now ... like the cornfield, it was in pieces; destroyed.

Even her dreams tormented her. The lemon that John had been cutting on that fateful day made an appearance, just before she woke. As John inserted the knife, a red fountain had spurted instead of lemon juice. The lemon had cried out in Sarah's voice, *If you cut me, do I not bleed?* Then the lemon turned into a heart and a hand shot out, curling talon-like fingers around it. The heart, still pumping, bulged out between the fingers, *Da-dum, da-dum, da-dum.* Josephina laughed manically, squeezing it tighter, bringing it close to her mouth, and then, with her perfect white incisors, ripped it open.

John had tried to ring again a few times then he'd resorted to texting her the day after she'd spoken to him.

> *I don't understand why you are being so cruel, Sarah. What was the point in phoning asking a few stupid questions and then, saying there's no us? And the new job – are you sure you want to do this, Sarah? This one is quite a biggy. You have already saved your nine and more, so aren't obligated at all to take a 'passing the time'. Yet another corruption. It actually means that a Stitch has backed out and passed time to someone*

else. My mother often used to take jobs that others had passed to her ... she did around ten missions in total, but then she was the best ever Stitch in my opinion.

Anyway, this one could save thousands ... I have no idea why, they won't reveal anything, so you're back to square one if you take it. A ballpark date – somewhere in the 1920s, and London again. There is disapproval about our relationship; 'they' weren't happy when we were together, but now they know it's over, they're worried that you don't really care and are just taking it on because you're desperate to escape ... you're not are you? I hate to admit it but I think they were right about you after all, especially after your call last night. You obviously don't love me enough, but I don't blame you; it was just all too much for you. Please be careful, Sarah, and don't do anything stupid. Love, John xx

She didn't love him enough! That was flaming rich when he had the bitch of the year mopping his fevered brow, and probably attending to other parts of his body as well! And he told a barefaced lie about having not seen her even though she was in his shop! She couldn't believe he had the gall to say that he thought they were right about her after all. And that line about the powers that be thinking she didn't care *really* got up her nose. Yes, she wanted to escape, that was true, but she still bloody cared! Why the hell did they think she'd accepted the crazy job in the first place? She could have been another Norman, buried her head in the sands of time and stuck two fingers up to 1940, 1913, and 1874, but she hadn't. It wasn't in her. She loved the idea that the past was alive and interlinked, held together by a thread of humanity.

Right from being a kid, she'd loved history – really interacted with the stories she learned in class and things her parents had told her. Sarah tried to imagine the smell, sights, sounds, and to 'walk in the shoes' of people in the past. It had always felt so important to know what had happened; she couldn't really put her finger on why, it just felt ... necessary; a requirement to her being a 'whole' person somehow. John's explanation had really fitted with what she had felt for years.

Sarah had replied:

John. I am not even going to comment on the bit about not loving you enough. There's no point. I'm tired of thinking about the whole sorry mess. I am taking the job because I care, and the medievally sleeved spindly ones can stick that up their arses, if they have arses. And the doing something stupid? I did that when I allowed you into my life. I am desperate, but for another adventure; it's got under my skin. Sarah.

After she'd pressed 'send message', she realised that John might be a bit puzzled about the 'medievally sleeved spindly ones' reference. He'd work it out though, from the arses bit. She felt a bit childish saying that she'd been stupid letting him into her life. It wasn't true, but the way Josephina had smiled at her in John's shop the other day burned white hot into her memory. And the way he'd lied to her so easily on the phone made her feel sick to the stomach. Besides, if he really cared as much as he said he did, why hadn't he come round and seen her face-to-face?

John had replied later, just to say that everything was set for this morning and he wished her luck.

Luck could tag along if it liked, but Sarah wasn't banking on it. Two cups of tea later, up, dressed, and once more ready to step into the breach, she felt resigned and ready for anything. No longer a time-travelling virgin, she was so much more prepared and knew more or less what to expect. Well, that is what she told herself. It made her feel confident, in control. She had actively chosen to do this. How difficult could it be? *OK, that's enough chest beating, Sarah, you'll end up in the jungle.*

Sarah wondered about the wisdom of that second cup of tea and trotted upstairs to the loo. Sitting there staring into space, she wondered what London in the 1920s would bring. I could pop back and see Rose; that would be a laugh. Sarah smiled and blinked her right eye rapidly. Damned bit of fluff or something. She tried to pick it out, blinked again, but no, it was still there. Ah, got it.

Wiping the object on the back of her left hand, she saw that it was an eyelash. An eyelash that appeared to be moving, spreading, changing shape ... what the fuck? Her right hand smacked the thing, hard, tried to dislodge it, but it wouldn't budge; it just kept growing until she could see a scene taking shape. The back of her hand had become a tiny cinema screen. A street, presumably London, 1920s' cars, people, buses, a busy workday ...

Sarah finished on the loo and began pulling up her knickers with her right hand, still staring open-mouthed at the back of her left.

The next minute she was standing on the steps of a large, grand, brown-and-white brick building, and a middle-aged couple stood nearby, looking at her aghast. Lowering her eyes, Sarah realised they were looking at her knickers. She'd managed to pull them up over her 'necessaries' but the black, longish dress she now appeared to be wearing had been hitched up under her armpits in the struggle to do so. There she was, slap bang in the middle of the busy London thoroughfare she'd seen on the 'cinema' screen, showing her knickers to the world!

'Look away, Edwin, she's obviously one o' them street

walkers.' The woman of the couple looked at Sarah and wagged her finger. 'We only stopped you to ask the time. You looked nice, respectable! But you never can tell these days, women cutting their hair and wearing trousers, and them "Flappers",' the woman said, tutting and shaking her head. She pulled at Edwin's sleeve, who didn't appear to want to look away, still having his eyes fixed firmly on Sarah's crotch.

'Oh my God, I'm sorry!' Sarah cried, pulling her dress down, her face crimson. She noticed a few knots of people had stopped in the street and were nodding and pointing over at her. She half-expected Danny Jakes and his crew to show up any minute, guffawing and yelling: 'You hoping to get lucky tonight, Miss?'

'Now she's taking the Lord's name in vain! Come on, Edwin, let's get away from her.' The woman had to practically drag Edwin away; he had a glazed look in his eye and a stupid smile on his face. Panicking, Sarah looked up the steps. At the top, high above some double doors, balustrades and grand arches, the words *St Mary's Hospital* had been carved into stone. That name rang a very faint bell, but her main concern was to escape all the prying eyes and pointing fingers. So, having no better idea, Sarah ran up the steps and inside.

The long, Victorian, arched corridors seemed even busier than the street outside. Porters pushed, doctors rushed, and cleaners mopped. One of the cleaners, a small squat woman in her fifties, grabbed Sarah's arm as she stood gawking. 'Oy, Sarah. Chef was looking for you earlier, said if you didn't turn up soon, you'd be out on yer ear,' the woman said, wrinkling her nose as if she had a bad smell under it.

Sarah raised her eyebrows. So this hospital was where she worked? That revelation hardly filled her with joy. Hospitals in her time were not the healthiest environments in which to work, so a 1920s' hospital could be potentially lethal. She wondered if she could actually catch something, or would she be immune, coming from another time? Ha! That would serve John right if she caught some horrible disease and died. Sarah rolled her eyes. *Yep, but you'd be dead; bit of a snag with that revenge plot, love.*

'No need to roll yer eyes at me, I'm just passin' the message on,' the cleaner said, wrinkling her nose again. Sarah realised there was a bad smell, and yes ... it was coming from the bucket. Ugh, she put her hand to her own nose.

'Stinks, don't it?' The woman said flashing a row of yellow teeth. 'Been doin' the toilets just now.'

Jeez Louise, this was a hospital, didn't they know about germs? They must have done; this was sometime in the 1920s, and Pasteur proved germ theory in 1861. 'Hadn't you better get clean water for these floors then if you've been doin' the toilets?' Sarah noted her 1913 accent had returned.

The woman wound her neck back as if Sarah had slapped her. 'I am in a minute, just mind your own and get to the bloody kitchen if you want yer job. I won't bother tipping you off next time,' she grumbled, picked up the bucket and stumped away, the mop head swinging from side to side over her shoulder.

Sarah shrugged, turned and made her way towards a door bearing a sign 'Strictly Staff'. Opening it and stepping through, she immediately caught the smell of food wafting on an updraft from some steps to her left. Oh goody, the kitchen ... again. Sarah hoped that Chef would turn out to be a bit nicer than Cook. She wouldn't hold her breath though. She was apparently late, and that wouldn't get her off on the right foot.

She walked down the steps and at last had a chance to get a better look at what she was wearing. Because of her embarrassing arrival she'd not really taken it in. Hmm, an ankle-length black dress and neat, black lace-up flat shoes. Patting her hair she found it to be cut in a long bob and, pressing her lips together, decided she must be wearing a touch of lipstick. No jewellery or earrings, but then that would have to do with working in a kitchen, she guessed.

On the next flight down, a wheezy whistle could be heard, accompanied by the slow slap of feet on concrete steps. Sarah stopped, and a few seconds later a man appeared, carrying across his shoulder half a pig and a string of sausages. She had to flatten herself against the wall on the stairs to let the butcher squeeze past. He was a typical old-fashioned butcher, complete with bloody blue-and-white striped apron and ruddy cheeks.

'Hello, lass,' he wheezed. 'Chef's on the warpath for you.' Hoisting the carcass higher and puffing out his cheeks, he set off again on his slow steady ascent.

'Yes, thanks, I know,' she called after him. It seemed as if the whole complement of staff knew she was late; Chef must be quite a presence. Sarah was beginning to get an anxiety rash. She stopped and looked behind her. Was that an indication that she should save the butcher? No, she didn't feel it somehow; it was just an anxiety rash. She scratched her neck as she walked down the last few steps.

As to her mission, she still had no clue. Her attire produced no real giveaways about the date. The woman who she'd managed to upset outside had mentioned Flappers. Sarah knew they were in vogue between about 1926 and 1928, and these young women had caused a stir when they had decided to wear daring, calf- and just-below-the-knee-length dresses. They had cut their hair into short bobs and smoked cigarettes. Their views on sexual practices were very risqué for the time, and some behaved promiscuously, even by today's standards. Sarah smiled when she thought of the tabloid press howling down ladette culture as if it were new. The Flappers were the first ladettes over eighty years ago.

'Oh, it's nice to see you smiling,' a tall gangly man remarked, stepping out of what looked to be a store cupboard opposite the foot of the stairs. 'You'd better wipe it off before you go in there. Chef is short-handed what with Maggie being off having the baby, *and* the butcher only just having brought the chickens.' He folded his arms and peered through round spectacles perched on a ski-jump nose.

'Yes, sorry, the er ... train was late.' Sarah smiled hopefully.

'Train? You only live a mile away, what were you doing on the train?' Gangly man narrowed his eyes.

Down the corridor, a door burst open and smashed back against the wall. A tubby man, in a chef's hat and grubby whites, stood in the doorway, his cheeks sucking in and out, puffing like an old bull.

'There you are, madam! Get in here and pluck those chickens if you still want a job at the end of the day!'

Sarah looked at him, rubbed her eyes and looked again. Nope, her eyes weren't deceiving her. The chef appeared to be Gary Keynsham. What the hell was her brain playing at now? She couldn't stand Gary, so if he was the one she had to save, shouldn't he be someone she liked?

'What you gawpin' at?' he said, almost apoplectic with rage. 'I'll give you five seconds and then—'

'I'm coming, Chef, sorry, Chef!' Sarah said, hurrying past him into the kitchen.

There looked to be about eight kitchen staff of various ranks. The ones of higher rank were shouting at the rest – the rest were running about like headless chickens. That observation led her to glance further across the room. On the table by a window overlooking a courtyard were six chickens. Sarah glanced at them and gulped. Her extent of chicken preparation hitherto had been taking the cellophane off, sometimes taking giblets out and then whacking it in the oven.

A thin-faced woman who had just sent an assistant scurrying out for lard marched across to Sarah and threw an apron at her head. 'Can you see the way Chef is eyeing you?' she hissed in Sarah's ear. Sarah glanced over to where Gary Keynsham was hacking a pork joint in half with an evil-looking cleaver. He was glaring at Sarah; his look matched the cleaver.

Sarah nodded.

'Well then, put that apron on and get plucking. I told you he'd be out for your blood if you turned him down.'

'Turned him down?' Sarah asked, throwing the apron on.

'Yes, when he asked you to the pictures last week of course. Now look busy.'

The woman scurried off to help a younger woman pick up a crate of potatoes and Sarah turned back to the chickens. She nodded and smiled over at Chef; he gave her a dirty look and carried on chopping. So Chef was like Gary in more ways than looks. A woman turns down his advances, his male ego is affronted, so he sets out to make her life a misery. Sexist pig. She wondered who the thin-faced woman was; she seemed like her only friend at the moment.

The chickens looked as if they had fallen asleep, and Sarah really didn't want to disturb them. She knew they were dead, obviously, but couldn't bring herself to touch them.

'Doris! Give Sarah her marching orders; she's just standing lookin' at them chickens as if she expects 'em to pluck 'emselves!' Chef bellowed to the thin-faced woman.

Sarah's heart sank. She'd not been here five minutes and she was already set to fail. *You opted for this mission, remember, snap out of it!* She turned to him. 'Sorry, Chef, I just feel a little queasy today ... I'll get to it now.'

Doris hurried over. 'Give her a last chance, Chef, I'll sort her.' She elbowed Sarah, and whispered. 'I know we are best friends, but there's only so much I can do to help you. Get on with it!' She turned her back on Chef and with lightning speed pulled a handful of feathers from the nearest chicken and shoved them in Sarah's hand.

'She's set to now, Chef!' Doris called, moving aside to allow the chef a clear view. He nodded grudgingly and walked off to shout at somebody else.

Gangly-man appeared silently at their side, as if he'd just risen up through a trap door. 'I'm not Kitchen and Cleaning Manager for nothing, I know what goes on around here, and you, madam,' he sneered down at Doris, 'will be tarred with the same brush as her if you don't watch out.'

'I don't know what you mean, Mr Ames,' Doris said, winking at Sarah and rushing off once more.

Mr Ames sidled close and put his hand on the small of Sarah's back. 'I think you should get on my good side if you want an ally against Chef, my dear.'

Sarah looked up into his rheumy grey eyes and was distressed to see a lascivious light kindling behind them. What was wrong with the men here? Were they all sex starved? She took a step to the side, coughed, and said in a small voice. 'Thanks, Mr Ames, I must get on with this pluckin'.' Though her movement had made him drop his hand, she could still feel the warmth of his handprint on her back. Shudder!

He folded his arms, leered at her and said, 'I bet you're a good plucker, aren't you, eh?'

Sarah looked at the chicken in front of her, and fuelled by pity and anger for all the poor women who had to put up with this kind of sexual harassment in the past, grabbed it and pulled out feathers almost as quickly as Doris. Ames smirked and sidled off again. God, he gave her the creeps; he seemed even worse than Chef, and that was saying something.

An hour later there were three un-plucked chickens remaining. Sarah had had no idea it would take so long. The smaller feathers were very fiddly and she had to use tweezers, which were making her finger ends sore. At least the tedious work had given her time to think. John had said that this trip was supposed to save thousands. Chef must be on the verge of discovering something like salmonella. Perhaps because he was angry about being turned down, he'd get careless, chop his finger off with his cleaver and bleed to death, and it was Sarah's job to stop that happening by agreeing to go out with him. She pulled a face and sighed. Still, if it saved thousands.

Blowing on her fingers, she picked up the tweezers and the fourth chicken. Hmm, salmonella and food contamination was known about by the 1920s, she was sure of it, so there must be another reason why Chef was so important. Her musings were halted by a milkman rattling a crate over in the far corner. He looked at a calendar on the wall, ticked off something and went out. 'I've ticked off today's delivery, Doris! Don't want Chef saying I forgot, like last week!' she heard him shout down the corridor.

The word 'calendar' jumped into her head and did a foxtrot. How had she missed that? She checked herself; she had been a bit preoccupied. It wasn't every day that a loose eyelash turned out to be the 1920s *and* then she'd had to contend with lecherous Larrys for the last hour. Served her right for thinking she was in control. Sarah wiped her hands on the front of the apron and rushed to the calendar; she must be quick before Chef returned. Lifting the cover, a black-and-white picture of the hospital, she saw 'September 1928'. She'd been close with the flapper reference of 1926–8 then.

A black tick had been drawn next to the number 28. Just then, Sarah heard footsteps coming along the corridor and flew back to her chickens.

The tweezers flew too, as she tried to rack her brains for a significant event happening on or around the 28th of September 1928 in St Mary's Hospital. Then it came to her like a lightning bolt slamming into her consciousness. Penicillin! Alexander Fleming worked here in the labs. He was Professor of Bacteriology!

'Danny, can you clear those feathers up that Sarah's plucked? And then, after break, that disinfectant needs takin' out to the labs. They delivered it here by mistake, stupid buggers, but it will give you a leg up if you know what I mean,' Chef bawled, as he stepped through the door.

'Yes, Dad, won't take me a minute.'

Sarah's fingers fell still, but her heart picked up speed; she'd know that voice anywhere. Turning round, she came face to face with Danny Jakes.

Chapter Twenty-Six

'Hello, Sarah, you look like you seen a ghost.' Danny smirked, as he swept an armful of feathers into a sack. Sarah was about to retort, 'Don't be rude, I think you'll find it's Miss Yates,' but stopped herself just in time.

'She ain't seen no ghost, she's seen unemployment loomin', that's what she seen, son,' Chef said, his chortle sounding like a gurgling cesspit.

'Ha ha, that's right, Dad, you gotta keep these women in their place. They may have got the vote a few months ago, but they should still do what us men tell 'em, right?' Danny looked at Chef and winked.

Sarah opened her mouth, closed it again and slapped the chicken down hard on to the table. Us men? Little shit couldn't have been much older than fourteen. *No point in getting angry. You have to figure out what the hell is going on here.*

She got to work on the chicken and kept one eye on Danny as he cleared the feathers and swept the floor. OK, so this was indeed the big one. She took a deep breath and allowed her knowledge of teaching GCSE 'Medicine Through Time' to run through her mind.

Sarah knew that mould that grew on bad fruit and cheese was spread by spores floating in the air. It had first been noticed by Lister in the 1870s. Spores had landed on the germs he was studying in his laboratory and weakened them. Though he found this fascinating, he'd not really done much with it; simply done a few experiments, made a series of notes and called the mould he'd discovered penicillium.

Fleming had 'discovered' it again accidentally in the same way, certainly in this year, and possibly on this day, yet it wasn't really made effective until Howard Florey and Ernst Chain got hold of it in the years leading up to WW2.

They had read an article Fleming had written about penicillin mould and set out to prove its worth by tests on mice and a willing human 'guinea pig'. They managed to get government backing and investment from big pharmaceutical companies to mass-produce it. It had been invaluable during the war and without it many lives would have been lost. Sarah couldn't believe how many times she'd set GCSE essays on this very topic. Students had to gather evidence about the input of Lister, Fleming, Florey and Chain and then write a conclusion about who was most important.

Sarah stopped plucking and felt a cold hand clutch at her soul. If she failed in whatever she had to do today, would that mean that when she returned to the future, penicillin wouldn't exist? That was a crazy responsibility to place on the shoulders of any one Stitch, or any number of Stitches for that matter. Surely, the powers that be wouldn't be so reckless.

A comforting thought suddenly occurred to her. John had said that time didn't always work like that – it was flexible. Perhaps there may be only subtle changes made to events, depending on the ability of the Stitch. She'd had fantastic reports so far, hadn't she, so why was she in a panic?

She sighed and answered her own question. Because, you daft bat, this is different to 1940, 1913, and 1874. Yes, she'd saved lives, and all were equally important in her book, whether Elspeth was the granny of a president or not. But this was penicillin they were talking about, one of the most important 'magic bullets' of the twentieth century and an invaluable antibiotic ever since.

Now she understood what John had meant when he'd said that this job could save thousands. By her reckoning, it had already saved millions and would continue to do so just so long as she got this right. She just wished to God she knew exactly what the consequences would be if she got it wrong.

Danny looked up from his sweeping and poked his tongue out at her. It looked like that little oik and his dad were the key to the riddle, and she wondered again, if she was supposed to save them, why hadn't her brain chosen someone she liked? More to the point, why would she *have* to save them? If she was here because of penicillin, wouldn't she have to save Fleming instead?

'Tea up, Sarah, Katherine, Jock and Fred,' Doris shouted, popping her head around a side-door. The named staff downed tools and trooped out. Sarah looked round and, realising that she must be the Sarah referred to, set down the one remaining un-plucked chicken and followed suit.

She found herself in a little offshoot kitchen. It had none of the state of the art (for 1928) facilities of the large kitchen, but it was cosy, had a long table and chairs, a fire and a stove. It reminded her a little of the one in 1913. 'Tea and biscuits there, you lot, no more than ten minutes as the other shift are waiting for their break too,' Doris said, and sipped her own tea. It seemed to Sarah that Doris was the backbone of the operation. Chef didn't appear to do much apart from make people's life a misery. Sarah slumped down at the table like a sack of spuds. Only an hour or so had passed, but she felt like she'd been there at least a day. A nagging headache was starting behind her eyes and she smelled like a wet chicken.

'Yes, help yourself to them, lad, I made 'em earlier.' Chef strutted in with Danny, pointed at the plate of biscuits and then scotched a young lad, Fred, Sarah thought his name was, across the ear. 'Keep your paws off them, the rest are for Danny. You've had at least four!'

Fred opened his mouth to reply, but a sharp glance from

Doris silenced him. Sarah heard him mumble under his breath, 'I've only had two.'

Danny's hand shot over Sarah's shoulder like a mechanical claw at a funfair, grabbed a huge handful of biscuits and withdrew quicker than the speed of light. He crunched his prize nosily, right next to her ear, and then picked up Fred's tea, slurping it down in one go. As a finale, he belched a thunderclap roll into her ear, too. Sarah dug her nails into her palms to distract her from leaping up and punching him in the face.

'Mr Flemin' back today, Fred?' Chef asked, pouring himself a cup of tea.

'Yes, I think so,' Fred muttered. He was still obviously angry about having his tea stolen and accused of eating loads of biscuits.

'You enjoy all that fetchin' and carryin' to the labs as well as doin' your kitchen duties then?'

'Yes, Chef, it makes for a bit of variety and that, you know?'

'And you think you might get to be a porter full time and go hobnobbin' with the professors and that when you get older, eh?' Chef winked at Danny over Fred's head.

Fred shifted uncomfortably. 'Um, I hope so, Chef.'

'So, you don't like the kitchen job, not good enough for you, is that it?' Chef folded his arms and frowned.

Fred looked up alarmed. 'No, Chef, that ain't it, I—'

''Cos Danny here, he loves the kitchen work and to be honest he's stronger than you. He might be able to do the fetchin' and carryin' to the labs an' orl.'

Fred said nothing, just looked panic-stricken.

'I might have a word to Mr Flemin' and one or two others about Danny; he's what's known as "grateful for his lot". He don't care about no variety, do you, Danny?'

'No, Dad, I just does as I'm told. I knows me place,'

Danny said, smirking at Fred with a nasty gleam in his eyes.

'Danny's gonna take that crate of disinfectant that got dumped here by mistake up to Mr Flemin', ain't ya, Danny? Save you the bother, Fred.'

'Yes I am, Dad. I best get to know all the lab assistants and professors before I gets the job, proper like.' Danny walked over to stand beside Chef.

Father and son wore the same peevish expression and glared a challenge to poor Fred. Poor Fred held their gaze for a few seconds, and then looked away; he was no match for such a formidable team of bullies.

Satisfied that they had won the point, father and son turned the talk to trivia, and the gathered staff made the most of the few minutes they had left of break. Sarah grabbed her cup and sipped her tea while watching Fred over the rim. The heat of his silent rage could have given the nearby fire a run for its money and Sarah's heart went out to him.

He looked to be about the same age as Danny, but lacked the other boy's confidence and mature stature. Fred was slight, pale, had mousy blond hair and, at the moment, looked totally defeated. He'd obviously set his cap at becoming a porter. Sarah imagined it wasn't much of a step up, but it was a step up nevertheless, and Chef had just moved the ladder – trampled on his dreams.

An idea was tiptoeing uncertainly around her mind, which involved Fred and the whole reason she was here. Sarah wasn't completely sure yet of how the whole thing was going to work but the crate of disinfectant scenario had made Sarah very excited. Sarah was so excited in fact that, whilst Chef had taunted Fred with it, she'd had to bite the inside of her cheek to keep from squealing.

Alexander Fleming had returned from holiday to work in his lab. Before he'd gone, he'd left a pile of Petri dishes containing bacteria in a container full of disinfectant waiting to be cleaned. The disinfectant hadn't covered all of the dishes, and spores of penicillium mould had floated in, probably from the kitchens below, and landed on the uncovered ones. When Fleming had examined those particular dishes, he found that the bacteria that had been covered in the mould were dead … the rest was history.

Sarah drained her cup and set it down in her saucer with a triumphant clatter. The idea formerly tiptoeing around her mind now stomped confidently towards a eureka moment. Tingles along her spine and hairs on the back of her arms standing up, confirmed her suspicions.

John had told her that she'd achieved her stitching in time and had saved her nine, even exceeded easily what was expected. But this was a different mission. Saving certain individuals was no longer her concern. She was now certain that Danny was unwittingly going to do something to jeopardise Fleming's discovery when he took the disinfectant up to the lab. She was also certain that the reason why Chef and Danny looked like the people she disliked was because she wasn't here to save them, she was here to stop them!

Break over, Sarah and the rest returned to their jobs in the big kitchen. Sarah knew she had to act fast, as Danny was going to take the disinfectant up to the lab after he'd finished eating everyone's biscuits. She had a plan; not a great one, but a plan nevertheless.

While ostensibly plucking the last chicken, she did a 360 degree sweep of the room. Doris was rolling pastry, Jock was chopping onions, Katherine was slicing bacon, and Fred was washing the floor. Chef was still having his break with the other staff. Just as Sarah was wondering exactly how to put her plan into action, Doris left the pastry, washed her hands and left the kitchen.

Sarah put the chicken down, took a deep breath and hurried over to Fred. ''Ere, Fred!' she hissed behind him. He jumped, knocked the mop heavily against the bucket, splashing water over his feet.

'Oy, look what you made me do.' He frowned at her. 'What you doin' creepin' and hissin' at folk?'

'Sorry, I need your help; it's a matter of life or death.' Sarah looked around to make sure Chef or Danny hadn't come in.

'Life or death?'

'Yeah, I haven't got time to explain, I just need you to take me up to Mr Flemin's lab, right now before Danny gets up there with that disinfectant.'

'Eh, what for?'

'I'll tell you on the way, so let's go.'

'You gotta be jokin'. Chef wants any excuse to get rid of me and give Danny all my jobs. If he catches me doin' that, I'll be sacked on the spot ... you an' orl.'

'I promise *you* won't be, and if I am, then so what? But we gotta go now.' Sarah took his hand and pulled him to the door.

'You'd better be right, Sarah. If I get the sack, me old mum will have no money comin' in. She's too ill to work 'erself.'

Fred led the way up three staircases and along two corridors. Sarah hoped this plan would work, because she would have Fred's 'old mum' on her conscience, as well as countless others, if it didn't. As they went, she told Fred that she had started 'walking out' with one of the lab assistants. The lab assistant had been angry when she'd told him about Chef's advances and Danny's nasty little ways, and he'd wanted to help teach them a lesson.

'But how did he know that Danny was going to start fetchin' and carryin' instead of me?' Fred puzzled. 'I didn't even know about it till just before.'

'Ah, well, there's been rumours goin' about.' Sarah tapped her nose. 'They've been plottin' a while, I think.' She then told him exactly what they must do once they were inside Mr Fleming's lab.

Fred shook his head. 'I still don't like it. What if it all goes wrong and *we* get into trouble, not Danny?'

'It won't; don't forget I have my young man to vouch for me, and Doris will back us ... probably.'

'I don't like that word "probably",' Fred grumbled, trotting up another flight of stairs. 'I've heard it too many times, an' it always turns out to be wrong for me.'

Fred stopped outside a room in a long corridor. He looked at her and rolled his eyes towards the door. Shoving his hands in his pockets, he looked repeatedly from left to right along the corridor so fast that Sarah thought his head would come loose.

'You trying to say this is the lab?' she asked, smiling at his attempts at non-verbal communication.

He nodded.

'Well, just stick your head in and see if the coast's clear. If Mr Flemin's already in there then we'll have to think again.' What she really meant was if Fleming was in there, then he'd probably be on the verge of discovering the mould on the uncovered dishes, and all would be well. She was almost sure he wouldn't be inside though, because if he were, there would have been no need for her mission in the first place.

'No, he ain't in there,' Fred said in a soft voice a few seconds later. He looked pale normally, but now he would be hard to find in the snow. Sarah hoped he wouldn't bottle it under the pressure of what she'd asked of him.

Pushing the door to the lab open, she shoved Fred in and then she slipped in quickly behind him. It was smaller than she had expected for the lab of such a grand discovery, but it was brighter and more personal, too. The walls were lined with shelves containing hundreds of glass bottles, test tubes and chemicals, but there was a window at the far end letting in sunlight. The light fell across a long, deep workbench under the window, and on that bench sat hundreds of Petri dishes, copper boilers, a few microscopes and Bunsen burners.

Hurrying to the bench, Sarah looked in the large tray and saw dozens of Petri dishes standing in disinfectant. There were indeed a few dishes not submerged under it. Her heart hammered in her chest, and adrenaline raced though her veins when she realised she was actually standing in the spot that would shortly hold a crucial place in the ranks of human discovery and progress.

Fred came up and stood by her side. He peered into the tray and then up at Sarah. 'What you lookin' so excited about? Hadn't we better do what you said before someone comes in?'

'Yes, you're right, we better had, Fred.' Sarah patted him on the shoulder and pointed under the workbench to the left.

A few minutes later, Fred was safely ensconced under the bench behind a stool and a few empty boxes. Sarah removed the white apron, crouched and slid behind a stool at the opposite end. She backed into the corner and on her knees, making herself as small as possible. She grabbed a box and placed that in front of her for good measure. Trembling with relief and anticipation, she felt as ready as she'd ever be. It wasn't a minute too soon.

Chapter Twenty-Seven

The door opened. Two pairs of legs entered. One was Danny's, the other was unknown. The unknown legs wore smart black trousers and shoes with a lab coat just visible above that.

'Thank you, Danny. Can you put the disinfectant on the floor at the side, and lift a bottle on to my workbench. I need to top up that tray. I haven't got round to cleaning the dishes in there. I'll be back shortly,' said the man in a cultured Scottish accent.

Sarah stared at the legs open-mouthed. Did they belong to whom she thought they belonged to? Danny answered her question.

'Right you are, Mr Flemin', sir, I'll do that right this minute. Is there anything else you'd like me to do while I'm here?'

'No, lad, that will be all, and don't touch anything, do you understand?'

'Yes, sir, I understand.'

'Can't think why Fred didn't bring it; he's normally such a good boy.'

'He's run off apparently, sir. You never know what he's goin' to do next my dad always says. Ee's always skivin' off any chance he gets, you know.'

Sarah glanced at Fred in the gloom under the bench and could see the glow of fury in his eyes and the murderous look on his face. Sarah caught his attention, held a finger of warning to her lips and shook her head. If Fred lost his temper and jumped out shouting the odds, the whole plan would sink.

'Really? He always seemed like a conscientious lad. Oh, well …' Fleming sighed and left the lab.

They watched Danny's legs walk to the side of the room and set the crate down. They could see there were two large glass bottles of disinfectant in it. Danny removed one and crouched down next to it. Sarah tried to flatten herself even further back into the shadows. *Please don't let him look over here under the bench!*

She needn't have worried; Danny was oblivious to anything but the task at hand. What was he doing? A squeaking, popping sound gave her the answer. He had just removed the stopper. Sarah guessed he was about to 'help' Mr Fleming by not just setting the bottle on the bench as he'd been asked, but by pouring some into the tray. He had expressly been told to not touch anything but, being Danny, was of course about to ignore that. She had suspected something like this and got ready to give Fred the signal. If they failed now, the Danny Jakes lookalike was set to deprive the world of penicillin.

Danny stood up and wiped his hands on his trousers. The smell of disinfectant was strong in the air. Danny bent, hoisted the bottle and walked towards them. Sarah thrust her thumb at Fred and he launched himself at Danny's legs like a Rottweiler. Danny hit the deck, cracking his head heavily against a stool. He rolled in agony, eyes closed, hands reaching up to his head. '*Aaargh* ... what the f—?'

Sarah shot out from her hiding place and wound her apron twice round his face and head. She pulled the material tight, stifling obscenities and his cries of surprise and anguish. Meanwhile, Fred smashed both disinfectant bottles to smithereens, ran to the door and held it open for Sarah. She unwound the apron at lightning speed, letting Danny's head bounce to the floor once more, and then sprinted over to Fred. Fred quickly checked the coast was clear, then they took off like greyhounds along the corridor.

At the far end, they turned a corner, stopped, and Fred

peeped back around. He flapped his hand at Sarah, signalling her to keep behind him. 'Mr Flemin's just come along and gone in his lab,' he whispered.

Next they heard a yell and then Danny shouting, 'I'm not clumsy, Mr Flemin', really I'm not! Somebody attacked me and smashed the disinfectant; they must have been big and strong, 'cos they overpowered me so quick!'

Sarah and Fred giggled at that.

'No, sir, I'm not lying ... yes, sir, I know how it sounds ... no there's no more disinfectant ... but ... well, can I help you pick up all this ...'

'GET OUT!'

Danny flew out of the lab into the corridor as if he'd been forcibly ejected on the toe of Fleming's shoe.

'Come on, Sarah, before he clocks us,' Fred said, taking her hand and running to the main stairwell.

Just before they arrived back at the main kitchen, Sarah stopped Fred and panted, 'We did it, Fred. Thanks so much for your help. We got our own back, didn't we? I reckon your job's a good 'un now.'

Fred beamed at her, his face flushed with triumph. 'We did. I just hope Mr Flemin' didn't believe all that about me skivin' and that.'

Sarah tied her apron strings behind her and smoothed out the wrinkles. 'He won't; he's just seen what a clown Danny is. Now just calm down and remember what we tell Doris and Chef when we go in there.'

'Where the bleedin 'ell have you two been?' Chef looked up from a soup pot, his face sour enough to curdle milk.

'I had a dizzy spell, Chef, and I asked Fred to help me out for some fresh air,' Sarah said, leaning heavily on Fred's arm.

'Dizzy spell? It would be nice if you were to have a "busy spell" for five minutes,' Chef snarled and continued stirring the soup. 'I've been chattin' to Mr Ames and we have come to the conclusion that you might not be required around here much longer. He said you told him some nonsense about a train, and now you've been missing for twenty minutes havin' a dizzy spell.'

'She did have one, Chef, she turned green like,' Fred chipped in.

'I was talkin' to the organ grinder, not her monkey; get on with washin' that floor!'

Just then Danny stumbled through the door, holding his head and swaying from side to side. 'Dad ... I've been ... done over,' he whined.

Chef left his stirring and yelled to Fred, 'Quick, get a chair before he faints!' He ran over and flung his arm under Danny, just as his knees gave way.

Sarah couldn't help it; she strolled over and said, 'Oh dear, Chef, looks like he's having a dizzy spell.'

Chef looked at her and bared his tombstone teeth. 'If I weren't supporting the weight of my injured son, so help me I'd swing for you.' He grabbed the chair from Fred and lowered Danny carefully on to it. 'Now get back to work, you heartless bitch. There's twenty pound of peas on that table want shellin'.'

Sarah went to the pea table, picked up a pod, but didn't begin work. Her work here was done. She giggled. That sounded like something a superhero would say. But as far as she was concerned she *was* a superhero; unless more disinfectant was miraculously found and poured over the penicillin mould before Fleming could come to his earth-shattering conclusion. Unlikely. She'd succeeded in her task again, and felt very proud of herself, elated even.

Sarah ran a thumb down the pod in her hand, picked out a few peas and popped them into her mouth. De-li-cious. It had been years since she'd had fresh peas ... Must have been at her grandfather's allotment when she'd been about eight. Thoughts of fresh vegetables and allotments took her straight back to John … and returning home.

Sarah watched Chef fussing over the miserable Danny and popped more peas. Home: where was that? Home was a place where she wasn't a superhero, where she was alone, where she had a job that she wasn't sure was for her anymore (apart from teaching her adorable Year 10) and, most gut wrenching, it was a place where the love of her life was now lost to the lovely Josephina. Elation gave way to emptiness. Did she even want to return home?

Fred looked up from his mopping, inclined his head towards Danny and winked at her. Doris and a few others were on the scene now, so Danny, pale faced and sipping water, made a Broadway production out of his unfortunate visit to the lab.

'There were three big strong men, Dad. I didn't get a good look at 'em 'cos they put a bag over me head.'

'Oh gawd, what did they do to you?' Katherine gasped, seemingly thrilled by the prospect of three big strong men wandering around the hospital.

'One bashed me on the head, the other stamped on me foot, and the last one punched me in the belly.'

Sarah raised her eyebrows at Fred and shook her head.

'But what were they after, I wonder?' Doris asked.

'Money I suppose,' Danny sniffed.

'Money, in a lab?' Doris frowned.

'Well, he don't know, does he? Why else would they attack him?' Chef snapped.

'Did they do any damage, Danny?' Jock asked.

'Yeah, they smashed those two new big bottles of disinfectant that I took up; went everywhere it did.'

Sarah opened another pod of peas and called over, 'Oh dear, I bet Mr Flemin' wasn't pleased about that, was he? I bet Mr Flemin' thought you were just clumsy and dropped it, and I bet Mr Flemin thought you were a liar for sayin' you were attacked.' Sarah smiled and winked. 'And I bet he don't want you near his lab no more, eh?'

Danny's mouth fell open. Perhaps he thought Sarah was a clairvoyant. Chef's face turned puce; he clenched his fists and started over to Sarah, but then a young girl, probably a cleaner, arrived at the door.

''Scuse me, but Mr Flemin' says I have to fetch Fred to go and help clean his lab. He don't want nobody else, he was very particular about that.'

Fred stopped mopping and beamed. Sarah popped more peas and gave him the thumbs up; she hoped this was the start of Fred's step back up the ladder.

Doris said, 'Well don't stand there like a simpleton, go and do as she asks, and take fresh water in that bucket; he won't want chicken feathers on his floor on top of everything else that's happened.'

Fred scuttled off and Chef stomped over to Sarah. His eyebrows knitted together in a crazy dog-leg furrow, beads of sweat, oozing from open pores, rolled down his face. He leaned in close, bared his teeth and hissed, 'Why you think you can talk to my boy like that I don't know, but you're out now, gel, and no mistake; there's no more last chances for you.'

Sarah took a step back, munched peas and shook her head. 'No, you'll never make it on to the stage, with that acting, Chef. We're not quite the Ray Winston villain type are we, sweetie?'

Chef's mouth worked but no sound was forthcoming. He obviously knew he'd been insulted but didn't really understand how. His hand shot out and grabbed Sarah's shoulder. Doris looked over, saw what was happening and flew over to stand between them.

'Now, Chef, you're a bit upset because of Danny, which is understandable ...'

Chef dropped his hand. 'A bit upset! She stands 'ere sayin' allsorts to our Danny and scoffing peas, she comes late and lies to Mr Ames, and then goes AWOL with Fred; of course I'm upset!'

Sarah was enjoying seeing him so angry. She was strangely unafraid and couldn't care less about what might happen to her anymore. She didn't belong here, but she didn't want to go home, either. It was about time the 1928 Sarah stood up for herself more, too. It should stand her in good stead for the future, because in her experience those who let sleeping dogs lie normally got bitten in the end. May as well go for the jackpot ... she leaned in, smirked and winked to everyone gathered, 'Oh, and don't forget to tell everyone the *real* reason why you're so upset with me, Chef.'

It was Chef's turn to step back. He avoided her eye, mopped his brow and coughed uncertainly. 'I don't know what you mean, and when Mr Ames gets here ...'

'Don't know what I mean? I think you do. It's 'cos I turned you down when you asked me to the pictures last week, ain't it?'

There was a collective gasp from the rest of the kitchen staff and Chef turned on them. 'Don't take no notice of her, she's a lyin' cow, and get back to work this minute!'

Ames drifted in like a bad smell. 'Is there a problem here, Chef?'

'There is, Mr Ames, and she's standin' right there,' Chef raged, pointing a chubby finger at Sarah. 'I know you persuaded me to keep her on a little longer earlier on, but now I want her sacked and out of here right now!'

Ah, so Ames had persuaded Chef to keep her on, had he? Perhaps she could do a little persuasion of her own. If it paid off, Doris, Fred and everyone else on the staff would have a happier life.

'Mr Ames,' Sarah said sweetly, 'may I have a word

with you privately about this matter?' Sarah fluttered her eyelashes for good measure.

Ames flushed. 'Well, I—'

'Don't let her talk her way out of it, Mr—'

'Thank you, Chef. If I need your advice I'll ask for it.'

Ames beckoned Sarah with a bony finger and turned on his heel. She followed him out and into the storeroom she'd first seen him come out of when she'd arrived earlier. It was much bigger than the offshoot kitchen. It was piled high with dried and canned goods and Ames seated himself at the end behind a large oak desk.

'Well, come up here and sit on that stool, I won't bite,' he said, arranging his thin lips into a lemon-slice smile.

Sarah walked down and perched on the stool. She pulled her dress up more than was necessary as she crossed her legs. Ames was afforded a full view of her stocking-clad knees. He ran a finger under his starched collar and cleared his throat. 'So, tell me your version of the story,' he breathed, not taking his eyes off her legs.

She shot him a warm smile. 'Well, you see, Mr Ames, I think Chef's got it in for me, all because I turned him down last week.'

'I see ... So you haven't done anything wrong?'

'No, I had a dizzy spell and he went potty when I got back,' she said, uncrossing and crossing her legs again. The hem of her dress slipped a few inches past her knee and further up her thigh.

Ames licked his lips and gaped at her stockings. He was almost incapable of speech. 'I know he can ... um ... act a little rashly ... at times.'

Sarah nodded and opened her eyes wide. 'Ain't that the truth. He says awful things about you behind your back, Mr Ames. Says you couldn't run a piss-up in a brewery and things like that, 'scuse my language.'

'Eh? Did he indeed?' Ames dragged his eyes from Sarah's legs for a second. He pursed his lips – lemon slice to cat's bottom in two seconds flat.

Sarah nodded and undid a few buttons on her dress. She fanned her hand over her chest. 'Yes he did. Don't you find it hot in here, Mr Ames?'

Ames swallowed and stared at her cleavage. 'Hot … um … yes … I …'

'Anyway,' she uncrossed and re-crossed her legs again in *Basic Instinct* fashion, 'I think you should go in there, sack him and his brat, Danny, too. That'll show 'em who's boss.'

Ames had a glazed look in his eyes; he seemed to be barely functioning above the neck. He leaned forward to get a better look down her dress. 'Yes, sack him … hmm.'

Sarah stood up, clasped his hand and slowly leaned forward, her chest inches from his nose. 'Oh, you will? That's marvellous, Mr Ames.'

Ames squeezed her hand and then ran his trembling fingers along her neck. 'But how will the kitchen,' he swallowed hard again, 'run without Chef?'

Sarah tried to control her revulsion as his clammy fingers moved on to trace the contours of her mouth. 'Doris runs the show anyway; she can cook just as well as him, I bet. You can get another chef tomorrow if you need to.'

'Really … though, Sarah, it's a big thing to ask, you know,' he whispered, running his fingers back down her neck and quick as a flash he undid another button. The top half of Sarah's bra was completely in view. He feasted his eyes on her ample breasts rising and falling inches from his face and she thought he might just collapse of a heart attack.

She sat back down, did her buttons up and looked at him coyly. 'Now, Mr Ames, that's naughty, but if you do as I ask, I will show you how grateful I can be.'

Ames gulped and wiped moisture from his top lip. 'What,

you mean that ... that ... you'll let me ...' He stopped and shook his head in disbelief.

'Yes, I've admired you from afar for some time now, and I'll let you do whatever you like ... but first, I want them permanently off the premises in the next ten minutes, alright?'

Ames nodded and then shot out of the storeroom like a speeding bullet. Sarah giggled and followed hot on his heels. She hoped she wouldn't be whisked back to the present before he could fulfil her wishes.

Hiding behind the door, she listened as Ames told Chef and Danny that their services would be no longer required. Chef obviously demanded to know why.

'It has come to my attention that you have been inappropriately making advances to female members of staff,' Ames said.

Sarah tutted in her head. That was rich coming from Ames.

'Is that what the cow said to you?'

'I do not wish to discuss the whys and wherefores.'

'But what about Danny, what's he supposed to have done?'

'He is rude and obnoxious; he has also smashed Mr Fleming's disinfectant. I saw the professor a little while ago, and he expressly ordered that Danny remain far away from his lab, or anyone else's.'

Yay! Sarah grinned. That bit must be true because she'd not told Ames. Fred hopefully would now be back on top.

'But I can't just up and go like that. Who will do the cooking? And anyway, I need a week's notice!'

Sarah peeped through the gap in the door. The kitchen staff were faffing around pretending to work but were obviously earwigging on the altercation at hand. There was open delight on many faces at the prospect of Chef's departure. Ames pulled Chef away from the rest of the staff and moved closer to the door. Sarah was able to hear every word, though Ames spoke quietly.

'Doris is more than capable of running the show, and if you keep arguing I may have to say why you were dismissed in any reference you may require. Now that wouldn't look good, would it? If you go now, I will say you left of your own volition.'

'That smacks of blackmail if you ask me,' Chef hissed.

'I'm not asking you, and if you don't get your things and your wretch of a child and leave, I will write a damning reference and add in a few embellishments. Do I make myself clear?'

Chef didn't answer; he turned and stormed over to Danny, who was still slumped on the chair pretending to be terribly injured. He yanked him up by the arm. 'Come on, get your things, we're off!'

'But wot have we done, Dad? Can't you stand up to that Mr Ames? He looks like a strong wind will blow him over ... give him a punch on the nose.'

'I'll give you a punch on the nose in a minute – now get movin'!'

Sarah had to put her fist in her mouth to prevent herself from guffawing. She put her eye to the gap again and saw Ames go over and whisper in Doris's ear. Doris took a step back and put her hand to her mouth. Then she smiled widely and nodded enthusiastically.

Behind the door, Sarah mirrored that smile. *OK, superhero, your work here is done ... again!* She hoped that returning to the future was imminent. Not that she wanted to go, but the situation with Ames could prove a little tricky now. Chef and Danny appeared a few minutes later from the offshoot, with murder burning in their eyes. She had a feeling that they wouldn't leave without coming to find her.

But where should she hide? That question was answered as Ames shot out of the kitchen ahead of them, grabbed her hand and dragged her into the storeroom again.

Ames slammed the door shut and rested his back against it. The lemon-slice smile had appeared again, and he started to unbutton his collar. Sarah didn't like the look in his eye. Surely he didn't think she was going to do it there and then in the bloody storeroom?

'Well, you certainly got rid of them, eh? Thanks, Mr Ames. We should arrange a trip to the pictures soon,' she said as lightly as she could muster, given the fact that Ames had just taken a key out of his pocket and locked the door.

'Pictures? You have got to be joking. No, we are going to do it right here and now. Get your dress off; in fact no, I'll take it off for you.' He ran over and pawed at her buttons.

'Hey, stop it! We can't do it here!'

'Oh yes we can. I just sacked two people for no reason, just because you asked me, and now I'm getting my reward.'

He pulled her hard to him and yanked her buttons open. She couldn't believe how strong he was for such a thin, gangly man. He pushed her against the wall and pinned one arm painfully up behind her back and ran his vile tongue across her neck and cleavage; at the same time, with lightning speed, he shoved his other hand up her dress.

Sarah yelled, clawed at his face and brought her right knee up with the aim of smashing it into his balls. Somehow though, he twisted her round just before she could make impact and forced her face to the wall. She could feel his erection against her bottom and he yanked her arm up again so hard that a white hot pain blazed the length of her shoulder, arm and back.

'Just stay still, you bitch. It was different earlier when you were teasing me. Now you want to go back on it. Well, that isn't an option, madam!'

'Leave me alone, you fucking bastard!' she yelled, trying to raise her foot and kick backward at his shins. She didn't manage it because he moved so quickly; he was as slippery as a bloody eel.

All of a sudden, she felt his grip slacken, his body jerk twice as if under the impact of an unseen force, and then, releasing her, he thumped to the floor. She spun round and saw that Ames was out cold, his ski-jump nose bent at an impossible angle, and blood pouring from his open mouth. She also saw the reason for his downfall.

John stood by the door nursing a bloodied fist. He winced, tucked it inside his jacket and looked into her eyes. 'I think it's time we left, don't you?' he said coldly.

Chapter Twenty-Eight

A second later Sarah stepped forward to hug John, but instead found herself stepping up on to decking. They were no longer in 1928 but standing in her garden under the pergola. Something in his eyes prevented her from hugging him now. He glared at her and sat on the bench, still cradling his hand. She couldn't see the extent of the injury as it was curled into a fist and covered in blood. Sarah sat down next to him. 'John, thanks for ... How did you ...?' Her words refused to form a coherent sentence as she noticed that anger darkened his face like clouds across the sun.

'Thanks, she says ... For fuck's sake, Sarah what were you playing at?'

She was taken aback. She'd seen him angry before, but never like this; he blew noisily down his nose and the corners of his mouth curled in a grimace. She lowered her eyes. Sarah couldn't bear the anguish in his when he looked at her. 'I wanted to make life better for Doris and Fred ... and it went wrong,' she mumbled to her feet.

'Went wrong? You could say that!' John jumped up and began pacing. 'You could have actually made life worse! I won't know until I see the report.'

'How could I have made it worse? Chef's gone and ...'

'Think about it, Sarah. I'm not sure Ames will be too chuffed with the 1928 Sarah, are you? Especially if he thinks she somehow broke his nose, smashed his front teeth in and laid him out cold. Didn't you even consider what would happen to her afterwards?' He stopped and shook his head at her. 'And if I'd not broken every Time-Needling rule and come to save you, you would have been raped.'

Sarah felt like a complete idiot and began to realise just

how incredibly stupid she'd been taking risks and playing with Ames like that ... playing with Sarah like that. 'What rules did you break?'

John stopped and held up his index finger on his uninjured hand. 'First, never go back in time without express permission. I told you that when we first met but I don't expect you remember.' He flicked up his middle finger. 'Second, never let emotions rule your head.' He flicked up his ring finger. 'Three, never touch anyone while you're there.'

Sarah raised her eyes. 'I really am sorry, John. I was full of triumph over what I'd achieved and I wanted to go that little bit further ... I guess it all went to my head ... I was reckless.'

'Oh, yes.' He glared at her and started pacing again. 'You were reckless, alright. Have you any idea what trouble you have caused me? You shouldn't have dabbled in things not related to the mission, should have kept your personal feelings separate from what's going on around you.'

That rankled. She tossed her hair and stood up to face him. 'Well, unlike you I can't just shelve how I feel. It was partly because I was so miserable about coming back home to emptiness and life without you that I did what I did.'

He stopped and waved his good hand in the air. 'Huh? Let me remind you, it was your decision to end it all between us! And shelve my feelings? Why the hell did you think I just risked everything to come and get you?'

She stuck out her chin. 'I don't know, John, why did you, considering I'm such a bloody liability?'

'Why? Because I love you, and you were in danger, you dopey mare!' He spat, wincing at the pain in his hand.

He loved her! His words did a pirouette in her heart and gathered up roses thrown on stage. Without stopping to think, she blurted, 'But how can you? You're with Josephina now!'

John pulled his head back, opened his eyes wide and stared at her in disbelief. He opened his mouth and took a deep breath.

What the hell did you say that for, Sarah? He looks like he's going to go crazy now.

But John didn't go crazy; he just ran his hand through his hair and looked at his feet. He flicked his head up and held her gaze for a few seconds; she saw hurt and bewilderment in his eyes. 'Oh, what's the point?' he said, and walked quickly away down the steps and up the garden path.

'John!' Sarah hurried after him.

'Bye, Sarah,' he tossed back and walked through her kitchen door.

By the time she'd done the same, he was nowhere to be seen. Sarah checked the living room, the bathroom and finally ran out into the street. Putting her hand to her head, she looked frantically up and down, but there were only a few people wandering along, none of them were John. He couldn't have left and jumped into his car in such a short time, not with his injured hand, so she concluded that he must have done one of his time tricks.

Sarah stepped back through the front door, slammed it shut and with her back against it, slid to her haunches. Tears welled and the emptiness in her heart threatened to engulf her. She dashed the tears away with the back of her hand, sniffed and quickly shook her head. There would be no luxury of wallowing in self-pity. She had made one hell of a balls-up, so she should take it like a woman, instead of a snivelling wimp.

Sarah stood, walked to the kitchen and filled the kettle. She needed to think, and copious amounts of tea always helped her come to decisions when she had dilemmas to sort. They were not always the right decisions, however, but

Sarah knew this time she had to get it right; her gut told her that this might be her very last chance.

An hour later she was showered, wearing a cotton floral yellow-and-blue halter-neck dress, had applied make-up with a light touch, had styled her blonde hair into loose curls and had chosen 'sensible' strappy wedge sandals. The mirror told her she looked just right and, as she kept telling herself, everything must *be* right.

Downstairs in the living room, she picked up the phone and went into the kitchen. On the side of her fridge were a few business cards under a magnet. She took one out and punched the numbers written across it into the handset.

'Yes, I would like a taxi as soon as possible, it's pretty urgent ... Um ... 10 minutes?' Sarah suddenly realised she had no idea of the time. She'd left for 1928 at around 5.15 a.m.; she didn't even know if it was still Saturday. 'Ah, half-one, yes, that's fine ... Great that you can come so quick on a Saturday ... where am I going? Handsforth, there's a market garden on the main through road. I need the cottage just before you get there.'

The countryside, dressed in its early summer finery, whizzed past the taxi windows. It was still Saturday. That gave her all weekend to do what was right; she just hoped she could do it. Five more minutes and she'd be there. An Amazon rainforest of butterflies flapped around her stomach and she absently picked the skin at the side of her fingernail until it bled.

It was a good job she'd not driven; she'd plumped for a taxi because she was a bag of nerves. In her head, she rehearsed again what she'd say to Josephina, what she'd say to John, and then what they might say back. Each scenario sounded like the dialogue of a bad soap opera, so in the end she abandoned it and decided to just go with her heart.

Watching the taxi disappear down the road, her tummy did a few somersaults, the rainforest of butterflies went round with it – tumble-dryer fashion. What if he wasn't in? What if he was in, but wouldn't let her in? What if Josephina slapped her and spat in her face? What if she slapped her back and they had full-on fisticuffs while John looked on, aghast? What if Sarah's head exploded with so many silly bloody questions hurtling around it?

She raised her hand and rapped tentatively on the door. It was only just loud enough to disturb a mouse with a hangover. Perhaps she should forget the whole thing and nip off now, before it was too late. Sarah sighed and smoothed her dress. Nope, she needed to get a grip. After all, she'd recently delivered a baby, saved lives in the Blitz, survived rattlesnakes, helped forward equality for women, and hopefully protected the discovery of a wonder drug. She knocked a second time, this time loud enough to start an avalanche in Switzerland.

The door opened. John stood there in black jeans and green T-shirt, accessorised with a white wrist-bandage and sling. *Blimey, his hand must really be in a bad way.*

Sarah looked up from his bandage. His face was expressionless, unreadable. Why didn't he say something? She expected questions, shouting, anything but silence.

'Um … are you alone, is it convenient for me to come in?'

John cocked his head on one side. 'Hmm, not really. I have three strippers in the kitchen, a few prostitutes waiting in the living room … oh, and I've a film crew coming over later to make a porno; they want me in the starring role.' He opened the door wide and walked to the kitchen.

Sarah followed him and then hovered by a chair next to

the table. John filled the kettle, raised his eyebrows at her and pointed at a cup. She nodded and slid on to the chair.

'Tea or coffee?' he asked

'Whatever you're having, don't put yourself out.'

'No, I would *never* do that for you, obviously,' he muttered, pulling milk from the fridge.

She flushed at the barbed remark and wondered how to proceed from there. Perhaps she should start with her daft comment when he'd opened the door.

'When I asked if you were alone, I meant was Josephina here. I didn't want to intrude, but I have a few things I'd like to say if—'

'Oh, not this again,' He slammed the milk carton down on the side. 'You're like a broken record; how many times do I have to tell you, she's history!'

Sarah blinked in disbelief. But what about the day she'd visited the shop and Josephina had told her she'd moved back in with John, about the photo, about her looking after him while he was ill? What about when she'd asked John on the phone if he'd seen Josephina and he'd lied through his teeth? What about all of it?

Though she could feel indignant anger building like a mini tornado she was mindful of John's mood and the fact that she wanted to get things back on an even keel. Sarah cleared her throat and tried to keep her voice calm and manner conciliatory.

'Sorry to harp on, but *she* told me she'd moved back in with you.'

John came over and set a mug of coffee before her. 'Eh, when did she do that?' He sat opposite, puzzled. 'When did you see her after that day here?'

'I came to see you after school at the shop last Wednesday. She was in the shop and she told me she'd moved back in and was helping out in the shop as you had flu.'

John leaned back in his chair, folded his arms and rolled his eyes at her. 'You came to the shop to see me last Wednesday and didn't tell me?'

She nodded. He made her feel like a naughty schoolgirl.

His emerald eyes fixed on hers, drew her in like a magnet. 'Why did you come to the shop?'

Sarah took a sip of coffee and sighed. 'Because I wanted to tell you I made a mistake, and that I wanted us to get back together,' she mumbled.

John's expression was a picture. He looked caught between tears and laughter and ran his hands through his hair. 'I don't believe this ... So, the ever-resourceful Josephina tells you that we're back together, and what, you just believe her and bugger off home?'

Trying to keep her voice calm and her manner conciliatory was proving to be a tougher task than Sarah had imagined. Nevertheless, she bit her tongue and said, 'Not at first. I mean yes, she was in the shop, but I guessed that could be down to you just being ill and desperate ... but there was something else ... something else she said which made me believe her. I was still prepared to give you the benefit of the doubt though, until I rang you later that night ... and then I did believe everything she'd told me without a shadow of a doubt.'

John leaned forward, his face pale and drawn. 'Really? I'm waiting.'

Sarah didn't like his attitude. Of course he was angry, had a right to be given what she had done earlier in 1928, but he seemed to be suggesting that she was gullible, stupid. What about the fact that he was a big fat liar? Calm and conciliatory abandoned her. 'Then I'll tell you, John. She told me that you had loved me once but that you would never take me back now because I was far too possessive and clingy. And what evidence did she have of my insecurity and clinginess?' Sarah stopped and leaned forward, mirroring

John's pose. 'She said that you couldn't believe that I was so jealous of the engagement photo that you had to remove it! So what would *you* have thought in my position? And the real gut-wrenching clincher was when I called and asked you if you'd seen her and you lied your bleeding head off!'

John pushed back his chair and jumped up, his face contorted in rage. His hand shot out, grabbed his half-finished coffee and hurled the mug across the room. Sarah put her hands over her ears as it smashed on the tiles. 'John, calm down. I'm sorry that I had to find out like that too, but I want to try and put it—'

'It didn't happen like that. God, if that bitch were here now I'd wring her fucking neck! All the heartache she's caused.' He thumped his good hand on the table. 'Yes, she came round again and found I was ill. She insisted on opening the shop and I didn't have the strength to argue, to be honest. If I had, you may never have taken that last job and I certainly wouldn't have had to come and save you.'

He came and knelt at Sarah's feet and took her hand. 'I never told her about you being jealous. She noticed that the photo was gone from the sideboard and asked was it because of you. I said yes, but because I had a new relationship and had moved on, *not* because you had been jealous about it. I wouldn't share things about you with her like that. She's a clever cow, guessed right and obviously knew just how to turn the screw, hey?'

'But why lie about it all when I asked!' Sarah pulled away and twisted her hands through her hair.

'Why the hell do you think? Can you imagine how you would have reacted, the way you were feeling? There's no way you would have believed the way it happened,' John exclaimed, his eyes beseeching hers.

She squeezed his hand and felt relief and a second chance slipping into view.

'Do you believe me now?' he asked.

She noticed his eyes were moist. 'Of course I do, and I might not have believed you if you told me the truth, but trust me, lying made things worse. And I am so, so sorry for the mess I got you into.'

'Let's not talk about that for a while, just let me hold you. You are right, I'm to blame, too. I shouldn't have lied. Lies are never the best option and I hardly broke my neck trying to get you back, either. But that was only because I didn't want you to be caught up in this freak show that I call my life.' John stood and pulled her to him, hugging her tightly with his one good arm. 'I've missed you so much,' he murmured into her neck.

'I've missed you so much too; in fact so much I thought I'd go crazy.' She cupped his face and drew his mouth to hers.

For a man with an injured hand, John had lacked nothing in the 'bedroom department'. (Another one of her gran's.) The kiss half an hour ago had gone from tender and loving to passionate and urgent in ten seconds flat, and here they were in John's bed, hot, sticky, out of breath and stupidly happy.

Sarah propped herself up on one elbow and placed little kisses along his chest. 'So did time stand still for you, Time-Needler?'

'Hey, you missed your vocation, you should do stand up.' He grinned.

'Stand up? I thought you preferred me lying down,' she said, replacing a kiss with a playful nip.

'Ouch, don't you think I'm in enough pain with my hand?'

Sarah frowned. 'What exactly happened anyway? Did it sprain when you smashed Ames in the gob?'

John sighed and closed his eyes. 'Not exactly ...'

She kissed the corner of his mouth. Why didn't he just tell her? '"Not exactly." OK, so what *did* happen to it then?'

'Let's just leave the twenty questions till later, huh? I think we deserve a bit of time away from stitching, needling and the rest of the world. I like just being here with you in our own little bubble.'

That worried her. She could tell that John was being evasive to try and stop her worrying, but that just had the opposite effect. 'I love being in our own little bubble as well, John, but I need to know what happened. How serious is the injury?'

He sat up and slipped out of bed. 'Look, why don't I get a nice bottle of wine out of the fridge, make a bite to eat and we'll take it outside?' He slipped on his jeans and turned to her. 'Sound like a plan?'

'I'd prefer it if you explained the whole thing to me first. Is what happened to your hand something serious … because of my stupid behaviour with Ames?'

'I'm afraid so, but I'd prefer it if we left it until we had a glass of wine in our hands and food in our bellies.' He avoided her eye and left the room.

Sarah flopped down on to the pillow. Damn, she had had a feeling in her gut all along that this was serious. Just what the hell had she done now? Had his finger been bitten off by Ames before he was knocked out? There had been quite a lot of blood around Ames's mouth … and perhaps Ames had got so mad with the 1928 Sarah after he'd picked himself off the floor, that he'd actually murdered her or something.

Just when everything seemed as if it were coming together and a glimmer of hope for the future was shining brighter by the second, her reckless behaviour in 1928 had fucked it up.

She picked up John's pillow, put it over her face and yelled at the top of her lungs into it.

If her actions had jeopardised her future with John, and perhaps the life of the 1928 Sarah, she'd never be able to forgive herself.

Chapter Twenty-Nine

'Want me to do anything?' Sarah asked, breezing in to the kitchen. John was cooking a chickeny pasta-type dish. She had set the table and poured the wine and kept her mouth shut about the elephant in the room. She reckoned that John would decide to raise it in his own time and with any luck, the elephant might pack its trunk and rumble back to the jungle. *The 1928 experience may just turn out to be a figment of your imagination, Sarah ... yeah, right.*

'You can grate the cheese if you like, and do you want garlic bread?'

'Only if you do; I'm easy.'

'Yes, I noticed earlier ...'

Sarah threw a bit of cheese at him. 'Watch it!'

The view from the patio seemed even more breathtaking today than it had last time she'd been here. The sky was blue and free of cloud. The hills were green, complete with sheep, and her ears were full of bird song. It couldn't have been more perfect if she'd have ordered it from the Perfect Scene Company. That would be something, wouldn't it? Going online and ordering a lovely spring day in the countryside, blue sky, temperature set to a comfortable 70 degrees and definitely no chance of grey cloud, please.

Sarah took a sip of perfectly chilled wine and a fork of perfectly cooked pasta and wondered if she had fallen on to the set of *The Stepford Wives*. But glancing at John's sling put the perfect day in perspective and she hoped the damned elephant would make an appearance soon, so they could try and move forward.

John picked up his glass and held it up to her. 'Let's have a toast.'

She raised hers and smiled.

'Here's to us, to being back together, starting afresh and to never being parted again.' He clinked his glass to hers. 'To us!'

'To us!'

They both took a sip of wine and then John resumed his meal. Sarah picked up her fork and then set it down again. She couldn't eat another morsel until he'd told her exactly what had happened in 1928. After a few seconds had passed he realised she wasn't eating.

'Something up with the grub?'

She pursed her lips and shook her head. She wanted to know, but there was no way she was dragging that pachyderm on to the patio. John told her he would tell her, so it had to be down to him.

'So why aren't you eating?'

A shrug and a sigh in return.

He scooped the last bit of pasta on to his fork. 'OK, you want me to spill the beans then, eh?'

'If you're ready to.'

He drained his glass and poured another. 'As ready as I'll ever be ... Look, why don't you do the twenty-question thing, or the hundred one in your case, and I'll answer. I'll leave what happened to my hand till last, if you don't mind.'

Now he'd said that she didn't know where to start. She took another sip of wine and sat back in her seat.

'OK, firstly, did I protect the discovery of penicillin?'

He shot her a wide grin. 'Yes, of course you did, you were bloody marvellous.'

She shook her head. 'I'm so relieved, but angry at the same time. Why the hell would the spindly ones put the weight of so many lives on the shoulders of one Stitch? So stupid if you ask me.'

'Spindly ones ... you mean the powers that be?'

'No, I mean the ones who make banisters for stairs, John.'

He laughed. 'OK, I asked for that. They do that kind of thing from time to time, no idea why. Perhaps they have no choice ... again, I don't know. Reading the background to the brief, I did realise that if you failed, penicillin wouldn't have been invented in time to save lives in the war. But reading between the lines, it *would* have been invented not long after.'

'Oh, that's alright then; if I'd have failed, thousands of soldiers would have died from their wounds. Bloody hell! How can they play with people's lives like that?'

'As I said, Sarah, I don't know; perhaps the spindly ones have no real control over anything. You'll just have to accept that we may never know. And, until you eat the rest of the meal I lovingly prepared, I won't answer another thing.'

A forkful or two later, Sarah ventured another question. 'So, did you get a chance to see if Ames did anything horrible to Sarah?'

'Yes, and no he didn't. He was so shocked about what he'd assumed she'd done to him that he steered clear of her. It appeared he thought she had special powers or something, so he daren't sack her, but he eventually left the hospital. Doris continued to run the kitchen and Fred became a trusted porter and sometimes even assisted Fleming in his tasks.'

Sarah started to enjoy her food again; things were certainly looking up. 'I see.' She grinned. 'I know I shouldn't have meddled, but it looks pretty promising so far.' She looked at his sling again and then back to her plate.

'That was better luck than judgement; don't *ever* think that what you did was acceptable, do you understand?'

Sarah looked up, startled at the anger in his voice. 'Yes, I'm sorry; I'm getting carried away with my success again, aren't I?'

He nodded and picked his glass up with a shaking hand. 'Yes, you are, Sarah.'

She lowered her eyes and continued to eat.

Poking the last little bit of pasta around the bowl, she thought she'd better get a few more questions in while she could, in case John became even more grumpy. 'Can I ask you how you knew I was in danger and how you managed to get to me if you don't normally travel in time, well not like me anyway, especially if you didn't have permission from the spindly ones?'

He smiled. 'I see, doing your trick of running one question into another again? OK, sometimes when there's a problem with one of my Stitches I get an alert, like a flag comes up on an email?'

She nodded.

'Well, normally, it's something like the Stitch needs to be brought back and I have to meet them at a certain place and calm them down or something, or it may be that the Stitch has become overly emotional and needs talking through a problem. This time though, I had three alerts come through *and* a message on my phone. That had never happened in all my time as a Needle – you had put yourself in grave danger ...'

He stopped and looked away over the hills. 'I had to make some big decisions ... potentially life threatening for me; luckily I got away with just this.' He nodded at his sling.

Sarah felt her heart beating faster as images of Ames biting John's finger off ran through her mind. 'God, John, what happened, please tell me.'

'Alright. I messaged them that I was going to get you. They said there was no way that was going to happen, and that I should just be on hand straight away after you got back. They said you would need a memory wipe, at least for the Ames bit, but they were so angry that they said they were tempted to wipe the whole experience, which of course would mean you wouldn't remember me at all. I know you said that's what you wanted, but I thought you still needed to have a choice about it when you got back.'

Sarah put her hand to her mouth and blinked back tears. 'So what exactly did you do?'

'I told them I was going in regardless, that I realised you had brought the situation on yourself, but I loved you and couldn't let it happen. In my last message to you I said that they were right about you, but I knew deep down you were just hurting and I guess I wanted you to stay away from me – to protect you. They said if I disobeyed them, I would be punished. I would have to come into physical contact with Ames, and would suffer the consequences.' He stopped and took her hand. 'I just went for it before they could stop me. I did a few time tricks and whacked Ames twice.'

Sarah didn't know what to say. How could she have ever doubted his love for her, even taking into account what Josephina had said? She should have gone to see John that Wednesday and just ignored the bitch. And now, because of her wrong-headedness, the poor man had something seriously wrong with his hand. But what exactly had happened to it?

'John, will you tell me just how badly injured your hand is?'

He sighed. 'I think it would be better if I showed you.' He carefully slipped his left arm out of the sling and placed his hand on the table. It was completely bandaged to just past his wrist and he flicked open the safety pin holding the bandage together.

Sarah was scared to look as he unwound the material, but

scared not to look, too. She clasped her own hands together and tried to calm her breathing and heart rate, both of which insisted on galloping away like a team of wild horses.

'I'll warn you, it isn't pretty,' John said as he prepared to unwind the last layer. A second later, the bandage sat in a heap next to his hand, or what was left of it.

'It isn't pretty' was the understatement of the century. Sarah couldn't believe her eyes. She wanted to put her fist in her mouth to keep from screaming. But she knew that she mustn't do that. John had sacrificed himself for her; the least she could do was sit there and take it.

His left hand looked as if it had been crushed, mangled and dislocated all at the same time. The thumb looked normal, though the other four fingers were bent, gnarled, twisted, and appeared almost welded together in a claw-like fist. She couldn't tell where one finger ended and the other started.

'Oh, John ... How the hell ... Have you seen a doctor?' She forced herself to hold back tears.

'No, there's nothing they can do for this. It doesn't hurt much now, it's just practically useless. I deliberately hit him with this hand, as I'm right handed and would be right up shit creek in my job without that. Mind you,' he held his ruined hand up to his eyes, 'it's not going to be easy working the garden with just one hand, anyway.'

Sarah couldn't help it. She burst into tears and put her hands over her face. She hated herself, for it was *all* her fault. She heard his chair scrape back and then he was beside her, hugging her to him. 'Hey, come on, stop that. I'll manage somehow.' He lifted her chin and wiped away her tears. 'I could always ask Josephina to come and help, what do you say?' His eyes twinkled and a mischievous smile curled his mouth.

She laughed, but it came out as a snort, along with an

attractive strand of snot. 'Over my dead body she will.' She blew her nose and took a big glug of wine. 'But I will help. I'll go part-time from September and work the rest of the time here with you. I have been thinking that I need a change for a while now. I'll try and keep my nice Year 10 class into Year 11, but not Year 9, they are the toughest year in my opinion. It will be a relief not to have to teach Danny anymore, there's no way that he would opt for history! And in the meantime I'll help out after school and at weekends. I'll be damned if your business will suffer because of my stupidity.'

'There's no need for that, I'll manage ...'

'There's every need.' She kissed his injured hand tenderly. 'I've already told you I wanted to cut my hours anyway, and I'm sure I'll love working here, especially alongside you.'

John pulled her up and held her tightly. 'Well, if you insist, how can I refuse? And if you're really sure, then I think it would be great.'

'I'm really sure,' she said, kissing his chin, then her lips brushed his mouth, jaw line and finally she placed small kisses all along his neck.

He sighed and looked into her eyes. 'Right, in that case we'd better go for it.'

'Upstairs again, you're insatiable.' She kissed him passionately.

He pulled away and shook his head. 'Upstairs? No, my girl, get your wellies on, we're off to have a look at some veggies.'

Chapter Thirty

Sunday morning at 7 a.m. found Sarah back in her overalls and already an hour into her task. She wiped the sweat from her brow with the back of her gardening glove and resumed a firm grip on the fork. Exhaling, she plunged it into the rich brown earth, stepped on the top with her wellington boot, eased her weight forward and tipped over a lump of sod. Watching the sod crumble and smelling the damp soil, she was taken back to Kansas. She smiled, leaned on her fork and looked across the English countryside.

Closing her eyes, she imagined the vast plain rolling away to meet the endless sky. She could almost feel the heat and smell the sage. Sarah's throat thickened and she had to swallow hard. What was all that about? When she'd been there, the living conditions were bloody awful, the situation was stressful, and she hadn't known if she'd ever get back home, so why was she so emotional?

It was very odd, but Sarah missed it in a strange way. She definitely missed the people. Martha was a bloody hero in her eyes, just like her 'poor ma'. The women of the plains back then had virtually nothing, but they just got on with it. When Sarah thought about the things in her life she took for granted, and all the things society are told they need, must strive for, her mind boggled.

Do we really *need* to hurry on down to Sofa Universe to get that half-price this or that? Do we really *need* to take the family to a land of people dressed as Mickey Mouse and various other cartoon characters, shovel our money into the already full coffers of that establishment, and all this just to show that we love our children?

Thoughts of children sent Artie's smiling face swimming

up before her eyes, so she opened them and shook her head. She missed him, too, and couldn't really grasp that he had grown up, grown old and died, many years ago.

Sarah resumed forking the earth and tried to shake Artie out of her mind. There was no point in dwelling on it, but emotions couldn't be switched on and off like a tap, could they? She admitted that she missed being someone's mother, too ... so it was no wonder she felt emotional, taking everything into consideration.

A few minutes later, she saw John walking towards her balancing a tea tray, but because of his hand, he wasn't having a lot of success. Sarah could hear him curse every so often as the tea slopped over the edge of the cups.

'What are you doing up and working so early?' he asked, setting the tray in a wheelbarrow.

'Well, you said this bit needed digging over so here I am. No point in lying abed when there's crops to be planted, cows to be milked and water to be hauled,' she said, in an over-exaggerated American drawl.

'Ha! Sounds like you're back in Kansas, eh?'

She nodded and picked up the half-cup of tea, flicking the drips from her fingers. 'I'd love to go back there one day with you, John. The scenery was breathtaking.'

'We can't just pop back through time on a whim, you know.'

'No, you daft sod, I meant jump on a plane and go over there. It wouldn't be the same, but there are still huge unspoiled bits. I've seen documentaries on it and stuff.'

He grinned at her and she realised that he'd known what she'd meant all along.

Sarah smiled back wistfully. 'I've been thinking about 1874 and getting a bit upset, to be honest.' She told him her thoughts and he drew her to him.

'That's why I love you. None of the holes needing your

expert stitching were just jobs, were they? You really cared about those people, wanted to do your very best for them.

'I still do care now. I miss them all.'

John went to the wheelbarrow and picked up his mug. He took a sip and gazed thoughtfully over the hills. 'I bet I can guess who you miss most of all out of all the ones you saved?'

Sarah walked over to him and slipped her arm through his. 'OK, guess away. I'll give you three.'

'I don't need three. It's Artie, isn't it?'

She looked up at him. 'Yes ... how did you know?'

'The spindly ones, as you call them, were moaning about it, but I knew anyway. It's obvious. We never did get the chance to discuss the fact that you had to be someone's mum and all the emotional baggage that went with that, did we? You think that your ex-husband robbed you of your chance to have babies.'

Sarah blinked rapidly. 'Well, yes, he did. When we'd talk about starting a family over the years, it was always, "Yes we will, but not yet," or, "We can't afford them just now," ... always an excuse. Then he has a one-night stand with my best mate and lo and behold she's pregnant. They get together and play happy families.'

'You're still very bitter about that, aren't you?'

She gave a huff and raised her eyebrows. 'Ya think; what gave it away?'

John sighed and held her close again. 'Now listen, there are a few things we have to discuss today regarding our future and the spindly ones. I have had a few email conversations with them while you were asleep. They urgently wanted to speak to me about the whole 1928 trip.'

Sarah stepped back; she didn't like the serious tone in his voice. What the hell had happened now? 'What did they say? Is there more bad news?'

‘I don’t think so, but we do have to make a few decisions. If we are going to be together properly, and hopefully start that family you have always wanted, we must answer their concerns.’

The words ‘start a family you have always wanted’ whirled into her heart and whipped her pulse into a crazy beat. ‘You want kids with me?’ Her voice trembled.

‘I thought it might be a nice idea, yes.’ John laughed, as he watched Sarah leaping around the freshly forked earth, laughing and yelling at the top of her voice like a demented hyena.

‘Come on then, breakfast and then email time,’ he said, grabbing her hood and dragging her back to the path.

An hour later, Sarah, still on cloud nine, collected the breakfast dishes from the table. John had gone up for a quick shower and then they were going to make contact with the spindly ones. He’d not told her very much about what they’d said to him so far, just that they needed assurances and certain conditions met. Sarah didn’t really care what they asked them to do; she’d do anything to make a life with John ... well, apart from murder, or handing over their first born.

First born ... Jeez Louise, she still had to pinch herself when she thought of the now-very-real prospect of having children. Her life at the moment was one very large see-saw. One moment she was down, as down as she could possibly be, the next she was soaring into the heavens, courtesy of Pink Fluffy Clouds R Us.

Even stacking the dishwasher and wiping down the counter filled her with delight. She looked around the kitchen and wondered if this lovely place would eventually become her home. It would be the logical thing to do. If she were to go part-time, she’d manage to just cover the mortgage, but if she sold her house and moved in here, things would be a lot more comfortable financially. It wasn't so long ago that she'd chastised herself for getting ahead of herself when she'd imagined living in this lovely old cottage. Now it wasn't a dream, but a real possibility.

Sarah pottered around the living room, straightening cushions and humming the 'Wedding March'. She presumed marriage would be on the cards; in fact, she would have to insist on it before children were planned. Though very liberal in most of her views, she still had the 'old-fashioned' idea that it was best to be married before having a baby. Explaining exactly *why* she felt like this wasn't easy, but ...

Blam blam blam!

Who was at the door at ten o'clock on a lazy Sunday morning? She hoped it wasn't a relative or friend. Much as she'd like to meet anyone who was close to John, they had very important business to attend to. Should she answer it or ...

'Can you get that, Sarah? I'm just getting dry, down in two minutes!'

Sarah opened the door and her heart and stomach had a race to see which could plummet the fastest. Josephina looked less than pleased to see Sarah, too. She removed her sunglasses, tossed her glossy hair and tutted. 'So, Seera, you're back on the scene, huh?'

Before Sarah could take charge of her faculties, Josephina barged past and into the kitchen. She threw her sunglasses on the table and whirled round, face flushed and eyes flashing. 'Where's John, I need to speak with him.'

Sarah's eyes quickly appraised her. Black shorts, emerald halter top, long tanned legs, red lips. Sarah hated her. Here *she* stood, barefoot, overalled and a bit grubby from her work in the field. Not waiting for a reply, Josephina stalked through to the living room, her unfeasibly high, high heels, clack-clacking on the tiles.

Sarah padded after her, her anger growing with every step. How dare she just flounce in here like this? 'He's in the shower, not in here, and I never actually invited you in,' she said, glaring at Josephina as she turned to face her.

'I need no invitation to *my* Johnny's home!'

Sarah felt her courage sweep up from her toes, gather momentum and then burst from her mouth. 'I think you'll find you do, and he's not *your* Johnny, he's *my* John!' Phew, that felt good; this is what she should have done before, fight not flight!

'Ha! He'll never be yours, look at the state of you, if you think ...'

She stopped as the door opened and John walked in. He wore jeans and a black T-shirt, his hair was still damp from the shower and his green eyes flashed in anger. Sarah looked from him to Josephina and she felt like she'd been hit with the ugly stick. Perhaps he would never be hers like Josephina said, why would he, when he could have ...

'What the hell are you doing here?'

'Darling! I thought I'd pop over and see if you needed anything ... You look fully recovered now, quite magnificent if I may say so,' Josephina purred. 'Oh my dear, you have a bandage, what happened?' She stepped towards him.

John held up his hand. 'Get the fuck out of my house before I do something I regret.'

'What? Why? What have I done?' Josephina put her hand to her mouth and slumped down theatrically on the sofa.

John didn't answer. He strode towards her, yanked her up with his good hand and propelled her out of the living room and towards the front door. Josephina protested and yelled all the way there and Sarah followed behind, stifling peals of laughter. Because she was being frogmarched along,

Josephina stumbled and tottered on the ridiculous heels, her legs even bowed once or twice; she had lost her glamour and appeared slightly cartoony.

John flung open the door and practically threw her out. Josephina's arms pinwheeled in an effort to keep her balance and she had to lean against her car for support.

She gasped and looked at John in disbelief. 'Johnny, how can you be so cruel, after everything we meant to each other?'

'Ha! Cruel? You wrote the book on that! I heard what you said to Sarah, and she's more of a beauty than you'll ever be, and the name's John. I *always* hated Johnny!' He went to close the door. Sarah's heart swelled with pride.

'My new sunglasses are in there!' Josephina wailed.

Sarah sped to the kitchen and returned with the flimsy diamante-edged shades. John took them and threw them at Josephina. 'Just like you, aren't they, Jose: expensive, flashy, but of no practical use whatsoever!' He slammed the door and turned to Sarah. 'That felt good!' he said and burst out laughing. She joined him and they leaned against the door howling like a couple of wolves until tears ran down their faces.

'OK, here goes,' John said, typing a series of letters and numbers into the address of his email. Sarah noticed it didn't have .com or co.uk after it, but then it wouldn't, would it? They were sitting cross-legged in the middle of John's bed and he had the laptop on his knee. Though Sarah had felt over the moon that Josephina had got her comeuppance, she was beginning to feel apprehensive about what the spindly ones wanted. A few elephants had arrived in her tummy and were limbering up for a cartwheeling extravaganza.

'What did they say to you whilst I was sleeping?' she whispered, as if the spindly ones were about to jump out of the wardrobe.

John sighed and moved a stray hair from her forehead. 'That they were angry about your behaviour and mine, too. Even though you were one of the best Stitches of all, you let emotions rule you too much. They said again that they wanted to wipe your memory and felt you couldn't be trusted. I begged them to reconsider, told them that you were extremely sorry, and they eventually agreed that you could be in on negotiations now.'

Sarah's elephants went into action. 'OK, better get on with it then.'

John wrote:

John Needler reporting. Sarah is here and willing to do whatever she can to allay your fears. What are your demands?

Seconds later a reply:

Sarah, you have shown yourself to be an outstanding Stitch and have compassion and love beyond measure for people in the past and we are eternally thankful for your endeavours. However, your last trip and your relationship with John have given us grave cause for concern.

There have only been three relationships between a Needle and a Stitch in the last 100 years. (One couple, as you know, were John's parents.) They were allowed only because we were entirely convinced that they would be true and long-lasting. We were also sure that the Stitch wouldn't try to stop the Needle doing his job and persuade him to settle down to a 'normal' job.

We are far from convinced that you will behave in a similar way and therefore wish to wipe your memory of all your stitching and consequently your relationship with John will be at an end.

Sarah looked at John open mouthed. 'Oh shit! What do we do now?'

John took her shaking hand and said, 'Don't panic, we're here to try and change their minds; if they were set on wiping your memory they would have done it by now.'

She nodded. 'Ask them why they're not convinced about us.'

'I think that's obvious, given the fact that you went a bit crazy in 1928 and I blatantly disobeyed orders to come and rescue you.'

'Yes, but there was the line about them not thinking we will be true and long-lasting.' She traced the line on the screen. 'That needs explaining.'

He shrugged but wrote:

Sarah wants to know why you aren't convinced that our relationship is true? She is willing to do whatever it takes to make you understand how much she loves me and assures you that she will never try to interfere with needling.

Before he pressed send he asked, 'Is that OK?'

She nodded and squeezed his hand.

Again a swift response:

Sarah was tested and found wanting. We deliberately told you that Sarah was due back later from 1874. When she came back early and found Josephina at your house, we had to be sure she loved you enough to fight for you – she didn't. This, coupled with the last debacle in 1928, means that we feel it would be kinder to disallow continuance.

Sarah flopped back on the bed and covered her face with

a pillow. She'd been right about all of that then. Of all the conniving, spindly, medievally-sleeve waving …

'Hey, help me here, come on, what do we say back?' John pulled the pillow away. She looked at his pinched expression and the fear behind his eyes. This was no dress rehearsal. The next email had to cut the mustard or she and John would be history. She guessed she would have to do something pretty drastic for them to change their minds.

She swallowed hard. 'Ask them if I'm allowed to type the next one.'

John raised his eyebrows but did as she asked. The request was granted.

Sarah wrote:

> *Thanks for letting me communicate directly. I realise how very stupid I have been and I can fully understand why you have arrived at this decision. I should have fought for John, but I was too scared of having my heart broken again. I recklessly strayed from my recent task and drew John in to save me with disastrous consequences for him. If you allow me to remain with him and make a life together, I will swear to do two things: 1) I will be available for stitching whenever you ask for the rest of my life, and will carry out my duties willingly and without straying from my task. 2) I will take John's injury instead. Please turn his hand back to normal and if you could be sure to maim my left hand, as I'm right handed.*
>
> *I hope these two things will assure you that I am serious about making amends.*

'You can't do that, I won't let y—' John stopped in shock as Sarah had already pressed send.

They waited in silence. The reply didn't come. Perhaps

they were having a chinwag about it all. A surreal thought forced its way through her anxiety. Did they actually have chins, or did they just have ...

'Sarah, my injured hand is burning!' John yelled, held it to his chest and grimaced.

'Here, let me see,' she said, unfastening the safety pin and slowly unwinding the bandage.

'It's stopped now, feels almost—' he murmured as Sarah revealed his hand '—normal.'

John's hand was indeed normal. He wriggled his fingers and turned it first one way and then the other. Sarah kissed it and then bravely held her left hand up, tuned her head away and screwed up her eyes. She waited ... and waited ...

A reply:

> *Sarah, it has been agreed that you have learned the error of your ways and are ready to make sacrifices to show your love for John. You will be spared injury, but not the first promise. You will be required to stitch as you described and should be prepared to journey to the past a month from now. If you ever renege on this promise in the future, yourself, John, or any offspring you may have will suffer. I trust you understand this is no idle threat.*

The laptop screen went black and it was clear the computer had shut down.

They both sat in silence looking at it for a few seconds and then John grabbed her round the waist and threw her back on to the bed. 'We won, Sarah! We're allowed to be together *and* my hand is completely healed.' He showered her face with kisses. 'You were so brave, I love you so much.'

She smiled and kissed him back. 'No braver than you were when you came to save me the other day.'

He stopped kissing her and frowned. 'You do realise you've just signed your life over to stitching? That was a huge thing to promise.'

'Yep, well you have signed your life over to needling, and I do enjoy it mostly. I'm still going part-time, so it won't be so stressful juggling school work with time travel. Besides, it will look great on my CV.'

John laughed. 'You are crazy, Sarah Yates, do you know that?' He started to kiss her neck and ran his hand along her leg.

'But you love me, right?' she murmured slipping her hands around his waist.

'Oh yes.'

'Hadn't you better stop all that? We have soil to dig, veggies to tend.' Her sky-blue eyes locked on to his.

'They can wait,' he said, and placed his mouth on hers.

About the Author

Amanda James (aka Mandy) was born in Sheffield and now lives in Bristol with her husband and two cats. In her spare time, she enjoys gardening, singing, and spending lots of time with her grandson. She also admits to spending far too much time chatting on Twitter and Facebook! Mandy recently left her teaching role to follow her ambition to live her life doing what she most enjoys – writing.

Follow Mandy:
Blog – www.mandykjameswrites.blogspot.co.uk
Facebook – www.facebook.com/mandy.james.33
Twitter – @akjames61

More from Choc Lit

If you enjoyed Amanda's story, you'll enjoy the rest of our selection. Here's a sample:

Vampire State of Mind

Jane Lovering

Jessica Grant knows vampires only too well. She runs the York Council tracker programme making sure that Otherworlders are all where they should be, keeps the filing in order and drinks far too much coffee.

To Jess, vampires are annoying and arrogant and far too sexy for their own good, particularly her ex-colleague, Sil, who's now in charge of Otherworld York. When a demon turns up and threatens not just Jess but the whole world order, she and Sil are forced to work together.

But then Jess turns out to be the key to saving the world, which puts a very different slant on their relationship.

The stakes are high. They are also very, very pointy and Jess isn't afraid to use them – even on the vampire she's rather afraid she's falling in love with ...

This is the first of a trilogy in Jane's paranormal series.

Visit www.choc-lit.com for more details including the first two chapters and reviews, or simply scan barcode using your mobile phone QR reader.

No Such Thing as Immortality

Sarah Tranter

I will protect you until the day I die ... forever!

A vampire does not have to feel any emotion not of his choosing. And Nathaniel Gray has spent two hundred years choosing not to feel. But when he accidentally runs Rowan Locke off the road, he is inexplicably flooded with everything she's feeling, and that's rage, and lots of it.

He is consumed with the need to protect Rowan at all costs including from himself. To Nate, what is happening is unthinkable and is pretty much as unbelievable as the existence of faeries.

But you see, 'There is no such thing as ... immortality.'

This is Nate's story ...

Visit www.choc-lit.com for more details including the first two chapters and reviews, or simply scan barcode using your mobile phone QR reader.

Out of Sight Out of Mind

Evonne Wareham

Everyone has secrets. Some are stranger than others.

Madison Albi is a scientist with a very special talent – for reading minds. When she stumbles across a homeless man with whom she feels an inexplicable connection, she can't resist the dangerous impulse to use her skills to help him.

J is a non-person – a vagrant who can't even remember his own name. He's got no hope, until he meets Madison. Is she the one woman who can restore his past?

Madison agrees to help J recover his memory, but as she delves deeper into his mind, it soon becomes clear that some secrets are better off staying hidden.

Is J really the man Madison believes him to be?

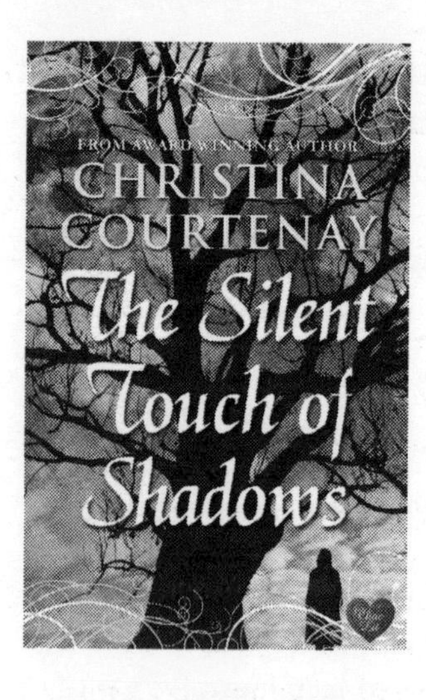

The Silent Touch of Shadows

Christina Courtenay

Winner of the 2012 Best Historical Read from the Festival of Romance

What will it take to put the past to rest?

Professional genealogist Melissa Grantham receives an invitation to visit her family's ancestral home, Ashleigh Manor. From the moment she arrives, life-like dreams and visions haunt her. The spiritual connection to a medieval young woman and her forbidden lover have her questioning her sanity, but Melissa is determined to solve the mystery.

Jake Precy, owner of a nearby cottage, has disturbing dreams too, but it's not until he meets Melissa that they begin to make sense. He hires her to research his family's history, unaware their lives are already entwined. Is the mutual attraction real or the result of ghostly interference?

A haunting love story set partly in the present and partly in fifteenth century Kent.

Visit www.choc-lit.com for more details including the first two chapters and reviews, or simply scan barcode using your mobile phone QR reader.

The UnTied Kingdom

Kate Johnson

Shortlisted for the 2012 RoNA Contemporary Romantic Novel Category Award

The portal to an alternate world was the start of all her troubles – or was it?

When Eve Carpenter lands with a splash in the Thames, it's not the London or England she's used to. No one has a telephone or knows what a computer is. England's a third-world country and Princess Di is still alive. But worst of all, everyone thinks Eve's a spy.

Including Major Harker who has his own problems. His sworn enemy is looking for a promotion. The General wants him to undertake some ridiculous mission to capture a computer, which Harker vaguely envisions running wild somewhere in Yorkshire. Turns out the best person to help him is Eve.

She claims to be a popstar. Harker doesn't know what a popstar is, although he suspects it's a fancy foreign word for 'spy'. Eve knows all about computers, and electricity. Eve is dangerous. There's every possibility she's mad.

And Harker is falling in love with her.

Visit www.choc-lit.com for more details including the first two chapters and reviews, or simply scan barcode using your mobile phone QR reader.

Dream a Little Dream

Sue Moorcroft

What would you give to make your dreams come true?

Liza Reece has a dream. Working as a reflexologist for a troubled holistic centre isn't enough. When the opportunity arises to take over the Centre she jumps at it. Problem is, she needs funds, and fast, as she's not the only one interested.

Dominic Christy has dreams of his own. Diagnosed as suffering from a rare sleep disorder, dumped by his live-in girlfriend and discharged from the job he adored as an Air Traffic Controller, he's single-minded in his aims. He has money, and plans for the Centre that don't include Liza and her team.

But dreams have a way of shifting and changing and Dominic's growing fascination with Liza threatens to reshape his. And then it's time to wake up to the truth ...

Highland Storms

Christina Courtenay

Winner of the 2012 Best Historical Romantic Novel of the year

Who can you trust?

Betrayed by his brother and his childhood love, Brice Kinross needs a fresh start. So he welcomes the opportunity to leave Sweden for the Scottish Highlands to take over the family estate.

But there's trouble afoot at Rosyth in 1754 and Brice finds himself unwelcome. The estate's in ruin and money is disappearing. He discovers an ally in Marsaili Buchanan, the beautiful redheaded housekeeper, but can he trust her?

Marsaili is determined to build a good life. She works hard at being a housekeeper and harder still at avoiding men who want to take advantage of her. But she's irresistibly drawn to the new clan chief, even though he's made it plain he doesn't want to be shackled to anyone.

And the young laird has more than romance on his mind. His investigations are stirring up an enemy. Someone who will stop at nothing to get what he wants – including Marsaili – even if that means destroying Brice's life forever …

Sequel to Trade Winds.

Visit www.choc-lit.com for more details including the first two chapters and reviews, or simply scan barcode using your mobile phone QR reader.

Introducing Choc Lit

We're an independent publisher creating
a delicious selection of fiction.
Where heroes are like chocolate – irresistible!
Quality stories with a romance at the heart.

Choc Lit novels are selected by genuine readers like yourself. We only publish stories our Choc Lit Tasting Panel want to see in print. Our reviews and awards speak for themselves.

Come and support our authors and join them in our Author's Corner, read their interviews and see their latest events, reviews and gossip.

Visit: www.choc-lit.com for more details.

Available in paperback and as ebooks from most stores.

We'd also love to hear how you enjoyed *A Stitch in Time*.
Just visit www.choc-lit.com and give your feedback.
Describe John in terms of chocolate
and you could win a Choc Lit novel in our
Flavour of the Month competition.

Follow us on twitter: www.twitter.com/ChocLituk, or simply scan barcode using your mobile phone QR reader.